The Collected Supernatural and Weird Fiction of Mrs. H. D. Everett

The Collected Supernatural and Weird Fiction of
Mrs. H. D. Everett

Sixteen Short Stories and One Novella of the Strange and Unusual Including 'Beyond the Pale,' 'Over the Wires,' 'The Death Mask,' 'A Girl in White,' 'The Pipers of Mallory,' and 'Iras: A Mystery'

Mrs. H. D. Everett

(Theo Douglas)

LEONAUR

The Collected
Supernatural and Weird
Fiction of
Mrs. H. D. Everett
Sixteen Short Stories and One Novella of the Strange and Unusual Including 'Beyond
the Pale,' 'Over the Wires,' 'The Death Mask,' 'A Girl in White,' 'The Pipers of Mallory,'
and 'Iras: A Mystery'
by Mrs. H. D. Everett

FIRST EDITION

First published under the titles
The Death Mask and Other Ghosts
and
Iras: A Mystery

Leonaur is an imprint of Oakpast Ltd

ISBN: 978-1-917666-26-8 (hardcover)
ISBN: 978-1-917666-27-5 (softcover)

http://www.leonaur.com

Publisher's Notes

Contents

A Girl in White

1

In telling the following story I give fictitious names. I do not wish the little house to be identified, nor would I do the owner of the property the slightest injury. It is, doubtless, a harmless place, where people have lived happily in the past, and will again in the future—ninety-nine people out of every hundred. That I happened to be the hundredth man who there, underwent a notable experience, may have had nothing to do with local influence. I write this, but add a query: perhaps one wiser than I will answer, and unravel the mystery which I merely present. I do not pretend to explain.

I took Riverside Cottage for my mother and widowed sister, for three months of the summer of 1914—mid-June to mid-September. They had both passed through a time of trial with which my story has nothing to do; quiet and change of scene became desirable, and mother wished to be within easy reach of London and of me. That was why I explored the Thames valley on their behalf, and was at once attracted to this house—a modern villa, with gay garden sloping to the water's edge, and boat moored at a small landing-stage overhung with trees: the stage and mooring-place shared, I may mention, with the villa next along the road, the garden of which joined with ours.

As soon as my mother and Lydia were settled in, I ran down for the week-end. They were satisfied with the place, and indeed could not praise it sufficiently, or the wisdom of my choice. The quiet delighted them, the privacy, as well as the outlook over the broad stream, which seemed to exercise a tranquillising influence in its flow. Also, the small house was sufficiently convenient; the two elderly servants were pleased, as well as the joint mistresses: what more could be desired?

Needless to say, I agreed with the encomiums and swallowed the reflected praise; but somehow there was a note which jarred. I was the discoverer of the cottage, its original admirer; but the very first night I slept under its roof, I began to wonder what attracted me to the place, and why I had thought it the right sort of nest for mother, who was old and tired, and Lydia, who was middle-aged and particular.

What was the jarring note? Did the "softness" of the valley, the near neighbourhood of a vast body of moving water, depress my spirits? No, for when we sat out in the garden, bright with flowers, and when I rowed Lydia a mile or so upstream, for the sake of floating down in the cool evening, I felt as usual. It was the house which overpowered me with its influence (I use the word in a non-committal sense)—the house where I became oppressed and ill at ease.

It is just the place where a fellow would cut his throat: that was my reflection the next morning, after a night of broken rest and uneasy dreams. My mother remarked at breakfast that I was not looking well, and Lydia made some joke to the effect that it did not suit me to be off the pavements. I went to church with the two women; for, as a matter of course, the dear souls were punctual church-goers, and expected me to be the same: returned to eat a light and digestible mid-day meal; and enjoyed a post-prandial nap in a basket chair under the trees, which made up for the disturbed night. Where could be a passing of time more commonplace, and less likely to foster morbid fancies? Yet it was after this, while still broad daylight of a summer afternoon, that I had my first glimpse of the white girl.

The staircase came down into the square entrance hall, close to the door of the dining-room (it will be understood that in the cottage there were no wide spaces; all was small and cramped). As I was descending the stairs, the figure of a girl in white passed quickly before me, from left to right, entering the dining-room. I felt a distinct shock of surprise, and, gaining the open doorway scarcely a minute later, paused to look into the room. There were no screens or recesses in which to hide, the room was plainly vacant, and here the bow-window did not open to the floor as in the other parlour. The latticed casements were set wide to admit the air, but they were narrow and high from the floor, and it would have needed a distinct effort for a grown person to squeeze through. I was still standing astonished in the doorway, when Lydia called to me from the garden. I was to make haste, for tea was ready; it had been carried out of doors.

Now the natural impulse would have been to tell out my uncanny experience, and inquire who was this girl in white who intruded upon us; but a curious reticence shackled my tongue and kept me mute. An inner voice might have been whispering—This is our secret, yours and mine, and you must reveal it to no other. I did not consider then the scruple about alarming my mother; that developed later. As I took the seat placed for me under the tree, the servant emerged from the house carrying hot scones covered by a napkin; she wore the usual black gown and white apron, and I knew the other domestic was similarly attired. Lydia and my mother both wore black; it could have been no mistake for any lawful inmate; none of them were in the least like my white girl. I drank my tea and kept up an indifferent conversation, but all the while I was trying to reconstruct the picture of what I had seen.

It was not easy. As a rule, I pride myself on quick perception and ready memory, receiving clear imprints, which are correctly retained; but in this case it was as if the surprise of the vision had blurred its details. The slender figure of a girl in white, no touch of colour in her array, which seemed of ordinary modern fashion—quickly passing the foot of the stairs, and disappearing into the room beyond. I had seen no face, that must have been turned from me; but I thought I could recall fair hair, so fair as to be almost flaxen, swept up smoothly from the nape of the neck, into twists worn high upon the head.

Again, at night I was ill at ease. The period of absolute darkness is brief at midsummer, and the first grey light was making lawn and flowerbeds visible when I drew away the screens from the window and looked out. There behind a rosebush, at the edge of the shrubbed border, was the same white figure. The girl might be stealing flowers before their owners were awake; I thought her action looked like it. Presently I saw her more distinctly, as she moved across the lawn to a heavy-topped standard, which had its own circle of root-room cut round it in the grass. She was welcome to our hired roses; but a desire beset me to accost her, and find out who she was, and whence she came. So, I hurriedly flung on my clothes.

A last glance from the window showed her still in sight. I went down to the drawing-room, opened shutters and glass door, and stepped out into the garden; but, as will have been divined, in vain. There was no girl in white, nor did the lawn show any track of footsteps, though my own were plainly traceable in the morning dew.

I was glad that morning to get back to London and my work; and felt distinctly reluctant to view the approach of Saturday, when I was again pledged to spend the weekend at Riverside. But on this, my second visit, I experienced nothing more abnormal than the burden of melancholy and foreboding which the cottage imposed on me before. Weighing on my spirits and driving away sleep. I saw no white girl, and evidently my mother and Lydia had seen nothing, for they seemed wholly contented and at ease. For the third week-end I was engaged elsewhere; but the fourth, a Saturday late in July, found me again at the cottage.

Expectant attention is supposed by some people to account for psychical happenings. I went thither prepared to see the figure, and I did see it, but under new conditions; no repetition of what occurred before.

My broken night repeated itself, though through the previous fortnight I had been sleeping well. I could get no rest in bed, and tossed there till I was almost in a fever. Plainly it was the house which affected me with this insomnia; and as soon as daylight began, I resolved to dress, take out a couple of cushions, and see if I could get to sleep lying in the boat. I crept softly downstairs, crossed the solitary garden, where all was wrapped in the Sabbath stillness of the early dawn, and, once in the boat, swinging to the silent flow of the great river, I slept delightfully and woke refreshed.

The servants were busy in the house when I went back, to bathe and shave and dress again, and doubtless they regarded me with wonder. To shave! I was presently at the glass, intent on chin-scraping—turned to moisten the lather—and, looking back, the face presented to me was not my own. Instead of the expected image, this was the countenance of a lovely girl, who looked at me with dark eyes full of sadness and appeal, whose lips moved as if to speak.

I cannot calculate how long the vision lasted; I only know it gave me full time to see—to note my own figure reflected behind her, shirt-sleeved and razor in hand, my head overtopping hers—to imprint on memory every feature of that face. Yes, I had been right; she was fair, the ghost girl, with hair so light as to be almost flaxen, which curled in rings on her forehead, while—an unusual combination—her eyes and eyebrows were of the darkest brown.

My ghost was pale, but it was not the pallor of death; her lips were warmly red, and on the left cheek there was a dimple ready to deepen had she smiled. Her dress was white. So far, I can describe her, though there is poverty about the written words. I stood frozen, gazing; and then the image melted into a haze of mist, which in its turn disappeared, and the mirror gave back nothing but my own swart reflection in the common way.

My hand shook, and I cut myself over the shaving which came after, which perhaps was not wonderful. The vision was not repeated, though several times that day I stood to gaze. And the second night was sleepless, like the first.

The experiment of the boat had answered well, so at dawn I betook myself thither as before. I fell asleep easily, but woke after the first hour, before the light was full. But it was sufficient to show plainly the slope of the garden, and there, wandering among the flower beds, was the white girl.

I did not spring up at once to confront her, something seemed to hold me paralysed and still. She came on towards me, walking uncertainly with spread hands, as I have seen the blind! On, till she stepped upon the wooden stage, and then, light as a feather, over the side into the boat.

It did not sway under the added burden. I lay in the stern, as I say, paralysed; and she went on to the bow, there turning to look back at me, and ringing her hands together as if in a passion of distress. Then—it all passed in a moment—she plunged into the river and was gone.

I was on my feet the instant after, but there was nothing to be seen. No swirling eddies, no bubbles coming to the surface, no human creature struggling and sinking in those dark depths. Then I remembered that I had heard no splash—all had passed in absolute silence—the boat had not swayed, as it must have done under a material weight. I was awake, I had not dreamed; but the being of my vision was not girl but ghost.

2

Close upon this last incident came the cataclysm we all remember, the outbreak of the war. I volunteered to rejoin my old regiment, was accepted, and in the hurry of preparation and equipment, last days in England slipped rapidly away. But I found time to prosecute certain inquiries about the past history of the river cottage. I could not ascertain that it had ever been the scene of a tragedy, but people are not always candid in answering such questions put by a tenant.

It was built some forty years ago, and the original owner died there, peacefully in her bed, and at an age exceeding the threescore years and ten. It was now the property of two middle-aged spinsters, who let it every year to cover the expenses of their autumn tour. All this was prosaic enough; the girl in white was not to be accounted for.

11

And, moreover, she seemed to have been visible to no one else; the vision was to me alone.

Of my own fortunes during the following twelvemonth, I shall speak only briefly. I was in the Great Retreat, and was twice wounded, but so slightly as to be able to return to duty after a brief sojourn in hospital. But in the early spring I received a third wound, which was a more serious matter, and sent me back to England for doubtful and difficult repair. My mother and Lydia came to London, where I was in hospital, occupying lodgings near me, and anxious, so soon as I should be pronounced convalescent, to have me handed over to their care. I was better, able to sit up, and discharge was well in sight, when my mother sprang upon me what she felt sure would be a pleasant surprise.

"Can you guess, Dick, where we are going so soon as you can be moved? We were so happy last year, Lydia and I, in the little house you found for us at G——, that I thought we could not do better than engage it again this summer, if it is still to be had."

And here the dear soul paused, plainly expecting my expressions of delight. I could not spoil her pleasure by avowing I hated the place, the cottage and its surroundings, and of my free will would never have set foot in it again. So, I swallowed down my distaste.

"And was it to let, mother?" I asked in my turn.

"Alas! no. Riverside Cottage had been snapped up before we inquired—and I don't wonder, it is so sweet a place. But I have taken the house next along the road, the one they call the Lodge, and I hope we shall like it as well. If you remember, the gardens join, and the landing-stage is shared between the two. The rooms are larger than at Riverside, and that will be an advantage when you are with us too."

Not Riverside Cottage after all, but the house next door. That was something of a reprieve, for I did not know how, under invalid conditions, my jarred nerves would stand the reappearance of the girl in white. But it was not probable, at least I thought not, that two houses could be made uninhabitable by one ghost.

I did not leave the hospital so soon as was expected—complications arose, and healing was deferred. So, I had time to receive a report, this time from my sister, of the neighbours at Riverside. The Tressidys were pleasant people, so I gathered; an old general who was subject to gout, and his maiden sister who kept house for him; also two unmarried daughters, both pretty and one charming, and the name of the charmer was Emily. The other daughter was, I gathered, something of

12

an invalid; and Emily was the mainspring of the family, full of spirits and fun. Lydia so evidently intended me to fall captive to Emily, that the spirit of resistance quickened, and I was not sorry to hear, on my arrival, that Emily was away on a visit, and the introduction would be deferred.

The Lodge appeared cheerful and comfortable that first evening, and I was not visited with the depression of the year before; also, in my airy bedroom overlooking the river, I slept well and undisturbed. It was not until the second day that I was introduced to the Tressidy family. Lydia came to summon me from the small sitting-room which was styled the library. The general had called, especially on me, bringing with him his elderly sister, and the younger daughter, Grace. A pretty girl, Lydia said, preparing me, but not to be compared with Emily. So, I was ushered into the room, halting with my stick.

There I was presented to a grizzled, choleric-looking old soldier, a meek elderly female, also grizzled; lastly to the girl. And how shall I describe my sensations, when from her seat in the background and the shadow, she turned on me the face of my ghost, and faintly smiled?

It was the very same face which looked at me out of the glass at Riverside Cottage, the dark eyes and eyebrows, the almost flaxen hair, even the hinted dimple on the cheek, which became more evident with her smile. Was it wonderful that I felt myself stricken dumb in those first moments, and then that I answered with some odd mis-statements in replying to General Tressidy, when he asked, as everybody does, about conditions at the Front, the service I had seen, and my wound. What the old man thought of my confusion I do not know; perhaps he concluded that the marring bullet had impaired, not body only, but also mind.

I had a chance to speak to Grace Tressidy later on when tea was served. The likeness persisted; it was no temporary hallucination. I wished she would have removed her hat, simple as it was, the ghost having been hatless; but in other ways she was dressed for the part, as her gown was white. She wished to relieve me of handing the cake, because I moved lamely, but this I would not allow; and when her wants were supplied, I sat down by her; the general was now talking to my mother.

Did she like the river valley, I asked, and did she know it well? I wanted to ascertain if she had been in the neighbourhood last year, but could not put so bold a question. It was all new to her, she replied, and all delightful; and then she caught her breath, and looked at me with the dark eyes of the vision, eyes with a question in them on her side: was it possible she remembered me, as I recognised her?

"You will think me very silly," she went on. "Emily laughs at me. I have never been here before, and yet it seems as if this place was familiar—even the house where we are staying. I knew every nook of the garden, and every turn of the road. It is as if I had visited it in a dream."

Was that in truth the explanation, and was my ghost nothing more than a perception of Grace Tressidy's dreams? I saw her several times in the days that followed, sometimes hatless, and twice I tried to draw the conversation again to this point, that I might ask her further, and perhaps confess; but each time she avoided it with timidity: had she taken herself to task for so unguardedly speaking out to a stranger, or was she afraid of what I might have to tell? The charming Emily was still away, and I was told, among her other virtues and merits, that she had been a constant nurse and guardian to this younger sister during a period of ill-health. My informant did not say the nature of Grace's illness, and she appeared now to have completely recovered. She walked and bicycled, and was as active as other girls; but the aunt would not let her go on the water, so the boat at the landing-stage was left to us.

I was disturbed by no ghost at River Lodge, but again I took to resting ill at night, though, up to now, mine had been the deep sleep of healthy convalescence. Perhaps I was thinking rather more of Grace Tressidy than was good for me, or would have pleased Lydia, who wished me to be attracted to her favourite, Emily. But, however caused, my insomnia returned; and the night it was at its worst, after tossing feverishly for a couple of hours, I recollected how, the year before, I had been able to sleep in the boat. There it still was, moored to the landing-stage between the two gardens, and a longing beset me to try anew the experiment which succeeded before. So again, I armed myself with cushions and went out, and, lying there in the stern, exacted to find drowsy peace.

The summer was not so far advanced as when I slept out the previous year, and the early mornings were somewhat chill. It seemed to be the chill which waked me, and, raising myself for a change of position, I looked up the slope of garden to the Riverside house with its drawn blinds. And lo! there again was my vision, on the lawn among the rose-bushes, recognised with a shock of heart which curdled through nerves and blood.

My white girl, who so strangely resembled, Grace Tressidy; or was it this time Grace Tressidy herself? She moved away from the bushes, and came slowly towards me with her hands spread out, like a blind person feeling her way.

Was I dreaming or awake? The ghost had acted so; the figure was but repeating the scene of a year before. I lay as if spellbound, and could neither move nor speak. She came on, and as she crossed the stage I saw that her feet were bare. Then, as before, she stepped into the boat.

This time it rocked and swayed under a material weight. The spell was broken. I sprang up, but not soon enough to prevent what followed. The figure at the prow made the despairing gesture I well-remembered, and then plunged into the water, now with a splash and scream.

The current in shore was slow, and what there was carried her past me. I seized her as she rose for the second time, and dragged her out drenched and gasping, but, thank Heaven, alive.

"I was asleep," she sobbed; and then—"What will Emily say!" and she fell again to weeping.

I could seek no explanation then and there. My task was to hurry her back at once, and rouse the inmates of Riverside for those ministrations of which she stood in need—hot bath, dry rubbing, bed. I could see that the accident caused all that household deep dismay, but it was everything that the girl was saved.

When I went round later to inquire, I was told Miss Tressidy wished to see me: this was not Grace, but the aunt.

We have no words to express our thanks. Captain Blake," she began. "I speak for the general too, for he is laid up in his room; the agitation has brought on a fit of gout. Our poor child would have been lost to us, but for you. It was just God's Providence that you happened to be there."

Then followed her story. Grace was a somnambulist. She had walked in her sleep as a child, but the tendency seemed to be outgrown, till it returned after an illness early in last year. Then it caused grave anxiety for a time, but the sister, Emily, was constantly at hand to watch, and so prevented harm. Grace was now well again as they believed; the trouble had not recurred for nearly a twelvemonth, so it was thought safe for Emily to leave.

The troubled period was, I gathered, in June and July of 1914, and so coincident with the appearance of my ghost, in a place unknown to Grace Tressidy, but where she was in the future to run so grave a risk to life.

Does this afford an explanation of the story I have told? It may, or it may not; but it is the only one I have to offer.

Someday I may tell the whole of my experience to Grace herself; but first there must be the telling of another tale I have in mind, and all will depend on whether she is disposed to listen. I think—I hope—she will be favourable to a war-worn soldier, but I do not know. Then I shall perhaps discover correspondences closer than those of which I am aware, and divine how it came about that we were drawn together, I as her preserver, she to yield the life I saved, to my care for days to come.

A Perplexing Case

He opened his eyes; consciously opened them for the first time since the blow and roar of the explosion which had seemed to blot him out of life; and looked about him, wondering. He was lying on his back in a narrow hospital bed, next but one to the wall, and in the next bed somebody was groaning: that was the first sound received by his understanding ears. His right side appeared to be stiff with bandages, but felt benumbed rather than painful;—he seemed to have no use in that arm. But his left arm lay out upon the covering, and he could move it without difficulty, and the fingers of the hand. And it was his hand which he was presently regarding with surprise.

If you had looked at the board hung over the head of the bed, you would have seen his name entered as Henri de Hochepied Latour, *Sous-Lieutenant* in a French regiment which co-operated with the British in a recent attack. His name as I have written it; his injury, wounds from shell-burst, and shock to brain—this a free translation of the surgical terms: and the date, five days before, on which he had been transferred from the dressing-station to this hospital behind the lines. Could the patient have lifted and turned himself to read, he might have challenged more than one item in this account; what these were will be apparent later. But for such an effort he had not the strength; he could only stare at his left hand, holding it before his face.

In this mischance that had befallen him, which he recognised as fortune of war, what had happened to alter that unwounded member? What he expected to see was a big brawny fist, with knotted joints and hard muscles; the hand of a working man, who, somewhat reluctantly and at the call of duty, had taken to shouldering a rifle. It might be whitened and attenuated by illness, but surely it still would be the same in form. What he did see was a hand delicately slender, olive in hue of skin, strong no doubt in a determined grip, but not with navvy's strength; the nails almond-shaped, daintily manicured and tended;

17

in all these details unlike his own. How could such a change have come about? He opened and shut the hand before his face, staring stupidly at it in his surprise.

Presently a nurse, who had been attending to the moaning patient in the next bed, bent over him and noticed that consciousness had returned.

"I will bring you presently some tea, *monsieur*," she said, to test whether he understood, speaking in slow careful French, the French of an Englishwoman.

The dark head moved on the pillow.

"Have you no English, Sister?"

This man had been in hospital before.

"Yes, of course I have. I am English. But I thought you would better understand my French, though I know it is not good."

"Good or bad, it would be all the same to me. I can say *bon jour*, and ask for bread and cheese, and that's about all. What did you say to me?"

"Only that I would bring you tea as soon as it is ready."

Sister Bennett glanced again at the board hung over the bed before she turned away. There must have been some mistake, for certainly Sous-Lieutenant Henri Latour ought to be able to speak his own language, and understand it when spoken, even by an Englishwoman. And he was a thorough Frenchman to look at, this wounded soldier, though he had an English tongue in his head, and not the most refined intonation of speech. But she made no comment in reporting to the doctor that Number Forty-nine had come to himself. If there had been a mistake, they would find it out soon enough without intervention of hers. And doctors and nurses were all closely engaged that night, as a fresh batch of wounded had come in.

But the next day there was further trouble. Number Forty-nine indignantly denied his identity with the French officer Henri Latour, declaring that he was one Richard Adams, lance-corporal, attached to the London Scottish. He persisted in this assertion with so much ruffled temper, that the doctor gave direction that he should be humoured. Confusion was a common enough consequence of shell-shock, so said the man of experience; but, for all that, this was not quite a common case. It was an odd coincidence that Richard Adams of the London regiment was lying unconscious in that very hospital. He had been injured, so it was believed, at the same time as young Latour, and by the bursting of the self-same shell; and, though his wounds were not considered serious, he had not yet come to himself.

Sous-Lieutenant Latour would be all right in a day or two, so Senhouse, the captain-doctor, forecasted. No doubt this young man had been in touch with Corporal Adams immediately before the catastrophe, and somehow—though how was unexplained—the impression of Adams' personality persisted in this condition of temporary aberration. That there could have been any actual mistake between the two was out of the question; the identification discs in each case furnished proof. And, beyond this, a friend of Latour's, visiting the hospital, had recognised him when he was carried unconscious from the ambulance.

Here was testimony enough, but further witness was forthcoming. The French lieutenant was presently inquired for by two ladies: Mademoiselle Ottilie Latour, his elder sister, and with her a charming girl whom she addressed as Julie, who was the young officer's betrothed. Might they be admitted to his bedside, such was Mademoiselle Latour's petition, just to look at him as he lay asleep, if they might do no more.

Senhouse the doctor was not hard-hearted enough to refuse. If the ladies could promise self-command, they could see the patient awake or asleep. His wounds were not serious, and recovery might certainly be hoped for. The shock of the explosion, however, had to a certain extent affected his mind. For this they must be prepared.

Mademoiselle Latour promised that neither she nor her companion would betray alarm or distress, and she held Julie's quivering hand fast in hers as they passed through the temporary ward, the eyes of broken men turning on them from their pillows of pain.

The young lieutenant was awake: he lay staring at the ceiling, still with a puzzled frown upon his brow, though he had thrust the slender olive hand, which was not the hand of Richard Adams, away under the bed-coverings: he could not bear the sight of it, it perplexed him too much,

Senhouse paused by the bed as the two women came beside it, standing opposite, and he glanced up at them from the face on the pillow. Yes, there could be no doubt that this was Henri Latour, the likeness between brother and sister was so strong; the clear-cut distinguished features seemed to have been struck from the same die. This Henri might have been thought somewhat effeminate-looking when clean-shaven: now his chin was disfigured by an eight days' growth of beard: but there could be no doubt that Ottilie, the sister who resembled him, was beautiful, of the very type of womanhood that Captain Senhouse most fervently admired, noble-looking now in her calmness and her grief.

"He is awake," she breathed in the lowest of whispers. "May I speak to him?"

Assent was signified.

"*Mon frere*," she began, bending nearer, with the younger girl also pressing close and leaning on her arm. The face which was Latour's turned to regard them, but his air of sullen indifference did not alter or lighten into recognition. He looked coldly at the anxious sister, and the tremulous young beauty who was his betrothed, made a slight movement of negation, and closed his eyes.

"These ladies have come to see you. They are speaking: don't you hear them?" Thus the doctor, in English.

The man addressed replied in the same tongue.

"I am obliged to them, but I don't know them. And I speak no French."

His manner suggested obstinacy as well as indifference. He did not know these people; he was annoyed by the emotion with which they seemed to regard him, and in his maimed state he was sensitive about pity: he wished they would go away. Ottilie Latour made another effort, naming the familiar home, the early interests they had shared; surely at such a hearing, the shattered memory would light up into renewed being, as might a smouldering fire! The younger lady fell on her knees, and her voice was broken by sobs.

"Ah, Henri—ah, Henri," she cried. "Don't you remember how we parted and what you said? Have you quite forgotten?"

The man opened his eyes again, but turned to Senhouse without notice of the appeal. He was fingering his chin, which showed a dark stubble of beard.

"Doctor," he said, "is there anybody here who can shave me? Nurse says I'm bound to ask you for the order. I hate to be like this."

English again, and rough-toned English to boot.

"It is of no use at present," Senhouse said to Mademoiselle Latour. "You are only distressing yourselves needlessly. Better to come away."

There were friends waiting who took the weeping Julie in charge, but the sister lingered behind.

"It is very strange," she said to Senhouse. "Do you often have such cases? Without doubt that is my brother, but it is not his voice. He would never speak like that; he is a cultivated gentleman. How is it

20

that he forgets his native tongue? I could understand shock stripping off later acquirements for the time, but not what is the bed-rock of nature." Here she paused, her earnest gaze striving to read the doctor's countenance, on which was written deep concern. "Do you think—really think—there is any hope?"

"We do not give up hope, we doctors, and you must not. The case is a peculiar one, that I grant; but others which have come under my notice have displayed equal confusion. Much may yet be done; we must have patience. Have you any knowledge of the man he seems to personate: one Richard Adams, a private soldier in the British army? Can you suggest any possible link between him and your brother in the past?"

Mademoiselle Latour shook her head, but she appeared to be considering.

"No, I recollect nothing. Of course, Henri may have known him. He was in England two years ago, and made many acquaintances; but not army ones, so far as I am aware."

"Oddly enough, a man of that name was wounded by the same shell-burst as Lieutenant Latour, and now lies in this hospital, also suffering from shock. Would it distress you too much—could you spare the time—to look at him? He is here, in this lower ward; the door on the right. You may recognise his face: if not likely, it is possible. I shall be greatly obliged."

Senhouse had a special reason for this urgency, one he did not avow. There seemed little or no ground for supposing the inspection could be of use. Mademoiselle Latour, however, assented willingly. She was quite at leisure; she would do whatever was wished. So together they entered the second ward.

Richard Adams was conscious and very restless, the Sister in charge said when interrogated; he had been talking strangely all the afternoon, as if delirious. There seemed no sense in it, but what he jabbered was in French. She was glad the doctor had come. That was Adams, in the middle bed.

Adams was a herculean young fellow of the Saxon type, fair and blue-eyed, and in the eyes was a cloud of trouble. He was tossing restlessly on his narrow couch, as if no position could be easy; but when he caught sight of the lady-visitor, his countenance became radiant with joy.

"Ottlie—Ottilie!" he exclaimed, stretching out two eager hands burning with fever." This is good, to see someone from home. How did you come? Have you been anxious about me at Les Rochers? Tell me, how is mother? And my Julie; how is she? You don't know what it is to lie here, and long to have word of them, if only a word. Now you are here, my dear sister, how long can you stay? Give me every moment you are able."

For a brief instant the sister seemed on the verge of fainting, but she yielded her hands to the grasp of those others which were strange to her. The voice was familiar, and the questions: who could have questioned her so, but Henri only?

"Mademoiselle Latour cannot stay long," said the doctor, bending down to him. "No doubt she will come again. And now you must not excite yourself."

"I want to hear of them all," the man went on; this rough English private soldier. "All of them—old Francois, and Madelon and Ninette: all, down to Ponto the dog. I dream of them at night, and I see them when I dream. Has mother been anxious about me? I feel sure she has."

The sister at last recovered power of speech.

"Yes, yes—indeed—she has been anxious: she is. She talks of nothing but Henri. I am here to bring her news."

"Tell her my last thought was of her. There was a blow which struck me—a great rushing, and a noise that stunned. The rush, sent me spinning with it, as if I had been a bullet from a gun: spinning—spinning through space. I thought I was going to her—to Rochers la Vallière, and I cried out her name. But I did not get to La Vallière: I did not go so far. Everything went dark, and I remember no more. I woke in this place, and I cannot make them understand what I want. Take me with you, Ottilie; take me home. Are they well there? The invasion has not touched them? Is mother well?"

"They are all well, and safe, and hoping for news of—of you—of Henri." As she spoke, she looked across at Senhouse in appeal: she knew not how much longer she could trust her self-command to keep up this farce: farce, was it, or fact and truth?

Not many more words were exchanged before the doctor asserted authority and led her away; and now she needed the support of his arm. Outside the ward she was thankful to sink into a chair, and drink the water he presently held to her lips.

"You did not know this Adams?"

"Not his face. But it was my brother speaking with his lips. My brother's body is in the other ward— his spirit here. *M. le docteur*, it is

22

terrible. Body and soul apart! What can be done?"

"You must forgive me for exposing you to such an ordeal. I suspected what was the matter, but I wanted to be sure. I wanted to see if this Adams, as he is called, would recognise you. Plainly he did so: he spoke to you at once by name. It will be easier to treat, now that we understand. There may be need of long patience. But, to my thinking, there is no reason for despair."

Mademoiselle Latour was gathering back her shaken self-control; she set down the glass of water.

"What can be done?" she repeated.

It was the question Senhouse had asked himself, and still he was groping in the dark after an answer. But he desired above all to reassure this noble-looking woman, who had been so sorely tried by his experiment. In replying, he assumed a confidence he was far from feeling, but hope was strong that it might be justified by the event.

"You will give me a free hand to do what I think best for M. Latour? There is a man, a Parisian doctor, who is great in these mysterious cases of—of brain-suspension, and confusion and all that. We will have him here in consultation, and he shall advise and treat the case. He has made some wonderful successes. You may be certain no pains will be spared by us to efface what now is wrong, and to restore the link of mind and body completely as before."

★★★★★★★★★★★★★★★★

Senhouse did not forget the apparent Latour's complaint about his sprouting beard, and he gave the required order that the lieutenant should be shaved—a simple matter, which had a somewhat unlooked-for result. The hospital orderly was sufficiently skilled to operate in this way upon the chins of the patients, and in due course of time he arrived with razor and lathering-bowl to shave the young French officer. He found the young French officer in sufficiently good spirits to be communicative. There was nothing, he averred, that did him so much good as a clean shave: it put him at once on right terms with himself and his world. And as (he hoped) his was a "Blighty" case of wounding, it would never do for him to go back to England with so much bristle showing. Liz, his wife, as good an old girl as ever stepped, would in that case have nothing to say to him.

"You think of crossing over to England, sir?" questioned the orderly, mindful of necessary respect when he was shaving an officer. But this officer had an odd way of talking, Frenchman as he was.

"Why, of course I shall be sent to England, and I hope it will be to

23

a London hospital. That will be convenient for Liz. She lives out Poplar way, and takes in fine sewing; and she has kept herself comfortable with that and the allowance—good old girl. And I know that, were it ever so, she'd never look at any one but me; not like some of the fellows' wives one hears of. We've got a kid, too; eight months old he is, and so far I've never set eyes on him. Liz'll bring him to the hospital when she comes to see me, you bet she does, for she's as proud of him as—as——"

The illustration failed, as the razor was now operating round the lower lip, and silence was only prudent. But in another couple of minutes, he would be released.

"There, sir, there's a clean shave for you. And, though I say it as shouldn't, one it would be hard to beat."

The patient fingered his chin somewhat doubtfully, with the one hand he could move; the hand which had caused him so much disquietude when he came to himself.

"I've got a glass here," said the soldier-barber. "'Tis but a little one, but if you look in it you can see for yourself. It has freshened you up above a bit, and you can't fail to be pleased."

The small vanity-glass was produced, and held at the right angle. The patient looked, and, looking, gave a cry—a yell of horror which rang through the ward, so that all the heads on all the other pillows turned to gaze, and the sister in charge came hurrying to learn what was the matter. This Latour, usually quiet and biddable, was suddenly wrought up into a state of fierce excitement.

"What have they done to me," he demanded wildly, "to make me look like that? I never had that sort of (blank-blank) face. I'll have the law of the (blank-blank) doctors, (blank) me if I don't. If I go to England with that face, Liz'll never believe I'm her husband." And so forth, in the teeth of regulations, and despite all persuasion, the protest garnished with sundry very forcible oaths which we omit, until excitement stilled away into exhaustion, and the sick man lost himself in sleep.

★★★★★★★★★★★★★★★★

The Parisian doctor who had become the referee in shock cases which do not yield to ordinary treatment, we will call Despard for the purpose of this narrative; it is not his real name. It became known very shortly that he had been summoned to the perplexing case at the B—— hospital, about which some rumour had gone abroad. Despard was supposed to pin his faith on hypnotism and such-like uncanny nostrums, and in consequence his name stank in the nostrils of one half of the surgical staff. He was going to hypnotise the shock case, that was the assumption; and some surprise was evidenced when it crept out through certain preparations, that Latour was to be treated by the more ordinary method of the transfusion of blood.

"I hope you've got a healthy subject to be donor," said the C.M.O., meeting Senhouse on the stairs. "And don't forget the saltwater admixture; for, whatever Despard says, I hold that to be essential." And then the C.M.O. bethought him to ask: "Who is the donor?"

"Well, sir, it is the other shock man, Adams. M. Despard has chosen him. He is healthy enough, I think, and a young Hercules for strength,"

"Tut-tut," said the great man, who very plainly disapproved, and to whom the hypnotist and his methods were *anathema maranatha*. "What!—two shock cases, and transfuse their blood! Never heard of such a proceeding in my life. What possibly can be gained by it but an aggravation of both their symptoms?" And so forth; and the C.M.O. may be written down as "left objecting."

★★★★★★★★★★★★★★★★

The experiment was tried next day in the operating-room of the hospital, Senhouse acting as one of Despard's assistants, the other being a coadjutor who accompanied him. The door was of course barred against intrusion, and what took place within was never precisely known. The process was a long one, and once while it was in progress Senhouse managed to slip away, so as to convey a modicum of comfort to the room below, where Ottilie Latour had been allowed to wait. She looked up at his entrance, eagerly expectant. She was pale to the lips with anxiety, but as beautiful as ever—at least Senhouse thought so.

"Is it over?" she asked.

"Not yet, and will not be for another hour. But I thought you would be relieved to know all is going well, and Despard is quite hopeful. He says it is a simple case compared to some which have passed through his hands, and he expects complete success. They went off into trance without difficulty, both of them, and neither saw the other, as a screen was put up between them. And they will be moved into fresh quarters directly after, so that there will be nothing to revive former impressions. I am sorry you have so long to wait."

"I do not mind how long; it is everything to be on the spot, and I thank you from my heart for getting me permission to wait here. I know you will bring me the earliest news."

"I will come to you the instant certainty is assured. But I don't expect Despard will give leave for you to see your brother today. Don't let that disappoint you."

Upon this, the messenger went back to his post at the theatre. There a certain amount of vital fluid was in process of interchange, and two spirits wrongly housed in their tenements of flesh were brought into touch by a force only partially recognised, though of existence coeval with human life.

After a while one of the patients began to stir and moan, and then to utter some querulous complaint.

"The young gentleman is coming round," said the assistant, calling Despard's attention. "*And he is speaking French.*"

Despard gave a grunt of satisfaction.

"Ah," he said, "if that is so, we have done well."

Some half hour later Senhouse went back to Ottilia.

"It is over, successfully over, and M. Despard confidently hopes the confusion will never be renewed. Your brother is in bed in the new ward, quite composed, and he remembers that you visited him. 'When is my sister coming again; my sister Ottilie?' he asked me. I told him you had been here today, but the doctor thought it unwise to permit a visitor on the day of operation. He said: 'Tell her to give my devotion to Julie and mother, and a message of remembrance to all at Rochers la Vallière.' And then he turned his face away on the pillow and fell asleep. That was your brother in his true form, not as before. You understand?"

Yes, Ottilie Latour understood, and her eyes were full of grateful tears.

★★★★★★★★★★★★★★★

Four days after, the second shock case was entrained for Blighty. Another shave had smartened him sufficiently to appear as Liz would wish and expect; and now when the glass was presented, he saw his own face in it—the face she would recognise and that he knew. And his hand was broad and muscular again, not the slim olive member the sight of which was his first perplexity. What had been the matter with him he queried, and was told on the doctor's authority he had suffered from shell-shock. And that to the victims of shock, confusion and dementia manifest themselves in many forms, including distorted vision, all owing to the temporary loss of balance by the brain.

A Water Witch

1

We were disappointed when Robert married. We had for long wanted him to marry, as he is our only brother and head of the family since my father died, as well as of the business firm; but we should have liked his wife to be a different sort of person. We, his sisters, could have chosen much better for him than he did for himself. Indeed, we had our eye on just the right girl—bright-tempered and sensibly brought up, who would not have said No, of that I am assured, had Robert on his side shown signs of liking.

But he took a holiday abroad the spring of 1912, and the next thing we heard was that he had made up his mind to marry Frederica. Frederica, indeed! We Larcombs have been plain Susans and Annes and Marys and Elizabeths for generations (I am Mary), and the fantastic name was an annoyance. The wedding took place at Mentone in a great hurry, because the stepmother was marrying again, and Frederica was unhappy. Was not that weak of Robert?—he did not give himself time to think. We may perhaps take that as some excuse for a departure from Larcomb traditions: on consideration, the match would very likely have been broken off.

Frederica had some money of her own, though not much: all the Larcomb brides have had money up to now. And her dead father was a general and a K.C.B., which did not look amiss in the announcement; but there our satisfaction ended. He brought her to make our acquaintance three weeks after the marriage, a delicate little shrinking thing well matched to her fanciful name, and desperately afraid of mother and of us girls, so the introductory visit was hardly a success. Then Robert took her off to London, and when the baby was born—a son, but too weakly to live beyond a day or two—she had a severe illness, and was slow in recovering strength. And there is little doubt that by this time he was conscious of having made a mistake.

I used to be his favourite sister, being next to him in age, and when he found himself in a difficulty at Roscawen he appealed to me. Roscawen was a moor Robert had lately rented on the Scotch side of the Border, and we were given to understand that a bracing air, and the complete change of scene, were expected to benefit Frederica, who was pleased by the arrangement. So, his letter took me by surprise.

"Dear Mary," he wrote, and, characteristically, he did not beat about the bush. "Pack up your things as soon as you get this, and come off here the day after tomorrow. You will have to travel *via* York, and I will meet you at Draycott Halt, where the afternoon train stops by signal. Freda is a bit nervous, and doesn't like staying alone here, so I am in a fix. I want you to keep her company the weeks I am at Shepstow. I know you'll do as much as this for—Your affectionate brother, Robert Larcomb."

This abrupt call upon me, making sure of response and help, recalled bygone times when we were much to each other, and Frederica still in the unknown. A bit nervous, was she, and Robert in a fix because of it: here again was evidence of the mistake. It was not very easy then to break off from work, and for an indefinite time; but I resolved to satisfy the family curiosity, to say nothing of my own, by doing as I was bid.

When I got out of the train at Draycott Halt, Robert was waiting for me with his car. My luggage was put in at the back, and I mounted to the seat beside him; and again, it reminded me of old times, for he seemed genuinely pleased to see me.

"Good girl," he said, "to make no fuss, and come at once."

"We Larcombs are not apt to fuss, are we?"—and as I said this, it occurred, to me that probably he was in these days well acquainted with fuss—Frederica's fuss. Then I asked: "What is the matter?"

I only had a sideways glimpse of him as he answered, for he was busy with the driving-gear.

"Why, I told you, didn't I, that it was arranged for me to be here and at Shepstow week and week about, Falkner and I together, for it is better than taking either moor with a single gun. And I can't take Freda there, for the Shepstow cottage has no accommodation for a lady—only the one room that Falkner and I share. Freda is nervous, poor girl, since her illness, and somehow, she has taken a dislike to Roscawen. It is nothing but a fancy, of course, but something had to be done."

"Why, you wrote to mother that you had both fallen in love with the place, and thought it quite ideal."

"Oh, the place is right enough, it is just my poor girl's fancy. She'll tell you I daresay, but don't let her dwell on it more than you can help. You will have Falkner's room, and the week he is over here I've arranged for Vickers to put him up, though I daresay he will come in to meals. Vickers?—oh, he's a neighbour on the opposite side of the water, Roscawen Water, the stream that overflows from the lake in the hills. He's a doctor of science as well as medicine, and has written some awfully clever books.

"I understand he's at work on another, and comes here for the sake of quiet. But he's a very good sort though not a sportsman, does not mind taking in Falkner, and he is by way of being a friend of Freda's—they read Italian together. No, he isn't married, neither is the parson, worse luck; and there isn't another woman of her own sort within miles. It's desperately lonely for her, I allow, when I'm not here. So, there was no help for it. I was bound to send for you or for the mater, and I thought you would be best!"

We were passing through wild scenery of barren broken hills, following the course of the river up-stream. It came racing down a rocky course, full and turbulent from recent rains. Presently the road divided, crossing a narrow bridge; and there we came in sight of the leap the water makes over a shelf of rock, plunging into a deep pool below with a swirl of foam and spray. I would have liked to linger and look, but the car carried us forward quickly, allowing only a glimpse in passing. And, directly after, Robert called my attention to a stone-built small house high up on the hill-side—a bare place it looked, flanked by a clump of firs, but with no surrounding garden-ground; the wild moor and the heather came close under the windows.

"That's Roscawen," he said. "Just a shooting-box, you see. A new-built place, raw, with no history behind it later than yesterday. I was in treaty for Corby, seventeenth century that was, with a ghost in the gallery, but the arrangement fell through. And I'm jolly glad it did"—and here he laughed; an uncomfortable laugh, not of the Larcomb sort, or like himself. And in another minute, we were at the door.

Freda welcomed me, and I thought her improved; she was indeed pretty—as pretty as such a frail little thing could be, who looked as if a puff of wind would blow her away. She was very well dressed—of course Robert would take care of that—and her one thought appeared to be of him. She was constantly turning to him with appeal of one sort or another, and seemed nervous and ill at ease when he was out of her sight. "Must you really go tomorrow?" I caught her whisper later, and heard his answer: "Needs must, but you will not mind now you have Mary." I could plainly see that she did mind, and that my companionship was no fair exchange for the loss of his. But was not all this exaction the very way to tire out love?

The ground-floor of the house was divided into a sitting-hall, upon which the front door opened without division, and to the right you entered a fair-sized dining-room. Each of these apartments had the offshoot of a smaller room, one being Freda's snuggery, and the other the gun-room where the gentlemen smoked. Above there were two good bedrooms, a dressing-room and a bathroom, but no higher floor: the gable-space was not utilised, and the servants slept over the kitchen at the back. The room allotted to me, from which Captain Falkner had been ejected, had a wide window and a pleasant aspect. As I was hurriedly dressing for dinner, I could hear the murmur of the river close at hand, but the actual water was not visible, as it flowed too far below the overhanging bank.

I could not see the flowing water, but as I glanced from the window, a wreath of white mist or spray floated up from it, stretched itself out before the wind, and disappeared after the fashion of a puff of steam. Probably there was at that point another fall (so I thought) churning the river into foam. But I had no time to waste in speculation, for we Larcombs adhere to the good ways of punctuality. I fastened a final hook and eye, and ran downstairs.

Captain Falkner came to dinner and made a fourth at table, but the fifth place which had been laid remained vacant. The two men were full of plans for the morrow, and there was to be an early setting out: Shepstow, the other moor, was some thirty miles away.

"I am afraid you will be dull, Mary," Robert said to me in a sort of apology. "I am forced to keep the car at Shepstow, as I am my own chauffeur. But you and Freda will have her cart to jog about in, so you will be able to look round the nearer country while I am away. You will have to put up with the old mare. I know you like spirit in a horse, but this quiet gee suits Freda, as she can drive her going alone. Then Vickers will look in on you most days. I do not know what is keeping him away tonight."

Freda was in low spirits next morning, and she hung about Robert up to the time of his departure, in a way that I should have found supremely irritating had I been her husband. And I will not be sure that she did not beg him again not to leave her—to my tender mercies I

30

supposed—though I did not hear the request. When the two men had set out with their guns and baggage, the cart was ordered round, and my sister-in-law took me for a drive.

Robert had done well to prepare me for the "quiet gee": a meek old creature named Grey Madam, that had whitened in the snows of many winters, and expected to progress at a walk whenever the road inclined uphill. And all the roads inclined uphill or down about Roscawen; I do not remember anywhere a level quarter of a mile. It was truly a dull progress, and Freda did not find much to say; perhaps she still was fretting after Robert. But the moors and the swelling hills were beautiful to look at in their crimson flush of heather. "I think Roscawen is lovely," I was prompted to exclaim; and when she agreed in my admiration I added: "You liked it when you first came here, did you not?"

"Yes, I liked it when first I came," she assented, repeating my words, but did not go on to say why she disliked Roscawen now.

She had an errand to discharge at one of the upland farms which supplied them with milk and butter. She drew rein at the gate, and was about to alight, but the woman of the house came forward, and so I heard what passed. Freda gave her order, and then made an inquiry.

"I hope you have found your young cow, Mrs. Elliott? I was sorry to hear it had strayed."

"We've found her, ma'am, but she was dead in the river, and a sad loss it has been to us. A fine young beast as ever we reared, and coming on with her second calf. My husband has been rarely put about, and I'll own I was fit to cry over her myself. This is the fifth loss we have had within the year—a sheep and two lambs in March, and the cart-foal in July."

Freda expressed sympathy.

"You need better fences, is that it, to keep your cattle from the river?"

Mrs. Elliott pursed up her lips and shook her head.

"I won't say, ma'am, but that our fences might be bettered if the landlord would give us material; as it is, we do our best. But when the creatures take that madness for the water, nought but deer-palings would keep them in. I've seen enough in my time here to be sure of that. What makes it come over them I don't take upon myself to say. They make up fine tales in the district about the white woman, but I know nothing of any white women. I only know that when the madness takes them, they make for the river, and then they get swept into the deeps."

When we were driving away, I asked Freda what the farmer's wife meant about a white woman and the drowning of her stock.

"I believe there is some story about a woman who was drowned, whose spirit calls the creatures to the river. If you ask Dr. Vickers he will tell you. He makes a study of folk-lore and local superstitions, and—and that sort of thing. Robert thinks it is all nonsense, and no doubt you will think it nonsense too."

What her own opinion was, Freda did not say. She had a transparent complexion, and a trifling matter made her change colour; a blush rose unaccountably as she answered me, and for a full minute her cheek burned. Why should she blush about Roscawen superstitions and a drowned cow? Then the attention of both of us was suddenly diverted, because Grey Madam took it into her head to shy.

She had mended her pace appreciably since Freda turned her head towards home, trotting now without needing to be urged. We were close upon a cross-roads where three ways met, a triangular green centred by a finger-post. There was in our direction a bank and hedge (hedges here and there replaced the stone walls of the district) and the right wheel went up that bank, giving the cart a dangerous tilt; it recovered balance, however, and went on. Freda, a timid driver, was holding on desperately to the reins.

"Does she often do this sort of thing?" I asked. "I thought Robert said she was quiet."

"So, she is—so we thought her. I never knew her do it before," gasped my sister-in-law, still out of breath with her fright.

"And I cannot think what made her shy. There was nothing—absolutely nothing; not even a heap of stones."

Freda did not answer, but I was to hear more about that cross-roads in the course of the day.

2

After lunch Freda did not seem willing to go out again, so, as I was there to companion her, we both settled down to needlework and a book for alternate reading aloud. The reading, however, languished; when it came to Freda's turn she tired quickly, lost her place twice and again, and seemed unable to fix her attention on the printed page. Was she listening, I wondered later. When silence fell between us, I became aware of a sound recurring at irregular intervals, the sound of water dropping. I looked up at the ceiling expecting to see a stain of wet, for the drop seemed to fall within the room, and close beside me.

"Do you hear that?" I asked. "Has anything gone wrong in the bathroom, do you think?" For we were in Freda's snuggery, and the bathroom was overhead.

But my suggestion of overflowing taps and broken water-pipes left her cold.

"I don't think it is from the bathroom," she replied. "I hear it often. We cannot find out what it is."

Directly she ceased speaking the drop fell again, apparently between us as we sat, and plump upon the carpet. I looked up at the ceiling again, but Freda did not raise her eyes from her embroidery.

"It is very odd," I remarked, and this time she assented, repeating my words, and I saw a shiver pass over her. "I shall go upstairs to the bathroom," I said decidedly, putting down my work. "I am sure those taps must be wrong."

She did not object, or offer to accompany me, she only shivered again.

"Don't be long away, Mary," she said, and I noticed she had grown pale.

There was nothing wrong with the bathroom, or with any part of the water supply; and when I returned to the snuggery the drip had ceased. The next event was a ring at the door bell, and again Freda changed colour, much as she had done when we were driving. In that quiet place, where comers and goers are few, a visitor is an event. But I think this visitor must have been expected. The servant announced Dr. Vickers.

Freda gave him her hand, and made the necessary introduction. This was the friend Robert said would come often to see us, but he was not at all the snuffy, old scientist my fancy had pictured. He was old certainly, if it is a sign of age to be grey-haired, and I daresay there were crowsfeet about those piercing eyes of his; but when you met the eyes, the wrinkles were forgotten. They, at least, were full of youth and fire, and his figure was still upright and flat-shouldered.

We exchanged a few remarks; he asked me if I was familiar with that part of Scotland; and when I answered that I was making its acquaintance for the first time, he praised Roseawen and its neighbourhood. It suited him well, he said, when his object was to seek quiet; and I should find, as he did, that it possessed many attractions. Then he asked me if I was an Italian scholar, and showed a book in his hand, the *Vita Nuova*. Mrs. Larcomb was forgetting her Italian, and he had promised to brush it up for her. So, if I did not find it too great a bore to sit by, he proposed to read aloud. And, should I not know the book, he would give me a sketch of its purport, so that I could follow.

I had, of course, heard of the *Vita Nuova*, who has not! but my knowledge of the language in which it was written went no further than a few modern phrases, of use to a traveller. I disclaimed my ability to follow, and I imagine Dr. Vickers was not ill-pleased to find me ignorant. He took his seat at one end of the Chesterfield sofa, Freda occupying the other, still with that flush on her cheek; and after an observation or two in Italian, he opened his book and began to read.

I imagine he read well. The crisp, flowing syllables sounded very foreign to my ear, and he gave his author the advantage of dramatic expression and emphasis. Now and then he remarked in English on some difficulty in the text, or slipped in a question in Italian which Freda answered, usually by a monosyllable. She kept her eyes fixed upon her work. It was as if she would not look at him, even when he was most impassioned; but I was watching them both, although I never thought—but of course I never thought!

Presently I remembered how time was passing, and the place where letters should be laid ready for the post-bag going out. I had left an unfinished one upstairs, so I slipped away to complete and seal. This done, I re-entered softly (the entrance was behind a screen) and found the Italian lesson over, and a conversation going on in English. Freda was speaking with some animation.

"It cannot any more be called my fancy, for Mary heard it too."

"And you had not told her beforehand? There was no suggestion?"

"I had not said a word to her. Had I, Mary?"— appealing to me as I advanced into sight.

"About what?" I asked, for I had forgotten the water incident.

"About the drops falling. You remarked on them first: I had told you nothing. And you went to look at the taps."

"No, certainly you had not told me. What is the matter? Is there any mystery?"

Dr. Vickers answered:

"The mystery is that Mrs. Larcomb heard these droppings when everyone else was deaf to them. It was supposed to be autosuggestion on her part. You have disproved that Miss Larcomb, as your ears are open to them too. That will go far to convince your brother; and now we must seriously seek for cause. This Roscawen district has many legends of strange happenings. We do not want to add one more to the

34

list, and give this modern shooting-box the reputation of a haunted house."

"And it would be an odd sort of ghost, would it not—the sound of dropping water! But—you speak of legends of the district; do you know anything of a white woman who is said to drown cattle? Mrs. Elliott mentioned her this morning at the farm, when she told us she had lost her cow in the river."

"Ay, I heard a cow had been found floating dead in the Pool. I am sorry it belonged to the Elliotts. Nobody lives here for long without hearing that story, and, though the wrath of Roscawen is roused against her, I cannot help being sorry for the white woman. She was young and beautiful once, and well-to-do, for she owned land in her own right, and flocks and herds. But she became very unhappy—"

He was speaking to me, but he looked at Freda. She had taken up her work again, but with inexpert hands, dropping first cotton, and then her thimble.

"She was unhappy, because her husband neglected her. He had—other things to attend to, and the charm she once possessed for him was lost and gone. He left her too much alone. She lost her health, they say, through fretting, and so fell into a melancholy way, spending her time in weeping, and in wandering up and down on the banks of Roscawen Water. She may have fallen in by accident, it was not exactly known; but her death was thought to be suicide, and she was buried at the cross-roads."

"That was where Grey Madam shied this morning," Freda put in.

"And—people suppose—that on the other side of death, finding herself lonely (too guilty, perhaps, for Heaven, but at the same time too innocent for Hell) she wants companions to join her; wants sheep and cows and horses such as used to stock her farms. So, she puts madness upon the creatures, and also upon some humans, so that they go down to the river. They see her, so it is said, or they receive a sign which in some way points to the manner of her death. If they see her, she comes for them once, twice, thrice, and the third time they are bound to follow."

This was a gruesome story, I thought as I listened, though not of the sort I could believe. I hoped Freda did not believe it, but of this I was not sure.

"What does she look like?" I asked. "If human beings see her as you say, do they give any account?"

"The story goes that they see foam rising from the water, floating away and dissolving, vaguely in form at first, but afterwards more like the woman she was once; and some say there is a hand that beckons. But I have never seen her Miss Larcomb, nor spoken to one who has: first hand evidence of this sort is rare, as I daresay you know. So, I can tell you no more."

And I was glad there was no more for me to hear, for the story was too tragic for my liking. The happenings of that afternoon left me discomforted—annoyed with Dr. Vickers, which perhaps was unreasonable—with poor Freda, whose fancies had thus proved contagious—annoyed, and here more justly, with myself. Somehow, with such tales going about, Roscawen seemed a far from desirable residence for a nervous invalid; and I was also vaguely conscious of an undercurrent I did not understand. It gave me the feeling you have when you stumble against something unexpected blindfold, or in the dark, and cannot define its shape.

Dr. Vickers accepted a cup of tea when the tray was brought to us, and then he took his departure, which was as well, seeing we had no gentleman at home to entertain him.

"So Larcomb is away again for a whole week? Is that so?" he said to Freda as he made his *adieux*.

There was no need for the question, I thought impatiently, as he must very well have known when he was required again to put up Captain Falkner.

"Yes, for a whole week," Freda answered, with again that flush on her cheek; and as soon as we were alone, she put up her hand, as if the hot colour burned.

3

I did not like Dr. Vickers and his Italian lessons, and I had the impression Freda would have been better pleased by their intermission. On the third day she had a headache and charged me to make her excuses, so it fell to me to receive this friend of Robert's, who seemed quite unruffled by her absence. He took advantage of the opportunity to cross-examine me about the water-dropping: had I heard it again since that first occasion, and what explanation of the sounds appeared satisfactory to myself?

The fact was, I had heard it again, twice when I was alone in my room, and once more when sitting with Freda. Then we both sat listening—listening, such small nothings as we had to say to each other dying away, waiting to see which of us would first admit it to the other, and this went on for more than an hour. At last Freda broke out into hysterical crying, the result of over-strained nerves, and with her outburst the sounds ceased. I had been inclined to entertain a notion of the spiritist order, that they might be connected with her presence as medium; but I suppose that must be held disproved, as I also heard them when alone in my own room.

I admitted as little as possible to Dr.Vickers, and was stout in asserting that a natural cause would and must be found, if the explanation were diligently sought for. But I confess I was posed when confronted with the fact that these sounds heard by Freda were inaudible to her husband, also present—to Robert, who has excellent hearing, in common with all our family. Until I came, and was also an auditor, no one in the house but Freda had noticed the dropping, so there was reason for assuming it to be hallucination. Yes, I was sorry for her trouble (answering a question pressed on me), but I maintained that, pending discovery, the best course was to take no notice of drops that wet nothing and left no stain, and did not proceed from overflowing cisterns or faulty pipes.

"They will leave off doing it if not noticed; is that what you think, Miss Larcomb?" And when I rashly assented—"Now perhaps you will define for me what you mean by *they*? Is it the 'natural cause'?"

Here again was a poser: I had formulated no idea that I cared to define. Probably the visitor divined the subject was unwelcome, for he turned to others, conversing agreeably enough for another quarter of an hour. Then he departed, leaving a message of concern for Freda's headache. He hoped it would have amended by next day, when he would call to inquire.

He did call on the following day, when the Italian lesson was mainly conversational, and I had again a feeling Freda was distressed by what was said, though I could only guess at what passed between them under the disguise of a foreign tongue. But at the end I recognised the words "not tomorrow" as spoken by her, and when some protest appeared to follow, she dumbly shook her head.

Dr.Vickers did not stay on for tea as before. Did Freda think she had offended him, for some time later I noticed she had been crying? That night I had an odd dream that the Roscawen house was sliding down from its foundations into the river at the call of the white woman, and I woke suddenly with the fright.

The next day was the last of Robert's stay at Shepstow. In the evening, he and Captain Falker returned, and at once a different atmosphere seemed to pervade the house. Freda recovered cheerfulness, I heard no more dropping water, and except at dinner on the second evening we saw nothing of Dr. Vickers. But he sent an Italian book with many scored passages, and a note in it, also in Italian, which I saw her open and read, and then immediately tear up into the minutest pieces. I supposed he wished her to keep up her studies, though the lessons were for a while suspended; I heard him say at dinner that he was busy correcting proofs.

So passed four days out of the seven Robert should have spent at Roscawen. But on the fourth evening came a telegraphic summons: his presence was needed in London, at the office, and he was bound to go up to town by the early express next day. And the arrangement was that in returning he should go straight to Shepstow and join Captain Falkner there; this distant moor was to be reached from a station on another line.

Freda must have known that Robert could not help himself, but it was easy to see how her temporarily restored spirits fell again to zero. I hope I shall never be so dependent on another person's society as she seemed to be on Robert's. I got up to give him his early breakfast, but Freda did not appear; she had a headache, he said, and had passed a restless night. She would not rise till later: perhaps I would go up and see her by-and-bye.

I did go later in the morning, to find her lying like a child that had sobbed itself to sleep, her eyelashes still wet, and a tear sliding down her cheek. So, I took a book, and drew a chair to the bedside, waiting for her to wake.

It was a long waiting; she slept on, and slept heavily. And as I sat and watched, there began again the dropping of water, and, for the first time in my experience of them, the drops were wet.

I could find traces now on the carpet of where they fell, and on the spread linen of the sheet; were they made, I wondered fantastically, out of Freda's tears? But they had ceased before she woke, and I did not remark on them to her. Yes, she had a headache, she said, answering my question: it was better, but not gone: she would lie quietly where she was for the present." The servants might bring her a cup of tea when I had luncheon, 'and she would get up later in the afternoon.

So, as I was not needed, I went out after lunch for a solitary walk. Not being governed by Freda's choice of direction, I determined to explore the course of the river, and especially how it flowed under the steep bank below the house, where I saw the wreath of foam rise in the air on my first evening at Roseawen. I expected to find a fall at this spot, but there was only broken water and rapids, alternating with smoother reaches and deep pools, one of which, I concluded, had been the death-trap of the Elliotts' cow. It was a still, perfect autumn day, warm, but not with the oppression of summer heat, and I walked with enjoyment, following the stream upward to where it issued from the miniature lake among the hills, in which it slept for a while in mid-course. Then I turned homewards, and was within sight of our dwelling when I again beheld the phenomenon of the pillar of foam.

It rose above the rapids, as nearly as I could guess in the same spot as before; and as there was now little or no wind, it did not so quickly spread out and dissipate. I could imagine that at early morning, or in the dimness of evening, it might be taken for a figure of the ghostly sort, especially as, in dissolving, it seemed to move and beckon. I smiled to myself to think that, according to local superstition, I too had seen the white woman; but I felt no least inclination to rush to the river and precipitate myself into its depths. Nor would I gratify Dr. Vickers by telling him what had been my experience, or confide in Freda lest she should-tell again.

On reaching home, I turned into the snuggery to see if Freda was downstairs; it must, I thought, be nearly tea-time. She was there; and, as I pushed the door open and was still behind the screen, I heard Dr. Vickers' voice." Mind," he was saying in English, "I do not press you to decide at once. Wait till you are convinced he does not care. To my thinking he has already made it plain."

I stood arrested, not intending to play eavesdropper, but stricken with surprise. As I moved into sight, the two were standing face to face, and the doctor's figure hid Freda from me. I think his hands were on her shoulders, holding her before him, but of this I am not sure. He was quick of hearing as a cat, and he turned on me at once.

"Ah, how do you do. Miss Larcomb? I was just bidding *adieu* to your sister-in-law, for I do not think she is well enough today to take her lesson. In fact, I think she is very far from well. These headaches spell slow progress with our study, but we must put up with delay."

He took up the slim book from the table and bestowed it in his pocket, bowed over my hand and was gone.

If Freda had been agitated, she concealed any disturbance, and we talked as usual over tea, of my walk, and even of Robert's journey. But she surprised me later in the evening by an unexpected proposition.

"Do you think Mrs. Larcomb would have me to stay at Aston

Bury? It would be very kind of her if she would take me in while Robert has these shootings. I do not like Roscawen, and I am not well here. Will you ask her, Mary?"

I answered that I was sure mother would have her if she wished to come to us; but what would Robert say when he had asked me to companion her here? If Robert was willing, I would write—of course. Did he know what she proposed?

No, she said, and there would be no time to consult him. She would like to go as soon as tomorrow. Could we send a telegram, and set out in the morning, staying the night in York, to receive an answer there? That she was very much in earnest about this wish of hers there could be no doubt. She was trembling visibly, and a red fever-spot burned on her cheek.

I wish I had done as she asked. But my Larcomb common-sense was up in arms, and I required to know the reason why. Mother would think it strange if we rushed off to her so, and Robert might not like it; but, given time to make the arrangement, she could certainly pay the visit, and would be received as a welcome guest. I would write to mother and post on the morrow, and she could write to Robert and send the letter by Captain Falkner. Then I said: "Are you nervous here, Freda? Is it because these water-droppings are unexplained?"

And when she made a sort of dumb assent, I went on: "You ought not to dwell on anything so trivial; it isn't fair to Robert. It cannot be only this. Surely there is something more?"

The question seemed to increase her distress.

"I want to be a good wife to Robert; oh, I want that, Mary. I can do my duty if I go away; if you will keep me safe at Aston Bury for only a little while. Robert does not understand; he thinks me crazed with delusions. I tried to tell him—I did indeed; hard as it was to tell." While this was spoken, she was torn with sobs. "I am terrified to be alone. What is compelling me is too strong. Oh Mary, take me away."

I could get no fuller explanation than this of what was at the root of the trouble. We agreed at last that the two letters should be written and sent on the morrow, and we would hold ourselves in readiness to set out as soon as answers were received. It might be no more than an hysterical fancy on Freda's part, but I was not without suspicion of another sort. But she never mentioned their neighbour's name, and I could not insult her by the suggestion.

The letters were written early on that Thursday morrow, and then Grey Madam was brought round for Freda's drive. The direction chosen took us past the cross-roads in the outward going, and also in return. I remember Freda talked more cheerfully and freely than usual, asking questions about Aston Bury, as if relieved at the prospect of taking refuge there with us.

As we went, Grey Madam shied badly at the same spot as before, though there was no visible cause for her terror. I suggested we had better go home a different way; but this appeared impracticable, as the other direction involved an added distance of several miles, and the crossing of a bridge which was thought to be unsafe. In returning, the mare went unwillingly, and, though our pace had been a sober one and the day was not warm, I could see she had broken out into a lather of sweat. As we came to the cross-roads for the second time, the poor creature again shied away from the invisible object which terrified her, and then, seizing the bit between her teeth, she set off at a furious gallop.

Freda was tugging at the reins, but it was beyond her power to stop that mad career, or even guide it; but the mare kept by instinct to the middle of the road. The home gate was open, and I expected she would turn in stablewards; but instead, she dashed on to the open moor, making for the river.

We might possibly have jumped out, but there was no time even for thought before we were swaying on the edge of the steep bank. The next moment there was a plunge, a crash, and I remember no more.

The accident was witnessed from the further side—so I heard later. A man left his digging and ran, and it was he who dragged me out, stunned, but not suffocated by the immersion. I came to myself quickly on the bank, and my instant thought was of Freda, but she, entangled with the reins, had been swept down with the mare into the deeper pool. When I staggered up, dizzy and half-blind, begging she might be sought for, he ran on downstream, and there he and Dr. Vickers and another man drew her from the water—lifeless it seemed at first, and it was long before any spark of animation repaid their utmost efforts.

That was a strange return to Roscawen house, she tenderly carried, I able to walk thither; both of us dripping water, real drops, of which the ghostly ones may have been some mysterious forecast, if that is not too fantastic for belief!

It was impossible to shut Dr. Vickers out, and of course he accompanied us; for all my doubt of him, I welcomed the service of his skill when Freda's life was hanging in the balance, and she herself was too remote from this world to recognise who was beside her. But I would have preferred to owe that debt of service to any other; and the feeling I had against him deepened as I witnessed his anguished concern, and caught some unguarded expressions he let fall.

I wired to Robert to acquaint him with what had happened, and he replied "I am coming." And upon that I resolved to speak out, and tell him what I had guessed as the true cause of Freda's trouble, and why she must be removed, not so much from a haunted house, as from an overmastering influence which she dreaded.

Did the risk of loss—the peril barely surmounted, restore the old tenderness between these two? I think it did, at any rate for the time, when Robert found her lying white as a broken lily, and when her weak hands clung about his neck. Perhaps this made him more patient than he would have been otherwise with what I had to say.

He could hardly tax me with being fancy-ridden, but he was aghast—angry—incredulous, all in one. Vickers, of all people in the world; and Freda so worked upon as to be afraid to tell him—afraid to claim the protection that was hers by right. And now the situation was complicated by the fact that Vickers had saved her life, so that thanks were due to him as well as a kicking out of doors. And there was dignity to be thought of too: Freda's dignity as well as his own. Any open scandal must be avoided; she must neither be shamed nor pained.

I do not know what passed between him and Dr. Vickers when they met, but the latter came no more to Roscawen, and after a while I heard incidentally that he had gone abroad. As soon as Freda could be moved, her wish was fulfilled, and I took her to Aston Bury. Mother was very gentle with her, and I think before the end a genuine affection grew up between the two.

The end was not long delayed; a few months passed, and then she faded out of life in a sort of decline; the shock to the system, so they said, had been greater than her vitality could repair. Robert was a free man again, war had been declared, and he was one of the earliest volunteers for service.

That service won distinction, as everybody knows; and now he is convalescent from his second wound, and here at Aston Bury on leave. And I think the wiser choice his sisters made for him in the first place is now likely to be his own. A much more suitable person than Frederica, and her name is quite a plain one—a real Larcomb name: it is Mary, like my own. I am glad; but in spite of all, poor Freda has a

42

soft place in my memory and my heart. Whatever were her faults and failings, I believe she strove hard to be loyal. And I am sure that she loved Robert well.

Anne's Little Ghost

We had planned to take a holiday as soon as I was demobilised, and I claim that we had abundantly earned it, Anne and I. She had been a war worker all the time I was serving abroad—(for there were, alas! no children to tie her to the duties of home)—and she needed relief and change as much as I. It was to be a real holiday and in full measure—no wretched scrap measured by days, but lasting several weeks, and at our own option to extend into months if we so pleased. This gave a peculiar feeling of wealth and spaciousness; for once we were to be millionaires in the holiday line. But from the £.s.d. point of view, a quite separate matter, the holiday was bound to be cheap. So, Anne decreed, and I left it to her to arrange what it should be, and where.

She was in high spirits the last time she came to see me in hospital, about a week before my discharge. She had heard of the very place for us, if I agreed—and of course I was ready to agree. Her friend Adelaide Sherwood recommended Deepdene, but there was no time to be lost; we must write or wire at once if we wanted to secure the rooms. Farmhouse lodgings in Devonshire; would not that be delightful?—with trout-fishing for me thrown in, and the sea not many miles away. It was really half a house, and the farm-mistress would board and cook for us: we could either bring a servant (we did not possess one) or a day-woman would come in from the village to order the rooms. Some friends of Miss Sherwood's had stayed there the previous autumn, and were abundantly satisfied with everything, cleanliness included; the charge was, besides, astonishingly low.

"Just think, Godfrey, of getting the farm produce fresh on the spot—eggs and vegetables, to say nothing of dairy luxuries beyond. And in such pretty country as they say it is. I cannot fancy getting tired of the quiet, but perhaps you may feel differently. A large sitting-room with glass doors on to a verandah, and such a view from it; the farm-buildings quite away on the other side. The bedroom is on the same floor: that will be right for your lame leg, will it not? And then upstairs two more bedrooms, roomy attics. We shall not need to use these, but they are part of the half-house, and are let with it. What do you say?"

A prompt telegram secured us the tenancy of the half-house, and a week later Anne and I were *en route* for our new abode. We took the journey leisurely—a fit prelude to a holiday which was to be all lei-sure—and stayed' a couple of nights at Exeter on our way. So, the jour-ney of the last morning, was a short one. We arrived at our destination soon after noon, to find all gilded with the cheer of mid-day sunshine, and a white-aproned landlady hospitably welcoming us at the door.

The house was neither picturesque nor old, but it promised com-fort, and seemed likely to justify the encomiums of Anne's friend and correspondent. Mrs. Stokes the landlady was openly proud of it, and showed us round expecting appreciation. The kitchen and offices oc-cupied the lower floor, but we had a separate entrance through the garden wicket up steps to the verandah, our private portion of it, which was cut off from the other set of lodgings by a light railing thrown across. This second set was at present vacant, but would be oc-cupied in another fortnight by two ladies, sisters, who came always at this time of year, bringing with them their own maid.

The attic rooms were also shown, though we were not intending to occupy them. My lame leg excused me from a further mounting of stairs, but Anne accompanied Mrs. Stokes aloft. The occupiers of both sets had an equal right to these stairs, and the attic accommodation was impartially divided, two falling to our lot, and two to that of the sisters and their servant.

They were airy rooms, Anne told me, and would make pleasant bedrooms, looking out through smaller windows on the same lovely view that we commanded on the lower floor. This was all that was said at the time, but later, when tea was spread and we were partaking of it, she told me more.

"People must have been here with children," she said presently in an interval of filling my cup. "The attic over our bedroom has evi-dently been used as a nursery, for there are coloured pictures pasted on the wall, and a child's bed is pushed into one corner. Mrs. Stokes said she would take it out if it was in our way."

There was just the slightest sigh with this communication, and the least possible droop at the corners of Anne's sensitive mouth, but enough to give me a clue to what was in her mind. I can often read

Anne's mind as plainly as the page of a book—though I do not tell her so; perhaps because of long association, to say nothing of affection. We two are singularly alone in the world, and so are drawn all the closer, each to each. We have been married rather more than eight years, and in our second year together we possessed, for a brief space of only weeks, a baby daughter.

So, brief a space that one might suppose both joy and grief would be easily forgotten; but those who so think, know little of a mother's heart—at least, little of Anne's. From the dear memory of that joy and that grief (the sword piercing her soul, as was foretold of another mother) comes the wistful interest she takes in all children. And I could divine her thought: "If only little Clarice had lived and had been with us here, the pictured attic would have been her nursery, and the little bed in the corner would have been ready made for her." But of this I said nothing.

"Perhaps Mrs. Stokes's own children sleep there when they are without lodgers," I suggested, but Anne shook her head.

"No, for I asked the question. They have only three big boys, all in their teens. The eldest works on the farm, and the other two are away at school. None of the Stokes family sleep under this roof; a stable is converted into quarters for them, so that the house may be set apart as lodgings"; and again there came the slight and smothered sigh.

I should be giving a false impression if it were thought from this that there is anything dreary about Anne. No one is more resolutely cheerful, or more keenly and alertly practical, than this wife of mine. These inner feelings of hers, tender regrets and constant thoughts, have their own secret chamber in her mind, the door of which is shut and barred; a sacred threshold, which even I dare not openly approach. No more was said about the empty cot and the pictures, and that first evening of our stay at Deepdene passed delightfully amid country sights and sounds, and the sweet Devonshire air. Miss Sherwood's recommendation was, we thought, justifying itself to the full.

And at night, when the veil of dimness, not quite darkness, was drawn over the garden and the hills, what a healing silence prevailed: bird notes stilled, and at last even the plaintive cry of a lamb which had wandered from its mother, satisfied and at rest. I slept profoundly, but presently what was this? Anne's voice: Anne shaking me awake.

"Godfrey! Godfrey, listen! Do you hear?"

I was for the moment deaf and dazed with sleep.

"No," I said. "What is it? What is the matter?"

"It is a child sobbing. A little child in trouble. A child that has been shut out. I cannot hear it and do nothing. Can you?" Anne was thrusting her feet into slippers, and was already arrayed in her dress-ing-gown—blue and white, the colours of the Virgin Mother. "I can't make out where the sound comes from—whether it is overhead or out of doors. Listen, and you will hear it too. There are no words, only cries and sobs. I heard it again the instant before you awoke."

I was out of bed by this time and broad awake. I heard no crying, but I did hear footsteps: a child's pattering run across the floor over-head, once from end to end of the room, and then again in return.

"Now I know," said Anne, quite composedly, proceeding to light a candle. "It is upstairs in the attic I told you of; the room like a nursery, which is over ours. I wonder what child it can be. Mrs. Stokes should have let us know. I am going up to see."

That was so entirely Anne-like I was not surprised. She went out carrying the light, and I followed on to the landing in case I should be wanted. As I went, I heard again the pattering feet overhead, and I think Anne heard them too. I waited at the foot of the stairs, not wishing to affright the child by the sight of a grim soldier-man in pyjamas. No child, not even the most nervous, could be frightened at the sight of Anne.

Waiting there, I could be certain that no living soul came down the stairs. I heard Anne pass from room to room, and then she called to me.

"Godfrey, I wish you would come up here."

I went up in the soft twilight that was not wholly dark, even in that enclosed place, entering where I saw her candle shine. She was in the attic with the pictured walls, sitting on the little bed, and her face was white and awe-stricken.

"I can't find anything," she said. "The rooms are all empty, and there is no place in which a child could be shut, I wish you would look too."

Of course I looked with her, and, equally of course, our search was fruitless. Then I persuaded her to go back to our room and listen there, while I hurried on some clothes and made search round the house outside. I talked some nonsense about the way in which sounds reflect and echo, and the difficulty there is about locating their direction, especially at night; but I do not think she believed me: unconvinced myself, I could hardly expect to convince another. And I was privately certain I had heard the footsteps of a child, not echoed over floors from a distance, but distinctly overhead. There must be some way of getting up to those attics, and down from them, that we did not know.

But in the morning Mrs. Stokes could tell us nothing, and had no explanation to offer. No child could have got in without her knowledge. It must have been one out of the village wandering round outside, scared by the darkness, and afraid to go home because it had been threatened with the stick. That was how the good dame dismissed the matter, and we might have been satisfied about the crying, but not as to those footsteps overhead.

It will be well believed that I was eager to sample the fishing, and the next day saw us on the banks of the stream, Anne sitting near me with a book. But somehow in the week following she managed to catch cold, and after that I had for a while to pursue my sport alone, and she spent solitary hours at the Deepdene farm.

I think it was on the second day of her seclusion that she said to me when I came back in the evening: "I have seen the child."

I had better mention here that in the interval we had heard no more of the sobbing voice at night, nor of the footsteps overhead. Anne looked as if something had moved her profoundly, even to the shedding of tears.

"Did you find out whose child it is, and why it is here?"

"No. She did not speak, and it seems so odd that Mrs. Stokes does not know. I was on the landing when I saw her first, and she was running upstairs. There is no carpet on those stairs, and I heard quite plainly the patter of her feet. A little girl. I went up after her, and she ran straight into that room which was a nursery, the room with the pictures."

"And you followed?"

"Yes, I followed, but she was not there. I was puzzled—almost frightened, and I went back again to the sitting-room. I think it must have been half an hour later when I saw her again. If you remember, it began to rain. It was so chilly; I was obliged to shut to the glass doors."

"Yes?" I said. Anne had paused again, with that odd breathlessness which was new.

"She was out there on the verandah, and the rain was slanting in upon her. Such a pretty little girl, and about the age——" (I knew what Anne so nearly said, and why she checked herself and altered the phrase to "about six years old." Clarice would have been six years old had she lived.) "Not a poor woman's child. She had a pretty white frock on, worked cambric and lace, and a silk sash of a sort of gera-

49

nium red. No cottagers' child would be dressed so. And she had such an appealing little face, as if she was longing to be sheltered and comforted. It was raining, you know, all the time."

"And what did you do?"

"Why of course I opened the window. I said, 'Come in my dear, you will get wet.' I held out my hand and she put hers into it—oh, such a cold little hand, as, cold and soft as snow. I can feel the touch of it still. I drew her into the room. 'We should be warm in here,' I said. No, I'm not crying, Godfrey; not really crying; but there was something in her face that touched me: a sort of surprise, as if no one had ever welcomed or been kind to her before. I asked her where she lived, but she only made a sign and put a finger to her lips. She heard me—I am sure she heard me, but I cannot help fancying the poor child is dumb.

"She heard me, for when I said, 'My darling, will you give me a kiss?' she put up both her little arms, and her face was close to mine. I would have had that kiss, only just then that tiresome Mrs. Stokes knocked at the door; the butcher, it seemed, had called, and she wanted to know if we would take a joint. The instant there came the knock, the child slipped away out of my arms. I had left the window open behind us, and she was gone."

"Mrs. Stokes did not see her?"

"No. She saw nothing, and could tell nothing; only I thought she looked a little *odd* when I was putting questions. I couldn't help wondering if there was any secret about it which she was bound to keep."

As the days went on, I began also to wonder this, and after a while that wonder shaped itself into action. But I anticipate.

That night we heard again the footsteps overhead, both of us heard them. It was still completely dark, and the rain, driven against our windows, was mixed with hail. The pattering steps crossed the floor above once, twice, and after an interval a third time. I was still awake, holding my breath to listen should they come again, when I heard another sound beside me. Anne was crying, very quietly, her face buried in the pillow so that all sound should be hushed. I put out my hand to touch her.

"What is the matter?"

"Oh Godfrey—oh Godfrey, that poor child," she sobbed. "It is so sad for her to be up there all alone in the cold and darkness, and only six years old. Six years old! Clarice would have been just that age. Can it be Clarice trying to come back to us? I felt as if she were Clarice when I held her in my arms."

I was not surprised. It was as if I had seen the thought taking shape, somehow as crystals form. But what could I do but dub it foolishness, born out of the sweet fond folly of a mother's love?

We heard no more that night. Next morning, without telling Anne of my intention, I went up to examine the attics for the first time by daylight. The rooms over ours were vacant, and in the one with pictured walls the little bed was gaunt and undraped, with its stripped mattress and uncovered pillow. There was no closet or recess in which it was possible for even the smallest child to hide, and as the walls were of thin modern building, secret entrances and passages were out of the question here.

I was to hear again later of that little bed. Nothing more passed between us touching that strange fancy of Anne's, the confession I had surprised from her in the night, until she said in a sort of shamefaced fashion (but again there were tears in her eyes):

"I made a pretence to Mrs. Stokes today; I hope it was not untrue enough to be wrong. I said we might be expecting a child visitor: we might expect any visitors you know, and some of our friends have children. And I asked her to have the pictured attic put ready, and the bed made up—in case. She did it this morning, and I did not want you to go up there and be surprised. It does not look nearly so miserable now the furniture is in order, and sheets and blankets are on the little bed. Anyone who was up there in the night, and who was cold and tired, could lie down."

What was I to say to this, but again that it was folly?—but I could not charge Anne with folly when she looked as she did then. And hardly a night passed without the pattering footsteps overhead.

The parish to which Deepdene belonged was a scattered one; the church was a long half-mile away, and a mere cluster of cottages called itself the village. That cluster, however, contained the post-office, and the inevitable general shop, which included among its wares a few toys of the simpler sort. One day Anne returned from a post-office errand the purchaser of a doll, pretty of head and face, but with its nudity barely covered by a scant chemise of waxed muslin. She said nothing of her intention, but for a day or two that doll lay about in our sitting-room, while her skilful fingers were busied shaping for it more befitting garments—pink and frilly, and with a pinafore of lace. Then it disappeared, but I did not remark, nor for a while did she explain, not until I asked her a week later if she had seen the child again.

"She often comes when I am alone, peeping in at me from the verandah," was the answer." And she was pleased when I gave her the doll. She took it from me and kissed me, but still, she does not speak."

She took the doll! With this the mystery grew. How could an immaterial creature, one we dimly guessed to be spirit and not flesh,' accept a material gift, removing it when she withdrew? Yet, Anne had given her the toy in exchange for a kiss, and the doll was certainly gone.

Next day when I came in from the stream, Anne was out, and some impulse urged me to go up again to the attic, the attic prepared for our supposed guests, which no one had arrived to occupy. It was vacant as before, but a couple of small vases held fresh flowers, of Anne's filling doubtless, and on the white pillow of the little bed there lay the pink-frocked doll.

I was beginning to be anxious about Anne. There was a change in her I did not like to see; a feverish spot on her cheek, and, slight as she was before, she had fallen away in the few weeks of our sojourn to be very thin. She laughed over it herself, and said her gowns must be taken in; but to me it seemed no laughing matter. Was vitality being drawn from her for the shaping of the child apparition in material form; and, if so, what would be the effect upon her health?

I am not instructed in such matters, but I vaguely recalled some of the explanations put forward—material forms built up from the medium, and life-substance drawn away. Ought I to make some excuse, and cut short our stay at Deepdene? That was one question, but another followed it. Now that she fancied the appearance might be that of her dead baby, our little Clarice, would Anne be content to go?

Our little Clarice! Mine as well as hers; the father's tie as valid surely as the mother's, if not so close and fond. If to one of us, why not to both? But in the end, I could no longer say this. Though only once, she was visible to me too.

Was it a projection from Anne's mind influencing mine? I have wondered since; but these are questions I can only indicate: they are beyond my power to answer.

We were sitting in the early twilight, the lamp unlit, as Anne had a headache: her head often ached in these days. The glass doors were open, and I dimly saw, first a glimpse of white on the verandah, misty and indefinite, which presently resolved itself into the figure Anne had described to me—the dainty figure of a girl-child in white frock and red silk sash, a cloud of dusky hair hanging about her little head.

She was peeping in at me and drawing back; then with more confidence peeping again. Anne took no notice; she was, I think, asleep. I remained motionless, scarcely daring to breathe, lest I should startle this exquisite small creature, as one might fear to might a bird. Presently she ventured as far into the room as where Anne was sitting, and stood resting her little elbows on her friend's knee, and looking me straight in the face.

I was able now to understand Anne's meaning about the child's pathetic eyes with their wistfulness of appeal, and also to appreciate something more: something that Anne herself had not noticed, was not likely to notice, as people seldom see likenesses to themselves. It was very marked—the eyes, the brow, the hair: here was Anne as she must have been a quarter of a century ago. Could I doubt that it was our child; and did a longing for the earthly parents' love draw her down to us, away from her safe and happy cradling in the satisfaction of Heaven?

I was still gazing when my wife moved and sighed, waking from her sleep; and the childish figure was gone in a flash, too abrupt for any real withdrawal. In spite of the evidence of those material-sounding footsteps—in spite of the handling of the doll—I never again thought of her as compacted of ordinary mundane flesh and blood.

I had seen her with my own eyes, and I could no longer doubt. But there was a point which I still desired to probe, despite that evidence of the resemblance. I wanted to find out whether the half-house we were renting could be haunted, and whether the child-ghost had been seen or heard by other people than ourselves.

It would be a difficult matter to ascertain, for in defence of their property against depreciation, very good people have before now thought it hardly a sin to pervert the truth. But I reflected that the clergyman of the parish had no interest in letting Deepdene. I would go in the first place to him, and then see what I could make of sounding Mrs. Stokes.

My errand to Mr. Fielding bore only negative fruit. He was a man advanced in years, a gentleman and a scholar, and he received me with suave politeness; if he could serve me in any way, he would be glad. But when I put my question, I could see that a faint flicker of amusement underlay his grave attention; he, the minister of the Unseen, was wholly sceptical as to its demonstration.

I said very little, merely asking did the house where we were lodging bear the reputation of being haunted? We—I, that is, for I left

Anne out of it—had heard sounds that could not be explained, and seen a small figure that appeared to vanish. I should like to know whether it was a matter of common report.

The answer to this was No. There might be some vulgar story of the sort, it was just possible, but it had never reached his ears. Had it done so, he would have discredited it. I would readily see on reflection how easy it was to mistake sounds and their origin; and not only did our ears trick us in such matters, but also our vision. A supposed phantom generally meant that the percipient would do well to resort to an oculist.

I did not argue the point. As I told him, I only wished to ascertain whether there was, or was not, any local tradition. I wished him good morning, and my next resort was to Mrs. Stokes.

Here I was met by indignation, and the good woman was not easy to appease. I was interested, I told her, I was not objecting; rather than otherwise, it increased my interest in Deepdene. I only wished to know if any of the other lodgers—and doubtless in the course of the year she would have many—had mentioned to her any similar sights or sounds.

Her first answer was a flat negative; but there was, I thought, an uneasy consciousness in the eye that did not meet mine as before, and presently modification came. For her own part she knew nothing, as she never slept in the house herself, nor did Stokes *père*, nor the boys—(was this, it occurred to me to wonder, a suspicious circumstance?) She had never seen or heard anything "worse than herself," and I might take that as on her Bible oath; but, now she came to think, some of the lodgers had mentioned a running about on those upper floors, happening when they had the rats in at threshing time. They got some virus when they heard of it, and there were no more complaints after that was put down. If I had been disturbed, no doubt the rats were getting in again. But, certain sure, there were no ghosts.

I wondered, and I wonder still, whether some houses have a psychical atmosphere which can be variously moulded and used; the child employing it to approach us, and the spiritual environment of others putting it to a quite separate use. I think this is not impossible, but as to the truth of the matter, who can say?

As I have shown, I gained nothing by my inquiries, and this is nearly all I have to tell. The end of our sojourn followed quickly. I remember once discussing psychical matters with a friend. He was a believer, and he said to me: "I always know how to distinguish a true ghost-story from a faked one. The true ghost-story never has any point, and the faked one dare not leave it out." This ghost-story of mine, though not faked, has a point, but it is one the ordinary reader would overlook, and I do not insist on it. I am abundantly content to be disbelieved, and Anne is content too.

It was Anne's health which brought our stay at Deepdene to an abrupt close. I think I have said that for some time I had noticed she was looking ill, and wondered vaguely whether her vitality could be drained away to supply material for those manifestations we had witnessed and heard. It was, however, no case of gradually lessened strength, but a threatened crisis which demanded prompt attention—surgeon's investigation and a nursing-home. So, in figurative language, we struck our tents, seeking another encampment, and Deepdene knew us no more.

Beyond the Pale

Without doubt the Hennikers' was a love-match. They had been married a couple of years, and it may fairly be said that neither party had found cause to repent. Rupert Henniker was sincerely attached to his wife, and she positively idolised him. The French proverb says that in all such unions there is one who kisses, and the other who permits the embrace. In this case Henniker was the one kissed, but he willingly yielded the cheek, and felt that Joan's adoration was well placed.

Joan began her married life with high ideals. She determined so to identify herself with her husband's pursuits, that she might everywhere be his unfailing companion; and to this young wife the nursery interests, which frequently alter such a programme, had not been vouchsafed by Providence. So, when Henniker laid his plans for a season's shooting in the wilds of Western America, Joan, as a matter of course, expected to go too.

She did not claim to shoulder a rifle beside him; that was not her way: but she could keep the rough little mountain dwelling which had been placed at their disposal, cosy and home-like for Rupert, and see that he missed no comfort that her care could supply. If on the spot, she could see that he changed into dry foot-wear when he came back of an evening; she could wash his socks and darn them, and contrive the best imitation possible of his favourite dishes over the stove, which there would be the sole substitute for an English kitchen-range.

She had some practical knowledge of these matters, though it was slight and inadequate; but she determined it should be sufficient, and everything in the adventure before them was seen through the rose-coloured medium of romance. The separation which might have been had she held back, was now no longer to be feared; and a prolonged *tête-à-tête* in the wilds would draw them together even nearer than before. Henniker had expressed himself as proud of his little woman's pluck, and she was determined to justify that pride and that praise.

Their solitude would not be absolute, as Arnott's ranch was distant only half a mile, which in that land of prairie wastes and wide distances, seemed almost as close as next door. Arnott and Henniker had been boys together and schoolmates, and it was upon his suggestion they were going out. Arnott's wife was said to be a good sort, and on Joan's arrival she would equip her with all needful knowledge.

So young Mrs. Henniker set out on her sea and land journey with a brave heart and bright anticipations, and her courage did not fail when at last they travelled on beyond railways and civilisation, into the great solitudes; climbing the spurs of the foot-hills, and looking up at the huge mountain wall and the high snows behind which the sun sank in the west. Perhaps the *adobe* hut when reached was something of a disillusion, though it was fairly commodious and not absolutely bare; the Arnotts had put in necessaries in the way of furniture, and had done their best to make it habitable.

It would look more home-like when Joan had had time to unpack and arrange her possessions and his—other than the precious rifles, which were not for feminine handling: and about all this Joan would have the aid of a "help" Mrs. Arnott had engaged for her, to soften the edge of hardship in this strange new housekeeping in the wilds. Nita, the half-bred Indian girl, could at least manage the stove, and wash and scrub the place down, if she could do no more.

Mrs. Arnott had of course her own establishment to look after, where a couple of pretty children added to the domestic cares and joys, so she could give Joan only occasional assistance; though a fount of practical advice was at her service whenever she cared to come up to the ranch. So, the next day Joan was left alone with her wild-looking "help" when Henniker went off to the hills.

Nita had a double tongue in her head, Spanish and Indian, on which a very little English had been grafted; and it was by the help of the very little English, that she and her new mistress were to exchange ideas and commands. Joan would have scorned to confess that from the beginning she stood in some awe of her assistant, but it was so in fact. Nita's service was utterly unlike any to which she had been accustomed, and there was something disconcerting about the girl's sudden lithe movements, and the keen regard of her black eyes.

At first mistress and maid were on good terms; and though Nita's ideas of necessary cleanliness were far from satisfying Joan, the young housekeeper hoped that admonition and instruction would have their due effect in time; and greater energy was displayed after the gift of a gay ribbon out of one of the Henniker travelling trunks.

But with the unpacking of these trunks came the development of an intense curiosity on the part of Nita concerning all kinds of civilised belongings, and, as Joan began uncomfortably to suspect, of a cupidity equally intense. The girl longed to deck herself out in imitation of her mistress, and pile on the few ornaments that were in evidence: Joan had, as a matter of course, left her jewel-case in the custody of an English bank.

Nita was nominally assisting arrangement upon shelves and drawers, and fingering the possessions that were laid away, when Joan first noticed the peculiar scar on her right wrist. Such a slender brown wrist it was, and at some time or other it must have been frightfully hurt. A deeply-seamed scar ran the whole way round the arm, or almost the whole way, as only about an inch of smooth skin was free from the ghastly indentation; and below this, nearer the hand, were a couple of lines of blue tattooing, twisted together at the back into a sort of device. Joan asked her how she had been hurt, but evidently Nita's English was not equal to the task of explanation; she frowned and drew back, pouring out a torrent of bastard Spanish, which left her mistress as wise as before.

Joan did not inquire further, but, thinking to please her, offered as a gift a string of coral beads which matched the ribbon. To her surprise Nita refused it, but snatched up a small miniature portrait taken from the trunk.

"Not those," she said, "I don't want those: I have beads enough. I will have this instead: give me this!"

The miniature was one of Joan's dead mother, and greatly valued by her; unluckily it was framed in a glittering oval of Paris paste. Joan was shocked at the greed and the demand, and wrenched the portrait out of those brown fingers which closed and clutched against her; there was indeed a struggle over it between the two.

"No, you cannot have that," she said, trying to disguise her displeasure—for what was the use of being angry with this child of nature? "You may have the corals if you care for them, but not this. It is the only portrait I have of my mother, and I value it more than all the world."

The girl looked sulky, but no more was said. Of course it was not the picture that she wanted, but the oval of shining mock gems. The attraction of this to one who had never before looked upon diamonds, real or imitation, was greater that Joan could divine. Yet civilised women have before now succumbed to such lures, so to covet possession may be reckoned less surprising in one beyond the pale. Joan was prudent enough again to lock the miniature in her travelling trunk, and when the key was turned, she dismissed the matter from her mind. But it was by no means blotted out of Nita's by that closed lid and turned key.

Several days went by, full of small jarring discomforts which need not be enumerated here. One afternoon Joan went up to the ranch to take counsel with Mrs. Arnott, and on her return she found the place deserted, her boxes broken open and ransacked, and, what specially moved her to wrath, the precious miniature was forced out of its frame and cracked across, while the glittering oval had altogether disappeared.

This was an outrage indeed. The actual thefts were of small account measured against this damage, the wrong of the disfiguring crack which split the beloved face in two. Joan cried out that the offender must be caught and punished, and Henniker was of the same mind; so, he and Arnott, who was sheriff's delegate for that part of the district, rode up into the hills in search of Nita, making their errand known.

The girl was supposed to have her abode with the old Indian woman her grandmother, who received them with wrath and curses, and swore to Nita's innocence—as doubtless she would have sworn to any statement which suited her, having small regard for truth. Also, she declared that she knew nothing of the grand-daughter's whereabouts, so the pursuing party returned baffled, after breathing forth vain threatenings.

Mrs. Arnott was with Joan when her husband and his friend returned.

"Did you really beard old Rachel in her den?" she asked, and looked more than a little concerned.

"Why of course we did. What else were we to do?" was his rejoinder.

"I suppose it was a matter of duty, but the old crone is what they call about here ill to cross, and likely to put ill luck upon you both. It was all very well for you to be out to catch a thief, but I wish you and Mr. Henniker had left old Rachel alone. You must know," she said, turning to Joan, "deserved or not, this grandmother of Nita's has the reputation of being a witch."

Of course they laughed at this as at an excellent joke, Joan and the two men, but there was an air about Mrs. Arnott as if she more than half believed in Rachel's malignant powers.

"I am more sorry than I can say that I sent Nita to you," she went on. "But the girl seemed teachable and promised to do well. There is nobody else but old Mercy Clew, our herdsman's wife, and she is coming up to you tomorrow. She is a rough specimen, but I have always thought her honest, and I believe your possessions will be safe with her."

The foregoing may be taken as the prologue to the drama, all of it commonplace enough, but needful to make clear what will follow.

Joan had spent a busy morning shepherding Mercy Clew—who was both deaf and obstinate—in the way of the help she required. It had been a strenuous time: a trial of patience as well as of physical strength in unaccustomed labours; and she had withdrawn into their living-room for a few minutes' breathing-space and rest, throwing herself into the one cushioned chair with a gasp of relief. Her eyes were closed, her muscles all relaxed, when *tap-tap* came behind her—the rapping of impatient fingers on the glass.

Mrs. Arnott sometimes tapped like that on her way to the entrance door; and Joan started round to face the window, feeling rather aggrieved by the intrusion. But Mrs. Arnott was not there. The tapping came again, and now she saw something where the glass was struck; only a shadow, but the shadow of a hand.

A hand reaching down from above. If the shadow was of any real substance, the intruder must be crouched upon the roof; the hut had, of course, no storey above the ground-floor. It must be Nita; that was her instant conviction: Nita playing some annoying trick: but with a warrant out against her it was surprising that she dared. Joan ran outside to see. No, there was no one on the roof, either above the smitten window or behind—no one hiding round the chimneystack, no one within sight; but, passing it on her return, she discovered that the smitten glass retained the print of a hand.

The hand had been pressed flat against the pane, palm and outspread lingers, and it seemed to have been dipped in something viscous and sticky, faintly streaked with blood. She looked at it from time to time during the day, and watched the gradual drying off of the mark in the keen hill air; but it was still faintly visible when Henniker returned, and his attention was called to it.

"Yes," he said, "whoever made that mark must have stretched down to do it from the roof. A daring trick, and likely, enough to be Nita's, unless indeed she has an accomplice. We shall catch her at it if she is foolhardy enough to come again."

There was no more tapping on the glass that night, to call attention to what was going forward; but when they got up the next morning a second window was marked. This one lighted the bedroom and looked to the other side of the house. Here there was no roof-slope above it but a gable, so it would have been more difficult, well-nigh impossible, to reach down to the glass from above. The print of the hand, however, was made precisely as before; wrist upwards and fingers downwards, a sticky impression streaked with blood. It was Henniker this time who discovered it when he drew aside the window screen to shave; he called to his wife, who was kindling a fire in the stove, and they both regarded it together.

"Somebody is trying to take a rise out of us"—such was Henniker's ultimatum. "No doubt it is supposed we shall be scared by these cursings of the witch. I'd like to get to the bottom of it before anything is known, so do not let us appear to take notice. I shall not say anything to Jack Arnott—yet, and do not you to his wife."

It was all very well to resolve on this course of action—or inaction, and easy to take no notice of a sticky mark on the outside of a window, which was presently effaced with a wet cloth. But the next demonstration, if it can be so called, was of a different nature and less possible to ignore. Mercy Clew came rushing in from her washbucket to where Joan was stirring a saucepan over the stove.

"Come you out here. Mis' Henniker. I cannot go on in the yard. They have been throwing stones at me this half hour!"

The woman had an air of passionate indignation, but together with the anger there was fear. Mrs. Clew's command of English was superior to Nita's, but Joan found her almost as difficult to understand.

"Do you mean that somebody is throwing stones, and at you? Who would dare to do such a thing? It must be a mistake."

"Come you out and see"—taking hold of Joan by the arm. "I wouldn't like to have you hurt, but I want you to believe. And if it is the doing of old madam, like enough she'll stone you too."

It was true that stones and pieces of rock were scattered over the beaten earth of the yard; but, for all Joan knew, they might have been there since the beginning of time. The woman showed the spot where she was standing, and the direction from which they struck her; and, the moment after, another stone fell plump into the water-bucket, and a second bruised Joan on the shoulder. Nobody was in sight.

"It is horrible of them. What have we done that we should be so persecuted! We must find out who is doing this."

She was angry rather than dismayed, and eager in searching round the dwelling-house and outbuildings. Except for these possible screens, Hunter's End stood in the open, away from trees and rocks. There seemed no possible cover to conceal the thrower of the stones, and yet again, immediately on their return, one was tossed into the yard.

"Bring your pail indoors into the kitchen," Joan commanded. "We shall be safe there."

But safe they were not, though shut in by walls and doors. The stones still struck them both, and fell within on the floor. The elderly "help" reached for her shawl and bonnet, which were hanging on the pegs,

"I'm sorry to leave you, marm, but stay I can't where there are such goings on. It's all through the old madam that your place has got bewitched. And, if I'm not mistaken, you'll have no more peace here, day nor night."

"Who is this old madam, and what do you mean about bewitching?" Joan held her back, almost by force, till she answered.

Mercy Clew dropped her voice to a whisper.

"'Tis not well to say the name of her, but she is kin to the girl you had here, her you sent after with a sheriff's warrant. It is well known that madam puts spells upon people, and has laid a spell upon the girl herself, if what one hears is true. She's an awful woman when she is angered, and you will have to get quit of her one way or another, or there will be no peace for this house. Mis' Arnott, she knows something of what has been done elsewhere, enough to pass her word to you that I am telling truth. And until madam's quit of you, I can tell you this. Not a soul about will come nigh the place, or drive their beasts past it. I'm sorry from my heart for what's before you, but you'll have to fend for yourselves."

And the Hennikers had in fact to "fend for themselves" in the days that followed. The witch, if truly a witch was in fault, had contrived to put upon them a boycott as stringent as any that existed in Ireland. And it was not only that the report of the stone-throwing had gone abroad, and the superstitious were afraid to venture into the bewitched quarter, animals, who could not be affected by hearsay, were also a prey to terror. Arnott's dog, who was used to accompany him in visiting Hunter's End, on the first occasion after these events began, hesitated when within twenty yards of the door, and appeared to scent danger: he then turned tail and fled for home, despite the calls of his master.

And one of the ranch horses, drawing a load of logs for the Henniker's use and led by Arnott, jibbed determinedly at about the same distance, and neither blows nor coaxing could induce, it to approach nearer. It was impossible to get help for Joan, other than what Mrs. Arnott could occasionally give; and Henniker did not like to leave her uncompanioned in the midst of such eerie happenings, so the guns were idle in their rack, except for the shooting of some rock pigeons and conies in the near neighbourhood of the hut.

Henniker's opinion had altered from the scornful disbelief professed in the beginning, to a mood of unwilling and annoyed conviction. The stone-throwing against old Mercy in the yard he had dismissed as nothing more than a spiteful trick; the tapping on the glass fell into the same category, and the impression of a human hand in an impossible position, might even have been made by a dummy pressed against the pane. But when it came to later experiences which he shared, occurrences when he and Joan were alone in the house, stone-throwing within shut doors which went on at intervals, the affair assumed a different complexion.

Stones—it is true they were small ones—Were thrown when the two were sitting at supper, first from one side of the room and then from the other; and a good-sized pebble was dropped from above into his coffee-cup, breaking the cup and spilling the contents. Even at night they were allowed no peace; articles left in the kitchen were brought through the shut door into their room and hurled upon the beds; the coverlets were grasped and dragged by something which remained invisible; fingers rapped a tattoo against the window; and, what seemed more extraordinary than all, running footsteps passed backwards and forwards overhead, where was nothing but the sloping roof.

Henniker started out again and again, gun in hand, but there was no target for his shot. Joan kept her courage wonderfully through those harassed days and nights; but when at last her husband accorded her a well-deserved meed of praise, she broke down and shed tears.

"I don't mind— that is, I can bear it so long as it only what we hear and feel. But if it should come to seeing anything dreadful, I am sure I could not go on being brave."

It was after this avowal that Henniker asked advice of Arnott, who had come down to see how they were faring; and it may be noted here that this friend had now been taken into the full confidence which was at first withheld.

"What would you do in my place? It's beyond endurance that we should be driven out by sheer devilry—for devilry it must be; but how can I stay on here when it is killing my wife? She won't leave me, or I would send her away, and stay and brave it out by myself."

"What would I do? Why, I'd be inclined to try what the half-breeds resort to in similar cases. Rank superstition you will say, and so do I; but it is possible there may be something in it as they say that it succeeds. They pit one witch against another, and let the two of them battle it out. There's a man up the river who goes by the name of the witchdoctor. If I were you, I'd have him over, and pay the dollars of his fee. I understand it is a big one."

"If we can be freed from this, I don't mind what I pay, or what absurdity I have to put up with."

"You will have to put up with absurdity, if his rites are of the sort I imagine. I have heard of them of course, living here, but I have never seen the thing done. I may as well say this is Cora's advice as well as mine" (Cora was his wife). "Very well, as you are willing, I will send Clew with the buggy at dawn tomorrow to fetch down Hill-of-the-Raven, and you must be prepared to receive him here."

Hill-of -the-Raven professed himself willing to undertake the job, and soon after mid-day Arnott brought him to Hunter's End. He was a very lean, very tall old Indian, who looked inappropriately garbed in European dress instead of his native paint and feathers. Arnott acted as interpreter, as his English was of the smallest; and he also mounted guard over the old man's bag of conjuring tools while Hill-of-the-Raven made first the outer round of the house, and then entered every room, standing and snuffing the air as a stag might who perceives a taint to windward, all the while muttering incantations to himself. Finally, he confabulated again with Arnott, who looked distinctly annoyed.

"Hill-of-the-Raven wants more money," he informed Henniker. "The old rascal says it is a worse job than he expected, and of a different sort: 'plenty magic here, and bad magic' He was to have cleared you out for ten dollars, but now he says he must have five and twenty."

For answer, Henniker counted the bills into his friend's hand.

"No doubt he is scoundrel enough for anything, but I will not stint the money. Tell him to go ahead with what he has to do."

"And he says the *senora* must help him. There is a woman in it, and there must be a woman against. Will Mrs. Henniker mind?"

Joan raised no objection, and the preparations went forward. The man stripped himself to the waist, wearing only his leather breeches. He then laid a sheet of iron on the wooden top of their table, and produced an odd-looking bowl of beaten metal, which he required Joan to fill with spring water, dipping into it the forefinger of each of her hands, first one and then the other, and stirring the water from left to right. He gazed into the bowl for a few minutes in silence, and then spoke rapidly to Arnott, who translated.

"He is enumerating the articles you have lost and wish restored. Some blouse-waists and a skirt, a belt and buckle, a scarf, and a circle of stones that glitter. That is right, is it not? But nothing more than he could have learnt from Clew."

This seemed only the preliminary. The witch-doctor now built up with great care four little pyramids of some stuff which looked like dried herbs, one at each corner of the iron sheet, the water bowl still occupying the centre. He took a hot coal from the fire and lighted these pyramids, one after another. As they smouldered, he began to speak, as if in conversation with some person invisible, upbraiding, commanding, threatening; and now the sweat stood in beads on his brow and rained from him with the effort he was making, though it appeared to be mental rather than bodily.

At intervals he sprinkled water round him in the room, finally snatching up the bowl and emptying it by tossing the whole contents upwards into the air. This in itself was a conjuror's marvel, as the water totally disappeared and nothing was wetted by it; but this crowning action had a result which astonished the three spectators. A material object fell from the ceiling and dropped upon the iron sheet. A woman's hand.

They all looked in amaze at this product of Hill-of-the-Raven's incantation.

"I have succeeded," the witch-doctor announced to Arnott. "The *senor* and *senora* will have no more trouble. But they must fold the hand in a fair white cloth, and bury it at sundown under the nearest tree. The *senora* will receive again what she has lost, but she will be asked to give back something in return. And that something she would do unwisely to refuse."

The Hennikers were by no means anxious to detain Hill-of-the-Raven, and he departed with Arnott to set out on his return journey in the buggy. Joan and her husband were left possessors of the strange

66

Thing which had fallen from the ceiling: could it really have been this slight small hand, now lying limp and dead, which had caused all the disturbance and trouble. A human hand, of natural flesh at least, though drained of blood; and—wonder the more, as Joan presently cried out in recognition, it was Nita's hand. It bore the double line of blue tattooing twisted into a knot, which she well remembered on the girl's wrist; and the hand appeared to have been severed exactly where Nita bore on her fore-arm that deeply indented scar. That the hand should have been hers, seemed to make the whole thing more horrible even than before. Joan shuddered away from the touch of it.

"Let us do what the man said: let us bury it out of sight."

"Yes, but not till sundown," replied her husband. "We had better keep to the letter of the instructions, absurd as they may seem. Find the white cloth he spoke of, and have it wrapped in readiness, and I will go and dig the hole under the tree."

So, the burial of the small limp hand took place exactly as Hill-of-the-Raven had enjoined, hastily and almost furtively conducted, at least to the consciousness of these two people; they felt almost as if they had been concerned in a murder, and were now hiding away the corpse. There was something solemn, too, in that still evening in which hardly a breath of air stirred, with sunset flush still lingering behind the mountain peaks, and a few faint stars beginning to look forth.

Henniker smoothed over the disturbed ground, and then shouldered his spade.

"That ends the trouble we will hope," he said.

Joan had kept her courage well in hand through the long strain upon it, but the events of that day had overtaxed her nerves.

"I am ready to hate out west," she sobbed. "When we have turned our backs on it, and are again in safe England, shall we ever believe that these things really happened, and were not from beginning to end an evil dream?"

A quiet night followed for the inhabiters of Hunter's End; there were no more tapping fingers, nor scampering feet above upon the roof. The next morning Mercy Clew came back to work, unafraid of further peltings, as she had full confidence in the witch-doctor's power of exorcism, and belief that all would now be well. And, more notable still, Arnott's horses driven by, no longer held back and sweated in terror, nor did the dog refuse to accompany his master. Whatever it was that had scared them from the place, was plainly removed and gone; and, now Joan had the companionship of Mrs. Clew, Henniker was released to carry his gun to the hills. This seems like the end of the story, but it is not. There is one more episode to be related, stranger than all.

Six days had gone by, and the seventh had dawned. It had been an undisturbed week, and the first vivid impressions of the witch diablerie were beginning to fade.

The first change that came was in the weather, which recently had been oppressive, heavy with heat, and scarcely a breath of air fanning down into the valley from blue heights and distant snows. The cup of it had doubtless been charged to the brim for a crisis of electrical disturbance.

Never had Joan in her English experience witnessed such lightning or heard such thunder: the jagged flashes seemed to leap from peak to peak, and the thunder was caught up by the mountain echoes and doubled and redoubled, rolling like a cannonade among the hills. Then followed torrential rain, driving and pitiless, scourging all before it, and creating, as it seemed in a moment, streams and rivulets where all had been as dry as dust. In the midst of this downpour a hail came from without: a buggy and pair of mules had halted at the gate, and two people were craving shelter, a boon that could hardly be denied.

Henniker opened the door, and a man staggered in supporting a woman wrapped in a hooded cloak, who seemed to be ill or faint. He placed her in a chair, and cleared the wet, lank hair out of his own eyes; he was a goodlooking young half-breed, about twenty years of age, and he had some broken English.

"This Hunter's End?" he asked, looking round. "And your name Henniker? My sister here is ill, having lost her hand. She has come to claim it again from you. And she has brought back the things she took away."

The fainting woman in the chair was Nita. The man opened a bundle on the table, and there, crumpled and soiled, were Joan's possessions, and rolled within them the oval frame of paste. As he took the bundle from her knee, the cloak that covered her fell apart, and showed that her right arm ended in a stump, about which a linen bandage was twisted, and the bandage was stained with blood.

"My sister's hand?" he continued, looking from Joan to Henniker, and back again to Joan. "You have it here. I bring you these in exchange: you have no claim to keep. If you do not restore her hand, she will die."

Joan whispered hurriedly to her husband.

"This was what Hill-of-the-Raven meant. The thing we were to

68

give back if it was demanded of us. You will have to dig it up."

"Are you afraid to be left with them?" he queried.

She shook her head, so he shouldered his spade and went forth to the tree-root to open again that small and uncanny grave, which was dug and filled in seven days before. He brought back the parcel in its folds of fair linen, from which he had shaken the dry earth; the rain which still fell without had not penetrated so deep.

The hand when unrolled from the cloth appeared to be un-changed, corruption had not set in. All this time Nita sat with closed eyes, leaning back in the chair, as if barely conscious of what was taking place. Now she moved when her brother addressed her in their native tongue, and held out the maimed stump of her right arm, from which he unwound the binding cloth, exposing the raw wound. He then united the severed parts, and Joan used afterwards to aver that she heard the bones grate together as they met. And when the bandage was rewound (a couple of pieces of bark folded in it to keep straight the wrist) she saw the dead fingers move, and the hue of life suffuse them once again.

This was the last of madam Rachel's magic, and of the uncanny events at Hunter's End. The brother lifted Nita to her feet, and half carried, half supported her to the waiting buggy, where his mules were hitched to the post. Both of them were apparently indifferent to the still falling sheets of-rain, through which they presently disappeared in the direction of the hills.

Fingers of a Hand

*"In the same hour came forth the fingers of a man's hand and wrote . .
. . and the king saw the part of the hand that wrote."*

The children were supposed to need a seaside change, and I daresay they did, poor wee things, as they had had whooping-cough in the spring, and measles to follow. As you know, we are taking care of them for Bernard, who is in India with his wife, and so we are even more anxious about them than if they were our own. That is one great use of unmarried aunts—to shoulder other people's responsibilities; and I, for one, think the world would be a poorer place if the "million of unwanted women" were, by some convulsion of nature, to be swept away. I only mention the children's measles as the reason why we took those lodgings at Cove at the beginning of July, for, now one has to economise, we should not have gone in for a seaside change as a luxury for ourselves.

The lodgings were clean and fairly comfortable, and we took them for two months certain, letting our own pretty cottage in the midlands for a similar term. And that was why we had no home of our own to retreat to when—— But I am telling my story upside down, as Sara says I always do. You would not be likely to understand, if I did not begin in the right place, with what went before.

The house was Number Seven, Cliff Terrace, a row of detached villas above the road, on the other side of which was the esplanade and the sea. There were no other lodgers, as we took both Mrs. Mills's "sets"; nobody in the house but ourselves and the bairns, and that important person Nurse, except Mrs. Mills herself, and her daughter who waited on us. So, you see there was no one who could have played tricks—— But again I am getting on too fast.

We had never been to Cove before, or to St. Eanswyth either, the larger watering-place which lies to the east of Cove; but we thought our choice of place for a summer holiday was amply justified by the pretty inland neighbourhood and the sweet air, and a safe beach close at hand, where the children could be out playing early and late under the guardian wing of Nurse. For the first fortnight we were all satisfied and happy, and, both in metaphor and actually, there was not a cloud in the sky.

Then the rain began, not brief summer showers and sunshine in between, but the worst weather of a wet July—a continuous downpour with hardly ten minutes intermission, and going on for days: such rain as Noah must have witnessed before the beginning of the Flood.

Of course, the poor children had to keep the house, and, though they and Nurse had the dining-room set to themselves, there was but little space for them to play about. Sara and I occupied the drawing-room, and she had been sketching from the window—not that there was much visible to make into a picture: a leaden sea and slanting lines of rain, and boats drawn up on the beach. At last, she pushed away colour-box and pencils.

"I can't stand this any longer," she said. "Rain or no rain, I am going out. It will be a good opportunity to test the resisting powers of my new cloak. You must stay in today, as I believe you have caught cold."

I did not dispute her fiat. Sara always decides what is, or what is not to be done, and I, who am a biddable person, submit to be ruled. And, to say the truth, I was not particularly anxious to get wet. I went on with my sewing till it was nearly time for Miss Mills to appear with the luncheon-tray, and then I began to clear the table of Sara's scattered possessions.

Some blank sheets of paper were lying about, besides the one pinned to her board with the half-finished sketch; and on one of these I noticed some large scrawled writing. Not Sara's writing, which is particularly small and neat; not the writing of anyone I knew. The words were quite legible, but they were very odd. GO—by itself at the top of the sheet; and the same word repeated twice below, followed by GET OUT AT ONCE.

Of course, I showed Sara this when she came in to luncheon, and she could not account for it any more than I. The sheets were unmarked when she took them out of her portfolio; of that she seemed to be certain.

"Someone has been playing a trick on us," she said. "If it is Mrs. Mills, it is an odd sort of notice"; and at this very mild witticism both

72

of us laughed.

But the idea of a trick being played was absurd: I had been in the room the whole time, as I said.

"Unless you think I dozed off while you were out, and did it in my sleep!"

Sara laughed again, and began to sort the loose papers back into place.

"Why, here is more of it," she exclaimed; and I saw on the sheet she held out, in the same large scrawl, a repetition of the words—GET OUT— GET OUT AT ONCE.

Now I could have sworn—had swearing been of any use—that I had looked those papers over on both sides after finding the first writing, and with that sole exception they bore no mark whatever. So, these last words must have been written after my discovery and before Sara's return, and while I was beside them in the room. Surely, they had been traced by no mortal hand!

You will not wonder that such a curious happening was the subject of discussion between us during the rest of that wet day. "I'd give anything to know who did it," Sara was saying, while I added: "I should like better still to know what it means." I am more credulous than Sara, and it seemed to me there must be some meaning in anything so unaccountable. I had this feeling from the very first, and, as you will see, both the conviction and the reason for it grew.

I pass on to the following Sunday. The weather was still wet, and the children were kept mainly to the house. For the sake of variety for them, Sara had little Dick and Nancy upstairs in our sitting-room for their Sunday lessons, which as a rule devolve on her to give, as she is a cleverer teacher than I. Lessons of the simplest, as they generally consist of showing pictures and giving explanations; and to be allowed to look at Sara's illustrated Bible is a frequent Sabbath treat. The children had gone down again to Nurse, and Sara was about to tidy the book away, when she gave a sharp exclamation.

"Grace, look here. Who can have done this?"

The volume was lying open at the nineteenth chapter of Genesis, and these words in the twenty-second verse were scored under blackly in pencil—*Haste thee: escape.*

Now Sara, who is particular in everything, is especially so about her books. She hates any soil or mark upon them, and nothing irritates her more than to have a lent volume returned with "purple passages" scored beside in the margin, whether in approval or otherwise. "Tut-

tut," she was saying, at the usual pitch of exasperation. "It is really unpardonable. *Where* is my india-rubber? I must see if I can take it out. It could not have been the children. And the Millses would never——! But there is nobody else."

"You would have seen, had it been the children. They are good little things, and would not: besides, they had not a pencil"—(thus I weakened an argument based on their righteousness). "And what odd words to have chosen to mark, when you think of the other scrawls. I wonder if this is all. It is possible there may be more."

"I shall look the book right through and see, and then I shall lock it in my box."

Sara sat down to her task armed with the piece of rubber, and by no means in a Sabbath spirit of peace and goodwill. She did find two other texts scored under, and these were the marked words:

2 Kings, ninth chapter and third verse. *Open the door and flee and tarry not.*

St. Matthew, seventh chapter and twenty-seventh verse. *The . . . house . . . fell, and great was the fall thereof.*

I was superstitious, because disturbed by these happenings. So, I was told, yet who would not have been affected in my place? I believe Sara too was disquieted in her secret mind, though she would not allow it. But then she was used to pride herself on being an *esprit fort.*

I kept saying to myself. What next?—and the next came quickly. I did not tell Sara what I purposed doing, but I left a couple of sheets of paper and a freshly-cut pencil displayed on the table when we were going out. More writing might be done with the opportunity given, and "it" might vouchsafe to make clear "its" meaning. I could not then have analysed what I meant by the convenient impersonal pronoun, nor am I clear of the exact meaning now.

We were about to do some shopping in the town, and I had stupidly left my purse on the mantel-shelf in the sitting-room, so I was obliged to turn back to get it. As I opened the door, my eyes fell at once upon the papers, and I saw some dark object moving across the white surface, and then quickly disappearing over the table edge. It was too big for a mouse; could it have been a rat? The thought of a rat gave me a nervous shiver; I think I would have a greater terror of rats than of ghosts.

I looked at the papers though I did not touch them; yes, a vague scrawl was begun upon the upper one, not developed into legible words. I had disturbed the writer too soon. But what could the writer be, coming in the form of a rat, or the shadow of a rat, and yet able to write words which appeared to convey a message? I left the papers as they were, but the scrawl was not continued; no doubt that unexpected first return had scared away the writer.

I said nothing to Sara of my failed experiment; but next day about the same time I laid my trap again, this time staying in the room, but retired into a distant corner, where I set myself to watch.

For a long while there was nothing. Then an object ill-defined and shadowy crept across the paper, stealing towards the pencil as it lay. I hardly dared breathe, the excitement was so tense. Over the pencil this shadow paused, and now became denser, taking solid form. It was not the whole of a hand, but a thumb and two fingers, forming something like a claw. But, if you consider, a thumb and two fingers are all a hand needs to manipulate a pencil, and "it" may not have cared to materialise anything superfluous. The pencil now slanted upwards between these fingers and the thumb, and—yes, no doubt remained—the claw was writing. Now we would know all, such was my sanguine thought, not forecasting how deep the mystery would remain.

It was Sara this time who interrupted, coming in. The pencil dropped, the claw from a solid form became a shadow, and slipped away over the edge of the table, as I had seen it vanish before. Sara noticed nothing; she was too full of her news, and of the letter open in her hand.

"Look at this. We ought to have had it two days ago, but there was a mistake in the address. It is from Mrs. Bernard's mother." (Mrs. Bernard is our brother's wife). "She is at Diplake for ten days before they go to Scotland, and she wants one of us to bring the children there just for the time they stay. She says she is sorry she cannot have us both, but it is a case of single room, as the house is full. She is expecting us tomorrow, so I shall have to wire, and tell Nurse to get ready. Will you go, Grace, or shall I?"

"Of course you must be the one. I should never get on at Diplake, and with a large, gay party. You must go, Sara, and put your best foot foremost, for Bernard's sake. And—I'm glad you have to take the children. For look what is written here!"

I showed her the paper on which the claw had scrawled. Over and over again the word DANGER, as if it could not be too often insisted on. Then, also repeated: GO. GET OUT. Then an attempt at *children*, afterwards clearly written: DANGER. CHILDREN MUST GO.

I think Sara was impressed at last, though she hardly believed in the claw I had seen writing. As to that, I must—she said—have been hallucinated, or else slept and dreamed. But little time remained for argument, as all was in a hurry of preparation—boxes to be packed, and the children to be consoled, for their enjoyment of the seaside pleasures was very keen, and the attraction small of going to stay with an almost unknown grandmother.

"But we are coming back?" said little Nancy. "We are coming back again here?" I believe I told her yes, but as to what will happen in the future, who can say?

They set out early next morning, Sara and the three children and Nurse, and I saw them off at the station. Sara said almost at the last:

"I don't half like leaving you alone here, Grace. If you find the lodgings too solitary, why not take a room at the hotel for the days I am away?"

I said I would think of it, but in truth I felt no special nervousness or concern, only an intense curiosity to see what would happen now we had (by pure accident) obeyed the dictation of the writing, and sent the children away.

The lonely evening passed for me without disturbance; Miss Mills came at the usual time to carry down my supper tray, and wished me goodnight, and shortly after this I went to bed.

I slept, and do not remember any warning dreams. But in the very early daylight I was suddenly startled broad awake—not I think by any noise, but by an alteration in the level of my bed. My head was low, almost on the floor, and my feet were high in air. Everything in the room was sliding and altering; basin and ewer slipped from the washstand, crashed and broke, and pictures flapped from the wall. Then came a greater crash like the jolting of a thunder-clap, and it was close at hand; chimney-pots falling, walls and roofs collapsing: was it an earthquake that had happened? I heard screams and shouts, but the sliding movement had stopped.

I struggled up and to my feet, for I had been half buried by the bedclothes falling back upon me; and there opposite was a great crack or rent in the outer wall, wide enough to admit my arm, with the new morning looking through, and a waft of air blowing in keenly from the sea. It was as if the house had broken in two. What but an earthquake could have caused such a disaster?—and again I heard people screaming. The often-repeated warning, the scored words in the Bible ran in my head. I could be thankful indeed that Sara and the children were safe at Diplake out of the way: what an agony had they been still here, and those screams possibly theirs!

I do not know how long it took me to scramble up the slanting floor, to find my clothes, my shoes, where all was confusion, so that if it were possible to get out of the house, I might go forth clad. Then I tried the door.

It was in some way jammed, and it seemed as if ages passed before I could wrench it open. When at last it gave way, the wreck revealed without was worse than the wreck within. The staircase was a heap of broken wood, and the back wall had fallen inwards; there was no getting down that way. What had become, I wondered, of Mrs. Mills and her daughter, and was it their screams that I heard? I called to them by name, but there was no answer.

Baffled so, I looked from the window, which had hardly a whole pane left. It was as if the terrace had disappeared: the road was broken up, and the house had been carried down with the sliding earth, many yards nearer the sea. A crowd had assembled, staring at this phenomenon, but at a safe distance. I shouted to them, and a man called up to me instructions to stay where I was, as a ladder would presently be brought.

I knew later that they feared at first to touch the house, lest it should collapse in total ruin like the one next on the terrace, where, alas! two people had been killed, overwhelmed and buried in their sleep.

This was a danger indeed, about which that warning came. The part of our house which fell, was where the children would have been sleeping. I was told that tons and tons of masonry had crushed in their little beds; even now it makes me sick to think of what we so narrowly escaped. The Millses, mother and daughter, were dug out of the basement quite unharmed, but I am afraid, poor people, they are heavy losers. I myself had not a scratch.

The great landslip at Cove, with all its damage and disaster, will surely pass into history: the slide of the undercliff down into the sea, the gaping fissure torn above, hundreds of feet in length—the alteration of the ground below, heaped into mounds and billows like the waves of the sea, while the buildings in the course of the slide are broken up and displaced like a set of children's toys, playthings in the hands of a giant. People who are wise about the geological formation, talk of a bed of slippery clay underlying the upper strata, and say water had percolated down to it owing to the wet spring, and, following upon that, the heavy rains of that dismal week in July. But they are wise after the event and did not forecast it: indeed, it was anticipated by no one other than the writer of those mysterious words.

Nevill Nugent's Legacy

From Mrs. Margaret Campbell to a Friend.

1

Yes, you are right; the legacy was a great surprise to us—the surprise of our lives, in fact; and we were ready to bless Cousin Nevill in the beginning—at least I was. Kenneth now says he always had his doubts. But I do not think he had many when he came in to me after the post delivery—just one step from the bedroom to the sitting-room of our flat, with that look upon his face, and the open letter shaking in his hand.

It seemed to have come to us straight from heaven, Cousin Nevill's bequest. For you must know we were at that time very hard up; almost, as the saying is, "stony-broke." Kenneth giving up his profession to join the army made a great change in our circumstances. We could not keep on our pretty house, of which I used to be so proud; and, as soon as I was alone, I moved into a tiny flat in town, and got work to do. But when Ken came out of hospital last January so ill and broken, my work had to stop, for I was needed to nurse him. Ever since then the money has been flowing out, with only a little—so little—trickling in: I cried over it only the night before, of course when Ken did not see. For it seemed as if even the wretched flat was more than we could afford, and I did not know where Tom's school-fees were to come from for another term—all important as his education is, the chance of life for such a clever boy.

You will judge what a breaking of sunlight into darkness was the great surprise. Ken's voice had a choke in it as he said: "I saw Nevill's death in the obituary, but I never dreamed it would benefit us."

"He was a rich man, was he not?" (I crowded my questions.) "Has he left us much money? *All* his money? What does the letter say?"

"All?—no, indeed! But a fair amount of property. It is a Mr. Bay-

79

liss who writes, an Edinburgh lawyer; and he would like to see me, as soon as I can make it convenient. Here, you can read for yourself."

He sank into the nearest chair, while I stood, devouring the communication; and now my hands were shaking too. Mr. Bayliss wrote that his client, Mr. Nevill Nugent, in a Will made the week before his death, devised the bulk of his property to Nugent relatives. To Kenneth, as representing his mother's side of the family, he gave the small estate of Mirk Muir, four miles distant from the manufacturing town of R——. It comprised the farms of South Muir, Bull Knowe, and Blackwater, and the residential property of Mirk Muir Grange, generally known as the Chapel House, and let off furnished, but now vacant. There was in addition a street of artisans' dwellings in R——, and most of these were in occupation. If well let, the entire property should bring in about £1,200 *per annum*.

"Twelve hundred a year! Oh, Ken! That will be riches indeed—for us!"

"I wish indeed it was likely. It isn't as good as that. Go on, and you'll see."

The drawbacks followed, and they were considerable. The rents received the previous year barely amounted to £600. An action at law was pending, which the new owner would do well to compromise even at a loss. There was also an annuity charge for an old servant, passed on to us. And finally, Ken was reminded that the death duties would be heavy. My first enthusiasm of greed was somewhat quenched.

"But, even so, there will be enough to make things better for us," I said more soberly. "Very—very much better. You can have the change you need so much—Tom's schooling can go on. And—"

"Yes, it will do all that, and more. It will be a change to go to Edinburgh. That is, the first thing we must do, Maggie; you and I."

Two days later we set out on our journey. Tom was left at school, as he was in the middle of a term; and though part of my rejoicing was that his lessons need not be disturbed by our failure to pay, I was irrational enough to regret that he could not be with us. He would have enjoyed the adventure of new scenes and new hopes; and I set out with the thought of my one boy very much in mind—which may have had its share in attuning me to what followed.

We had not exhausted our wonderment during those days of hasty preparation. Ken remarked more than once:

"I'd give a good deal to know what made Nevill think of me at the last. Since he had that row with my dear old dad, we haven't been on speaking terms. And it must be a dozen years since last we met. If I am right in remembering, it was just before Tom was born."

"I never saw him," I chimed in. We were now in the great express on our way to Edinburgh—third-class travellers in spite of our accession of fortune. "Tell me what he was like."

"Oh—Nevill was a fellow with a crook in him, and looked it all over. He was always queer—about religion, as well as in other matters. Didn't hold with any of the recognised forms, and used to preach as a free-lance when he could get anybody to listen. I've no doubt he meant well. I believe he built a chapel for himself."

"Is that why Mirk Muir Grange is called the Chapel House?"

"I daresay it is. I'm glad he did not saddle his bequest with the provision I should do parson. There are disadvantages enough without that."

We were to hear more of the disadvantages from Mr. Bayliss in Edinburgh. He was a stiff, dry sort of man, but he became slightly more genial on finding Ken willing to take his advice about compounding the action, and selling a portion of the property to meet charges and duty, instead of putting a mortgage on the farms. He thought Ken would be wise to keep on a certain McGregor as his factor, as he had served Nevill Nugent for half a lifetime, and knew the place and the people. We might expect to get something like £300 in the course of the first year, but it was not likely to be more, unless a tenant could be found for the Chapel House: he called it that, I noticed, rather than the Grange. But we had better not be sanguine, as the house was not an easy one to let.

Ken asked why—a question on the tip of my tongue too, though it got no further.

Mr. Bayliss did not seem very ready with his answer. It was a good deal out of the way, he said at last. "Drains bad?" Ken suggested, but was answered no; all the sanitary arrangements had been put in complete order for the last tenant. Of course something might be done by advertising, as the autumn season was coming on; and Mrs. Wilding, who was left in charge, was said to be an excellent cook.

Ken turned to me.

"I don't see why we shouldn't go there ourselves, as it is standing vacant. For a few weeks at any rate, until a tenant offers. What would you say to the plan? It would give us the opportunity of looking round."

I caught at the idea.

"I shall like it of all things," I exclaimed. "And you can settle everything else from there."

It struck me Mr. Bayliss looked relieved.

"Yes, you would do well to go, Mr. Campbell," he said. "You will understand better about the property after seeing over it, and consulting with the factor. I think I told you the Chapel House cannot be alienated so long as Mrs. Wilding lives. You are bound to keep it up to afford a home for her, though she works there as a servant. The Will provides for that, as well as for the annuity charge of which I spoke."

A curious provision this, if you come to think of it; and it will be an odd position for us—for me—with a servant in the house over whom I can have no authority, as it is her home by as clear a right as it will be my own. I cannot bid her go, however much she may transgress. But I said nothing of this to Ken, for I did not want to make difficulty; and if it is true we cannot let the Grange, it will be cheaper to live in it ourselves than to pay rent elsewhere. Then the query came up, why could not the Grange be let?—this after we had left Mr. Bayliss, and were discussing the matter between ourselves.

"Do you think it can be haunted?" I suggested, but Ken laughed aloud in scorn of the idea.

"What are you fancying about it, Maggie? It isn't an ancestral castle, hundreds of years old, but just an ugly modern house, without a scrap of romance. Ghost, indeed! It's too far from a station, or up and down too many hills on a bad road. Those are the reasons that keep houses vacant, not humbug about ghosts."

2

Ken was right in part of his description.

Mirk Muir *was* a long way out from R——, and on a hilly road; and the Grange certainly was an ugly house. Indeed, it could hardly have been plainer, or presented a more dismal exterior, than it did when we turned in through the open gate, one wet cloudy evening on the edge of dusk. The walls were faced with stucco and painted drab, the windows flat, and the slate roof dark with rain. The house itself looked square and compact as it fronted us and the gate; but to the left was a long annexe of one storey only, which appeared to be built of wood. "By George, that must be Nevill's chapel," Ken exclaimed. And then our "machine" drew up at the door.

It was opened to us by Mrs. Wilding, a tall gaunt woman, with quite the saddest face I ever saw. She made me think of those people who after a great grief are said never to have smiled again. But she was quite civil, even anxiously so; hoped we should not be inconvenienced because only two rooms had been made ready, but the notice was short, and she could only get in a girl to help. The dining-room was open, and presently there would be the service of a meal; the bedroom we were to occupy looked to the front immediately above. On the morrow, any changes we desired should of course be made.

It would do very well, we told her; and while Ken directed the driver about carrying up our luggage, I turned into the dining-room and sat down. There a lamp was lighted, and the table ready spread with a white cloth; there was even the cheer of a glowing fire which smelt delightfully of peat, and which the chill of the wet evening made welcome, summer as it was. I recognised comfort; but somehow, I knew not why, my spirits had sunk down to zero. There was no visible cause, but I seemed, on entering the house, to have stepped into a cloud of depression which engulfed and swallowed me up. I felt properly ashamed of myself when Ken came in, rubbing his hands.

"Really, this is very snug," he said. "And you will be pleased with the room above, for it has three windows, and a view each way. Early Victorian, of course, and a four-post bed with curtains at every corner, but nothing missed out that we can want. The luggage has been taken up, so you can go there when you like."

To have Ken pleased and cheerful—what more could I desire? I roused myself with an effort, and departed to unpack and make ready. Through the hall window I saw our driver climbing to the box of his vehicle, preparatory to driving away; and a boy was going out and closing the door behind him—a boy of about Tom's age; no doubt he had been got in to assist with the luggage.

I did not give him a second thought, but lighted the two candles which stood ready on the toilet-table, and prepared to change from my travelling-dress. Presently Mrs. Wilding brought me a jug of hot water. She seemed anxious to be attentive, and I was ready to like her, only that it gave me a chill at heart to see her face, from which all hope seemed to have gone out.

She served our meal, but not quite in the ordinary way, putting it on the table for us to help ourselves. She was alone in the house, she said, except for the girl who came in, and her husband, who was paralysed and a cripple. She thought she could manage for us with the girl's help; that is, if we were satisfied with what she could do. We might find it difficult to get a regular servant to stay. Here again there was reticence and no reason given; and something seemed to tie my tongue from asking why.

I broke Ken's rest that night by an outcry in my sleep, and when he roused me to know what was the matter, I was weeping and trembling, and at first beyond speech. I had heard Tom calling for me, that was my dream; his voice screaming "Mother—mother!" as if in awful trouble or unbearable pain. I woke with the cry still ringing in my ears, and it needed all Ken's common sense to console me. Even then I could not forget. Something terrible had happened to our child: that was my fear, but what I could not tell. I did not see him in the dream; it was a dream of sound and not of sight; the cries seemed to break out of some strange place which was his prison.

Ken talked to me and comforted me till the grey morning light stole into the room, and after that he slept again, but I could not sleep. It was true what he said. Tom had always seemed perfectly happy at school, and the house-master and his wife were our friends, and would let us know at once if any ill befell the boy. And, as he reminded me, they knew of our changed address, as I had written from Edinburgh to say we were going on to Mirk Muir.

The post of that morning brought no ill news; in fact no news of any kind. After breakfast, Mrs. Wilding suggested I might like to see the house, and I went alone with her, as Ken had gone to call on McGregor the factor.

There was not a great deal to see: upstairs our bedroom was the only apartment of any size, though there were a number of smaller rooms. One of these I fixed on as a dressing-room for Ken, and another (in my own mind) as just right for Tom, if we stayed on at Mirk Muir and he came for the holidays. On the ground-floor there was a drawing-room, and a small nondescript third sitting-room. The drawing-room, a drab little place, was to the left of the entrance hall; it had only a single window, but on one side of the fireplace was another door, which Mrs. Wilding unlocked with a key taken from the pocket of her apron.

"This is the room Mr. Nugent built on to serve as a chapel," she said, drawing back to allow me to look in.

I found myself at the head of about six steps, leading down into an interior chill as a vault. It was a spacious place, bare of furniture, but with a sort of dais at the further end. It was lighted by four windows high in the wall, bordered by ugly strips of blue glass; and a large stove for heating purposes had a black chimney-pipe carried up into the roof. There was also an outer door, which Mrs. Wilding said led into the garden.

"McGregor keeps the outer key, but of course he will give it up to Mr. Campbell; and I will now leave this one, so that you can enter when you like from the drawing-room. Yes, the chapel-room does strike cold, in spite of the wooden floor having been put in when it was used as a schoolroom. It was all stone flags to begin with, and the stones are still there underneath. Mr. Nugent did not use it many times, after going to all the expense of the building. He took a dislike to Mirk Muir and went away; and the tenant next after kept a school for boys, and made it into a class-room—the house has been through many hands in the last eight years."

"And you have been here with all the changes?"

"Yes, for that was Mr. Nugent's wish. I was matron when it was the school; but with the others I have cooked and kept house. Will you like to see the kitchen side?"

I was willing to see all she cared to show, but I understood by a slightly hinted reserve, that the back premises were her own peculiar domain, on which I was not to intrude except by invitation. And I did not wonder when I discovered what was there.

The best kitchen is a spacious apartment, where, I imagine, cooking is rarely done, as there is another and more modern range in the second kitchen behind. There was a fire, however, and set beside it in an elbow chair was the helpless figure of a man.

He was paralysed below the waist, having sustained some injury to the spine, and the malady was creeping upwards; but he must once have been of uncommon strength, with a large and powerful frame. He still had the use of one hand; and he kept a stick beside him. At first, he did not appear to notice my entrance, as he kept his eye on a collie-dog, a nice creature, which was sidling round to find a resting-place within the radius of warmth. I shall not soon forget the murderous look on his face, as he struck at the animal with his stick—missing it, happily, for the blow fell harmless on the floor.

"Leave the dog alone," his wife commanded sharply. And then: "This is the new mistress, Mrs. Campbell," she said as we passed through.

The man then made some sort of civil salutation, but I could not bring myself to speak to him, except with the merest good day. If from a man's countenance you may judge the quality of his soul, in this afflicted body must have dwelt a very demon. In the work-a-day kitchen beyond, a stout servant-lass was busy washing dishes at the sink: she had heard what passed, and the blow of the stick on the floor.

"Bassett'll be the death of that dog, missis, just as he was of the other," she remarked as she bent over her task.

"Who is Bassett?" I asked, though feeling sure what would be the answer.

"The man you have just seen—Thomas Bassett, my husband."

"But you are Mrs. Wilding?" I exclaimed, perhaps unwisely.

"I have taken back my former name, because I will not any longer be called by his. Did not Mr. Bayliss tell you?" was her counter-question, to which I answered No.

The tour of inspection ended, I wandered out into the garden, for it was now fine overhead, though everything was still drenched by yesterday's rain. Presently I discovered I had dropped my handkerchief, and as I knew I had it when Mrs. Wilding was showing me the drawing-room, I turned in there on re-entering. There it lay on the drab carpet; but I was surprised to come upon the boy who—as I believed—helped over night with our luggage. Certainly, he could have had no business there, in a room I was likely to occupy. Again, he was in the act of slipping through a door: it was the front door the night before, and now he was disappearing into the chapel by the entrance Mrs. Wilding had left partly open. This time I followed, as I was curious to find out who he was and what was his errand; but the chapel-room was empty.

I shut the door upon the steps and turned the key, though I left it standing in the lock. Then I went back to the dining-parlour and sat down, for I felt suddenly weak.

The surprise of that complete disappearance was something of a shock to me, but not such as I would have supposed must be the effect on a living person of seeing what is called a ghost. Indeed, I hardly admitted the haunting possibility to myself, even then: my mind was running on the fear of something having happened to Tom. I had heard of doppelgangers and apparitions of the living, and this boy was about Tom's size and age, though I could not say the figure was in his likeness: the face I did not see.

I said nothing to Ken when he came in, full of his business with the factor, and wanting me to walk over to South Muir with him in the afternoon, where he had an appointment to view the farm. Nothing then, or through the evening; and I rested quietly that night with no recurrence of my dream. But the next morning I saw the boy again.

I was about to cross the hall, and there he was on the staircase, mounting quickly, but full in view. I called to Mrs. Wilding, who was in the room behind me, collecting our breakfast-china on a tray.

"Who is the boy who has just gone upstairs, and what does he want?" I asked.

Mrs. Wilding put down the cloth she was folding; she did not seem surprised.

"I do not know, ma'am, but I'll see,"—and she ran up, while I waited below. I heard her pass from room to room, and then she came down to me. "There is nobody there," she said.

"Then what is it? You must tell me. I have seen this figure twice before. Is it a ghost?"

"Mr. Bayliss wrote that we were not to name it to you, but now you have seen for yourself I have no choice. People say it is a ghost, and some see it and some don't. I have never seen it for my part, though I have lived at Mirk Muir for years, and been through the house at all hours, day and night. I doubt if it is a ghost myself. There is no reason for a ghost to be here."

She looked strangely agitated, as she stood plucking at her apron with nervous hands, while two spots of feverish colour burned on her tragic face. The apparition seemed in some way to concern her nearly, though she professed to disbelieve.

"What do you think it is?"

"I have come to fancy—it is like to be—something made up out of my thoughts, which shows to others, though not to me—never to me. I'm always dwelling on my great trouble, that my son has gone away."

Here a sort of dry sob choked her voice, but presently she went on.

"He was but a slip of a lad, much like the figure they talk about, when he ran away to sea because his stepfather was cruel. I knew it was in his mind to go. 'Mother,' he says to me, 'I can't bear it any longer, and don't you fret. Whatever hard usage I get on board ship, it can't be as bad as what I've had here; and I shan't write, for I won't be sought for and brought back. But when I've got to an age and a weight so that Bassett can't touch me, then I'll come again to you, and we'll go away together.' Bassett had beaten him cruel, not once but hundreds of times. And the next day he was gone."

"And that is—how long ago?"

"Eight years and two months. It was when the chapel room was building. And within a year after that, Bassett fell off a ladder and was fixed helpless. Martin need not have feared him then, but I could not tell where my boy was, to let him know. I did put an advertisement in papers I thought he might see, but no notice came. Ma'am, they say that marriage is an honourable estate, and a married woman is respectable. I thought it would be good for me to be married; but I say now that the worst day's work that ever I did, and the wickedest, was when I married Bassett. To give him power over myself, body and soul, was bad enough, he being what he was; but the sin was to give him power over my child. I haven't said it out so plain to anyone else; but I believe it is my thoughts dwelling on Martin that make the ghost, and not anything real."

Ken looked worried when he came in to lunch, after another confabulation with McGregor.

"I doubt more and more whether Nevill meant well to us when he left us Mirk Muir," he said when we were alone. "He has had no end of trouble with the tenants—money going out for repairs and claims, and precious little coming in. And this house won't let at any price; nobody will look at it. There is some confounded story which has got about—"

"The story of a ghost: is that what you mean? The ghost of a boy?"

"Who has been telling you about it?" he asked, frowning.

"I have seen it for myself, three times since we came. I saw it again this morning by broad daylight, and then I asked Mrs. Wilding: She says it is seen by some people, and always the same; but she thinks it is a sort of thought-shape, and not a ghost. I am not afraid of it, so you need not mind. What, did McGregor tell you."

"He appears to believe in it, unless he was pulling my leg. He says it has played all manner of what he calls 'pliskies,' and it began to be active when Grant took the house and brought his school. He was the next here after Nevill. McGregor has a notion Nevill saw it himself, and that was why he gave up living here, after going to the expense of building on that outside room. McGregor says the ghost was never heard of till after the chapel room was built; the house was quiet up till then, and of good reputation. It was as if the building disturbed something; though that, of course, is absurd. Now tell me what you saw, and what Mrs. Wilding said."

★★★★★★★★★★★★★★★★★★

I had the opportunity of questioning McGregor myself that evening, as he came round to see Ken. He is a pawky old Scot, with a twinkle of humour in his eye, but I believe he was sincere in what he told me. Oddly enough, his errand was to ask Ken if he would be willing to sell the chapel room. He had just received an offer for it from a certain contractor, who would take it down at his own expense, to re-erect for some purpose connected with the war. The contractor would bind himself to take away the brick foundation and stone flagging, as well as the wooden part, and smooth the garden over to be as it was before. The price offered was less than a third of what it cost Nevill to erect, although all materials have gone up in value; but Ken was glad to realise even so much money, and well inclined to consent.

"I didn't tell him he might be buying the ghost along with it," said the factor with a wag of his head and a smile. "The ghost came with the chapel room, and maybe the ghost will go with it. And if it does, so much the better for the Grange."

"I wish you would tell me what you know about the ghost, Mr. McGregor. I'm very interested and not nervous, and my husband will not mind. It seems a very harmless sort of apparition, and I do not see why anybody should be afraid."

"Just so, ma'am, and I don't know that ever it did harm but once, and that most likely was accident and not intent. We first began to hear about it when Mr. Grant was here with his school of twenty boys, and we thought of it at the first as nothing but the young lads' mischief and a tale. To look at it was much the same as one of them, and they got into scrapes being supposed to go up to the dormitories at wrong hours, and that. Then the *dominie*, counting heads, would find too many boys in class, and when he counted again, they were right: he could not make it out.

"But the thing that began the trouble was a scribbling on the exercise-books and writing copies and that, scribbling done in pencil, not real writing, but W.W. or M.M., like this"—tracing with his finger on the table—"the same over and over again. I saw some of it myself. Nobody could make out who did it; and at last, Mr. Grant locked the books in his own desk; but they were scribbled on even there. He got very angry, and vowed he would flog the whole school, from the senior lad down to the youngest, unless the one that played the trick would come forward and confess. And then there started up a boy who was a stranger and not one of the scholars, and went up to the master's desk with a copy-book in his hand.

"The *dominie* was about to take it from him; but no sooner were they face to face than Mr. Grant fell down in a fit, and that before ever he touched the book. And in the confusion that followed, the stranger boy disappeared, and no one could say where he came from or how he went. That was the biggest pliskie that was played. Those who came here after, have just seen him going through the rooms to vanish in some shut up place, and sometimes they have heard cries and knockings, but all the appearances have been much the same."

3

My last letter ended with McGregor's narrative, did it not, dear Susan?—and now you write to say you are interested, and ask me what more has happened. No more apparitions have happened. I have not seen the boy again, nor has Kenneth seen him: he says he shall not, he is not so made; and, if a healthy scepticism is any safeguard, I imagine he will not. But on the other hand, no eager credulity could in my case have made visible that of which I did not know.

I believe I told you Ken decided to sell the chapel room, and have it taken away. It is needed for some war object, I am not sure what; so for every reason we are glad to have it go. The contractor's men have been busy all this week taking the timbers to pieces as if it were a child's puzzle, and putting it, not in a box, but on a couple of big lorries. Now they are at work upon the brick foundations and the floor; and the door which led into it from the drawing-room is to have glass panels, and be our way out into the garden.

Only one other event is worth naming since I wrote. That horrible old husband of poor Mrs. Wilding's has been taken ill, and I believe the doctor thinks seriously of his state. He hates any sort of change, Mrs. Wilding says, and he excited himself over hearing the chapel room was to be taken away. Imagine this: the first night after the work began, he crawled, nobody knows how, out of the kitchen and through the hall and drawing-room, and himself undid that door.

Then I suppose he fell down the six steps, for he was found at the foot of them in the morning, only half alive. It is almost incredible that he could have done it without help. Since then, he has had two epileptic fits, and talks the strangest nonsense, so his wife tells us. I wish he could be taken to a hospital—for her sake, poor thing, as well as ours. Ken is going to speak to the doctor, and see what can be arranged.

You ask about Tom. We have had good news of him; two cheery letters, all about cricket, and having got into the first eleven, the height of his ambition. My dream could have meant nothing wrong with him; and now I begin to think it must have been what McGregor calls a "pliskie" of the ghost's.

★★★★★★★★★★★★★★★★★

I was interrupted yesterday; but now in continuing I can tell you I have seen the boy again. I went out through the drawing-room to look how the work was getting on. The wooden floor has been removed, and now the men are taking up the stone slabs which were underneath, with care not to break them, as they are to be used elsewhere. There were two men at work over this, and the boy was talking to one of them. He seemed to be speaking very earnestly, and pointing to a part of the floor a yard or two away; and the man looked up in his face, and said something (I thought) in answer. I felt a cold shiver pass over me, but in spite of this I walked down the steps into the wrecked place, and, as I approached the group, the boy's figure seemed, to slip behind the man with the pickaxe, and so was gone.

"What was that boy doing here, and what did he say to you?" I asked, though my breath almost failed me over the words.

I fancy the workers knew about the ghost, but both of them shook their heads. They had seen no boy, but something was a-whispering in the place—always a-whispering behind them, but they could not make out what it said.

I had but just written that down, when there was a stir outside, of men calling and shouting. Mr. Campbell was wanted, and somebody else was bidden to run for the police. I did not know what was the matter, but Ken now tells me "human remains" have been found under that stone floor. It is very horrible. We have no notion how they came there, but there will, of course, be an investigation. Don't you think we may have happened on a reason for the ghost?

I must post this letter now, if it is to go tonight. I will write again when we know more.

★★★★★★★★★★★★★★★★★

(*Five days later.*) Oh Susan, this has been a terrible business, and Mrs. Wilding is almost out of her mind with grief. The body was that of a boy twelve or fourteen years of age, and from the clothing and certain things found with it, there can be no doubt that it was Martin Wilding, her son. Bassett must have caught him about to run away, and either have killed him on purpose in a homicidal outbreak, or so beaten him that he died; and then buried his body under the floor of the chapel room, the flags of which were being laid down at the time. Mrs. Wilding has charged her husband, and will give evidence against him; and the wretch has been taken away. She says she hopes he will be hanged, but Ken thinks it is not likely the law will go to that extreme, as he is not in his right mind. But he will be shut up as a criminal lunatic for what is left to him of life.

I wonder whether Nevill Nugent foresaw the troubles that would come upon us when he left us the ghost as his legacy! Martin Wilding's remains have been coffined, and will be buried tomorrow. Ken got me some flowers, and I have made a cross of white lilies for Mrs. Wilding to lay on the grave. Is it not strange to think I should have seen him four times, looking as he must have done in life, when all the while his body was lying there? Poor, poor boy, to think what he must have suffered, not able to let his mother know! Now the mystery is cleared up, I don't suppose Mirk Muir Grange will be haunted any more, and Ken may succeed in letting it. As for ourselves, I do not think it likely we shall remain here. Ken says he would rather not, as the associations are too painful: odd that the objection should come from him, the one who saw nothing, and not from me!

Over the Wires

Ernest Carrington, captain in the "Old Contemptibles," was in England on his first leave from the front. There he had a special errand, hoping to trace a family of the name of Regnier, which had been swept away in the exodus from Belgium, then of recent date. Two old people, brother and sister, harmless folk who had shown him the kindest hospitality before their home was wrecked and burned; and with them their niece Isabeau, who was his chosen love and his betrothed wife. He had endured agonies in these last weeks, receiving no news of them, though he fully believed they had escaped to England: it was more than strange that Isabeau did not write, as she knew his address, though he was ignorant of hers.

A friend in London had made inquiry for him where the thronging refugees were registered and their needs dealt with, but nothing seemed to be known of the Regniers. Now he would be on the spot, and could himself besiege the authorities. Hay might have been lukewarm over the quest, but it seemed impossible that he, Carrington, could fail. His friend Hay, with whom he was to have stayed, had just been transferred from Middlesex to the coast defence of Scotland, but had placed at Carrington's disposal his small flat, and the old family servant who was caretaker.

The flat was a plain little place, but it seemed luxurious indeed to Carrington that first evening, in sharp contrast to his recent experiences roughing it in the campaign. His brain was still in a whirl after the hurried journey, and it was too late to embark upon his quest that night; but the next morning, the very next morning, he would begin the search for Isabeau.

Only one item in Hay's room demands description. There was a telephone installation in one corner; and twice while Carrington's dinner was being served, there came upon it a sharp summons, answered first by the servant, and; secondly by himself. Major Hay was wanted, and it had to be detailed how Major Hay had departed upon sudden orders for Scotland only that morning. Now the meal was over and cleared away, and the outer door closed, shutting Carrington in for the night. Left alone, his thoughts returned to the channel in which they had flowed for many days and nights.

Isabeau—his Isabeau: did the living world still hold his lost treasure, and under what conditions and where? And—maddening reflection—what might she not have suffered of privation, outrage, while he was held apart by his soldier's duty, ignorant, impotent to succour! He could picture her as at their last meeting when they exchanged tokens, the light in her eyes, the sweetness of her lips: the image was perfect before him, down to every fold of her white dress, and every ripple of her hair. His own then, pledged to him, and now vanished into blank invisibility and silence. What could have happened: what dread calamity had torn her from him? Terrible as knowledge might be when gained, it was his earnest prayer that he might know.

A groan burst from his lips, and he cried out her name in a passion of appeal.

"Isabeau, where are you? Speak to me, dead or alive!"

Was it in answer that the telephone call began to ring?—not sharply and loudly, like those demands for Major Hay, but thin and faint like their echo. But without doubt it rang, and Carrington turned to the instrument and took down the receiver.

"Yes," he called back. "What is it?"

Great Heaven! it was Isabeau's voice that answered, a voice he could but just hear, as it seemed to be speaking from far away. "Ernest—Ernest," she cried, "have you forgotten me? I have forgotten many things since I was tortured, but not you—never you."

"I am here, my darling. I have come to England seeking you, with no other thought in mind. Tell me, for God's sake, where I can find you. Can I come tonight?"

There was a pause, and then the remote voice began again, now a little stronger and clearer.

"Ernest—is it really you? I can die happy, now you tell me that you love me still. That is all I wanted, just the assurance. All I may have in this world—now."

"Darling, of course I love you: you are all in all to me. Where are you speaking from? Tell me, and I will come?"

"No, no: it is all I wanted, what you have just said. It will be easy now to die. I could never have looked you in the face again—after

94

I am not fit. But soon I shall be washed clean. What does it say—washed? And they gave them white robes!"

The voice failed, dying away, and when Carrington spoke there was no answer. He called to her by name, begging her to say if she was in London or where, but either the connection, had been cut off, or she did not hear. Then after an interval he rang up the exchange. Who was it who had just used the line? But the clerk was stupid or sleepy, thought there had been no call, but was only just on after the shift, and could not say.

It was extraordinary, that she could know where he was to be found that night, and call to him. And how was it that the voice had ceased without giving him a clue? But surely, surely, it would come again.

To seek his bed, tired as he was, seemed now to be impossible. He waited in the living-room, sometimes pacing up and down, sometimes sitting moodily, his head bent on his hands: could he rest or sleep when a further call might come, and, if unheard, a chance be lost. And a call did come a couple of hours later; the same thin reedy vibration of the wire. In a moment 'he was at the instrument, the receiver at his ear, and again it was Isabeau's voice that spoke.

"Ernest, can you hear me? Will you say it over again: say that you love me still, in spite of all?"

"Dearest, I love you with all my heart and soul. And I entreat you to tell me where you are, so that I can find you."

"You will be told—quite soon. They are so kind—the people here, but they want to know my name. I cannot tell them any more than Isabeau; I have forgotten what name came after. What was my name when you knew me?"

"My darling, you were Isabeau Regnier. And you were living at Martel, with your old uncle Antoine Regnier, and his sister, Mademoiselle Elise. Surely you remember?"

"Yes; yes. I remember now. I remember all. I was Isabeau Regnier then, and now I am lost—lost— lost! Poor old uncle Antoine! They set him up against the wall and shot him, because they said he resisted; and they dragged the *Tante* and me away. But the *Tante* could not go fast enough to please them. They stabbed her in the back with their bayonets, and left her bleeding and moaning, lying in the road to die. Oh, if only they had killed me too. Don't ask me—never ask me—what they did to me!"

"Do not think of it, Isabeau dearest. Think only that I have come to seek you, and that you are safe in England and will be my wife. But I must know where you are, and when I can come to see you."

"I will tell you some time, but not now. The nurse says I must not go on talking; that I am making myself more ill. She's wrong, for it cannot make me ill to speak to you; but I must do as I am bidden. Tell me that you love me; just once again. That you love what I was: you cannot love what I have become."

"Darling, I loved you then, I love you now, and shall love you always. But tell me—you must tell me where."

She did not answer. This seemed to be the end, for, though he still watched and listened, the wire did not vibrate again that night, nor for many following hours.

He did not spend those hours in inaction. He was early at the London office, and then took the express to Folkestone, but at neither place was there knowledge of the name of Regnier. Nor had he better fortune at the other seaports, which he visited the day following. But where there had been such thronging numbers, despite the organisation vigilance, was it wonderful that a single name had dropped unnoted? And if what had been told him was correct, about the murder of her uncle and aunt, she must have reached England alone.

His next resort was to a private inquiry office, and there an appointment was arranged for him at three o'clock on Friday afternoon.

He had arrived in London on the Monday, and it was on Monday evening and night that those communications from Isabeau came over the wire. Each of the following nights, Tuesday, Wednesday and Thursday, he had spent in Hay's rooms, but from the installed telephone there was no sound or sign.

No sign came until mid-day on Friday, when he was just debating whether to go out to lunch, or have it brought to him from the service down below. The thin, echo-like call sounded again, and he was at once at the receiver.

"Isabeau! Is it you? Speak!"

"Yes, it is I." It was Isabeau's voice that answered, and yet her voice with a difference: it was firmer and clearer than on Monday night, although remote—so remote!

"Where are you? Tell me, that I may come to you. I am seeking you everywhere."

"I do not know where I am. It is all strange and new. But I rejoice in this: I have left behind what was soiled. I would tell you more, but something stops the words. I want you to do something for me: I have a fancy. You have done much, dear Ernest, but this is one thing more."

"What is it, dearest? You have only to ask."

"Go to the end of this street at two o'clock. That is in an hour from now; and wait there till I pass by. I shall not look as I used to do, but I will give you a flower—"

Here the voice failed; he could scarcely distinguish the last words. Strange, that one thing could be said and not another, never what he craved to know. But in an hour, he would see her—speak to her, and their separation would be at an end. Not as she used to look! Did she mean changed by what she had suffered? But not so changed, surely, that he would not know, that she would need to identify herself by the gift of a flower. And was the change she spoke of, of the body or the mind? A chill doubt as to the latter, which had assailed him before, crept over him again. But even if it were so, there would be means of healing. She was ill now, shaken by what she had suffered: with love and care, and returning health, all would be well.

He was punctual at the place of appointment. A draughty corner this street-end; but what did he, campaign-hardened, care for chill winds, or for the flying gusts of rain? The passers-by were few for a London street; but each one was carefully scrutinized and each umbrella looked under—that is, if a woman carried it. There was not one, however, that remotely resembled Isabeau. Taxis went by, now and then horse-drawn vehicles; presently a funeral came up the crossing street. A glass hearse with a coffin in it, probably a woman's coffin by its size. A cross of violets lay upon it within, but a couple of white wreaths had been placed outside, next to the driver's seat. A hired brougham was the only following.

They had done better to put the wreaths under shelter, but perhaps no one was in charge who greatly cared. As the cortege came level with the corner, a sharper gust than before, tore a white spray from the exposed wreath, and whirled it over towards him; it struck him on the chest, and fell on the wet pavement at his feet. He stooped to pick it up: he loved flowers too well to see it trodden in the mud: and as he did so, a great fear for the first time pierced him through. What might it not signify, this funeral flower? But no, death was not possible: scarcely an hour ago he had heard her living voice.

He waited long at the rendezvous, the flower held in his hand, but no one resembling her came by. Then, chilled and dispirited, but still holding the flower, he turned back to his lodging. It was time and over for his appointment at the inquiry office, but the rain had soaked him through, and he must change to a dry coat.

The servant met him as he came in.

"A letter for you, sir. I am sorry for the delay. You should have had it before, but it must have been brushed off the table and not seen. I found it just now on the floor."

Could it be from Isabeau?—but no, the address was not in her writing. Carrington tore it open: it was from the Belgian central office, and bore date two days back.

"We have at last received information respecting Mademoiselle Regnier. A young woman who appeared to have lost her memory, was charitably taken in by Mrs. Duckworth, in whose house she has remained through a recent serious illness, the hospitals being over full. She recovered memory last night, and now declares her name to be Isabeau Regnier, formerly of Martel. Mrs. Duckworth's address is 18, Silkmore Gardens, S. Kensington, and you will doubtless communicate with her."

Here at last was the information so long vainly sought, and it must have been from the Kensington house that Isabeau telephoned, though her voice sounded like a long-distance call. He would go thither at once; his application to the inquiry office was no longer needed: but still there was a chill at his heart as he looked at the white flower. Was some deep-down consciousness aware, in spite of his surface ignorance; and had it begun to whisper of the greater barrier which lay between?

As he approached the house in Silkmore Gardens, he might have noticed that a servant was going from room to room, drawing up blinds that had been lowered. At the door he asked for Mrs. Duckworth.

"I am not sure if my mistress can see you, sir," was the maid's answer." She has been very much upset."

"Will you take in my card, and say my business is urgent. I shall be grateful if she will spare me even five minutes. I am a friend of Mademoiselle Regnier's."

Carrington was shown into a sitting-room at the back of the house, with windows to the ground and a vision of greenery beyond. It was not long before Mrs. Duckworth came to him; she wore a black gown, and looked as if she had been weeping.

"You knew Isabeau Regnier," she began with a certain abruptness. "Are you the Ernest of whom she used to speak?"

"I am. She is my affianced wife, so you see I inquire for her by

98

right. I have been searching for her in the utmost distress, and until now in vain. I have but just heard that you out of your charity took her in, also that she has been ill. May I see her now, today?"

The lady's eyes filled again with tears, and she shrank back.

"Ah, you do not know what has happened. Oh, how sad, how dreadful to have to tell you! Isabeau is dead."

"What, just now, within this hour? She was speaking to me on the telephone only at midday."

"No—there is some mistake. That is impossible. She died last Tuesday, and was buried this afternoon. Her coffin left the house at a quarter before two, and my husband went with it to the cemetery. I would have gone too, only that I have been ill."

At first, he could only repeat her words: "Dead—Tuesday—Isabeau dead!" She was frightened by the look of his face—the look of a man who is in close touch with despair.

"Oh, I'm so sorry. Oh, do sit down, Mr. Carrington. This has been too much for you."

He sank into a chair, and she went hurriedly out, and returned with a glass in her hand.

"Drink this: nay, you must. I am sorry; oh, I am sorry. I wish my husband were here; he would tell you all about it better than I. It has been a grief to us all, to everyone in the house; we all grew fond of her. And we began quite to hope she would get well. When she came to us her memory was a blank, except for the wrong that had been done her. That seemed to have blotted out all that was behind, except her love for Ernest—you.

"But she said she could never look Ernest in the face again, and she wanted to be lost. She took an interest in things here after a while, and she was kind and helpful, like a daughter in the house—we have no children. And then her illness came on again; it was something the matter with the brain, caused by the shock she had sustained. She was very ill, but we could not get her into any hospital, all were too full. But she had every care with us, you may be sure of that, and I think she was happier to be here to the last. So, it went on, up and down, sometimes a little better, sometimes worse. Last Monday evening delirium set in. She fancied Ernest was here—you—and she was talking to you all the time. It was as if she heard you answering."

"Have you a telephone installed? Could she get up and go to the telephone?"

"We have a telephone—yes, certainly. But she had not strength

99

enough to leave her bed, and the installation is downstairs in the study."

"I declare to you on my most solemn word that she spoke to me over the telephone—twice on Monday night, and once today. It is beyond comprehension. Can you tell me what she said, speaking as she thought to Ernest?"

"She asked you to remind her of her forgotten name. We did not get Regnier till then, nor Martel where she lived; it was as if she heard the words spoken by you. I wrote at once to the organising people to say we had found out: I had no idea then that her death was so near. With the recollection of her name came back—horrors, and she was telling them to you. It seems she lived with an old uncle and aunt: would that be right for the girl you knew? They shot her uncle, the Germans did, when they burnt the house, and stabbed her poor old aunt and left her to die. I can show you a photograph of Isabeau, if that will help to identify. It is only an amateur snapshot, taken in our garden, at the time she was so much better, and, we hoped, recovering. It is very like her as she was then."

Mrs. Duckworth opened the drawer of a cabinet, and took out a small square photograph of a girl in a white dress sitting under a tree, and looking out of the picture with sad appealing eyes.

Carrington looked at it, and at first, he could not speak. Presently he said, answering a question of Mrs. Duckworth's:

"Yes, there can be no doubt."

He had heard enough. Mrs. Duckworth would fain have asked further about the marvel of the voice, but he got up to take leave.

"I will come again if you will permit," he said. "Another day I shall be able to thank you better for all you did for her—for all your kindness. You will then tell me where she is laid, and let me take on myself—all expense. Now I must be alone."

There was ready sympathy in, the little woman's face; tears were running down, though her words of response were few. Carrington still held the photograph.

"May I take this?" he said, and she gave an immediate assent. Then he pressed the hand she held out in farewell, and in another moment was gone.

★★★★★★★★★★★★★★★★★

The sequel to this episode is unknown. Carrington sat long that night with the picture before him, the pathetic little picture of his lost love; and cried aloud to her in his solitude: "Isabeau, speak to me, come to me. Death did not make it impossible before: why should it now? Do not think I would shrink from you or fear you. Nothing is in my heart but a great longing—a great love—a great pity. Speak again—speak!"

But no answer came. The telephone in the corner remained silent, and that curious far-off tremor of the wire sounded for him no more.

Parson Clench

Stoke-St. Edith is a small and deeply rural parish, a complete back-water; at least it was so fifteen years ago, and changes move so slowly within its boundaries that I should doubt it being greatly altered, even now. It has been said about the Stoke-St. Edith people that they just begin to realise they are born when it is time for them to die, and that it takes at least as long to convince them they are dead. And by the latter proposition hangs a tale.

As sometimes happens, though the case is rare, this retired and unimportant parish has a fatly endowed living, such as was reckoned in former times a suitable provision for younger sons. And some two-and-sixty years before the period of this story, the Albury younger son of that date not being of an age to take orders, the Reverend Augustus Clench was put in to keep the benefice warm for him.

But when the time came for Mr. Clench to surrender his cure, the younger son had developed other views, and the warmer was undisturbed. And so, the long procession of years went on, and the old gentleman—whom none of us could picture as ever having been young—became more and more autocratic, more deeply conservative, more blind to all advantage in change, even when change was plainly for the better. It seemed to us juniors that he must have been born in a black gown and bands, bald-headed and wearing spectacles—(no doubt the bald head was fact)—and that of all things at Stoke-St. Edith he was the least mutable. So, it came as a shock to us all, then scattered far and wide, when among the newspaper announcements we read that the Reverend Augustus Clench was no more.

I was not a resident in the parish when the following events took place, but I heard of them from a faithful correspondent, and later supplemented her account by personal inquiry on the spot.

The next presentation to the living was in the gift of the widowed Mrs. Albury at the Hall, who had long designed that fat provision for her nephew, the Reverend Basil Deane. He was working as curate in an East London parish, and when Mr. Clench's death took place, he had his doubts whether he would be justified in exchanging strenuous duty so early in his career, for the soft cushion of rural ease. But it was now or never for his chance in life; his Aunt Emmeline, good gentle soul, was a confirmed invalid, and at her death the Albury property, with the presentation right, would pass under her husband's will to a distant cousin, who would have no concern or care for any Deane.

Mr. Clench was only just buried when Mrs. Albury wrote:

I want you to come down for this next Sunday and take the services here, as the churchwardens are in a difficulty, and then we can arrange about your succession to the living. You know it is my earnest wish to have you settled at the Rectory. I cannot be thankful enough that I returned from France to be here at this time. I do not generally leave the Riviera so early in the spring, and it really was as if I had been led. But I caught a severe cold on the homeward journey, and am obliged to keep to my own two rooms, which I know you will excuse."

Mrs. Albury used to spend the greater part of the year abroad, and Basil's visits to her had hitherto been paid either at the Riviera villa or in London: he had not seen Stoke-St. Edith since his childhood. So, he came with only the faintest recollection of what the place was like, and none of the old man it was proposed he should succeed.

He was unable to get away from his London duties till the Saturday, and his first appearance at the village church was shortly before the eleven o'clock service: there was, he had been told, no celebration, as that took place only once a month, and had been held the Sunday before, after the funeral sermon. Basil reflected that he would change all that, but it was too early yet to announce intentions: at the present moment he was called upon to do no more than carry on the services in the well-worn rut of many previous years.

The clerk, an elderly man wedded to Stoke-St. Edith ways, awaited him in the vestry. ready with instructions, and looking somewhat askance at the coloured stole Basil took out of his vestment bag. "We aren't used to that sort of thing here," the official ventured to hint; but Basil proceeded to assume it, despite the disapproval. It was likely to be a lengthy service. The Litany was expected of him, and also the ante-Communion office, but Basil reflected he might shorten his sermon, and took the opportunity to glance at the notes he had prepared.

The choir were not surpliced, so he would have to go in alone; a final instruction from Aldridge dictated where he was to read the service.

"When you come to the chancel, sir, you'll see two reading-desks, one on the right-hand side and one on the left. 'Twas the one on the left hand the old rector always used, and that will be your place. We keep the other for a visiting parson when there is one, like as may be a missionary coming to preach for the Gospel in Foreign Parts collection. I think I mentioned there would be no collection today."

But when Basil marched into church, feebly accompanied by a voluntary on the wheezy old harmonium, he found the desk on the left of the chancel already occupied, so turned into the other. He felt some slight surprise, concluding he had mistaken Aldridge (who was frowning disapproval from one of the back pews at this insubordination on the part of his pupil). And, when the music ceased and he opened his book, he looked across at his *vis-à-vis*.

It was an elderly clergyman who was seated opposite, wearing a black skull-cap to cover his baldness, and spectacles over which a pair of very keen eyes critically regarded the younger man. He did not stand for the opening of the service, so Basil concluded he was infirm as well as aged; as old, or nearly so, as the nonagenarian priest who had officiated there for so many years. Probably he was a retired parson resident in the village, who came in to give assistance in some part of the service—a part he had not yet reached, but Aldridge ought to have told him.

He made a slight pause on arriving at the Lessons, both the first and the second, but the opposite parson did not budge; and again before the Litany, with the same absence of result. He did not rise for either of the Creeds, but was observed distinctly to frown when Basil turned to the East, which doubtless had not been Mr. Clench's practice. When it came to sermon time, however, he got up very alertly, and ascended the pulpit stairs just as Basil was approaching them. Then from that elevation he looked back at the younger priest with a distinctly malicious smile.

What was Basil to do? He could not challenge the usurper of his pulpit then and there, or drag him out in the face of the watching congregation and take his place. He went back to the reading-desk as if for a book; and then, the loudly shouted hymn having come to an end, he became aware that the man in the pulpit was not intending to preach, though he occupied the legitimate place of the preacher. There was an awkward—an extremely awkward—pause. Aldridge was fidgeting at the bottom of the church; the sparsely filled aisles displayed a *vista* of astonished faces. So, in desperation Basil came forward to the chancel step, and from there delivered his address.

He had been in priests' orders close upon four years, and during that time had faced many congregations; the nervousness of the raw hand was no longer his, or so he flattered himself. Why should it be harder to speak to these country bumpkins than to the keener people of the towns? But on this occasion his nerve failed him, he stumbled over his words, lost the place in his notes, and recovered the thread of the argument with agonising difficulty, while a cold perspiration broke out over him, and he turned from red to white, and then to red again. Yet, had he been cool enough to analyse his feelings, he would have discovered the disturbing element emanated from one only among his hearers, the strange old man who had mounted into the pulpit, and who now bent forward over the tasselled cushion, staring him in the face, and smiling with a sort of evil amusement and triumph.

He had intended to shorten his address, and short it was indeed, as he stumbled through it to a premature and pointless close. The blessing followed, the wheezy harmonium struck up with renewed spirit, and as he turned towards the vestry, the old man descended the pulpit stairs as if to follow him thither. But on reaching the door which Aldridge was holding open, there was no one to be seen.

Aldridge shook his head more in sorrow than in anger, as he prepared to help Basil off with his vestments.

"People here always make such a talk over any little difference. I'm afraid, sir, they won't half like you preaching to them from the floor, when they have been used to take their sermons out of the pulpit. Begging your pardon, sir, have you always been accustomed to preach so?"

"I have often done so," Basil answered. "But today, as you would see, I had no choice. Who was the old clergyman who sat on the left side of the chancel, and then went up into the pulpit, though he did not preach? It was impossible for me to ask him to give place."

"Old clergyman, sir? I didn't see no old clergyman. Where was he, did you say?"

"In the reading-desk when I went in, and he went up before me into the pulpit. Where do you sit in the church, that you did not see—?"

"I could have seen right enough anything that was there," blurted out Aldridge, forgetful of his manners. "The pulpit was open to you the whole time, and the reading-desk as well, sure as I am here a living man. Begging your pardon, sir, for being positive." And then the clerk paled from his usually healthy colour, as a strange thought occurred to him. "Might I ask, sir, what the gentleman you saw was like?"

"An old clergyman in a surplice and a black stole. An Oxford hood he had too, for I saw the crimson silk as he went up the pulpit stairs. He had on a black skull-cap and spectacles, with sharp eyes looking over them. Bushy white eyebrows, and thin bony hands, with the veins standing out on them."

"The Lord have mercy upon us!" Aldridge was staring with his jaw dropped. "It was Parson Clench himself, and you not knowing! And him buried a fortnight come Wednesday! Lord save us: what is to be done?"

"Come, come, my good man, this is rank nonsense." But Basil was dismayed as well as angry, and a horrid creeping shiver about his scalp might verily have raised his hair had it not been so short-cut." Mr. Clench is dead and buried. It could not have been Mr. Clench in church."

"It would be him if it was anyone at all," the clerk said doggedly. "He was buried in his vestments just as you saw him. I went to the Rectory for a last look before the coffin was closed, so I know. And I daresay you've heard tell how bent he was on preaching to the last, even after he began to fail. He hated letting anyone else up into his pulpit, and he wasn't one to change. I'd lay odds a feeling he had in life wouldn't be so much different now. Heaven itself would have a tough job to alter Parson Clench, where he had set his mind; begging your pardon, sir, for speaking free. But to think of him in the church, and seen by you!"

This was a last mutter, as Basil assumed his coat. He said no more to Aldridge in the way of assertion or contradiction, but he went out of the vestry utterly dazed. The church as he glanced round it was empty, except for a girl sorting music at the harmonium—no doubt the "organist" who had officiated at that wheezy instrument: she looked completely undisturbed. Had no one else shared his vision? Basil was of course aware that there were records of such happenings, and that popular interest in them (or curiosity?) had of late years greatly increased; but hitherto he had been indifferent if not sceptical, and utterly unexpectant of any such experience happening to himself.

He would fain, even now, have withheld belief, but it was difficult to remain incredulous when he had seen, and had been able minutely to describe, a man who was a stranger to him, with whose appearance in life he was unacquainted, and of whom he had no thought other than indifference in coming to Stoke-St. Edith to fill his place.

He returned to the Hall and the waiting luncheon much perturbed in mind. It was not easy to face Aunt Emmeline and her affectionate interest: what did he think of the church, and was it easy to fill (a matter of voice)— also had he a full congregation, and did they appear attentive and interested? He hated himself for giving such half-hearted replies to her enquiries, and was sensitively aware of her disappointment in them; and yet how could he help it and what could he say, wishing as he did that, he had never seen the Stoke-St. Edith church, and might never set foot in it again. And a renewal of his ordeal was before him as close at hand as three o'clock, the custom there dictating that the evening service should be read in the afternoon.

Mrs. Albury's catechism did not last long on this occasion, as the butler came to say luncheon awaited him in the dining-room; his aunt had her tiny invalid meal served to her upstairs. "I shall see you again this evening, my dear, and then we will have a, *real talk*," she said as she dismissed him. Alas! a real talk must mean his acceptance of the Stoke-St. Edith living, or a confession of the barrier of the ghost.

As he walked across to the church, which was situated at no great distance from the Hall, he reflected that perception of this species of appearance, may happen to a man on some isolated occasion, once in a lifetime, never to be repeated again. He might take the duty at Stoke-St. Edith year in and year out, and never again encounter the wraith of the late incumbent, though the fact that he once had done so would be an unforgotten and unforgettable experience. But, despite all reasoning, the ordeal before him made heavy demands upon his courage, and it was a very dour-looking young man who walked into the vestry, and was assisted by Aldridge to robe.

"I can't make out that anybody else saw what you saw, sir, in the church this morning," that functionary whispered. "But I've been told since, there's a talk about in the village that the late rector *walks*. There are some who met him in the lane when he was on his death-bed, stricken so that he could not move; and one at least who saw him going by, out of her cottage window, the day after he was buried. People will tell such-like stories as you know, fancies running away with them; and there are few that heed."

The wheezy harmonium struck up a voluntary, and Basil went on into the church. Approaching the chancel, he saw that both reading-desks were vacant, and he fully purposed to take possession of the left hand one, which was his own. But he found himself powerless to carry intention into action. It was as if he was firmly seized by the shoulders, and pushed into the right-hand seat by a force he could not resist, or was unable to do so without a struggle, which would have been unseemly in the face of the congregation. What Aldridge was thinking in his place at the west end, Basil could only conjecture, but probably his guess only erred by falling short of the fact.

For the first part of the service the left-hand reading-desk remained empty, but on returning to his seat after the second Lesson, he found that it was filled by the same appearance as before, the old man in his vestments and skull-cap, peering at him over spectacles with unfriendly and defiant eyes. It was almost a relief when the presence externalised and became visible, instead of being merely felt in every fibre of his bodily frame.

What was to happen when sermon time arrived? The figure opposite made no movement when Basil was about to leave the desk, and yet in a moment, instantaneous as a flash of light, there it stood at the bottom of the pulpit stairs, barring his way, and facing him with a malignant smile.

Basil did not contest the passage. He delivered this second address from the chancel step, and when he turned at the conclusion, the figure had disappeared.

"Did you see him again, sir?" demanded Aldridge, who was waiting in the vestry, and Basil briefly assented: he was in no humour to discuss the marvel a second time, and Aldridge had no fresh explanation to advance.

There was nothing for it now but to be candid with Aunt Emmeline, and how she would take the communication he dreaded to think: women were always a mass of nerves, especially invalid women. But his aunt was more reasonable than he had ventured to expect, and was ready to respond to his wish that they should keep the matter to themselves.

"I do not want to be labelled as a man with a supernatural extra sense, or to give Stoke-St. Edith a bad name. I am afraid the matter may to some extent have gone abroad through Aldridge, but I'll try to see him tomorrow, and give him an injunction not to talk."

"Yes, my dear," the aunt acquiesced. "It was wonderful, of course, that you should see, and be able to describe a perfect stranger. But it may never happen again, to you or to anybody else. And Basil, I hope,

I do trust, that this will not set you against accepting the Living. We know it is likely—I suppose it is likely—that the spirits of the dead are about us always: you know it speaks in the Bible of the great cloud of witnesses. So surely, we need not take it as extraordinary if we see one of them now and then. And Mr. Clench was a good man. He would do nobody any harm."

His aunt might have thought differently, Basil reflected, had she seen the malignant eyes of the apparition which barred his way.

"If it went on happening, I could not stay here. Better for someone to come who would not see."

"I don't want you to decide in a hurry; take a week or two to think it over. I will not have you give me a definite answer tonight. Things may look different on reflection. It is such a chance for you, my dear; and it would be so happy for me to know you were here looking after the people, when I am obliged to be so much away. And there is such an excellent rectory-house, quite a country gentleman's place, the best rectory in the county, so they say, and in very good repair. You need not open the whole of it, if you thought it too large for you alone. It could be made so nice. I was not going to tell you just at once, but I have five hundred pounds put aside to help you with the furnishing!"

What was he to say to all this kindness—how was he to repulse the soft entreating hands held out to him full of gifts? It would make no difference, of that he could be certain; but yes, if she wished he would take a longer time to think the matter over, and he would see the Rectory on the following morning, as he need not take train for London till the afternoon. And then he endeavoured to tell her how deeply he felt her kindness, and what a disappointment it would be to him too, so to put the great chance of his life away.

That ended the Sunday evening, and after Monday's breakfast he went across to the Rectory, in fulfilment of the promise given over night.

The red-brick Georgian mansion, with its stone pediments and cornice, and formal garden-court, was surely an attractive dwelling, cheerful to look at in the Spring sunshine, a home of which any young divine might well be proud. Probably Parson Clench had some such thoughts of it, when he came into possession at Stoke-St. Edith two-and-sixty years before. But he would not have had the same shrinking from the habitation in which his predecessor lived and died, that now disquieted Basil Deane.

Mr. Clench's housekeeper opened to him. She was staying on as caretaker, so she told him, until Mr. Clench's relatives decided what would be done about the sale. Nothing had been disturbed as yet, she was waiting instructions; and it was what the poor old gentleman had wished, that everything should be kept on just the same. He had spoken of it when he was wandering at the last, thinking he had a journey to go, but that he was coming back.

"Yes, sir, they are handsome rooms, both upstairs and down. A fine old house, just right for a family, but rather large and lonesome for one alone. The dining-room is on this side as you see, with a small breakfast-parlour behind, though it never was used for breakfasting, not in my time. Maybe you are the gentleman who is to succeed Mr. Clench, and who preached yesterday up at the church?"

Basil told her that he took the services only as a visitor, and that nothing was decided yet about the living: the last not quite the truth, for in his own mind the decision against taking it was already made.

"Most gentlemen admire the staircase, which is oak as you see, and real old. And here is the drawing-room, but not in order, as we put up the bed you see for Mr. Clench when he got feeble at the last, and it was here that he died. It was convenient, being next to the study. A fine room the study is, and looks handsome lined with bookcases. It was a lot of books Mr. Clench had, and he was that particular over them. We have put a fire in here to keep away the damp, as I know he would have wished."

She was opening the door as she spoke, and holding it for Basil to enter. Yes, there was a fire on the hearth, and in a chair drawn near it was seated an old man, a man in a black cassock and skull-cap, with sharp eyes peering over spectacles: the old man of the church, though the white surplice was no longer worn. And there was the same hostility in the silent gaze which met and held his own.

Basil drew back.

"Who is the old gentleman who is using the room?" he asked in a low voice of the housekeeper.

"No one is using the room, sir. There is nobody in the house but myself."

"Why there he is, just before you, sitting by the fire."

The woman looked round in a scared way, and then shut the door again.

"Are you meaning to put a fright upon me, sir?" she said as they stood together in the hall; she seemed both indignant and alarmed.

Basil disclaimed any such intention.

"I am perfectly serious. I would be the last to wish to frighten you. I saw him so plainly sitting there, that I thought you must see him too. An old man in a skull-cap."

The housekeeper wrung her hands.

"If I was to see him, I could not stay here, no, not for double the wage. People in the village make a talk about the old parson *walking*, but I never heed such tales. I saw him die, and I saw him buried. It is altogether past belief."

Basil declined to visit the upper floors: what was the use? It should never be his house; upon that he had now unalterably determined. It remained only to break the decision to Aunt Emmeline, and then to return to the mill-horse grind of the East London toil.

★★★★★★★★★★★★★★★★★★

Some ten days later he received the following letter :—

My dear Nephew,—I have had you much in mind since we parted, and yesterday our solicitor, Mr. Kempson, came down to see me. I wanted to consult him what I could best do in your interests about the vacancy at Stoke-St. Edith. He thinks it will be quite possible to arrange an exchange of this benefice now vacant for the right to present to another one likely to fall vacant before long, of the same, or nearly equal value.

Of course, I did not tell him why you had refused Stoke-St. Edith; I left him to suppose you were too much engrossed in your present work to wish to give it up just at once. But, oh my dear Basil, it is indeed a cruel disappointment to me not to have you here.

Your affectionate Aunt,

Emmeline Albury.

P.S.—The £500 for rectory furniture will now be invested in your name, ready for you when the time comes, whether I live or die.

The Crimson Blind

1

Ronald McEwan, aged sixteen, was invited to spend a vacation fortnight at his uncle's rectory. Possibly some qualms of conscience had tardily spurred the Rev. Sylvanus Applegarth to offer this hospitality, aware that he had in the past neglected his dead sister's son. Also, with a view to the future, it might be well for Ronald to make acquaintance with his own two lads, now holidaying from English public schools.

Mr. Applegarth was a gentleman and a scholar, one who loved above all things, leisure and a quiet house: he retained a curate at his own expense to run matters parochial in Swanmere, and buried himself among his books. The holidays were seasons of trial to him on each of the three yearly occasions, and it would not be much worse, so he reflected, to have three hobbledehoy lads ramping about the place, and clumping up and down stairs with heavy boots, when it was inevitable he must have two.

The young Applegarths were not ill-natured, lads, but they were somewhat disposed to make a butt of the shy Scottish cousin, who was midway between them in age, and had had a different upbringing and schooling from themselves. Ronald found it advisable to listen much and say little, not airing his own opinions unless they were directly challenged. But in one direction he had been outspoken, afterwards wishing devoutly he had held his tongue. Spooks were under discussion, and it was discovered—a source of fiendish glee to the allied brothers—that Ronald believed in ghosts, as he preferred more respectfully to term them, and also in such marvels as death-warnings, wraiths, and second-sight.

"That comes of being a Highlander," said Jack the elder. "Superstition is a taint that gets into the blood, and so is born with you. But I'll wager anything you have no valid reason for believing. The best evidence is only second-hand; most of it third or fourth hand, if as near. You have never seen a ghost yourself?"

"No," acknowledged Ronald somewhat sourly, for he had been more than sufficiently badgered. "But I've spoken with those that have."

"Would you like to see one? Now give a straight answer for once,"—and Jack winked at his brother.

"I wouldn't mind." Then, more stoutly, "Yes, I would like—if I'd the chance."

"I think we can give you a chance of seeing something, if not exactly a ghost. We've got no Highland castles to trot out, but there's a house here in Swanmere that is said to be haunted. Just the thing for you to investigate, now you are on the spot. Will you take it on?"

It would have been fatal to say no, and give these cousins the opening to post him as a coward. Ronald gave again the grudging admission that he "wouldn't mind." And then, being Sunday morning, the lads said they would take him round that way after church, and he should have a look at the window which had earned a bad repute. Then they might find out who had the keys in charge, if he felt inclined to pass a night within.

"I suppose, as neither of you believe, you would not be afraid to sleep there?" said Ronald, addressing the two.

"Certainly, we would not be *afraid*." Jack was speech-valiant at least. "As we believe there is nothing in it but a sham, like all the other tales."

Alfred, the younger boy, did not contradict his brother, but it might have been noticed that he kept silence.

"Then I'll do what you do." This was Ronald's ultimatum. "If you two choose to sleep in the haunted house, I'll sleep there too."

But, as the event fell out, the Applegarths did not push matters to the point of borrowing keys from the house-agent and camping out rolled in blankets on the bare floors—an attractive picture Jack went on to draw of the venture to which Ronald stood committed. After the morning service, the three lads walked some half mile beyond the village in the direction of the sea shore. Here the houses were few and far between, but two or three villas were in course of building, and other plots beyond them were placarded as for sale.

Swanmere was "rising"—in other words, in process of being spoiled. Niched in between two of these plots was an empty house to let, well placed in being set some way back from the high road, within the privacy of thick shrubberies, and screened at the back by a belt of forest trees.

A desirable residence, one would have said at a first glance, but closer acquaintance was apt to induce a change of mind. The iron gates of the drive were fastened with padlock and chain, but the young Applegarths effected an entrance by faulting over the palings at the side. Everywhere was to be seen the encroachment and overgrowth of long neglect: weeds knee high, and branches pushing themselves across the side-paths, though the carriage approach had been kept clear. The main entrance was at the side, and in front bowed windows, on two floors, were closely shuttered within, and grimed with dirt without.

The boys pushed their way round to the back, where the kitchen offices were enclosed by a yard. But midway between the better and the inferior part of the house, a large flat window on the first floor overlooked the flower-garden and shrubbery. This window was not shuttered, but was completely screened by a wide blind of faded red, drawn down to meet the sill. Jack pointed to it.

"That is where the ghost shows—not every night, but sometimes. Maybe you'll have to watch for a whole week before there is anything to see. But, if rumour says true, you will be repaid in the end. Whatever the appearance may be."

Ronald thought he saw a wink pass between the brothers. He was to be hoaxed in some way; of that he felt assured.

"I'll go, if we three go together, you and Alfred and I. If there is a real ghost to be seen, you shall see it too. What is it said to be like?"

"A light comes behind the red blind, and some people see a figure, or the shadow of a figure, in the room. Perhaps it is according to the open eye, some less and some more. You may see more still, being Highland born and bred. Very well, as you make it a condition, we will go together."

"Tonight?"

"Better not tonight. There's evening church and supper, and the governor might not like it, being Sunday. We will go tomorrow. That will serve as well for you."

The fake, whatever it might be, could not be prepared in time for that first evening, Ronald reflected. He was quite unbelieving about the red blind and the light, but firm in his resolve. If he was to be trotted out to see a ghost, the Applegarth cousins should go too. It was a matter of indifference to him which night was chosen for the expedition, so Monday was agreed upon, the trio to set out at midnight, when all respectable inhabitants of Swanmere should be in their beds.

When Monday night came, the sky was clear and starlit, but it was the dark of the moon. One of the lads possessed an electric torch, which Jack put in his pocket. And when it came to the point, it appeared that only Jack was going with him. Alfred, according to his brother, had developed a sore-throat, and Mrs. Dawson the housekeeper, was putting him on a poultice which had to be applied in bed.

So, it was the younger Applegarth who had been chosen to play the ghost, Ronald instantly concluded: he had no faith at all in the poultice, or in Mrs. Dawson's application of it, though he remembered Alfred had complained of the soreness of his throat more than once during the day.

There was little interchange of words between the two lads as they went. Ronald was inwardly resentful, and Jack seemed to have some private thoughts which amused him, for he smiled to himself in the darkness. Arrived at the Portsmouth road, they got over the fence at the same place as before; and now Jack's torch was of use, as they pushed their way through the tangled garden to the spot determined on as likely to afford the best view of the window with the crimson blind. Neither blind nor window could now be distinguished; the house reared itself before them a silhouette of blacker darkness, against that other darkness of the night.

"We can sit on this bench while we wait," and young Applegarth flashed his torch on a rustic structure, set beneath overshadowing trees. "I propose to time ourselves and give an hour to the watch. Then, if you have seen nothing, we can come away and return another night. For myself, sceptic as I am, I don't expect to see."

He could hardly be more sceptical than Ronald felt at the moment. Certain that a trick was about to be played on him, all his senses had been on the alert from the moment they left the road, and he felt sure that as they plunged through the wilderness of shrubbery, he had heard another footstep following. He did not refuse to seat himself on the bench, but he took care to have the bole of the tree immediately at his back, as some protection from assault in the rear.

Some five or six minutes went by, and he was paying little attention to the house, but much to certain rustling noises in the shrubbery behind them, when Jack Applegarth exclaimed in an altered voice: "By Jove, there is a light there after all!" and he became aware that the broad parallelogram of the window was now faintly illuminated behind the crimson blind, sufficiently to show its shape and size, and also the colour of the screen. Could young Alfred have found some means of entrance, and set up a lighted candle in the room?—but somehow he doubted whether, without his brother to back him, the boy would have ventured into the ghostly house alone. The fake he anticipated was of a different sort to this.

As the boys watched, the light grew stronger, glowing through the blind; the lamp within that room must have been a strong one of many candle-power. Then a shadow became visible, as if cast by some person moving to and fro in front of the light; this was faint at first, but gradually it increased in intensity, and presently came close to the window, pulling the blind aside to look out.

This was so ordinary an action that it did not suggest the super-natural. A moment later, however, the whole framework of the win-dow seemed to give way and fall outwards with a crash of breaking glass. The figure now showed clearly defined, standing outside on the sill with the red illumination behind; but its pause there was one only of seconds before it leaped to the ground and came rushing towards them; a figure so far in ghostly likeness that it appeared to be clad in white. Following the crash of glass came other sounds, a pistol-shot and a scream, but the rush of the flying figure was unaccompanied by noise. It passed close to the bench where they were seated, and young Applegarth grasped Ronald's arm in a terror well-acted if unreal.

"Come away," he said thickly. "I've had enough of this. Come away."

The light behind the blind was dying out, and presently the win-dow was again in darkness, but these spectators did not stay to see. Jack Applegarth dragged Ronald back towards the road, and the younger lad broke from the bushes and followed them, sobbing in what seemed to be real affright, and with a white bundle hugged in his arms. They climbed the palings and went pelting home, and not till the distance was half accomplished did any one of them speak. Then Ronald had the first word.

"Why Alfred, I thought you were in bed. I hope your throat will not suffer through coming out to trick me with a sham ghost. I made sure all along that was what you and Jack would do."

Alfred hugged tighter the bundle he was carrying: did he fear it would be snatched off him and displayed?—it looked exceedingly like a white sheet.

"I had nothing to do with that thing," he blurted out between chattering teeth. "I don't know what it was, or where it came from.

But I swear I'll never go near the blamed place again, either by night or by day!"

2

Whether there was any natural explanation of what they had seen, Ronald never knew. His visit to his Applegarth relatives was drawing to a close, and, shortly after, the old Rector died suddenly during the service in church. The home was broken up, the two schoolboy cousins had their way to make in the world, and, whether ill or well made, this history knows them no more. And between the just concluded chapter, and this which is now begun, must be set an interval of twenty years.

Ronald had done well for himself in the meantime. He had become an alert hardheaded business man, a good deal detached from the softer side of life, for which, he told himself, there would be time and to spare by-and-bye. But now, at thirty-six, there began to be a different telling. He could afford to keep a wife in comfort, and it seemed to him that the time for choice had come.

This does not pretend to be a love-story, so it will only briefly chronicle that it was the business of wife-selection which took Ronald again to Swanmere. He happened to act as best man at his friend Parkinson's wedding, and one of the bridesmaids seemed to him an unusually attractive girl, happy herself, and likely to make others happy, which is better than mere beauty. Probably he let fall a wish that he might see Lilian again; anyway, sometime later, he was invited to run down and pay a weekend visit to the newly-married pair, when Lilian was at the same time expected to stay. And, as it happened, the Peregrine Parkinsons had settled at Swanmere.

"Do you know this place at all?" queried Mrs. Parkinson, who was meeting him at the station with the small pony-carriage, of which, and of her skill as a whip, she was inordinately proud.

"I was here once before, many years ago," was Ronald's answer. "I was only a schoolboy in those days, visiting an old uncle, who then was rector of the parish. Swanmere seems to have grown a good deal bigger than I remember it, or else my recollection is at fault."

"Oh yes, it has grown; places do grow, don't they? There was a great deal of new building before the war; villas you know, and that style; but 1914 stopped everything. Peregrine and I were fortunate in meeting with an older house, in a quite delightful well-grown garden. Oh no, not old enough to be inconvenient, and it has been brought up-to-date for us. We were lucky to get it, I can assure you: it is so difficult in these days to find anything moderate-sized. They are snapped up directly they are vacant, the demand is so much in excess of the supply."

Ronald did not recognise the direction taken, even when the pony willingly turned in at an open pair of iron gates, which he had last seen chained and padlocked—or if not these gates, their predecessors, as gates have a way of perishing in untended years. All was trim within, pruned and swept and gravelled, and the garden a riot of colour with its summer flowers. But the front of the house, with double bows carried up to the first floor, did strike a chord of association. "I wonder!" he said to himself, and then the wonder was negatived. "No, it isn't possible; it would be too odd a coincidence." And upon this he dismissed the thought from mind.

It did not return during the evening, not even when he went up—in a hurry, and at the last moment—to dress for dinner in the bedroom allotted to him; a spacious and well-appointed one, where his portmanteau had been unpacked and habiliments laid out. After dinner there was the diversion of some food music; Mrs. Parkinson played and Lilian sang. The Swanmere experience of twenty years ago was quite out of mind when he retired for the night; pleasanter thoughts had pushed it into the background and held the stage. But the recollection was vaguely renewed last thing, when he drew aside the curtains and opened the window, noting its unusual square shape, divided into three uprights, two of which opened casement fashion.

It was the only window in the room, but so wide that it nearly filled the outer wall. Certainly, its shape recalled the window of twenty years ago which was screened by a crimson blind, and his watch in the garden with Jack Applegarth. He was never likely to forget that night, though he was far from sure whether the ghost was ghost indeed, or a sham faked by the Applegarth boys for his discomfiture. Probably these suburban villas were built all upon one plan, and an older foundation had set the note of fashion for those that followed. He never knew the name or number of the haunted house, or locality, except that it was entered from the Portsmouth road, so in that way he could not identify it. And again, he dismissed the idea, and addressed himself to sleep.

Neither this recollection nor the dawning love-interest was potent to keep him awake. He slept well the early part of the night, and did not wake till morning was brightening in the east. Then, as he opened

119

his eyes and turned to face the light, he saw, and was astonished seeing, that the window was covered with a crimson blind, drawn down from top to sill.

He could have declared that nothing of the sort was in place there overnight. The drawn-back curtains had revealed a quite ordinary green Venetian, which he had raised till it clicked into stoppage at its height. To all outward seeming this was a material blind, swaying in the air of the open casement, and with no light behind it but that of the summer dawn.

And yet, for all that, he lay staring at it with nerves on edge, and hammering pulses which beat thickly in his ears and throat: something within him recognised the nature of the appearance and responded with agitation, despite the scepticism of the outward man. That was a bird's song vocal outside, wheels went by in the road, the ordinary world was astir. He would rise and assure himself that the blind was a mundane affair, palpable to touch, it had of course slipped down in the night owing to a loosened cord, and was hung within the other.

And then he discovered that his limbs were powerless: it was as if invisible hands restrained him. He writhed against them in vain, and in the end, despite those rapid pulses of the affrighted heart, he fell suddenly into trance or sleep.

He had had a seizure of nightmare, he concluded when he awoke later, with the servant knocking at the door to bring in tea and shaving-water, and the open window cheerful and unscreened, letting in the summer air.

His first act was to examine the window-frame, but—of course, as he told himself—there was no crimson blind, nothing but the green Venetian, and the curtains drawing on their rod. He had dreamt the whole thing, on the suggestion of that memory of a schoolboy visit long ago.

He was well assured of the folly of it all, and yet he had again and again to reason the thing out, and repeat that it was folly—himself in colloquy with himself. This was still more necessary when in the course of the morning he strolled out into the garden and round the shrubbery paths. Though the wild growth of long ago had been pruned back and certain changes made, he had no difficulty in finding the spot—what he thought the spot—where he and Jack Applegarth had watched. There was still a rustic seat under the trees, full in view of the square window of his room where the red blind no longer was displayed. He sat down to light a cigarette, and presently his host appeared, pipe in mouth, and joined him on the bench in the shade.

"You have a nice place here," Ronald said, by way of opening conversation.

"Yes," Parkinson agreed. "I like it, and Cecilia likes it, and in every way, it suits us well. Convenient for business you know, and not too pretentious for young beginners. We both fell in love with it at first sight. But I heard something the other day" (poking with his knife at a pipe which declined to draw) "something that rather disturbed me. Not that I believe it, you know; I'm not that sort. I only hope and trust that no busybody will consider it his, or her, duty to inform Cecilia."

"What did you hear?"

"Why, some fools were saying the house used to be haunted, and that was the reason why it stood long unlet, and fell into bad repair. Stories of that sort are always put about when a place happens to be nobody's fancy, whether the real drawback is rats or drains, or somebody wanting to keep it vacant for interests of their own. As you know. In this case I should say it was the latter. Because the man told me lights were seen when the place was shut up and empty. A thieves' dumping ground, no doubt. Or possibly coiners."

This in pauses, between whiffs of the pipe. Parkinson ended:

"I don't want Cecilia to know. She is fond of the place, and I wouldn't like her to be nervous or upset."

"Couldn't you warn the man?"

"I did that. But there are other men who know. And, what is worse, women. You know what women's tongues are. Especially when they think they have got hold of something spicey. Or what will annoy somebody else!"

"Why not tell your wife yourself, and trust to her good sense not to mind. Better for her to learn it so, than by chance whispers from a stranger. She won't like it if she thinks you were aware, and kept it up your sleeve."

But Parkinson shook his head. Fond as he was of his Cecilia, perhaps his opinion of her good sense had not been heightened by the experience of four or five months of marriage. And Ronald checked his own impulse to communicate the history of that former episode, together with the odd dream—ii it was a dream—which visited him the night before. But he had found out one thing: now it was beyond doubt. This smartly done-up villa with its modern improvements, was identical with the closed and neglected house of long ago.

That day was Saturday. He had been invited to stay over the weekend, so there were two more nights that he was bound to spend at the villa. He did not enjoy the anticipation of those nights, though some slight uneasiness would cheaply purchase the intermediate day to be spent with Lilian. And what harm could any ghost do him, and what did it matter whether the window was covered with a crimson blind, or a white or a green!

It mattered little when regarded in the day, but during the watches of the night such affairs take on a different complexion, though Ronald McEwan was no coward. He woke earlier on this second night: woke to be aware of a faint illumination in the room, and of—he thought after, though it was hardly realised at the time—the instantaneous glimpse of a figure crossing from wall to wall. One thing he did distinctly see: over the window there hung again—the crimson blind! Then in the space of half a dozen heart-beats, the faint light faded out, and the room was left in darkness.

This time the paralysis of the night before did not recur. He had been careful to place within reach at the bedside the means of striking a light, and presently his candle showed the window unscreened and open, and the door locked as he left it overnight. He did not extinguish that candle, but let it burn down in the socket; and he was not again disturbed.

During Sunday he debated with himself the question to speak or not to speak. That spare room might next be occupied by someone to whom the terror of such a visitation would be harmful; and yet, he supposed, all turned on whether or not the occupier was gifted (or shall we say cursed?) with the open eye. He felt thankful he had been quartered there and not Lilian. Finally, he resolved that Parkinson must be warned, but not till he himself was on the point of leaving—not till he had passed a third night in the haunted room, disturbed or not disturbed. And, after all, what had he to allege against it in this later time? Could a room be haunted by the apparition of a crimson blind?

Saturday had been brilliantly fine throughout, but Sunday dawned upon unsettled weather, and a wet gale rushing over from the not distant sea. He went to rest that night resolved to keep a light burning through the dark hours, but found it necessary to shut the window on account of the driven storm. He strove to reason himself into indifference and so prepare for sleep, which visited him sooner than he expected, and for a while was profound. It was somewhere between two and three o'clock when he started up, broad awake on the instant, with the consciousness of something wrong.

It was not the moderate light of his candle which now illuminated the room, but the fierce glow of mounting flames, though he could not see whence they proceeded. The red blind hung again over the window, but that was a negligible matter: some carelessness of his had set the Parkinsons' house on fire, and he must give the alarm. He struggled up in bed, only to find he was not alone. There at the bed-foot stood gazing at him a man, a stranger, plainly seen in the glare of light.

A man haggard of countenance, with the look of a soul that despaired; clad in white or light-coloured garments; possibly a sleeping-suit.

Ronald believed he made an attempt to speak to this creature, to ask who he was and what doing there, but whether he really achieved articulate words he does not know. For the space of perhaps a minute the two stared at each other, the man in the flesh and he who was flesh no more; then the latter sprang to the window, standing on the low sill, and tore aside the crimson blind. There was a great crash of glass like that other crash he remembered, a cry from below in the garden, and a report like a pistol-shot; the figure had disappeared, leaping through the broken gap. Then all was still and the room in darkness; those fierce flames were suddenly extinguished, and his own candle had gone out.

He groped for the matches and struck a light. The red blind had disappeared from the window, there was no broken glass and no fire, and everything remained as he had left it overnight.

No one else appeared to have heard that shot and cry in the dead middle of the night. After breakfast he took Parkinson into confidence, who heard the story gloomily enough, plainly discomforted though unwilling to believe.

"You have been right to tell me, my dear fellow, and I am sure you think you experienced all these impossible things. But look at probability. Those Applegarth boys hoaxed you years ago, the impression dwelt on your mind, and was revived by discovering this house to be the same. Such was the simple cause of your visions; any doctor would tell you so. As for my own action, I don't see clear. It is a horribly awkward affair, and we have been to no end of expense settling in. Cecilia likes the place, and it suits her. So long as she does not know!"

"Look here, Parkinson. There is one thing I think I may ask—suggest, at least. You have another spare bedroom. Don't put any other guest where I have been sleeping. Couldn't you make it a storeroom—

box-room—anything that is not used at night?"

Parkinson still was doubtful: he shook his head.

"Not without an explanation to Cecilia. She happens to be particularly *gone* on that room on account of the big window. It was just a toss-up that she didn't put Lilian there, and you in the other. And—if in time to come a nursery should be needed, that is the room on which she has her eye. She would never consent to give it up for a glory-hole or a store-room without a strong reason. A very strong reason indeed."

Ronald could do no more: his friend was warned, the responsibility was no longer his. It was some comfort to know that Lilian was leaving two days later, going on to another visit, and the fatal house did not seem to have affected her up to now.

After this, a couple of months went by, during which the Parkinsons made no sign, and he for his part kept his lips entirely sealed about his experiences at Swanmere. It might be, as Jack Applegarth said long before, his Highland blood which rendered him vulnerable to uncanny influences, and the Parkinsons and their Southron friends might remain entirely immune. But at the end of two months he received the following letter:

Dear Old Chum,—It is all up with us here, and I think you will wish to know how it came about. I am trying to sub-let Ashcroft, and hope to find somebody fool enough to take it. I haven't a fault to find with the place, neither of us have seen or heard a thing, and really it seems absurd. The servants picked up some gossip about the haunting, and then one of them was scared—by her own shadow, I expect, and promptly had hysterics. After that, all three of them went to Cecilia in a body, and said they were willing to forfeit their wages, and sorry to cause us inconvenience, but nothing would induce them to stop on in a haunted house—not if we paid them hundreds—and they must leave at once.

Then I had to have it out with Cecilia, and she was not pleased to have been kept in the dark. She says I hoodwinked her—but if I did, it was for her own good; and when we took the place, I had not the least idea. Of course, she could not stay when the servants cleared out—and nor could I; so, she has gone to her mother's, and I am at the hotel—with everyone asking questions, which I can assure you is not pleasant. I shall take jolly

124

good care not to be trapped a second time into a place where ghosts are on the loose.

There is one thing that may interest you, as it seems to throw light on your experience. The house was built by a doctor who took in lunatic patients—harmless ones they were supposed to be, and he was properly certificated and all that: there was no humbug about it that I know. One man who was thought quite a mild case suddenly became violent. He locked himself into his room and set it on fire, and then smashed a window—I believe it was *that* window—and jumped out. It was only from the first floor, but he was so badly injured that he died: a good riddance of bad rubbish, I should say.

I don't know anything about a red blind or a pistol-shot: those matters seem to have been embroidered on. But the coincidence is an odd one, I allow.

We were pleased to hear of your engagement to Lilian, and I send you both congratulations and good wishes, in which Cecilia would join if here. I suppose you will soon be Benedick the married man.

Yours ever,

Peregrine Parkinson."

The Death Mask

"Yes, that is a portrait of my wife. It is considered to be a good likeness. But of course, she was older-looking towards the last."

Enderby and I were on our way to the smoking-room after dinner, and the picture hung on the staircase. We had been chums at school a quarter of a century ago, and later on at college; but I had spent the last decade out of England. I returned to find my friend a widower of four years' standing. And a good job too, I thought to myself when I heard of it, for I had no great liking for the late Gloriana. Probably the sentiment, or want of sentiment, had been mutual: she did not smile on me, but I doubt if she smiled on any of poor Tom Enderby's bachelor cronies. The picture was certainly like her. She was a fine woman, with aquiline features and a cold eye. The artist had done the features justice—and the eye, which seemed to keep a steely watch on all the comings and goings of the house out of which she had died.

We made only a brief pause before the portrait, and then went on. The smoking-room was an apartment built out at the back of the house by a former owner, and shut off by double doors to serve as a nursery. Mrs. Enderby had no family, and she disliked the smell of tobacco. So, the big room was made over to Tom's pipes and cigars; and if Tom's friends wanted to smoke, they must smoke there or not at all. I remembered the room and the rule, but I was not prepared to find it still existing. I had expected to light my after-dinner cigar over the dessert dishes, now there was no presiding lady to consider.

We were soon installed in a couple of deep-cushioned chairs before a good fire. I thought Enderby breathed more freely when he closed the double doors behind us, shutting off the dull formal house, and the staircase and the picture. But he was not looking well; there hung about him an unmistakable air of depression. Could he be fretting after Gloriana? Perhaps during their married years, he had fallen into the way of depending on a woman to care for him. It is pleasant enough when the woman is the right sort; but I shouldn't myself have fancied being cared for by the late Mrs. Enderby. And, if the fretting was a fact, it would be easy to find a remedy. Evelyn has a couple of pretty sisters, and we would have him over to stay at our place.

"You must run down and see us," I said presently, pursuing this idea. "I want to introduce you to my wife. Can you come next week?"

His face lit up with real pleasure.

"I should like it of all things," he said heartily. But a qualification came after. The cloud settled back over him and he sighed. "That is, if I can get away."

"Why, what is to hinder you?"

"It may not seem much to stay for, but I—I have got in the way of stopping here—to keep things together." He did not look at me, but leaned over to the fender to knock the ash off his cigar.

"Tell you what, Tom, you are getting hipped living by yourself. Why don't you sell the house, or let it off just as it is, and try a complete change?"

"I can't sell it. I'm only the tenant for life. It was my wife's."

"Well, I suppose there is nothing to prevent you letting it? Or if you can't let it, you might shut it up."

"There is nothing *legal* to prevent me—!" The emphasis was too fine to attract notice, but I remembered it after.

"Then, my dear fellow, why not? Knock about a bit, and see the world. But, to my thinking, the best thing you could do would be to marry again."

He shook his head drearily.

"Of course it is a delicate matter to urge upon a widower. But you have paid the utmost ceremonial respect. Four years, you know. The greatest stickler for propriety would deem it ample."

"It isn't that. Dick, I—I've a great mind to tell you rather a queer story." He puffed hard at his smoke, and stared into the red coals in the pauses. "But I don't know what you'd think of it. Or think of me."

"Try me," I said. "I'll give you my opinion after. And you know I'm safe to confide in."

"I sometimes think I should feel better if I told it. It's—it's queer enough to be laughable. But it hasn't been any laughing matter to me."

He threw the stump of his cigar into the fire, and turned to me. And then I saw how pale he was, and that a dew of perspiration was breaking out on his white face.

"I was very much of your opinion, Dick: I thought I should be happier if I married again. And I went so far as to get engaged. But the engagement was broken off, and I am going to tell you why.

"My wife was some time ailing before she died, and the doctors were in consultation. But I did not know how serious her complaint was till the last. Then they told me there was no hope, as coma had set in. But it was possible, even probable, that there would be a revival of consciousness before death, and for this I was to hold myself ready.

"I daresay you will write me down a coward, but I dreaded the revival: I was ready to pray that she might pass away in her sleep. I knew she held exalted views about the marriage tie, and I felt sure if there were any last words she would exact a pledge. I could not at such a moment refuse to promise, and I did not want to be tied. You will recollect that she was my senior. I was about to be left a widower in middle life, and in the natural course of things I had a good many years before me. You see?"

"My dear fellow, I don't think a promise so extorted ought to bind you. It isn't fair—!"

"Wait and hear me. I was sitting here, miserable enough, as you may suppose, when the doctor came to fetch me to her room. Mrs. Enderby was conscious and had asked for me, but he particularly begged me not to agitate her in any way, lest pain should return. She was lying stretched out in the bed, looking already like a corpse.

"'Tom,' she said, 'they tell me I am dying, and there is something I want you to promise.'

"I groaned in spirit. It was all up with me, I thought. But she went on.

"'When I am dead and in my coffin, I want you to cover my face with your own hands. Promise me this.'

"It was not in the very least what I expected. Of course I promised.

"'I want you to cover my face with a particular handkerchief on which I set a value. When the time comes, open the cabinet to the right of the window, and you will find it in the third drawer from the top. You cannot mistake it, for it is the only thing in the drawer.'

"That was every word she said, if you believe me, Dick. She just sighed and shut her eyes as if she was going to sleep, and she never spoke again. Three or four days later they came again to ask me if I wished to take a last look, as the undertaker's men were about to close the coffin.

"I felt a great reluctance, but it was necessary I should go. She looked as if made of wax, and was colder than ice to touch. I opened the cabinet, and there, just as she said, was a large handkerchief of very fine cambric, lying by itself. It was embroidered with a monogram device in all four corners, and was not of a sort I had ever seen her use. I spread it out and laid it over the dead face; and then what happened was rather curious. It seemed to draw down over the features and cling to them, to nose and mouth and forehead and the shut eyes, till it became a perfect mask. My nerves were shaken, I suppose; I was seized with horror, and flung back the covering sheet, hastily quitting the room. And the coffin was closed that night.

"Well, she was buried, and I put up a monument which the neighbourhood considered handsome. As you see, I was bound by no pledge to abstain from marriage; and, though I knew what would have been her wish, I saw no reason why I should regard it. And, some months after, a family of the name of Ashcroft came to live at The Leasowes, and they had a pretty daughter.

"I took a fancy to Lucy Ashcroft the first time I saw her, and it was soon apparent that she was well inclined to me. She was a gentle, yielding little thing; not the superior style of woman. Not at all like——"

(I made no comment, but I could well understand that in his new matrimonial venture Tom would prefer a contrast.)

"——But I thought I had a very good chance of happiness with her; and I grew fond of her: very fond of her indeed. Her people were of the hospitable sort, and they encouraged me to go to The Leasowes, dropping in when I felt inclined: it did not seem as if they would be likely to put obstacles in our way. Matters progressed, and I made up my mind one evening to walk over there and declare myself. I had been up to town the day before, and came back with a ring in my pocket: rather a fanciful design of double hearts, but I thought Lucy would think it pretty, and would let me put it on her finger. I went up to change into dinner things, making myself as spruce as possible, and coming to the conclusion before the glass that I was not such a bad figure of a man after all, and that there was not much grey in my hair. Ay, Dick, you may smile: it is a good bit greyer now.

"I had taken out a clean handkerchief, and thrown the one carried through the day away crumpled on the floor. I don't know what made me turn to look at it as it lay there, but, once it caught my eye, I stood staring at it as if spell-bound. The handkerchief was moving—Dick, I swear it—rapidly altering in shape, puffing up here and there as if blown by wind, spreading and moulding itself into the features of a face. And what face should it be but that death-mask of Gloriana, which I had covered in the coffin eleven months before!

"To say I was horror-stricken conveys little of the feeling that possessed me. I snatched up the rag of cambric and flung it on the fire, and it was nothing but a rag in my hand, and in another moment no more than blackened tinder on the bar of the grate. There was no face below."

"Of course not," I said. "It was a mere hallucination. You were cheated by an excited fancy."

"You may be sure I told myself all that, and more; and I went downstairs and tried to pull myself together with a dram. But I was curiously upset, and, for that night at least, I found it impossible to play the wooer. The recollection of the death-mask was too vivid; it would have come between me and Lucy's lips.

"The effect wore off, however. In a day or two I was bold again, and as much disposed to smile at my folly as you are at this moment. I proposed, and Lucy accepted me; and I put on the ring. Ashcroft *père* was graciously pleased to approve of the settlements I offered, and Ashcroft *mère* promised to regard me as a son. And during the first forty-eight hours of our engagement, there was not a cloud to mar the blue.

"I proposed on a Monday, and on Wednesday I went again to dine and spend the evening with just their family party. Lucy and I found our way afterwards into the back drawing-room, which seemed to be made over to us by tacit understanding. Anyway, we had it to ourselves; and as Lucy sat on the settee, busy with her work, I was privileged to sit beside her, close enough to watch the careful stitches she was setting, under which the pattern grew.

"She was embroidering a square of fine linen to serve as a tea-cloth, and it was intended for a present to a friend; she was anxious, she told me, to finish it in the next few days, ready for despatch. But I was somewhat impatient of her engrossment in the work; I wanted her to look at me while we talked, and to be permitted to hold her hand. I was making plans for a tour we would take together after Easter; arguing that eight weeks spent in preparation was enough for any reasonable bride. Lucy was easily entreated; she laid aside the linen square on the table at her elbow. I held her fingers captive, but her eyes wandered from my face, as she was still deliciously shy.

"All at once she exclaimed. Her work was moving, there was growing to be a face in it: did I not see?

131

"I saw, indeed. It was the Gloriana death-mask, forming there as it had formed in my handkerchief at home: the marked nose and chin, the severe mouth, the mould of forehead, almost complete. I snatched it up and dropped it over the back of the couch. 'It did look like a face,' I allowed. 'But never mind it, darling; I want you to attend to me.' Something of this sort I said, I hardly know what, for my blood was running cold. Lucy pouted; she wanted to dwell on the marvel, and my impatient action had displeased her.

"I went on talking wildly, being afraid of pauses, but the psychological moment had gone by. I felt I did not carry her with me as before: she hesitated over my persuasions; the forecast of a Sicilian honeymoon had ceased to charm. By-and-bye she suggested that Mrs. Ashcroft would expect us to rejoin the circle in the other room. And perhaps I would pick up her work for her—still with a slight air of offence.

"I walked round the settee to recover the luckless piece of linen; but she turned also, looking over the back, so at the same instant we both saw.

"There again was the Face, rigid and severe; and now the corners of the cloth were tucked under, completing the form of the head. And that was not all. Some white drapery had been improvised and extended beyond it on the floor, presenting the complete figure laid out straight and stiff, ready for the grave. Lucy's alarm was excusable. She shrieked aloud, shriek upon shriek, and immediately an indignant family of Ashcrofts rushed in through the half-drawn *portières* which divided the two rooms, demanding the cause of her distress.

"Meanwhile I had fallen upon the puffed-out form, and destroyed it. Lucy's embroidery composed the head; the figure was ingeniously contrived out of a large Turkish bath-sheet, brought in from one of the bedrooms, no one knew how or when. I held up the things protesting their innocence, while the family were stabbing me through and through with looks of indignation, and Lucy was sobbing in her, mother's arms. She might have been foolish, she allowed; it did seem ridiculous now she saw what it was. But at the moment it was too dreadful: it looked so like—so like! And here a fresh sob choked her into silence.

"Peace was restored at last, but plainly the Ashcrofts doubted me. The genial father stiffened, and Mrs. Ashcroft administered indirect reproofs. She hated practical joking, so she informed me; she might be wrong, and no doubt she was old-fashioned, but she had been brought up to consider it in the highest degree ill-bred. And perhaps I had not considered how sensitive Lucy was, and how easily alarmed. She hoped I would take warning for the future, and that nothing of this kind would occur again.

"Practical joking—oh, ye gods! As if it was likely that I, alone with the girl of my heart, would waste the precious hour in building up effigies of sham corpses on the floor! And Lucy ought to have known that the accusation was absurd, as I had never for a moment left her side. She did take my part when more composed; but the mystery remained, beyond explanation of hers or mine.

"As for the future, I could not think of that without a failing heart. If the Power arrayed against us were in truth what my superstition feared, I might as well give up hope at once, for I knew there would be no relenting. I could see the whole absurdity of the thing as well as you do now; but, if you put yourself in my place, Dick, you will be forced to confess that it was tragic too.

"I did not see Lucy the next day, as I was bound to go again to town; but we had planned to meet and ride together on the Friday morning. I was to be at The Leasowes at a certain hour, and you may be sure I was punctual. Her horse had already been brought round, and the groom was leading it up and down. I had hardly dismounted when she came down the steps of the porch; and I noticed at once a new look on her face, a harder set about that red mouth of hers which was so soft and kissable. But she let me put her up on the saddle and settle her foot in the stirrup, and she was the bearer of a gracious message from her mother. I was expected to return to lunch, and Mrs. Ashcroft begged us to be punctual, as a friend who had stayed the night with them, would be leaving immediately after.

"'You will be pleased to meet her, I think,' said Lucy, leaning forward to pat her horse. 'I find she knows you very well. It is Miss Kingsworthy.'

"Now Miss Kingsworthy was a schoolfriend of Gloriana's, who used now and then to visit us here. I was not aware that she and the Ashcrofts were acquainted; but, as I have said, they had only recently come into the neighbourhood as tenants of The Leasowes. I had no opportunity to express pleasure or the reverse, for Lucy was riding on, and putting her horse to a brisk pace. It was some time before she drew rein, and again admitted conversation. We were descending a steep hill, and the groom was following at a discreet distance behind, far enough to be out of earshot.

133

"Lucy looked very pretty on horseback; but this is by the way. The mannish hat suited her, and so did the habit fitting closely to her shape.

"'Tom,' she said; and again, I noticed that new hardness in her face. 'Tom, Miss Kingsworthy tells me your wife did not wish you to marry again, and she made you promise her that you would not. Miss Kingsworthy was quite astonished to hear that you and I were engaged. Is this true?'

"I was able to tell her it was not: that my wife had never asked, and I had never given her, any such pledge. I allowed she disliked second marriages—in certain cases, and perhaps she had made some remark to that effect to Miss Kingsworthy; it was not unlikely. And then I appealed to her. Surely, she would not let a mischief-maker's tittle-tattle come between her and me?

"I thought her profile looked less obdurate, but she would not let her eyes meet mine as she answered:

"'Of course not, if that was all. And I doubt if I would have heeded it, only that it seemed to fit in with—something else. Tom, it was very horrible, what we saw on Wednesday evening. And—and—don't be angry, but I asked Miss Kingsworthy what your wife was like. I did not tell her why I wanted to know.'

"'What has that to do with it?' I demanded—stoutly enough; but, alas! I was too well aware.

She told me Mrs. Enderby was handsome, but she had very marked features, and was severe-looking when she did not smile. A high forehead, a Roman nose, and a decided chin. Tom, the face in the cloth was just like that. Did you not see?'

"Of course I protested.

"'My darling, what nonsense! I saw it looked a little like a face, but I pulled it to pieces at once because you were frightened. Why, Lucy, I shall have you turning into a spiritualist if you take up these fancies.'

"'No,' she said, 'I do not want to be anything foolish. I have thought it over, and if it happens only once I have made up my mind to believe it a mistake and to forget. But if it comes again—if it goes on coming!' Here she shuddered and turned white. 'Oh Tom, I could not—I could not!'

"That was the ultimatum. She liked me as much as ever; she even owned to a warmer feeling; but she was not going to marry a haunted man. Well, I suppose I cannot blame her. I might have given the same advice in another fellow's case, though in my own I felt it hard.

"I am close to the end now, so I shall need to tax your patience very little longer. A single chance remained. Gloriana's power, whatever its nature and however derived, might have been so spent in the previous efforts that she could effect no more. I clung to this shred of hope, and did my best to play the part of the light-hearted lover, the sort of companion Lucy expected, who would shape himself to her mood; but I was conscious that I played it ill.

"The ride was a lengthy business. Lucy's horse cast a shoe, and it was impossible to change the saddle on to the groom's hack or my own mare, as neither of them had been trained to the habit. We were bound to return at a foot-pace, and did not reach The Leasowes until two o'clock. Lunch was over: Mrs. Ashcroft had set out for the station driving Miss Kingsworthy; but some cutlets were keeping hot for us, so we were informed, and could be served immediately.

"We went at once into the dining-room, as Lucy was hungry; and she took off her hat and laid it on a side-table: she said the close fit of it made her head ache. The cutlets had been misrepresented: they were lukewarm; but Lucy made a good meal off them and the fruit-tart which followed, very much at her leisure. Heaven knows I would not have grudged her so much as a mouthful; but that luncheon was an ordeal I cannot readily forget.

"The servant absented himself, having seen us served; and then my troubles began. The tablecloth seemed alive at the corner which was between us; it rose in waves as if puffed up by wind, though the window was fast shut against and wandering airs. I tried to seem unconscious; tried to talk as if no horror of apprehension was filling all my mind, while I was flattening out the bewitched damask with a grasp I hardly dared relax. Lucy rose at last, saying she must change her dress.

"Occupied with the cloth, it had not occurred to me to look round, or keep watch on what might be going on in another part of the room. The hat on the side-table had been tilted over sideways, and in that position, it was made to crown another presentation of the Face. What it was made of this time I cannot say; probably a serviette, as several lay about. The linen material, of whatever sort, was again moulded into the perfect form; but this time the mouth showed humour, and appeared to relax in a grim smile.

"Lucy shrieked, and dropped into my arms in a swoon: a real genuine fainting-fit, out of which she was brought round with difficulty, after summoned help of doctors.

"I hung about miserably till her safety was assured, and then went as miserably home. Next morning I received a cutting little note from my mother-in-law elect, in which she returned the ring, and informed me the engagement must be considered at an end.

"Well, Dick, you know now why I do not marry. And what have you to say?"

The Lonely Road

"I am awfully sorry, Tom, I am indeed, and after all your kindness in coming down to see me about that tiresome business, but we can't drive you to the station this evening as I promised. The mare has been kicking in the stable again, and Summers has just discovered she is dead lame. You must really make up your mind to stay another night, and we will get a conveyance over from Ardkellar first thing tomorrow. If I write at once I shall catch the post: we haven't a telegraph office in the village, or I would wire. Summers has only just made the discovery, so he tells me. Now do be reasonable, and say you'll stay."

"That is kind of you, Margaret."

Tom Pulteney fixed again in his left eye the single eyeglass that was always dropping out. This so that he might look at his widowed cousin with the right expression, and she was good to look at, though no longer in her first youth.

"A few more hours here is a temptation; a greater one than I can say. But I'm positively bound to get back to Dublin tonight, and somehow or other I must contrive to catch the 8-50. I'm not such a weakling that I can't walk the distance. How far do you call it to the station?"

"It is eight miles good from here to Ardkellar. And it is a lonely road——"

"Well—I shan't need company for that short distance. I shall be too full of regrets after tearing myself away from you—to say nothing of Adelaide. Though you know very well that Adelaide does not count."

"'I don't know anything of the sort.' But I hate you going—all that way on foot, and at such an hour."

"Hate my going by all means—I'd wish nothing better. But for a different reason."

"Oh, Tom, do be serious: but if you must go, take care. The road has

137

had a bad character of late; there have been assaults and robberies. Of course you don't go about with a revolver—here. But do you carry a heavy stick?"

"I didn't bring one. But I've got my fists, and I know how to use them."

"You must have a stick. I will lend you Laurence's; it is loaded at the head. I know you will sometime let me have it back."

"If it will make you easy about me——"

"It will make me easier. I am vexed about the mare—and not knowing till the last minute. I am afraid you will have to set off at once if that train is to be caught. And it is getting dusk even now."

The farewells followed, which Tom Pulteney made as affectionate as he dared. It was something of a triumph to him that Margaret was really concerned about the possible risk he was running, on a lonely stretch of road where there had been at least one attempted murder; and he set out with that conviction kept warm at heart.

To him an eight-mile walk was truly a light matter, but he happened to be burdened carrying a suitcase made heavy by expensive fittings, and before the end of the first half mile he began to wish he had slipped his pet razors into his pocket, and asked his cousin to send the case after him, which without doubt she would have done. And for a reason other than the weight: if thieves were abroad, and he was attacked by two, it would be easily snatched by a confederate while one of them knocked him on the head. And a good sound leather suitcase, all but new, is worth stealing now-a-days apart from what it may contain.

The contents of Tom's were also of value, things that he could ill spare—among other oddments a handsome finger-ring which he had brought from town, hoping he might find courage to offer it to Margaret as a *gage d' amour*. The parcel had not been opened: opportunity had not served, or else he had feared to damage his own cause by speaking too early in her widowhood. These articles would, he reflected, be safer if carried on his person, and then he could abandon the suitcase with less reluctance should there be need.

He was now far beyond Ballymacor, and the road before him was solitary. On a sudden impulse he deposited the case under the hedge, unsnapped the locks, and sought in the fast-fading light for his more treasured possessions. These he secured in innermost pockets, again shouldered his burden, and went on whistling under his breath, as might a man light-hearted and unafraid.

But was he unafraid? Was he not assuming the pretence of a bold-ness he did not possess? In the midst of that search into his luggage, a doubt beset him that the action there and then had been unwise; for at the same time, he heard, or thought he heard, a rustle of movement behind the hedge. There was nothing for it then but to go on, and trust he had been mistaken, or the presence and movement wholly in-nocent. But presently he imagined—imagination first, but soon there was no doubt—that he heard footsteps following. He swung round twice and glanced behind him, but so far as he could see in the dusk the road was clear.

The sound went on, and now the footsteps approached nearer, quickening upon his, and he was already bracing every nerve, prepar-ing for the encounter he expected.

At this critical moment a huge white dog leaped over the fence on the right.

"Why, Boris," he exclaimed unthinking, and the creature came beside him with wagging tail: surely in the event of attack, here would be a formidable ally.

The dog was friendly, and appeared to answer to the name called. Margaret had had such a dog in her husband's lifetime, a Russian wolf-hound of which she had been fond; Pulteney had often seen them together, the tall elegant woman followed by the noble hound. Surely this must be Boris; and yet he had a dim recollection of some mischance mentioned in a letter of Adelaide's, an accident in which the dog had been injured, and he thought killed. Certainly, he had not seen Boris on any recent visit to Ballymacor. If only he could keep the dog beside him, he would, he thought, be safe. So, he spoke to the creature by name, and spoke again; and each time Boris responded in dog fashion, pleased by the recognition, or so it seemed.

The footsteps still were following; and now, bolder because ac-companied, he glanced over his shoulder. Yes, there were two men, and they were close behind, of villainous aspect in the dusk. The dog also looked round and growled, showing his teeth, formidable white fangs, set in a jaw like an alligator's: if the creature was strong enough and fierce enough to pull down a wolf, he would surely be a match for any man. But supposing the followers were armed, and their object murder and not mere robbery, what then?

The sky by this time was clearing, and behind the breaking clouds there came some shining of the moon, showing the way in front and the white hound beside him, and, as he remembered after, both their shadows. From time to time, he spoke to his four-footed companion, and also put out his hand to pat the dogis neck; but somehow, he never succeeded in touching him—the white rough coat seemed always just beyond reach, though there was no shrinking away to avoid contact.

Pulteney all the while was on the strain to listen, and though he still heard the following footsteps, double footsteps, it seemed to him that they were falling further behind. He could not now be far from Ardkellar, his destination; the railway-line here crossed the road high up on bridge and embankment, and a luggage train lumbered over before him, with gleaming lights and a long rattle of trucks. Not far beyond there was a crossroads, and here the footsteps stopped. Pulteney glanced again over his shoulder, and saw that the two men had halted there, and seemed to be consulting together.

He turned and went on, and now he heard no more the pursuing feet. He was close to the outskirts of the country town, and, he concluded, in comparative safety. He could still see the dog beside him, and was beginning to wonder how he could best dispose of his companion in safety, and contrive to let Margaret know; as Boris who had befriended him, must certainly have strayed from Ballymacor. They had reached the first row of houses and the outpost of street lights, when he noticed that the form of the dog was altering, becoming shadowy in outline, instead of substantial as before.

Still the creature kept step by step beside him, though a figure compacted of white mist growing more and more transparent, till at last, at the passing of the third lamp, this ghostly likeness of Boris faded into nothing and was gone. Tom Pulteney walked into the station of Ardkellar, grateful for his escape, but a bewildered man.

He wrote the history of that night's adventure to his cousin Margaret.

> Upon my word of honour, this is the literal truth, though you will find it difficult to believe. I made sure the dog was yours, as he seemed to know me, and evidently would have shown fight had I been attacked. And I believe the men saw him just as I did, and were deterred from carrying out their plan. It is true I could not touch him, though I tried; but no one could have been more astonished than I was when he dissolved into something like white smoke and then was gone. It was an experience I shall never forget.

To him, Margaret in reply.

I do believe your story, and to me it is altogether convincing, though so strange. My dear Boris died two years ago: there was an accident I cannot bear to think of, even now. He was caught by a touring car going at speed, and caring nothing for the life or safety of a dog. I had him shot in mercy; I never say destroyed. And what you saw that night is witness that under other conditions he is in existence still. He was so good, so faithful: I never called on him in vain, and he knew almost my thought before I spoke. I was thinking of him that evening. I said to Adelaide—she will tell you—how I wished I had had Boris here, for I would have sent him with you on that lonely walk, and then you would have been safe. For I was very anxious. I believe my thought, my wish, did send him, dear, dear fellow. But I cannot expect you to receive this as I do, or think that it explains.

Tom Pulteney to Margaret.

I am convinced, indeed. It was you who worked the miracle, and you worked it for me. Your letter, which explains so much, tells me one thing more: may I hope it is the one thing I would give the world to know? You were anxious—you cared what became of me. Could you care always—could you care enough? I pray that the post may bring me the answer I long for; but I am ever your devoted lover, however you reply."

The Next Heir

1

Fryer and Fryer, solicitors, of Lincoln's Inn, the original firm and their successors, have for the past hundred years acted as guardians of the interests of the landed gentry, buying and selling portions of estates, proving wills, drawing up marriage settlements and the like. And a glance at the japanned deed-boxes in their somewhat shabby office would discover among the inscriptions, sundry names of note.

The original Fryers have long been dead and gone, but there is still a Fryer at the head of the firm. And on a certain day of spring, this ruling Fryer was alone in his private office-room, when his clerk brought in a message.

"Mr. Richard Quinton to see you, sir. He has no card to send up, but he says you will know his name and his business, as he has called to answer an advertisement."

Without doubt Mr. Fryer did know the name of Quinton, as it was legibly painted on a deed-box full in view, but something in his countenance expressed surprise. He signified his willingness to see Mr Richard Quinton, and presently the visitor entered, a pleasant-faced youngish man, brown of attire, and indeed altogether a brown man, except for the whitish patch where his forehead had been screened from the sun. Bronzed of skin, brown of short cut hair, and opening on the world a frank pair of hazel eyes, which looked as if they had been used to regard the wide spaces of waste lands, and were not fully used to the pressure and hurry and strenuousness of our over-civilised older world.

"I have called, sir, about an advertisement inserted by Fryer and Fryer in a Montreal paper. I have it here to show you. It was posted to me at the London hospital, where I have been since my wound, I see that the representative of Richard Morley Quinton, who emigrated to Canada in 1827, will hear on applying to you of something to his

143

advantage."

"*May* hear of something," corrected the man of law. "Are you the representative in this generation?"

"I am, sir. Richard Morley Quinton was my grandfather."

"Great-grandfather, surely? You are under thirty, and he was twenty-six years old when he left England."

"No: grandfather. He had a hard struggle in his first years on the other side. His English brother was not the sort to help him, and he never asked for help: he would not. He did not marry until late in life, and my old dad was the only son who survived infancy. There was a daughter who married and had children. But I don't suppose you want to know about her."

"We want the male heir. Or at least to know where he might be found."

"My dad married earlier, but he had no children by his first wife. He was well over fifty when he married my mother, and I am their only child. I can put you in the way of getting all the certificates you want, and vouchers from responsible people who have known the family. And now, tell me. Why am I advertised for? Is it an inheritance?"

"Not at the present moment, but it may be."

"Of Quinton and Quinton Verney—is that so? My dad would have been pleased. He thought much of Quinton, hearing about it from his father, who was born at the Court."

"If the present Mr. Quinton, your second cousin, makes no will, the Quinton property goes to the heir-male of your mutual great-grandfather. But he has the power of willing the whole where he pleases—to a hospital, or to a beggar in the street. You can count on no certain inheritance. You understand?"

"Then why ——?"

"We advertised because Mr. Quinton wished to ascertain who represented the Canadian branch of the family, and also to make your personal acquaintance. We can give you no certainty, but I gather from what he has written, that, if your cousin likes you, and if you agree to certain stipulations respecting the property, he intends to make you, his heir. When the particulars you give me are verified, you will have to go down to Quinton, but he will reimburse any expense you may be put to, through loss of time and detention in England. You can hold yourself at our disposal?"

"If military orders do not interfere—yes, gladly, for the sake of a

144

look at old Quinton Court, even with nothing to come after. But perhaps Mr. Quinton may prefer to meet me in London."

"You will have to go down there. Mr. Quinton is a complete invalid, and keeps a resident doctor: he is still under sixty, but most unlikely, I should say, to marry. His father was killed in the hunting-field; he had not been long married, but his wife, who was one of the Pengwyns, gave birth to twin sons, posthumous children. This Clement was the younger of the two, but his elder brother died at nineteen, also from an accident. There you have the family history in a nutshell. Give me an address, where a letter will certainly find you when I have looked into this."

Richard had not long to wait for the expected letter. Mr. Clement Quinton seemed disposed to take his young kinsman on trust, without holding aloof till his story was verified. Mr. Fryer was still in correspondence with Canada when the summons came for Richard to present himself at Quinton Verney. The young Canadian was prompt in obeying, and on the day following he took train for the nearest railway point. No day or time had been named for arrival, so, after changing at the junction and alighting at a small wayside station, no conveyance was there to meet him. Nor, on enquiry, was any trap to be hired. His portmanteau could be sent by a returning cart in the course of a couple of hours, but for himself there was no alternative. He would have to walk the four miles, or rather more, which separated the station from Mount Verney.

Mount Verney, these people styled Mr. Quinton's dwelling, and not Quinton Court as he expected; the Quinton Court his old father used to talk of, told by the grandfather reminiscent of his youth. Why had the original name been changed?—that should be a first question when the time for putting questions came. Meanwhile he was not ill-pleased to be approaching Quinton on foot and alone, and a walk of four miles and over was but a light matter.

Four miles of lovely country verdant with the early green of spring, hill and dale unfolding wooded glimpses here and there, and the ancient Roman road stretching its white line before him, enduring still after all these centuries. He could hardly mistake the way, but after a while he thought it better to ask direction. There were iron gates and an avenue leading to Mount Verney, so he was told, and when he came to the iron gates, he must turn in.

Gates and an avenue! His father had spoken of no such appendage to Quinton Court, but no doubt they were additions of a later time.

He had his father much in mind during that walk, and the interest he would have felt in this possible—nay, probable—inheritance for his son. His grandfather too; the grandfather who died before his birth: it was as if the two old men went beside him along the green-fenced way, made fair by the sunshine of late April. And he had another person in mind, one who up to now has not been named.

Nan, his girl, who waited for him far off across the Atlantic, full of love and faith. If this succession truly came to pass, if it were even an assured future to him and to his heirs, marriage would be no longer an imprudence, it might be entered into at once on his return, released from war-service. That hope was enough to gild the sunshine, and spread the pastures with a brighter green. And then he came to the gates, and they stood open.

Mount Verney did not boast a lodge, though the drive was a long one. The avenue had been closely planted with ilex and pine, too closely for the good of the trees, and it was consequently dark in shadow: as he turned in, he was conscious of a certain chill.

The open gates were hung on stone pillars, and the ornamentation of these uprights caught his eye. On either side, inwards and outwards, a face was carved in relief, but a face that was not human: the mask of a satyr, with pricked animal ears and sprouting horns, and an evil leering grin. Richard had seen nothing of this sort in his backwoods experience, though possibly other things that were starker and grimmer. The leering faces filled him with repugnance; they should not remain there, he thought, to watch over the comings and goings of the house, did ever that house become his own.

The dark avenue had a bend in it; he could not see to the end, but he thought he knew well what he would find there, the old Quinton homestead had been so often described to him. The grey stone house, with its gables and mullioned windows, diamond-paned; the steep roof, up and down which the pigeons strutted and plumed themselves; the paved courtyard with its breast-high wall and mounted urns. He had a clear picture of if in his mind, and this was what at the turn of the avenue he expected to see. But when the turn was reached, his joyful anticipations fell dead. This was quite another place. Had he been misdirected after all?

What lay before him was a white stuccoed villa, spreading over much ground, but so pierced with big window-spaces that it presented to the beholder scant solidity of wall. This was the entrance side; towards the valley the walls rounded themselves into two semicircles with a flat central division, and here again were the big sash windows of plate-glass, overlooking the view. But there was no mistake. This was Mount Verney.

A grave-looking elderly manservant answered the bell, and it became evident the Canadian visitor had arrived too soon. Mr. Richard Quinton was expected, yes certainly, but the day had not been named, and Mr. Quinton was at present out in the car, and Dr. Lindsay with him. If Mr. Richard would step into the library, tea should be brought to him—unless he preferred sherry. His room had been so far prepared that it could be quickly made ready; he, Peters, would tell the housekeeper. And would Mr. Richard come this way?

So tea was served to Richard in the library, and his first meal under the Mount Verney roof was taken in solitude, as the master of the house did not return. The library possessed one of the wide bows overlooking the valley, but in spite of the tall sash windows the room was a dark one. They were, it is true, heavily draped with crimson curtains, and the furniture was also heavy, and of an inartistic period. He tried to picture Nan in these surroundings, sitting in the opposite big chair (it would have swallowed her up entirely unless she perched on the arm) and pouring out for him from the huge old teapot, but the effort was in vain.

The fancy portrait of his little love would not fit into this frame, but doubtless the frame could be altered: like the grinning masks on the gates, there was much it would be possible to change. Meanwhile hurrying footsteps were heard on the floor overhead, housemaids, were busy there; and presently Peters came again to ask if he should conduct the guest to his room.

Richard left the dull library with a sensation of relief. The chamber immediately above had been prepared for him, of equal size, and with windows commanding the view. Richard made some appreciative comment, which seemed to please the old servant.

"Yes, sir," he said, "this is the best bedroom, it has the finest lookout. Mr. Quinton himself gave orders for it to be yours. It used to be Lady Anna Quinton's."

"Lady Anna Quinton!" Richard repeated the name in his surprise. "I did not know Mr. Quinton had ever been married."

"No, sir, and he never was. Her Ladyship was his mother. She went away to France and died there; it is getting on for thirty years ago, but Mr. Quinton couldn't bear to take the room to be his, though it is the best in the house. I'll send up your portmanteau, sir, directly it arrives."

And with that, Peters withdrew.

Here Richard was certainly well lodged. He stood at the middle window which had been set open, and looked out over a wide prospect. The sun was now beginning to decline, and the first flush of rosy cloud was reflected in the chain of pools which filled the valley to the right, widened out almost to the dimensions of a lake—no doubt artificially formed by damning up the natural stream, which rushed over a weir out of sight. In the middle distance, between the house and the water, was a grove of young oaks, not thickly set like the planting of the avenue, but high-trimmed and rising tall and bare-stemmed out of evergreen undergrowth. The shimmer of water was visible through them in the background, not wholly concealed though it might be when leafage was full.

The name of Quinton Verney was familiar, cherished among those legends of the importance of the family which the Canadian branch had preserved and handed down; but the lake was to Richard another innovation and surprise. Was it good fishing water, he wondered, and would rainbow trout flourish and breed there? As he stood looking, a boat shot out from the headland to the right, and, crossing the field of view, was lost behind the grove: it was only after it had disappeared that Richard began to wonder what had been the motive power. He could not recall any flash of oars or figures of rowers, or indeed any occupier of the boat.

This might have puzzled him still more, but his attention was diverted by the sound of an arrival below. A car had drawn up at the entrance, voices were now heard in the hall, footsteps on the stairs. After a brief interval, a sharp, rather authoritative knock came at his door and a man entered, a man still on the younger side of middle-age, reddish-haired and short of stature, with a close-trimmed bristly moustache.

"Mr. Quinton?" Richard exclaimed, coming forward. If this was his host, he was quite unlike the fancy picture he had formed. But then at Mount Verney everything was unlike and unexpected.

"No—my name's Lindsay—I'm the doctor. Mr. Quinton is sorry you were not met, but he had not understood you were arriving to-day."

"I hope my coming has not been inconvenient?"

"Not at all—not at all, unless to yourself. But I do not suppose you minded the walk from the station; it is pretty country, and you came here especially to acquaint yourself with the place and its surroundings. One thing more. I have to ask you to excuse Mr. Quinton for this evening, and put up with my company only. Mr. Quinton is, as you know, an invalid, and I have been with him today to his dentist for some extractions under an anaesthetic. He is a wreck in consequence"—here the little reddish man shrugged his shoulders—"and will not leave his own rooms again tonight. You are comfortable here, I hope?"—this after Richard had expressed concern at his host's condition. Now it was necessary he should praise his quarters, which he did without stint.

"Mr. Quinton would have it that Lady Anna's room should be made ready for the heir, and we were all surprised, as it has been long out of use. Well, *adieu* for the present: come down as soon as you are ready. Dinner is at seven: we keep early hours here in the country. What! your portmanteau not come? Then never mind about dressing; we will not stand on ceremony for tonight."

With that, Lindsay the doctor took himself off. But, after he had closed the door, some of his last words kept repeating in Richard's mind. *Made ready for the heir!* That was taking intention for granted in a way for which he was not prepared; and, suddenly, he felt strangely doubtful of his own wish in the matter. Did he really desire to be the owner of the Quinton property, and, if not, from what hidden root did disinclination spring?

Presently a gong sounded from below, and he went down to find the dining-room lighted up, though it was scarcely more than dusk without, and the window-screens were still undrawn. The table was set out with some fine old silver and an abundance of flowers, the service of the meal was faultless, and Lindsay made an excellent deputy host. Good food has a cheering influence, and the causeless depression which had threatened to engulf Richard's spirit was lifted, at least for the time.

"I hope you will like Quinton Verney," Lindsay was saying with apparent heartiness. "Mr. Quinton is particularly anxious that you should like the place, and take an interest in his hobbies. He will explain better than I can what they are. But be prepared to hear a great deal about Roman remains in Britain, and to be cross-questioned about your knowledge."

"Then I can only avow ignorance. It is a study that has not come in my way, but I am at least ready to be interested."

"Ah, well, interest won't be difficult in what has been discovered on your own land, for that is his especial pride. A fine tessellated pavement down there by the pools, and an altar in what is now the grove. I am a duffer myself in these matters, but Mr. Quinton is a downright enthusiast about the old pagans and their times. It was he who re-planted the grove where it is supposed that a sacred one existed, and set up in the midst of it a statue of Pan copied from the antique. I chaff him sometimes about it, and tell him I believe there is nothing he would like better than to revive the Lupercalia, and convert the entire neighbourhood. That's an exaggeration, of course, but the element of mystery appeals to him. As you will discover."

Following this touch of personal revelation, Richard remarked:

"You know Mr. Quinton very well. I suppose you have been with him a long time?"

"Eighteen months—no less, no more. But you can get to know a man pretty well in that time, especially when you happen to be his doctor as well as his house-mate. He has been an invalid for many years—since boyhood in fact: a sad case: you'll know more about it after a while. I was at the war before that: got knocked out, and when free of hospital could only take on a soft job, and fate or luck sent me here. Quinton and I have got on well together. Indeed, I may tell you in confidence that he offered to leave me all he possessed, provided I would bind myself by his conditions."

So, the Quinton inheritance had been offered and refused else-where. Here was a matter that might well give Richard food for thought.

"And why did you not——?" he began impulsively.

"Why didn't I grasp at such a chance? Well, I allow it was tempting enough, to a man who is a damaged article—a damage that will be life-long. But I couldn't consent to bind myself as he would have me bound; and there was another reason. I would have been suspected of using my position here to exercise undue influence, and that I couldn't stomach. It was I who suggested to Mr. Quinton that he should seek out his next of kin—eh, what; what is the matter?"

The query was to Peters, who was whispering at his elbow.

"Pray excuse me. I am sorry, but my patient is not so well." And the little doctor hurried away.

Peters brought in the next course.

"Dr. Lindsay hopes you will go on with the dinner, sir, and not wait for him. He may be detained some time."

For the rest of the meal Richard was solitary. He declined after din-ner wine and dessert, so Peters, who felt himself responsible towards the guest, suggested that he might like to smoke in the library, and coffee would be brought to him there. Richard rose from the table, and, as he did so, turned towards the unscreened window behind his chair, and experienced the shock of a surprise. There stood a strange-looking figure, gazing in at him and at the room, with face pressed against the glass. His exclamation recalled Peters, who was in the act of carrying out a tray; but by the time the old butler returned, the figure had disappeared. Who, or what was it? But Peters could not tell.

"I'll have it inquired into, sir. No one had any call to be there. These windows look into the enclosed garden, that is always kept private. A man, did you say, sir? Like a tramp?"

"A man," Richard assented, but he did not add in what likeness. Surely it must have been some freak of fancy that suggested those lineaments, the white leering face which resembled the bestial masks at the gate of the avenue, with their pricked ears and budding horns; and suggested also the naked torso, of which a glimpse was afforded by the light.

Peters brought word with the coffee that no one was found in the garden, but he meant to be extra careful in locking up, "lest it should be somebody after the plate." And indeed, were ill characters about, the unscreened window was likely to bring danger, as the display of silver on sideboard and table might well excite the cupidity of a looker-in.

Dr. Lindsay came down an hour later, but it was only to ask whether Richard had all he wanted for comfort and for the night.

"I shall be sitting up with Mr. Quinton," he explained. "Unluckily, haemorrhage has followed these extractions, and he is morbidly affected by the sight and taste of blood. No, not a sufficient loss to be alarming: it will be subdued by tomorrow I don't doubt: it is serious only as it affects his special case. You'll give Peters your orders, will you not, and tell him when you wish to be called, and all that. I understand your portmanteau has arrived."

So, Richard found himself back again in the best bedroom at an early hour, with the night before him, and his luggage unpacked, and despatch-case set on the writing-table. Now was the time for the letter he had promised Nan, with his first impressions of Quinton Verney, about which she was naturally curious; the old homestead he had described to her, which might someday be his home and hers. But when he spread paper before him, he felt an overmastering reluctance to write that letter. What could he say if he told her the truth—and

151

surely nothing less than the truth and the whole truth was due to Nan, however much it might disappoint and puzzle her.

Could he tell her, with no reason to allege, of the distaste he felt for this place, for the house and all that it contained?—a distaste which began with the first sight of those leering masks at the avenue gate: how tell her of that other living face which resembled them, seen peering into the lighted dining-room, pressed against the glass of the shut window a couple of hours ago? Better delay, than that he should fill a letter with maunderings such as these, when another day's experience, or a personal interview with the invisible cousin, might bring about an altered mind.

He was tired and out of spirits, and though he rejected with scorn the suggestion that a walk of less than five miles could have fatigued him, he was only lately out of hospital, and it was long since so much pedestrian exercise had come his way. And there had been throughout a certain excitement of highly strung expectation, from which no doubt reaction played its part. No, he would not attempt to write to Nan; the letter should be postponed until the morrow. And he would betake himself at once to bed.

2

It has been said that the chamber allotted to him was spacious and well-appointed, a private bathroom opened from it, and with one notable exception, it fulfilled every modern requirement. The rest of the house had been wired, and electric light installed, but here there were no means of illumination but candles, and, though these had been abundantly supplied on toilet and mantelpiece, and also at the bedside, the result was curiously dull. It was as if the walls and hangings of the apartment absorbed and did not reflect the light; a room of ordinary size would have been as well illuminated by a farthing dip.

One of the windows was opened down a hand's breadth behind the curtains, and they stirred faintly in the air. Richard drew them apart to push up the lower sash, and then was struck by the beauty of the scene below. The valley had put on a veil of silvery mist, so delicate as hardly to obscure, and away to the left the moon was rising, a full yellow moon, magnified by its nearness to the horizon.

How still it all was. He had been used of late to the roar of a great city, audible even through hospital walls; before that to the thudding of great guns, and the scream of shell. How silent, and how peaceful: but presently not completely silent, for music broke into the stillness.

Somebody down below was playing on the flute, long-drawn notes and a simple air, but of enthralling sweetness. The music was difficult to locate; sometimes it seemed to come from near the house, sometimes from the grove of trees, and now to be a mere echo from a greater distance still. Could some rustic lover be serenading a house-maid? but no, that seemed impossible. Richard was himself no musi-cian, but he knew enough to appreciate the rare quality of the per-former. And then the final notes died away, and silence reigned under the rising moon.

He dropped the curtain over the window, leaving it open, and now applied himself quickly to prepare for bed. Tired as he was, he expect-ed to sleep as soon as his head touched the pillow: such was his custom in high health, and the habit had served him in good stead when re-cruiting strength. But on this first night at Mount Verney sleep and he were to be strangers. No doubt there was some excitement of nerve or brain, the cause of which might be looked for entirely in himself. This at first; but by-and-bye there was something external, something more, though it was nameless and undefined.

A change had set in: this was no restlessness of his own that he was suffering, it was the misery and torture of another; a misery all the greater that it could not be expressed. It seemed to him that he was divided; he recognised that he was lying on the bed, but he was also walking the room from wall to wall, with tossed arms, with hands clenched and threatening, and then spread open; gestures foreign to his nature under any extreme of passion. He, or the entity which ab-sorbed him, did not weep: no tears came to the relief of this distress, and his own voice was dumb in his throat; there could be no cry of appeal. Whether the passion which tore him was fury solely, or grief solely, he could not tell; or whether in its extreme anguish it com-bined the two.

For a while he was completely paralysed by this strange experi-ence: he was walking the room with the sufferer; he *was* the sufferer: and then again, he knew the personality and the agony were not his own; that his real self was stretched upon the bed, though he could neither lift a finger nor move a limb. How long did this endure in its alternations? Keen as was his after memory, he could not tell: mo-ments count as hours when under torture, and in an experience so abnormal time does not exist, even as we are told it will be effaced for us hereafter. One fragment of knowledge informed his brain; how he knew cannot be told, for no voice spoke. The entity was a woman.

153

It was no man's agony into the vortex of which he had been drawn; this was a woman who knew both love and hate, a mother who had possessed and also lost.

Then, in a moment, the strain upon him snapped: he could move again, he had the government of his limbs, he was in his own body and not that other, if the other was a body indeed. Candles—the means of striking a light—were at his hand; in less time than it takes to write, both flames were kindled: the whole room was plain to see, and there was nothing, nothing but empty air. And yet he knew, he knew that the woman was still there—that she was pacing up and down from wall to wall—that she was still torn with fury, from the vortex of which his own spirit was scarcely yet set free, as consciousness of it remained.

This would have been a staggering experience, even to one versed in psychic marvels, but of such matters Richard Quinton was completely ignorant. To him the ordeal he had passed through was as unique as it was unaccountable—a horror to have so penetrated another's being, and also in a way a thing of shame, to be covered up shuddering from the light of day. He leapt out of bed; he must seek the window, the free air, if he would not choke and die. In his rush forward it seemed as if he encountered and passed through the frantic figure that yet was invisible and disembodied; but the collision, if it was collision, affected neither: roused as he was, the grip of individuality was too strong. He tore the curtains apart, and there at last was the cool night, the serene moon, the wafting of free air, in which, behind him in the room, the lighted candles flared.

The moon was now high in heaven, the scene was bathed in white light, the shadows, where shadows fell, were black and sharply defined. The silvery mist of the earlier evening had disappeared, the light veil of it withdrawn, rolled up and swept away before that stirring of air. There was a path of reflected light across the quiet water of the pool, the headland stood out dark. And, strange to relate, from behind it again shot out the mysterious boat, the boat he had seen before, but now there were two men on board. He saw, or thought he saw, one man attack the other; for a dozen seconds they were locked together struggling. Then the rocking boat capsized and sank, and the men also disappeared.

Richard saw this, and yet in some dim way he realised that he had witnessed no actual disaster for which he need give the alarm: it was a scene projected into his mind from the mind of another. It did not even occur to him that there, within a bowshot of the house, were men drowning who might be saved. The moon-path on the water was smooth again now, undisturbed by even a ripple, the night utterly still. But a moment later the silence was broken by the same flute music which had discoursed so sweetly earlier in the night. It was, however, tuned to a livelier measure this second time, one that might accompany dancing feet. It sounded from the grove, and underneath the clear light Richard could distinguish moving figures, leaping among the trees.

There were five or six of them apparently, men or boys, and the figures looked as if naked above the waist. And the dance was not solely a dance, for they seemed to be chasing, or driving before them, some large animal which fled with leaps through the undergrowth, a goat possibly, or a sheep. The animal and the pursuing figures disappeared among the trees, and then appeared again as if they had made a circuit of the grove; the goat (if it was a goat) leaping in front, and the others pursuing. This was the end; a cloud drifted over the moon, and when it passed there was no more sign of movement in the grove, and the jocund fluting had ceased.

Richard turned back into the room, and now his perception of that fury and distress, if not wholly effaced, was dulled as if here, too, was the shadowing of a merciful cloud. But stretch himself on that bed he could not, nor address himself to sleep, lest it should be renewed with all the former horror. He would keep the lights burning, if only he had a book, he would occupy himself with reading, but literature had formed no part of his light luggage.

He might seek one in the library below, treading softly in stocking-soles so as not to disturb the sleeping house.

But as he issued forth, candle in hand, he found a burner switched on on the landing, and the dressing-gowned small doctor crossing over from an opposite door. Lindsay at once accosted him.

"Can I do anything: what is the matter?—oh, can't sleep, and want a book: is that it? I can find you one close at hand, and mine are livelier than the fossils in the library. Come this way."

Lindsay's room opened over the entrance, next to Mr. Quinton's bedchamber. A set of bookshelves filled a recess.

"Help yourself. The yellow-backs on the top shelf are French—I daresay you read French. But you'll find English ones below, and perhaps they are more likely to put you asleep." He snapped on an extra light, and then turned for a fuller scrutiny of his companion. "You look pretty bad," was his remark. "Does a sleepless night always knock you up like this? I'm doctor to the establishment you know, and I prescribe a peg. Whisky or brandy will you have? Both of them are here, and so is a syphon. Sit down while I get it ready. Three fingers—two—one? Good: you do well to be moderate. Get outside that, and you'll feel better. And then you can pick your book."

Lindsay did not question further as to the cause of disturbance, though he looked inquisitive, as if suspicions were aroused. Richard for his part remained tongue-tied, time was needed to digest and try to understand his experience: he might speak of it later on, but not now, while still his nerves were vibrating from the strain. The human companionship was, however, reassuring, and by the time the prescribed dose was swallowed, he felt altogether more normal. He inquired for Mr. Quinton, sat for a while conversing on indifferent subjects, and then departed with a book.

He did not venture again to lie down, but installed himself in a deep chair, the candles burning at his elbow. The effect of the novel may have been soporific, though he was an inattentive reader. After a long interval he fell asleep, and waked to find morning already brightening in the east.

The night was over, its perplexities and distresses had sunk into the past, and a new day had begun. It was refreshing to spirit as well as body to wash and re-clothe, to undo the bolts and chains which guarded the front door, and find himself in the free air. Though it was still the air which breathed over Mount Verney, he was delivered from the evil shadow of that roof. He retraced his steps of the day before, down the dark curving drive, out through the satyr-headed gates, to the highroad which was free to all, the road traversed by Roman legions in centuries that were past. He turned to the right, with the eastern sky behind him, and walked on, without object, but steeping himself in the freshness of the newly awakened world.

At first, he appeared to be the only person astir and observant, but presently an old man of the labouring class pushed open a gate some way ahead and came towards him, a shepherd accompanied by his dog. Richard would have liked to exchange ideas with an English working man, but felt too suddenly shy to venture on more than a good-morning as they drew abreast. The man, however, stopped and accosted him.

"Beg pardon, master, but as you came along, did you mebbe happen on a straying sheep? A ewe she is, and has taken her lamb with her, one getting on in size, as it was dropped early. Me and the dog have been after her since first it was light."

Richard had no information to give; he had not seen the ewe and her lamb. And then he bethought him.

"I stayed last night at Mount Verney, and, looking out in the moonlight, I saw a sheep leaping about in the grove, the coppice of oaks by the water. Would that be the one you have lost?

The man shook his head.

"No, sir, that would be Mr. Quinton's sheep. I drove it down myself, a prime wether, only a day ago; and my heart was sore for the poor thing. It seemed as if the dog here was sorry too, for he didna like the job. Mr. Quinton he buys one at the spring full moon, and again at harvest, of my master or one of the other breeders, always to be driven into the coppice and left there, and I doubt if ever the creatures live as much as two days. What he wants them for 'tis beyond me to say.

"Seems a waste of good meat and good wool, for it is just a hole in the field and dig them under, so I am told, and not a soul the better. Some folks will eat braxy mutton, meat being dear as it is; but not one of them would touch a sheep that had died up there in the wood, poisoned as like as not. 'Tis just a mystery to all of us. But I've no call to be passing remarks, seeing you know Mr. Quinton, and are staying at Mount Verney.

Richard might have replied with truth that he did not know Mr. Quinton, their acquaintance was still to make. But he asked instead for direction, and was told to, cross a stile to the right into a certain field-path, which would bring him out opposite the house, by the bridge over the water.

The bridge was a rustic affair of planks and a hand-rail, and beyond it the way diverged to right and left, the path on the left entering the grove, barred only by a light iron turnstile. Was it curiosity, or another sort of attraction which drew Richard thither, to see by daylight the spot on which he had looked down under the moon the night before? Now it seemed ordinary enough; the paths cut through it were grassed over and green, but here and there, where the turf was soft, he noticed they were trampled by divided hoofs, larger than those of sheep. The trees, young and slender, shorn of their lower branches, were now faintly green with unexpanded leafage; the undergrowth, which was chiefly rhododendron, was here and there breaking into purple and pinkish flower.

While still some way from it, he could distinguish among the trees the statue of which Lindsay had spoken. It was mounted on a pedestal, and was, as he said, a modern copy of the antique. Pan with his pipes in bronze, an abhorrent half-animal figure; the brooding face less repulsive perhaps than those of the satyrs at the gate, but the regard it appeared to bend on the observer who approached, had a keener expression of intelligence and evil power. Richard as he drew near, his attention riveted on that face and crouching figure, almost stumbled over an object lying at the foot of the column.

It was the dead sheep. Had it been dragged thither with a purpose, or hunted till it fell exhausted where it lay? There was no mark upon it that he could see, of the knife of the executioner, but the swollen tongue protruded from the half open jaws, and thick blood had flowed from both nostrils, staining the ground.

Truly Mount Verney was a spot where there were strange happenings. The shudder of the night again passed over Richard, and he had now no least desire to linger in the grove, or to make further discoveries. Passing through another gate he gained a steep slope of lawn, leading up to the gravelled terrace on which the windows of the library opened. His approach had been observed, and here was Lindsay waving him a cheerful greeting, with the intelligence of waiting breakfast.

3

"Been for an early ramble?—that was well done. Mr. Quinton wants you to see as much as possible of the place before he speaks to you of the future. A lovely morning. And this house stands well, does it not, above the valley? Gives you a first-rate view."

Richard assented. And then put the question he had been meditating.

"Was this house built on the site of another, do you know? The house my father used to speak about was called Quinton Court. It was built long before his father's time, and was of stone; it had a walled courtyard and mullioned windows. I don't suppose it was ever a grand mansion. But that was what I expected to find in coming down here."

"Quinton Court is still in existence; the man lives there who has the farm. It is a fine-looking old place, but I expect it has gone a long way downhill since it was given up as the family residence. You will find it about a mile from here, on the other side of the hill."

"I should like to see it. I should greatly like to see it!"

"Make it the object of your next walk. Go the length of the lake to the head water, and through the field beyond, and you will come upon a cart-road. I would show you the way, but I may have difficulty in leaving. And perhaps you would rather go alone."

That he would prefer to make the visit alone was so true that Richard left the suggestion uncontested. Lindsay passed lightly to another subject; one on which he was not improbably curious.

"I hope the novel and the 'peg' helped on to sleep? I hate to lie awake myself, but sometimes a strange bed——! There is fish, I think, under that cover. Or do you prefer bacon?"

"I am a good sleeper usually, in any sort of bed, strange or familiar. Dr. Lindsay, I am sorry to be a troublesome guest, but can I change my room? And, if you will allow me, I will do so before tonight."

"You can, without doubt. There are other guest-rooms, though with fewer advantages than the bow-room, as we call it. I will see about the exchange. But—may I be so indiscreet as to ask why? Because Mr. Quinton will put the question to me, and I had better be prepared to answer him."

"Then perhaps I may put a question on my side. I understand that bedroom has been long out of use. I know nothing about ghosts, and have never believed in them, but—it is not like other rooms. Is it supposed to be haunted? And, if so, why was it chosen for me?"

"I can't tell you much about it; remember I only came here eighteen months ago. As for why it was chosen, you must ask Mr. Quinton: it was his doing, not mine. I never heard of any ghost being seen there. The only queer thing said about the room sounds like illusion, and could not disturb a sleeper. Nor would it, I suppose, be visible at night. But perhaps you, as a Quinton, would be more sensitive than a stranger."

"What is the queer thing?"

"Why it seems absurd, but they say whoever looks through that window sees a boat on the lake. I saw something like it myself on one occasion, but I expect it is a flaw in the glass. Was there a ghost last night?"

"No ghost in the sense you mean, but such an impression of misery—and not misery only, anger—that I found sleep impossible. That is all I have to tell. If Mr. Quinton is affronted by my wish to change, I must find quarters elsewhere till he is ready to speak to me."

"Nonsense: he won't be affronted; it would be absurd. I doubt if you will see him today, but he is decidedly better, and I shall not need to sit up another night. You'll like him, I think. He has his eccentricities, that must be allowed. But you would be sorry for him from your heart if you knew all."

"He is eccentric? I heard a strange story about him this morning, from an old shepherd I met in the road. Is it true that he purchases a sheep twice a year, and that it is driven into the grove to die? There is one lying dead there now, at the foot of the statue of Pan."

Lindsay shrugged his shoulders.

"I told you he was half a pagan, and I don't defend the sheep business. That sacrifice is one of the things he wants continued, and makes a condition; but I told him straight out that no successor would pledge himself to a thing so out of reason, and you had better be firm about it when he speaks. Of course, it is natural he should wish Mount Verney kept up as the residence of the owner; there one can be in sympathy. His grandfather built it, and his father planned the grounds, and the ornamental water and all that. Odd about the lake, seeing what happened after. Why, don't you know. The elder son was drowned there. Mr. Quinton's twin brother. Archibald, his name was. He was the Quinton heir."

Richard saw again, in a flash of memory, the two figures struggling in the boat and disappearing under water; but where was the good of taking Lindsay into confidence? He had said enough, and made it plain he would occupy the room no more, nor look from it over the lake: he did not care to what sort of apartment he was transferred; it would serve him for the time, however mean.

The doctor hurried away as soon as they had breakfasted, apologising for his enforced absence, but Richard was well content to be alone. He wanted to think out the warning again given about conditions. That which concerned the sheep was unthinkable, and could hardly be pressed; but evidently there were others, by reason of which Lindsay had refused the offered heirship. If he was required to live at Mount Verney in the future, and make it his home and his wife's home—what then? In one way the prospect of the inheritance was tempting enough to him, and would be to any man—an inheritance that would at once convert him into a person of importance, with a stake in the country as the saying is; a good position to offer his wife, ample means, provision for the children that might be born to them.

But if what he began dimly to suspect was fact; if the place had somehow fallen under a curse, in pagan times or now—such a curse as affected inanimate building, and tainted the very ground—it would be no fit home for her. And Nan was not covetous of riches—she would not mind struggling on with him and being poor; she would approve, so he justly thought, of a refusal made for the sake of right.

160

There was nothing to detain him indoors, so with these cogitations in mind, he set out in the direction Lindsay had indicated, following the north shore of the artificial lake, and crossing the headland which, viewed from above, had been the departure point of the mysterious boat. On the western side of the headland, furthest from the house and half hidden by the bank, were the remains of what certainly had been a boathouse; but in these days no boat sheltered there, and the timbers of the roof had rotted and fallen in decay. He passed through the gate by the headwater, a clear and fast running stream; found and followed the cart-road, which after a while was merged in a superior approach, now well-nigh as worn and deeply rutted as the other.

He came upon the old Court suddenly, round a fold of the hill, and there he stood for a while, his heart moved by a mysterious feeling of kinship—if not utterly fantastic to suppose flesh and blood can feel itself akin to walls of stone. The old homestead had fallen from its first estate, but there was a dignity about it still, the dignity of fine proportion and high quality, differing widely from the jerry building of today. The grey gables were there as of old, the roof of slabbed stone, the panes of diamond lattice; there the flagged courtyard with its breast-high boundary wall, and five of the six urns mounted in place; the sixth had fallen, and lay broken at the foot.

The front door was fast shut, an oak door studded with iron, but Richard drew near and knocked, treading the very stones the footsteps of the dead had worn. Why, why had the later degenerates forsaken this dear place, and fixed their abode at Mount Verney?

A neatly-dressed young woman opened to him, and looked inquiringly at the stranger.

"I'm sorry, sir, my father is not in, if so be as you come seeking him."

No, Richard said, that was not his errand; but might he be allowed to see inside the house, if only a couple of the rooms?

"Why certainly, if you are thinking of taking the place. I didn't know as it had got about that we are leaving, but news do fly apace. But we shall not be out until September."

"My name is Quinton, and I am from Canada. My great-grand-father lived here, and it was here that my grandfather was born. I am anxious to see the Court now I am in England. If you would be so good as to allow——"

"Come in, sir, and look where you like; you are kindly welcome. My father would make you so I know, for he is the oldest tenant on

161

the estate. We have no fault to find with the place, but the farm is too big for father now he has no son with him, and the house too large for us too. I am the only one at home, and mother is laid by with the rheumatics. These long stone passages take a lot of cleaning, to say nothing of the many rooms, though more than half of them we shut away."

So, upon this invitation Richard had his wish, and saw over the house upstairs and down. In some of the rooms put out of use there were still pieces of old furniture, Quinton property, his guide told him: an oak chest or two, corner cupboards with carven doors, a worm-eaten dresser, chairs in the last stage of decrepitude. They were let with the house, having been thought unworthy of removal to Mount Verney. In the best parlour sacks of grain were stored, and on the threshold of two of the empty bedrooms he was warned to step warily, as the floors were thought to be unsafe.

Quinton Court had fallen from its first estate, but it was still lovely in the eyes of this late descended son. It had been cleanly kept, however roughly, and there was an air of purity about its homeliness, of open casements and scents of lavender and apples. He could picture his Nan here, a happy house-mistress under the ancient roof of his forefathers; but not as the chatelaine of Mount Verney with all its wealth: never at Mount Verney. Ah, if only Mr. Quinton would make this place his bequest to the next heir, the old Court and the surrounding farm which he might work for a living; and leave Quinton Verney and his accumulated thousands, where else and to whom else he pleased!

4

Such were Richard's thoughts as he walked back along the green shores of the lake, and under the mid-day sun. He and the doctor were again *tête-à-tête* at luncheon; but he was told Mr. Quinton desired to see him that afternoon in his private room above stairs; also, that he intended to dine with them, being greatly better than the day before. So, the first interview with his host came about earlier than he had been led to expect.

The appearance of his elderly cousin took him by surprise. Mr. Clement Quinton was strikingly handsome, though older-looking than his two and fifty years. He might have been taken for a man advanced in the seventies, though his tall thin figure was still upright. He owned a thick thatch of grey hair, a close-cut white beard, and bushy grey eyebrows above eyes of steely blue, rather unnaturally wide open.

He welcomed Richard cordially, shaking him by the hand: a cold hand, his was, and yet the younger man felt uncomfortably, the instant they were palm to palm, that he touched something sticky and moist. Mr. Quinton's left hand was gloved, and Richard remembered after that he held a dark silk handkerchief in the other while they talked together.

There was nothing embarrassing or noteworthy about the earlier conversation. Mr. Quinton appeared kindly interested in Richard's past history, asking about his father and home, how he had been educated and where, and also the details of his military service. They had been talking together for half an hour, before any reference was made to the future.

"I want you to be interested in this place," he said with emphasis. "I want you to be particularly interested. For there are various things I am bound to leave to the doing of others, and much will depend on their punctual carrying on. It will smooth my pillow—as the saying is—if I may be assured of the co-operation of my successor."

This was not very easy to answer, as Richard could not assume successorship on a hint so vague. So, he struck out into an account of his visit to Quinton Court, and pleasure over the discovery that the old house of which his grandfather had spoken with affection, was still solidly existent.

"I was afraid it had been pulled down, and Mount Verney built on its site."

"No, we destroyed nothing. My respect for antiquity is too great. As I will show you later, it has been my great desire to—call back into life, I may say—associations from the dead past of an earlier period still. Traces of what had been, were thick on the ground hereabouts: you shall have the complete history of how, and why, and what. You will find it remarkable indeed. I will tell you frankly, my young cousin, it is here and on Mount Verney I want your interest focussed. This place dates back to the Roman occupation of Britain, and in comparison, with the relics here, Quinton Court is but a thing of yesterday."

"Dr. Lindsay told me Roman remains had been unearthed. I think he said some portions of a pavement."

"There was a villa here, on this very spot; baths in the valley, with the water running through them; and an altar where you see the grove, which was once a dense thicket of wood. I have other means of knowing, besides conclusions drawn from the fragments that remain, and these communications the excavations have strikingly confirmed.

I was directed where to dig. There was a special cult connected with this place. The worship of Pan."

"I observed the statue in the grove."

"It marks the site of the old altar. Pan is a deity about whom little has been known and much mistaken. From the sources of information at my command, I have compiled a treatise. And that is one thing I require of my successor. If unpublished at the time of my decease, I wish it given to the world."

The posthumous publication of a treatise! It would be well if other conditions were no more formidable than this.

"Some writers have made the mistake of confounding Pan with Faunus; surely an extraordinary error. My theory is entirely different. Cain was his prototype. Cain."

Here the recluse seemed to be stirred by some inward excitement, and he got up to pace the room.

"Cain!" he repeated." Of course, you know the scriptural narrative, and probably little else about that founder of an early race. There are mistakes in that account—it is libellous, the fabrication of an enemy. Eve put about unworthy slanders. If Cain did truly kill his brother, it was in self-defence, or in a fury of panic anger: I say if, for I do not allow it to be the truth. Abel, the favourite, was a sneak and a coward, and he knew whatever lie he set up, so long as it was against the other, would stand as unassailable truth. He was better blotted out, than left to be the father of a degenerate race. Cain was at least a man—— And it is said the Lord put a mark on him. What did that mean, think you?"

"I have not the least idea. Does anybody know?"

"I know this much, that it was the curse of the partly animal form. Cain was crippled into that likeness, and some of his sons took after him. Not the daughters, for they were in the likeness of Eve. And it is on record that they were beautiful. The sons of God saw the daughters of men that they were fair. But that does not come into the argument, nor concern us now. It was because of the mark set on him that Pan loved solitary places, the cool depths of caves and the shadow of woods. It was he in the beginning, and not Abel, who was the keeper of flocks. Abel did nothing but laze in the sun and watch the fruits ripen, and then gather them for an offering. I told you that the record lied. Do you wonder how I know all this?"

Richard could do nothing but assent.

"I will tell you—show you. I wish to instruct you in my methods, that they may be yours hereafter. It is not all who have the gift of sight.

164

Lindsay is psychically blind. But something tells me you have it, or will have it. Come here with me."

He opened a door and showed an inner, smaller room, probably intended as a dressing-closet in the original design of the house. There was a writing-table and chair in the sole window, but the only other furniture was a high stand, on which was some object covered over with black velvet drapery. Mr. Quinton turned back part of the covering, and directed, Richard to seat himself before it. The lifted flap revealed the smooth and shining surface of a large crystal, or ball of glass, set into a frame.

"You know what this is, and what its use? I want to test whether I can make a scryer of you. The black cloth is used only to prevent confusing lights. Now look steadily into the crystal, and tell me what you see."

Richard looked, in some amusement and complete incredulity.

"I see the reflection of my own face," he said presently. "Nothing more. Except—yes—something which looks like smoke."

"Go on looking, and be patient. There will be more."

As Richard gazed, his own reflection disappeared, the smoke cleared away, and there were the gates of the avenue with the leering faces, exactly as he saw them the day before. Then the cloud of smoke returned, blotting them out; cleared again, and showed the spy of the evening, peering in at the window of the dining-room. Succeeding this, came the scene of the grove by moonlight, with the figures leaping among the trees, and driving the doomed sheep.

"I am seeing a procession of scenes," he replied to a further question. "But only what are in my mind and memory. Nothing new."

"Go on looking," was again the command. "What is new will come."

The next scene was, as Richard half expected, the grove as he entered it that morning, with the statue of Pan on its pedestal, and the sheep before it lying dead. This persisted, not small as dwarfed within the limits of the ball, but now as if a window opened before him on the actual scene. But a change was taking place in the figure of the god. The bronze seemed to soften and warm into flesh, the terrible, wise face was no longer serene and meditative, the eyes looked into his, and now there was mockery in them, revelling in his surprise. The thing was alive, moving, surely about to descend.

But no. The figure, without leaving its pedestal, stretched out one hairy ape-like arm, and clutched the body of the sheep, drawing it up to rest on his crossed hocks, while the mocking face bent closer, as if to snuff or lick the blood. Was the monstrous creature about to tear the victim open, ready to devour? The action of the hands looked like it.

Richard could look no longer. A sweat of horror broke out over him, and stood in beads on his forehead; he started up gasping for air.

"Let me go," he cried out wildly: "let me go!"

Mr. Quinton replaced the velvet covering.

"That is enough for today," he said. "I am sufficiently answered. You can see."

Richard hardly knew how he got out of the room, whether it was by Mr. Quinton's dismissal or his own will. Or how long a time elapsed before, finding himself alone, he happened to look at the palm of his right hand, which had felt curiously sticky after contact with Mr. Quinton's. The smear on it was dry and easily effaced by washing, but without doubt what he had touched was blood.

Mr. Quinton seemed to have been in no way affronted by Richard's abrupt withdrawal. He was in a genial mood when he joined the two younger men at dinner, now with his loose wrapping gown put off, and faultlessly attired in evening dress. A handsome man; and Richard noticed that his hands were beautifully shaped and white. But, to the guest's vision, there was one striking peculiarity about his appearance, a peculiarity which seemed to increase as the meal went forward. Perhaps the opening of Richard's clairvoyance, artificially induced some hours before, had not wholly closed. For doubtless what he now perceived, would not have been visible to ordinary sight.

Most of us in these later days have heard of the existence of *auras*, a species of halo which is supposed to emanate from every mortal, indicative of spiritual values and degrees of power; but it is doubtful whether our backwoodsman was aware. What he saw, however, was an *aura*, though formed of shadow and not light. It encompassed the seated figure of his host with a surrounding of grey haze, spreading to a yard or more from either shoulder, and equally above the head; not obstructing the view of the room behind him, but dimming it, as might a stretched veil of grey crape.

It was curious to see Peters waiting on him and passing through this, evidently unaware; his hand and the bottle advancing into the full light as he filled Mr. Quinton's glass, and then withdrawing to leave the veil as perfect as before. Mr. Quinton made an excellent dinner, and chaffed Richard on his want of appetite; he also drank freely of the wines Peters was handing round, and pressed them on his guests. The glasses were particularly elegant, of Venetian pattern, slender stemmed and fragile.

Peters had just replenished his master's glass, when Mr. Quinton in the course of argument, lifted and brought it down sharply on the table with the result of breakage. The accident attracted little notice; Peters cleared away the fragments and mopped up the spilt wine, and another glass was set in its place and filled. But as Mr. Quinton raised the fresh glass to his lips, Richard noticed that blood was dripping from his right hand in heavy spots, staining his shirt-cuff and the cloth.

"I am afraid, sir, you have cut yourself," he exclaimed impulsively; and almost at the same instant Peters appeared at his master's elbow offering a dark silk handkerchief.

Mr. Quinton did not answer, but uttered an exclamation of annoyance, and abruptly rose from table and left the room. Lindsay followed him, but presently returned, looking unusually grave. Richard inquired if the cut was serious.

"Mr. Quinton did not cut his hand," Lindsay answered. "I am charged to tell you what is the matter. Though it is as far as possible kept secret, he thinks it better you should know."

The gravity of Lindsay's countenance did not relax. He poured out half a glass of wine and drank it, as if to nerve himself for the telling of the tale.

"When I came here as resident doctor eighteen months ago, I heard the story: it was, of course, necessary I should be informed as I had to treat his case. I shall have to go a long way back to make you understand. Lady Anna, Quinton's mother, had twin sons, born shortly after her husband's death. She must have been a strange woman. They were her only children, but almost from infancy she made a difference between them, setting all her affection on Archibald, the elder, and treating the other, Clement, with coldness and every evidence of dislike.

"Quinton says he can never remember his mother caressing him, or even speaking kindly. He was always the one held to blame for any childish fault or mischief, and pushed into the background, while everything was for Archibald the heir. We cannot wonder that this folly of hers led to bad feeling between the lads. It was active in their school days, though they were educated at different schools, and met only in the holidays. Whenever they met, they fought. What the last quarrel was about I cannot say, but Archibald was entering an expensive regiment, and the army could not be afforded for Clement, though it was his great desire: he owns to having been very sore. They were in a boat on the lake, and they fought there, and the boat capsized.

"It was said that Archibald hadn't a chance; he had been stunned by a blow on the head, or else had struck his head in falling. They both could swim a little, but he went down like a stone, and Clement reached the shore: the distance could not have been great, nor could one have expected such an accident to result in anything worse than a ducking. The horrible part of it was that Lady Anna saw what happened from her window in the bow room."

"Ah!"

"Yes, the room you had, and where you were disturbed last night. She saw the fight and the struggle, and was convinced of Clement's guilt: that he had plotted the occasion and killed Archibald, so that he might take his place. She wanted to have the boy tried for murder; ay, and would have had her way, had it not been for her brother, Lord Pengwyn, who was guardian to both the lads. He got the thing passed over as an accident, as no doubt it was. But the point I am coming to, though I've been long about it, is this. When Clement was drawn from the water, and brought in, sick and dazed.

"Lady Anna met him in a fury of passion. He was Cain over again, the first murderer who slew his brother: I wonder, did Eve do the like! 'Your brother's blood,' she said, 'will be upon your hands for ever.' Quinton says he would not have cared, after that, if they had hung him then and there. He had an illness, and the palms of his hands began to bleed—from the pores as it were, without a wound—and they have continued to bleed at intervals from that day to this. You saw what happened tonight."

"It sounds like a miracle. Is there no cure?"

"Everything has been tried—styptics, hypnotism even. Sometimes the symptom remits for two or three weeks, and the bleeding is generally early in the day; he thought himself safe this evening. Miracle? no, unless the power of the mind over the body is held to be miraculous. You have read of the stigmatists—women, ay and men too—on whom the wounds of Christ have broken out, to bleed always on Fridays?"

"I have heard of them—certainly. But I set it down as a fraud—a monkish trick."

"It is as well vouched for as any other physical phenomenon. And this case of Quinton's is nearly allied, though horror created it in his case, and not saintly adoration. It has spoiled his life; for over thirty years he has been an invalid, and will so continue to the end. His aberration of mind has all arisen from this root: his queer fancies about Cain and Pan, blood-sacrifices to Pagan gods—satyrs and fauns and hobgoblins, and I know not what!"

"You speak of aberration, and yet assert that he is sane?"

"He is sane enough for all practical purposes—a good man of business even, with a sharp eye to the main chance. Take him apart from these cranks of his, I like him—I can't help liking him. You'll like him too, when you know him better. You have seen the least attractive side of him, coming down like this, with the misgiving he is driving you into a corner. I'd have you stand up to him and speak your mind about what you will and will not do. And I believe he will hear reason in the end."

★★★★★★★★★★★★★★★★★

Next morning's post brought Richard a letter, forwarded on from London: a notice requiring his appearance before a certain Medical Board, and obliging his return to town. He sent a message to Mr. Quinton by Lindsay, explaining his abrupt departure, but saying he was willing to return if desired. The reply message requested an interview, in the same upstairs room as before.

It proved to be a long one. Lindsay, waiting in the hall for the car to come round, wondered what was the delay, and what was passing between the two. At last, a door in the upper regions opened and shut, and Richard came down the stairs. He was white as chalk, staggering like a man dizzy or blind, and a cold sweat stood in beads on his forehead, as happened after the scrying of the day before. Lindsay sprang forward to meet him, and propped him with a hand under his arm. He leaned against the wall, and gasped out:

"It's all over—I've refused—you were right to refuse too. The thing he asks is impossible. This house is full of devils—of devils, I tell you—and they come out of Quinton's crystal. He made me look again—against my will, and I saw—what I can't speak of—what I never can forget!"

"Come into the dining-room with me, and I'll give you a dram. You have been upset; you may think differently when you are calm."

"No—no. Never this place for me. He is beyond reason: he is given over to the fiend. I told him I would thank him for ever for just Quinton Court and a farm, but he would not part the property. It had to be all or nothing. And not even to gain Quinton Court would I be owner here. No, I'll have no dram. I want to get away."

The car was now heard coming round, and drawing up at the door.

169

"Goodbye, Lindsay, and thank you for your kindness. We may never meet again, but I shall not forget."

These were last words, and the next moment he was shut in and speeding away, the open gates with their watchful faces left behind.

5

Richard reached London only to fall ill. The doctor diagnosed influenza, but seemed to think his system had received a shock: as to this he was not communicative. He had a week in bed, and another of tardy convalescence, a prey to depression and all the ills resulting from exhaustion. A fortnight had gone by since he left Mount Verney, when he received a communication from Fryer and Fryer asking for an interview. Mr. Fryer wished to see Mr. Richard Quinton on a matter of business, and would be obliged if he could make it convenient to call.

"I ought to have written to the old bird, to tell him I am out of the running," was Richard's comment, spoken to himself. "But, as I have been remiss, I had better go and hear what he has to say. I shall have to take a taxi."

He had no strength left for the walking distance, and even the office stairs were something of a trial. He was shown in at once to Mr, Fryer, and began with an apology.

"I have only just ascertained your address," said the man of law. "Are you aware, Mr. Quinton, that your cousin and late host is dead?"

"Indeed no, sir, I was not aware." And that Richard was shocked by the intelligence was plain to see.

"He died suddenly of heart-failure the night after you left. And, so far as Dr. Lindsay and I can ascertain after a careful search through all his papers, he has left no will"

This communication did not seem to inform Richard; he was still too dazed by what he had just heard.

Mr. Fryer tapped the blotting-pad before him, which was a way he had when irritated.

"You don't realise what that means? The whole property goes to you, both real estate and personal. Mount Verney, and all that it contains."

Richard gave a cry, which sounded more like horror than elation.

"You are telling me—that I am the owner of Mount Verney?"

"If no will is discovered later, certainly you are the owner."

"And does this bind me to live there? Because I cannot—I will not. I told Mr. Quinton so before leaving, and, as he made it a condition, I refused the inheritance."

"So, I understand from Dr. Lindsay. No, you are bound to nothing. You can live where you please. And, as soon as the legal processes of succession are gone through, you can sell the property, should you prefer investment abroad."

Richard still sat half-stunned, slowly taking it in. He could rid himself of Mount Verney and all that it contained, and Quinton Court, the home of his desire, would be his own.

"You would have wished, of course, to attend your cousin's funeral, but you had quitted the address left with me, and we were unable to let you know in time. He was cremated, according to his own often-expressed desire. There is one thing, Mr. Quinton, I would like to say to you—to suggest, though you may think I am exceeding my province. Your cousin's intestacy benefits you, but there are others who suffer by it. Old Peters, a servant who had been with him from boyhood: he would have been provided for without doubt. Probably there would have been gratuities to the other domestics, according to their length of service; and his resident doctor, Lindsay, would have come in for a legacy. Of course it is quite at your option what to do."

"I will thank you, sir, to put down what you would have advised Mr. Quinton in all these cases, had you prepared his will, and I will make it good."

It was not always easy to divine Mr. Fryer's sentiments, but he seemed to receive the instruction with pleasure. Lawyer and client shook hands, and then Richard was in the street again, hurrying away. O, what a letter—what a letter he would have to write to Nan!

★★★★★★★★★★★★★★★★★

Legal processes take time, and summer was waning into autumn before Richard was fully established as owner of the Quinton property. Up to now he had sedulously avoided Mount Verney, though he had been in the near neighbourhood, and had several times visited Quinton Court. He knew only by the agent's report that his orders were carried out, the heads removed from the gate-pillars and the statue from the grove, which was a grove no longer, as the young oaks had been felled and carted away.

The Roman relics had been presented to a local museum, and the house was now shut up, and emptied of most of its furniture. Lindsay, at Richard's desire, had chosen such of the plenishings as he cared for and could make useful, receiving these in addition to the money gift advised by Mr. Fryer.

All this was accomplished, the last load removed, and now the big white villa was shut up and vacant, and Clement Quinton's heir was about to enter for the first time as its possessor. But, strange to say, he had elected to make the visit late at night and in secret, so planning his approach across country that his coming and going might be unnoticed and unknown. A thief's visit, one would have said, rather than that of the lawful owner, who could have commanded all.

The latter part of the journey was made on foot, and throughout he carried with him, under his own eye and hand, a large and heavy gladstone-bag. He had studied incendiary methods when serving in France, and materials for swift destruction were contained within.

It was a wild evening; a gale, forestalling the equinox, hurtled overhead, tearing the clouds into shreds as they flew before it, and making clear spaces for some shining of stars. Rain was not yet, though doubtless it would fall presently. The wind would help Richard's purpose, rain would not, though he thought it could hardly defeat it. That intermittent shining of the stars gave little light. The night was very nearly "as dark as hell's mouth," and Richard had much the feeling that he was venturing into the mouth of hell.

It had needed the mustering of a desperate courage, this expedition on which he was bent, but he could entrust his purpose to no other hand. Purification by fire: there could be, it seemed to him, no other cleansing. He intended no oblation to the infernal gods, that was far from his thought: what he dimly designed was a final breaking of their power.

With this purpose in mind he turned into the dark avenue, the shut gates yielding to his hand, between the pillars from which the satyrs' heads were gone. Did faces pry on him from between the close-ranked trees? He would not think of it: and for this night at least he would shut the eyes of his soul, the eyes with which he had perceived before, or he might happen upon something which would make him altogether a coward. In the darkness he left the road more than once, and blundered into the plantation, needing to have recourse to the electric torch in his pocket before he could find the way. But at last, he came upon the open sweep of drive, and there was the villa before him, stark and white, eyeless and shuttered, the corpse of a house from which the soul had gone out.

This new owner had been careful to carry with him the keys which, admitted. He unlocked a side door and entered, and now the torch was a necessity in the pitch darkness which prevailed within. His first act was to go through the lower rooms, unshuttering and opening everywhere, so as to let in a free draught of air. Here a certain amount of the heavier furniture still remained: Lindsay had been moderate in his selection, though he might, with Richard's approval, have grasped at all. Then he mounted to the attics, opening as he went, and here the incendiary work started. The flames were beginning to creep over the floors and about the back staircase, when he turned his attention to the better apartments on the first floor, entering and igniting one after another. He left Mr. Quinton's private rooms until the last; the rooms where those momentous interviews had taken place, and where the devils had issued from the glass.

The private den had been wholly stripped, both of furniture and books; no doubt Lindsay, who was free to take what he pleased, had valued these mementoes of a patient who was also a friend. Richard was glad to find the apartment empty; there was less to recall the past. But as he moved the illuminating torch from left to right in his survey, it seemed to him for an instant that a tall figure stood before him—long enough to realise its presence, though gone in the space of a couple of agitated heartbeats. He never doubted that it was Quinton, present to reproach him, to arrest the course of destruction if that were possible. But in spite of what he had seen—if indeed he did see—he gritted his teeth and went on.

The inner cabinet was next to enter. Here nothing had been removed or changed; the writing-table in the window still had its equipment of inkpot and blotting-pad, and on the latter, Richard noticed, a sheet of blank paper was spread out. The velvet cover thrown over the high stand, no doubt concealed the uncanny crystal into which he had been forced to look. No one would look into it again after the destruction of this night! And then somehow, he knew not how, his attention was drawn to the white paper on the table.

Most of us have seen the development of a photographic plate, and how magically the image starts into view on a surface which before was blank. That was what appeared to happen under his eyes upon the paper, and the image was the imprint of a large hand, a man's hand, red as if dipped in blood.

The same awful sensation of sick faintness experienced before with the crystal, overcame him once again. It was a marvel to him afterwards that he did not fall unconscious, to perish in the burning house. He saved himself by a desperate effort of will, flinging what was left of his incendiary material behind him on the floor. As he gained the staircase, a rush of air met him from below, and this was perhaps his salvation. But the house was now filling with smoke, and from the upper regions came already the crackle of spreading flame.

The crackle of flame, and something more. Something which sounded like the clatter of hoofs over bare floors, and a cackle of hellish laughter; unless his senses were by this time wholly dazed and confused, hearing bewitched as well as sight. He found the door by which he entered, locked it behind him and fled into the night, now no longer bewilderingly dark, but faintly illuminated by the rising moon.

He did not take the direction of the avenue and the road, but climbed fences and made his way up the hill behind; and when on the wind-swept summit he turned to look back. He had done his work effectually; the white villa was alight in all its windows, fiercely ablaze within, and, as he still lingered and watched, a portion of the roof fell in, and flame and smoke shot up into the sky.

From the local paper of the following Saturday.

We regret to state that the mansion of Mount Verney, recently the residence of the late Clement Quinton, Esquire, and now the property of Mr. Richard Quinton, was destroyed by fire on Tuesday night. The origin of the fire is wrapped in mystery, as the house was unoccupied and shut up, and the electric light disconnected, so there could have been no fusion of wires. Much valuable property is destroyed, and part of the building is completely gutted. The blaze was first noticed between twelve and one o'clock, by a man driving home late from market. He gave notice to the police, but by the time the fire-engines arrived, the conflagration had taken such bold that it could not be checked, though abundant water was at hand in the Mount Verney lake. The loss to Mr. Richard Quinton will be very considerable, as we understand no part of it is covered by insurance.

From the same-paper in the following December.

We understand that a gift has been made to our hospital fund, of the shell of the Mount Verney house with the grounds that surround it, to be converted into a sanatorium for the treatment of tuberculosis, and Mr. Richard Quinton also adds to the subscription list the sum of £1,000. This munificent donation of money and a site, will enable the work to be put in hand at once; and it is believed that what is left of the original mansion can be incorporated in the scheme.

The Mount Verney house, which, as will be remembered, was destroyed by a disastrous fire about three months ago, was not insured, and Mr. Richard Quinton had no wish to rebuild for his own occupation. He will, we understand, make his future residence at Quinton Court, the ancestral home of his family, so soon as he returns from Canada with his bride.

The Pipers of Mallory

1

While my last letter was flying out to you in India, dear Margaret, and your reply flying back to me, a great deal has been happening.

My last letter was all about Jack, wasn't it?—how we met and fell in love and how he was under orders for the war, and so we had to be married in a desperate hurry—such a hurry that it shocked Aunt Winifred, glad as she was to get rid of me.

I told you what I was going to wear, and Jack says I made rather a nice-looking bride (he put it more strongly than that). He was, of course, in khaki, and looked dearer than ever, and half an hour or less turned me into Mrs. Frazer. We had only nine days for our honeymoon instead of the three weeks we hoped for, but they were nine lovely days. Then there was the dreadful going away; but, before that came about, the question had to be settled—the question you ask, my dear cousin—what was to become of me while Jack was away in France fighting those horrible Huns?

It was over this Jack and I had our first difference—not a serious difference, for we kissed and made it up at once—when I found out what he wanted me to do. He actually wished me to make my home with his mother in Scotland—fancy that—to bury myself for months and months in the wilds with a woman I did not know, who would be worse than Aunt Winifred twice over. I had never been free in my life, but always in leading-strings, and I made up my mind I would be free now, quite on my own, to make up for what I should suffer through Jack being away.

I didn't tell Jack that—about wanting to be emancipated, he would not have understood. I told him what was quite true—that I wanted to make my V.A.D. training of use, and do war work of sorts in a London hospital, like Violet Power. And my plan was that Violet and I should take a flat together, a tiny flat, which would cost next to nothing (I thought), near enough to her hospital to be convenient, a hospital which needed helpers, and would find work for me, too.

Jack did not like it. Dear fellow! He is one of the old-fashioned sort who thinks women should be hedged about and protected, and give themselves up to looking after their household concerns; but he gave in when he saw I was determined.

That was nearly at the end of our time together—our lovely time. He had planned to take me up to Mallory, to say goodbye at the end of his leave, but having to go off suddenly altered that. However, he made me promise I would go there alone as soon as he left, to pay my mother-in-law a long visit before I settled down with Violet in the flat. Over that I was obliged to yield (with some private reservation about the long), for, as you will understand, I could not say "No" to him just then.

Well, we parted, and it was a hard parting. He put me in the night train for the North, before he left to cross over to France. Peters, his mother's servant, was to meet me in Edinburgh and take care of me from there; you see, I could not get away from the "take care."

Now you will know from my letter, the "Jack" letter, that I had never seen Lady Heron. She is always more or less of an invalid, and bronchitis, or something like that, prevented her taking the long journey to be present at our wedding. Fancy having attacks of bronchitis, and yet living up there in the North! She has been a widow for many years, and Jack is her only son; there is a son by a former marriage, Jack's half-brother, who is now Lord Heron. The Frazers are poor in these days, but Jack's mother has an income of her own, though I do not think it is a large one. Mallory is the old family place—mind you pronounce it right—Mal-lory, and not the other way. I suppose Lady Heron would not live there if Heron married, but he is still a bachelor, and with the regiment somewhere in France. Jack does not say much about his half-brother. I fancy the two are not very good friends.

Peters was waiting for me on the Edinburgh station, and by that time I was feeling rather better, and able to take an interest in what was new. Breakfast was ready for me at an hotel, with no bill for it, as Peters paid everything. I was "her leddyship's guest," he said, and it was by Lady Heron's orders; he seemed quite hurt when I offered. A very good breakfast it was, and I was hungry, for I had been far too wretched to eat any dinner the night before. Then, after rest and refreshment, I had to sally forth again to a different station, Peters carrying my hand-luggage. And when we gained the street—that wonderful street

178

with the Castle opposite, standing up grey against the morning sky—there was a skirl of wild music coming towards us, with the tramp of marching feet.

A skirl. That is the right word for bagpipes, as perhaps you know. I daresay you have heard them in India, as there are Scottish regiments there, but I had never heard them before. Their music may be barbaric—people say so; but there is something about it that fires the blood—that fired my blood, though I am only a Scotswoman married and not born. I could understand how it put spirit into the tired feet which were following, muddy from a long route march, as they kept time to the swing and beat of the brave tune. Jack belongs to a Highland regiment, of course, the same that Heron is in. And at the moment I felt prouder than ever to be Jack's wife.

"I suppose Lady Heron has a piper at Mallory, has she not?"

It was the first question I had put to Peters. I had the notion that a piper must be a necessary appendage to every Highland family of importance; Lady Heron would not of course detain a young man, but she might so employ some old retainer, past the age to be of service in the war. But the servant shook his head. He, too, is quite elderly—did I say?—and speaks broad Scotch, though his name might as well be English.

"No, mom," he answered, "we hef no piper at Mallory. Her leddyship does not like the pipes."

Not like the pipes! How odd of her, I thought. And upon this scrap of information the latent opposition which I had felt towards Jack's mother from the beginning swelled and took shape. How strange of a woman who had soldier sons—a son and a stepson—and who wrote as if she were proud of them and their calling; and of one who I knew from Jack was Highland bred to the backbone!

Throughout the journey north-west, now with great hills looming up through mist, now by the side of rushing streams, I was thinking of my mother-in-law, and how much easier it would have been to meet her for the first time if Jack had gone with me to Mallory. I was afraid of her, to tell the truth, and that made me brace myself beforehand to be defiant, picturing a great lady who would stand on her dignity, and think Jack might have done better for himself than in marrying me, an Englishwoman of no particular family and small fortune. She would condemn, she would dictate, she would want to interfere.

The day wore on; the train was not a fast one, and there were frequent stoppages, and every hour Peters would come to the window to know whether I wanted anything. But at last, there came the station where we alighted for Mallory.

There was a car to meet us, and in less than half an hour Mallory came into view. Not the fine place I had been picturing to myself, only a moderate-sized country house, but possessing a tower with corner-turrets in the Scottish fashion, which gives it some distinction. The rest of the house is low, with thick walls of undoubted antiquity. The windows are small, but beyond them there are lovely views.

It was only a confused impression I derived from that first entrance—of a hall warm with firelight, decorated with heads of beasts, and skins and weapons, of a room beyond, also warm, and of a frail little lady rising from her chair at the window, and coming lamely across to greet me with an embrace and a kiss.

Such a frail little lady to be the mother of a great, strong man like Jack She, like the house, was not what I expected, but I was right in two particulars. She is *grande dame* to the finger-tips, and I am certain she views me critically.

2

On further acquaintance I like Lady Heron better than I expected, and I have been able to express myself somewhat enthusiastically in writing to Jack; this will please him. I would give a good deal to know what her letter—the long letter I saw her writing—said to him about me. She is kind to me, painstakingly kind, but still, we are strangers to each other, and I think it likely we shall be strangers to the end. That she is fond of Jack ought to knit a bond between us, but somehow, I strongly suspect it is the very thing which holds us apart.

She is always testing and appraising me, though not in the way I expected; she tells me little anecdotes of Jack's youth, and watches to see if I receive them with the enthusiasm I ought; she shows me some cherished pictures—stupid, old- fashioned photographs—of Jack as a baby, Jack as a toddler learning to walk, and upwards at various stages of his boyhood. It is plainly my duty to care about these, but I don't particularly; they seem too far removed from the Jack I know. The pictures bore me, and I shudder inwardly when a new anecdote is presented. And, sitting here in the chair of truth, I must confess it—I find Mallory dull.

My chief amusement is going out for rambles by myself, rambles Lady Heron is too lame to share; she can only walk up and down the terrace with her stick by way of exercise, and that at the sunniest time of the day. The surroundings here are certainly beautiful, and the Highland people interest me. I talk to them when I have a chance, and try to get accustomed to their way of speech. It was from one of these Highlanders I found out the reason why Lady Heron does not like the pipes.

I never put the question to her. I do not know why not, as it would have been a simple thing to ask, but whenever it came into my head, something happened to divert the thought and keep the words unspoken. But that thrilling pibroch heard in Edinburgh seemed to haunt me here at Mallory, though not always the same tune. I dreamt of it the first night I was here; it waked me from sleep, as a real thing might have done but when I listened in the deep, country stillness and the darkness of the unfamiliar room, there was not a sound. And each time I walked in the direction of Glen Fruin I heard it with my waking ears, very faint and far in the distance, but I could be certain it was there.

I went some way up the Glen on the third occasion, hoping to get nearer to the sound, but it seemed to recede as I approached; the preliminary skirl, and two or three bars of a tune, as if the musician were practicing, and then a fault and silence. Presently my watch warned me I should return, for Mallory is a punctual household, and Lady Heron would be waiting tea. I was well on my way home when I met an old shepherd I had spoken to before, and, as I still heard the music at intervals, I bethought myself to ask him:

"Who is it about here who plays the pipes? Somebody is practicing away there in the Glen."

Highland fashion, he met my question by another, and his shaggy brows drew together.

"You be the leddy Frazer, be you not?" I was Mrs. Frazer, I told him.

"Eh, weel, ye are Frazer married, and so have a right to hear. 'Tisn't lucky for the Frazers when the pipes are sounding in Glen Fruin, but the Lord be thankit that they don't come lower down! I do not look to hear them mysel', being nobbut Steenson that was once Macgregor."

This was pretty well Greek to me.

"Why isn't it good for the Frazers?" I demanded.

"Ye've never heard the legend? Mebbe 'tis not for the likes of me to tell ye, but seeing as ye ask—Time gone by the chief of the Frazers had his pipers equal with the best, always seven of them in his tail, and callants growing up to take the place—and a proud place it was—of them as were short-winded or old. Glen Fruin was full of folk in those days, where there's nought now but a wheen ruins, or a square in the green to mark where walls have been. And custom was that Frazer's pipers should be chosen from the Glen Fruin folk.

"That was a time of battles, same as now, and the Frazers were up in arms. I don't mind the name of the battle, no, nor how long ago, but there was a great slaughter, and the Frazers fell to a man, and the pipers with their chief. It is said there was none to fill their places, for the callants had not been instructed, and the head of the clan was nobbut a wailing Cairn. And since that day the Frazers have had no pipers—the Frazers of Mallory. Mebbe that is why the dead men are not content, and when a Frazer is about to die, they are heard piping in Glen Fruin."

I am putting down the old man's words as nearly as I remember them, but I daresay I spell them wrong. As I listened a cold shiver went down my spine and crept among the roots of my hair; if my hair had been undone, I think it would have stood up with fright.

"Why, you don't mean to say," I stammered—"you don't mean to tell me that what I have been hearing is a ghost? A ghost in broad daylight and in the open air! And who is it who is going to die?"

"You needn't be afeared, my leddy, for him as is your own. There's a many Frazers at the war besides, and the pipers pipe the same for a death in bed. There's John Frazer near his end at the Mill, and mebbe 'tis for him. He has a son fighting, and Donald Frazer, farmer, has two more. Ye need na fear for the heads of the clan, or for their women-folk, unless the pipers come right down to Mallory, and go round the house."

"Do they come as close as that?" I asked, shuddering.

"Ay, my leddy, that they do. And they are heard by all of the Frazer name, and sometimes by them as are not so called, but I never heard tell of their being seen. It is just a sound and no more, sometimes a lament on the pipes, sometimes a fine march for them as fall. And they go once round for a woman, and twice for the heir, and three times for the head of the clan. They went three times round the house when the late lord died, and there was many who heard them, together with my Leddy Heron hersel'. And ever since then she hasna been able to bear the pipes, the real pipes, and they are warned not to come nigh."

After that I wondered no more at what Peters had told me in Edinburgh. The faint, far-off skirling, which had sounded even while old Steenson was speaking, ceased as I hurried back, but Mallory looked a

182

dark blot in the prospect, dismal as it had never seemed before. Was it because of this superstition that Lady Heron had grown old and grey before her time? It would be awful, I thought, to live here year in and year out, eternally listening for those notes of doom. What should I do, I, a married Frazer, if I heard them circling round the house, and if it meant that Jack—I tell you frankly what was my first impression afterwards; some healthy scepticism came to my relief. An old man's story of impossible ghosts—where was the need to credit it?

Through that day and the next everything moved on velvet—the quiet, regular hours, the careful service, the slightly formal ways with an old-world atmosphere about them, which I found piquant and attractive when not in one of my impatient moods. And I was perhaps more patient, more inclined to be appreciative, because the weeks of my visit had nearly run out; very soon now I should be setting out to establish myself with Violet at the flat, in the midst of London and life.

I was softened, too, because Lady Heron appeared to recognize my right of choice as to what I would do in Jack's absence. All she said was:

"Your home is here, my dear, when you care to have it so. When you wish to come back to Mallory you have only to let me know." Then I heard her sigh softly to herself, perhaps because she recognised that I did not care. I thanked her and said I would write, and she replied:

"I think I shall know without telling." An odd thing to say.

On the next evening, which was the last but one, we were sitting together in the half-light with the windows open, for although it was late October the weather was still warm. I was holding wool for Lady Heron to wind, and was so close in front of her and could clearly see her face, when, in the distance, and a mere thread of sound, but perfectly distinct, I heard the skirl of the pipes.

I do not think my hands trembled, held out stiffly with the skein, but hers did in the effort to wind.

The thin, faint music came near, nearer, and then seemed to turn away. Not to the house; for all my cherished unbelief, I was thankful that it was not coming to the house.

Lady Heron had dropped her ball of wool, and now stooped to regain it.

"We will not wind any more now, my dear," she said. "I am obliged to you, but I shall have enough." And then she crossed the room and rang the bell, a hanging bell-pull, old-fashioned like all else at Mallory.

Peters came quickly; was it only my fancy that he looked disturbed.

"We will have the windows closed now and the lamp lit." Such was her commonplace order. I heard no more of the pipes that night, but next morning came the news that John Frazer, the tenant of the Mill, had passed away.

It was no doubt a coincidence, nothing more, but we may put it down as an odd one. That was the day before yesterday. I left early yesterday morning, Peters going with me as far as Edinburgh, and I have been busy writing, writing, all these hours in the train. What a packet you will have to wade through!

3

You have been good, dear Margaret, in liking my letters about the hospital work, although while I was so busy they could only be scraps. (And, what was worse, I am afraid my letters to poor old Jack in the trenches were scrappy too. Ungrateful, perhaps, for I have lived all this while on his scraps to me.)

But to go back to the hospital. You will be surprised to hear that I have had to give up my work there, which is a great disappointment. But everything has been horrid of late. I am alone in the flat. The beginning of the upset was that Violet turned horrid; wasn't it nasty of her, when we had been such chums? I told you about Captain Bridgwater, who used to come to see us after he left the hospital; he was cousin to some of Violet's people, and an old schoolfellow of Jack's. It seemed right and natural to be friends, as that was so I liked him in the beginning—really, I liked him very much, and was pleased when he showed that he liked me. But Violet liked him in a different way, and expected a flirtation they had begun years before to have a serious meaning; she declares it would have meant something serious if it had not been for me. So, we had a quarrel, and she said dreadful things, and I was indignant, as I had a right to be, and was not sorry when she packed her boxes and gave up her share of the flat, leaving me alone.

I was not sorry, but I was shaken by it, and it so happened that when Captain Bridgwater came in, he found me crying. Then he was horrid, too, and said things—things that at first, I did not understand, and that he had no business to say to Jack's wife, he who had been Jack's friend. I shall never speak to him again, you may be sure.

After this I went to the hospital, to my work as usual, but I did not feel a bit like myself. I had a fainting fit for the first time in my life, and they were a long while in bringing me to. Afterwards the doctor told me I should have to give up V.A.D.-ing. I am not strong enough.

I am wondering what I ought to do. Jack would not like me being here by myself. He only consented to the plan because Violet was joining me, and I do not know of anybody else. But nothing on earth will induce me to go back to Aunt Winifred.

★★★★★★★★★★★★★★★★★

I was interrupted there, and now where do you think I am continuing my letter? I am writing in the train, the Scotch express, and I am on my way to Mallory. There is a surprise for you, and a surprise for me, but I begin to think it is the best solution of the difficulty that could have been found. Lady Heron sent for me, and the queer thing is how she could have known or guessed. I begin to think my mother-in-law must be a bit of a witch.

Where I broke off above was when the servant came in to say a man named Peters had called and had brought a letter. It was a kind letter, so kind a letter that it made me cry, though that is saying little, as tears have been close to my eyes of late. The rigors of winter were past, Lady Heron wrote; the days were already lengthening into spring; a visit would give her the utmost pleasure, and she fancied it might now suit me to come to her again. Peters was her messenger instead of the post, and if I were willing Peters would arrange my journey, and spare me all trouble about it, as indeed he has done. And it was not necessary for me to write.

Peters would send her a wire, and a warm welcome would await me.

So here I am travelling North. And I think you will agree it has been a wise decision, and one that will please Jack as things are. I shall post this to you in Edinburgh, my dear, and write again from Mallory.

4

Really, Margaret, I am happy to be here, much happier than I was before. Lady Heron is so kind, and I think we understand each other better than we did. I have a lovely room on the south side of the house, and the air is far milder than you would suppose. We never say anything about the pipes, but I fancy they must have been heard twice at least while I was in London, because two more of the Frazers have fallen; sons of the people at the farm; and another of the clan name died in hospital the week before my return.

Alas! We have heard the pipes again, and I will tell you how. They came at the edge of dusk, not what they call here the murk of the night, but while there was still light enough to see, had there been bodily presence to be seen.

Lady Heron likes me to play to her, and I was sitting at the piano, recollecting old airs, and sometimes crooning a bit of song half to myself, when it seemed as if my music had an echo outside the house. My fingers fell from the keys, and in another moment, I was sure what it was, and where.

It came with a sweep, swiftly, devouring space, heard afar, and then immediately close, passing our window, which looked out upon nothing—nothing, not a shadow even, nor the print of a foot. The wild pibroch passed by, but it went circling round the house, and, oh, it was coming back? We both sprang up and met in a close clasp together, each of us calling the other by name. "Mother!" I cried to her—the first time I have called her so, but it seemed rent from me without thought. It passed the second time, and now there was a cry with it, like a human voice in pain, and again it went circling through the air which had been still, but was rising with a gust of storm.

Twice for the heir! That was what the old man Steenson said, and, oh, me! Jack was the heir. There was a pause of seconds, and then it passed for the third time, the pibroch and the shriek. Afterwards there was a great silence. The wind which had swept with it fell also—if it were wind indeed; and we two women drew apart and looked at each other. Her face was ghastly, and I expect mine was no better.

"Cecily," she said, "you know!" And then, "Who told you?"

Soon afterwards Peters came in to light the lamps, and the old servant's hands so trembled as he performed his task that the glasses clashed and clattered—he who was usually noiseless. He, too, had heard; of that I made no doubt; he had heard even as we.

It was the sign for the head of the house. Lady Heron heard it just so before her husband died. There was some small comfort to us both in the belief that it came for Heron and not Jack. But that comfort did not last. The telegram from the War Office came two days after— "Wounded and missing, believed killed"—the intimation to Lady Heron about both her sons, Lieut.-Colonel Lord Heron, and Captain the Hon. John Frazer; not one alone, but both.

I cannot write about that time. A chink was left to us through which hope came, but one could hardly look at it in face of the awful doubt. And the sign for the head of the house would stand also for Jack, provided Heron had been the first to fall.

Looking back, I cannot think how we endured the suspense. Counted by days the measure of it was not long, but it seemed as if ages went by. We tried to comfort each other; Lady Heron was an angel to me through all her own pain; but for her I would have died.

I cannot write about it; you must take it for granted, and I hurry on to the end.

We were sitting together, we two alone, as we were when the sign came. Lady Heron was knitting, feverishly knitting at those socks for Jack which she would not lay aside, little as either of us believed they would be worn. We were together, as I said, when Peters rushed into the room with another telegram on his silver tray. (I wonder he remembered the tray.) Lady Heron tore it open; it was addressed to her.

"Home slightly wounded. With you and Cecily tomorrow.—Jack."

My mind takes a leap from that moment to another when he stood at the door. Lady Heron would not let me go to the station because I had fainted again, and as I might not, she would not either; she said it would be unfair to take the advantage. Jack at the door, a figure in soiled khaki, very pale, with his head bandaged and his arm in a sling; Jack himself, alive and still to live. My Jack; and I do not mind now, as once I did, that he is his mother's Jack as well.

He has been through dreadful things. Heron fell—poor Heron—and was left in No Man's Land, and Jack went after him. At the utmost risk to himself he dragged out his brother from under a pile of dead, and into the shelter of a shell-crater.

There they existed for three days under incessant fire, all hope of them being abandoned; existed by a miracle, for it was death to move. Heron was fearfully wounded, but Jack, wounded himself, managed so to bandage him that the bleeding stopped; and then he found some emergency rations on which they sustained life. If there ever were a coldness between the brothers, as I thought, it must have melted away in those dreadful hours.

On the fourth day our troops attacked again on the farther side of the wood, which diverted attention, and then Jack began the task—the difficult and painful task—of half-carrying, half-dragging Heron to where he could be helped, as his only chance of life. All this time Jack was wounded himself, in the head and on the shoulder and side, but the burst of shrapnel which shattered his arm did not happen till they were close to our own lines. By this Heron was wounded again, but in any case, Jack thinks he could not have survived; the doctor at the dressing-station said so. Heron died there, but not till some hours later, and Jack was with him to the last.

So, the pipers were right and not wrong when they bewailed the head of the house who had fallen. What it meant to Jack I did not consider then, and it came on me with a shock of surprise when Peters, sometime later, addressed him as "My Lord."

But I think more—much more—of the fact that he has been recommended for the Cross.

The Whispering Wall

My story begins before the war, though not long before. We were a party of light-hearted undergraduates in Jack Lovell's rooms at Cambridge, and we had been laughing uproariously over some story of psychical marvels. Jack was the only one of us who took the matter seriously.

After the others had gone, I said to him: "Surely you didn't believe that farrago of nonsense Smith was telling, did you? I was surprised to hear you argue that it might be true."

"Only that it might be true, not that it was. I saw no impossibility; that was all."

"Why, old man, you do surprise me! You are the last fellow I should have thought likely to give in to spooks."

Jack was smoking; he knocked out his pipe before he answered, and began to fill it with deliberation.

"And you would have been right, when the evidence was hearsay. But the position alters to one who has heard and seen."

"Why, you don't mean to say that you have—"

Jack had his pipe between his teeth again, so he merely nodded. But the nod was enough.

"My dear old Jack! But you haven't reflected what cheats these mediums are. They are past masters as conjurers—have to be, and all their spooks are faked. I know a fellow who is a Psychical Researcher, and he says—"

"I have not been to mediums. My people live in a house up north which has a queer reputation. The old wing is practically shut up, because of what you call spooks: a ghost that is heard rather frequently, and sometimes seen."

"And you do not suspect anyone of playing tricks?"

"What for a hundred and fifty years on end?" Jack seemed to consider the question, and then he shook his head. "There's no trick about it. No."

"Before I believed, I should have to hear and see for myself, and investigate a lot to make sure. I would rather like to try."

"Then come down to Marchmore with me next week. We go down then, as you know. You will be very welcome. You are not fixed anywhere else."

I had no fixtures, and I accepted the invitation then and there. I received the welcome he promised me, and Jack did not proclaim me a ghost-hunter, or give me away."

Marchmore was a larger house than I expected: Jack was not one who said much about his family. It was built on three sides of a quadrangle, of which the iron gates supplied the fourth, and surrounded by a stretch of parkland. The centre was the family dwelling, with an older wing on your left as you faced the entrance, and a quite modern one on the right, which contained the servants' quarters. The guest-chamber allotted to me was in the centre building, but Jack's rooms, bedroom and sitting-room together, were on the first floor of the old wing, which was supposed to be the habitat of the ghost.

I went off to smoke with Jack when we retired for the night, and found him pleasantly established, with cheerful light and fire, lounge-chairs, and every comfort. I suppose I was impatient, for I said as soon as we were alone: "When is the entertainment going to begin, and where is it to be held?"

I do not think Jack quite liked his spooks taken in that spirit. "I told you I could not answer for it, and you might be disappointed," he returned with some sharpness in his voice. "It may happen at any moment, or you may have to wait for it—days, or even weeks. But as to where it happens, I can show you now. Come upstairs with me."

He took up the lamp, and led the way out to the landing, where he unlocked a door which shut in an enclosed staircase leading to the attic floor.

"Come up here whenever you like," he said; "you will have a better chance alone."

The stairs were uncarpeted, with a window behind them at the top, which lighted a narrow passage under the pitch of the high tiled roof. A closed door faced us at the end, and there were also doors to right and left.

"You can look into all these rooms," Jack said. "You will find them empty, as we do not use them, even for limber. But it is here in the passage that you must listen for the voice."

The place was grim enough. Confess I did not care for it, but I was not going to show the white feather.

"You haven't told me yet what I should hear."

"It is a sort of whispering which travels along the wall on the left, beginning quite away at the end; and as it draws near and passes you it gets distinct." He touched the side wall of the passage as he spoke.

"Hum—some acoustic peculiarity?" I suggested.

"Very likely! I have often thought that, but the sound shapes itself into words, and sometimes—not always—they have meaning. Probably they differ to each hearer. I cannot say how they would come to you."

We stood in silence for a while, and nothing happened; the place was close and oppressive with its one window closed—indeed, there seemed to be some unnatural deadness about the air. Jack moved first.

"It will not come tonight, so we had better go down," and he led the way with his lamp. At the foot of the staircase, he locked the enclosing door, but left the key standing; and I confess to a certain relief when we were back in his pleasant sitting-room, and the ghost hunt was over for the night.

Marchmore had other attractions, but I tore myself away from them next morning on the pretext of letters to write in Jack's room. I did write one or two, that there might be some correspondence of mine in the letter bag as a result; but these epistles were of the briefest. Then I sought the attic staircase, closing the door after me to prevent surprise from below. The narrow passage, with its blank surroundings of shut doors, lighted only from the window behind me, was hardly more cheerful on a daylight view. I did not believe in it; but, despite my scepticism, I experienced a creeping thrill about the spine, and an odd sensation in my ears, which were strained to listen.

The silence, however, was absolute. Of course, I said to myself, that happened to be a still day, and no doubt the phenomenon depended on the wind whistling round the caves and crannies of the old house. Then I turned my attention to the five shut doors.

Those on the right and left opened into four narrow garrets, empty as described to me; two of them lighted with small dormer windows, the other two by oblongs of thick glass let into the slope of the roof; dismal chambers, which, apart from the ill reputation of this upper floor, would hardly be chosen for occupation.

The fifth floor at the end of the passage opened into much a larger and more cheerful room, which had the advantage of a broad, low window, nearly the width of the front gable, and also of a rusty fire-place at the side. Probably at some distant date children had used it for a playroom; it was empty of furniture, but in one corner was a dilapi-dated rocking-horse, and a lidless box half full of broken toys.

I wondered who were the children who had once played here, unafraid; and then as I turned away from the toybox, as if caused by its suggestion, I had the brief illusion that one of them stood beside me; a little fair-haired lad in a belted pinafore. Of course, it was a trick of the imagination, and I quickly saw how it was caused. This room also had a glazed pane let into the roof, and sunshine through the parting clouds had thrown down, on to the floor below, a shaft of light.

After that I went downstairs, but I resolved not to mention that odd fancy of mine to Jack, as he might attach to it some psychical meaning. He had described to me no visible ghost; he had spoken only of the whispers, and these I had not heard.

I was in Jack's room the third evening of my stay, and we had been discussing quite other matters. I had not even the ghost in mind, when there was a patter of footsteps overhead, quite small footsteps, like a child's. They seemed to run across the large attic and along the passage, and presently back again over the uncarpeted floors.

"What is that?" I exclaimed.

Jack did not give a direct answer. "It often comes before the whis-pers," he said. "If you come upstairs now, I believe you will hear."

He took the lamp and led the way. I noticed that he needed to unlock the door shutting in the staircase. His light showed the passage empty and doors shut, and the pattering footsteps had ceased.

We stood as before, facing the wall on the left; and presently, at the far end, the whispering began. However caused, it was undistin-guishable from a human voice, and, as the whisperer approached, the vague sounds formed themselves into spoken words, but words with-out meaning. "*Ah Mont,*" and again "*Ah—Mont,*" and then, with a sort of sighing gasp, it added, "*Year.*"

The voice died away to our left, above the hollow of the stairs; and then, after the interval of a couple of minutes, began again by the shut door. The same words were repeated as it approached us the second time, and after that the stillness was unbroke. Jack, still holding up his lamp, opened the five doors one after another, and showed the rooms empty.

Then we went down into the smoking-room, locking in the ghost as before. "Well," he said, "can you account for it?"

192

"No," I answered.

After we had settled back in our respective chairs and relit our pipes Jack asked: "Did you distinguish any words?"

"Yes," I replied, and told him what I had heard. "Is it always the same?"

"I heard it just as you did, and the phrase was new. I have no idea what it means. The words sometimes are: "Come and play"—as if a child spoke them."

The impression was too recent and vivid to allow of jesting, as I might have jested once. I enquired if there was any legend which explained the haunting.

"No legend. But there is a saying that if one of us Lovells sees the child, he will not live to have children of his own."

I heard no more while I was at Marchmore, and the day after, my visit came to an end.

That fateful summer of 1914 brought many changes. Jack Lovell and I ceased to be students at the university. We both joined the army, and went out immediately after the retreat, so we were in the November fighting, half-forgotten now amidst all that had come after, but it was mentioned in the dispatches as "heavy".

A village was held by our regiment against stubborn assaults, repulsed with the bayonet. Jack Lovell was wounded, how severely we others did not know, for there was much confusion.

He was sent to the base hospital; and two days after that I got a shrapnel tear on the shoulder—a surface affair, but it began to look angry, and so I was ordered down. I asked at once for Jack, and was deeply distressed to be told his hurt was serious, and he was not expected to live.

I was allowed to see him, and presently was at his bedside, with his hand in mine. His face looked grey and pinched; it was hardly the face I knew.

"You'll be going back to England, Eccles, lucky fellow!" he said presently, and he smiled—such a wan smile it was.

He would come too, I answered; he mustn't lose heart about himself; you know the sort of thing one says, even when it is a lie.

"Yes, but not the way you will," he answered. "The child at Marchmore wants me; he was always whispering for me to come and play. And you know what you heard at the wall; what we both heard there. I've been thinking about it tonight. You know the place where we were fighting? Tell me the name of it—Eccles—tell me!"

Was he wandering? I thought so. But, of course, I answered him.

"It was near Armentières."

"Wasn't that what the voice whispered? You heard it too. *Ah-mont-year.* Why, of course it was! I know what he was driving at, though I did not understand it then. It's all as it should be."

And then again, he smiled, and, turning his face from me, appeared to fall asleep.

I went home for my wound to heal, but he remained behind. That is, what was mortal of him; for I left the best pal I ever had laid in a soldier's grave in France.

The Wind of Dunowe

It was growing late, the Autumn evening was advanced out of the long northern twilight to be on the edge of dark, when Reginald Noyes left the Dunowe smoking room where he had been chatting to his host, and dashed upstairs, two steps at a stride, to dress for dinner. The warning bell had rung some time before, so he was not surprised to find his wife already attired in her evening gown. She was seated with her back to him, warming her toes at the wide and glowing fire of peat.

Noyes would have been just as well pleased not to find her there—a moderate statement of his sentiments. It was a case of the grey mare being the better horse, and the young man had not always an easy time with his chosen partner. To one sensitive to such indications, the psychic atmosphere of the big state bedroom was charged with displeasure, and this was accentuated by a shrug of an averted shoulder. Surely something more was wrong than the mere fact that Noyes was behind time.

"Why, Flossie, what's the matter?"

The frivolous nickname ill-fitted Mrs. Noyes, at least in her present mood. And at all times she was rather of the severe type of beauty, even when the sun shone—the metaphorical sun.

"Matter? Matter enough! It's no use: I can't stick it out here for another ten days, to the limit of our invitation. I'm bored to death. Coming to Dunowe has been altogether a mistake. You must make some excuse for a change of plan, and take me back to town."

"Why—you wanted to cultivate the MacIvors: you even schemed to be invited. You were as pleased as I was when we were both asked—every bit. The shooting is excellent, and MacIvor such a good fellow. And I'm sure his mother received us with every kindness. Have you and she fallen out?"

"Do I ever fall out with anyone? I've no patience with you when

195

you are absurd. Of course there has been no quarrel. But I'm sick to death of this ghostly old barrack. There isn't the least chance here of bringing off any *coup*. And, as you know very well, if we don't between now and Christmas—!"

Here there was an effective pause. Noyes winced. Probably he did know what was meant. But he put up a further objection.

"You said, with a view to *coups*, that this visit was the very thing you wanted—to get into a house-party with Mrs. Noel MacIvor, and have a chance to draw the feather over her. By George, Noel was a lucky man when he married her, in spite of the snub nose and the American accent. A girl with two millions to her fortune, and likely to have as much again when Poppa dies. And when all the MacIvors are as poor as rats, and he the second son!"

"Two millions—yes. But it seems they were dollars, not pounds sterling, as we heard. And the girl is as sharp and as well able to take care of herself and her money as—as the paternal Yankee himself."

"Well—she can be fairly generous when she likes. MacIvor tells me she offered to restore Dunowe for him—put the castle in complete repair. That was pretty well for a sister-in-law. But of course, he wouldn't consent."

"More fool he to refuse such an offer. But in other ways she is downright stingy: dresses herself like a schoolgirl of seventeen, sweet simplicity unadorned. Not a jewel, even. And she should have had plenty of toilets and jewels in those Saratoga trunks we saw carried in!"

"I daresay you would have liked to have the ransacking of them!"

"I thought of that. But the Noels are far off in the other wing, and she has a dragon of a maid who seems always to be on guard."

"Good heavens, Flossie! I hope you won't do more than think of it. That sort of thing never pays. And we should be marked for ever!"

"Nonsense. What marks one is not the doing, but being found out. I don't mean to run risks. I said, there is the maid. And I doubt if the jewels are there, though they ought to be. It isn't worthwhile. But we are bound to get hold of the money—or money's worth—by Christmas.

Probably Noyes winced for the second time at this renewed reminder, but he was at the moment out of sight. He had plunged into the dressing-room, and was throwing things about there in the course of a hurried toilet. The door between the two rooms was set wide, and now and then he came to the opening to speak.

196

"I thought you were depending on your bridge. You wanted to play Auction with Mrs. Noel—that was the tale in London. You never said a word about her jewels."

"Right: I meant to play here, and win from her. But the little fool hates cards. And the old lady is puritanical, and hates them too. They are practically barred, or allowed with a limit of sixpenny stakes."

"Can't you work it some other way? Flatter the heiress, and creep up her sleeve. Get her to restore us, as MacIvor won't let her do up the castle!"—a laugh here, which was presently extinguished in the folds of a towel.

"I can get round most—girls, but she doesn't take to me. She's like a—a glacis with no vantage for the foot. The only human bit about her is that she's curious. She's curious about the ghost here, and wants to find out. I told her I would try to help her—"

"*You* would help her! Why doesn't she question the family? They would know if there is anything in it. But of course, there isn't."

"It is the solitary point on which we touch. A sympathetic interest in ghosts is better than no fellow-interest at all. I've given myself out as psychical—save the mark!"—and here the lady laughed. "I might personate the ghost, and get at the boxes that way. But the clue of how to make up is still to seek. We do not know what sort of figure is seen."

"Surely she could ask her husband!"

"Noel told her something, and then he shut up, and would say no more. Lady MacIvor can't bear the subject mentioned, and Sir Ian is just as bad. And she thinks Noel must have been laughing at her. He said the ghost was a gale of wind: a gale which blows inside the castle when the real weather is still. Now a gale of wind won't help me to the boxes. But it is mixed up somehow with an ancestress. I can't find out which, though I asked all the questions I could, quite innocently, about the pictures. Ghosts apart, I tell you there is no chance here, and the sooner we get out of this the better. I wrote today to Juliet in Hampshire: you know she wanted me for her bridge parties, though she says I must not sweep the board as I did last winter. But of course, that was only her joke. Gracious, there's the second gong. I must go down at once, and leave you to follow."

Dinner was served in the hall at Dunowe Castle, a noble but somewhat bare room, stone-floored, and so lofty as to be open to the rafters. The diners were, however, well protected from any chill; a great fire blazed, and the table was set within folding screens of Spanish leather, while a thick carpet was spread under foot. Dunowe knew nothing of the modern luxury of electric light, and the moderate illumination of the table was effected by candles in tall silver holders. This was all very well within the screens, but the corners of the big room were abandoned to gloom, and only a single lamp burned overhead in the gallery. The piquant little American bride looked round her with a shiver as she descended the staircase. Here was hiding more than ample for dozens of ghosts, and that shrewd draught from the gallery which blew on her uncovered shoulders might be the precursor of the supernatural wind which was supposed to be the MacIvor family omen.

It was not a numerous party which assembled at the table. A married pair with a couple of clever daughters had quitted the castle that morning, frigid old people, and the girls plain and elderly: impecunious also, and of no account from the point of view of Mrs. Noyes. There were Noel MacIvor and Reginald Noyes, and four other men who were "guns," seven in all with the host; but the American bride and Mrs. Noyes were the only ladies remaining, with the exception of the stately old dame who sat at the head of the table, and was Sir Ian MacIvor's mother. Sir Ian had placed the lady guest on his right hand, and his sister-in-law opposite.

Mrs. Noyes was still in a clouded humour and had little to say, but she must have been well entertained by the pretty American's lively chatter. Ian MacIvor was a handsomer man than his more fortunate brother, but the family honours seemed to have brought with them a weight of care, not to say melancholy, and he looked old beyond his years.

"I went over to Eagles' Cairn today with the mater," said the bride, whose Christian name was Caryl. "You know they are all coming to Dunowe for the dance next week, and Mollie Campbell sent you a very particular message. She says they are going to put on fancy dress, as it makes it just twice the fun, and she hopes all the women you expect will do the same. Of course, you men will wear the tartan. The mater did not seem to mind. I said I'd be delighted, and I thought Mrs. Noyes would dress up too." Then, with an appeal also to her *vis-à-vis*: "Say, that was right, was it not?"

"Quite right, if you ladies do not mind the trouble for such a small impromptu affair. It was just like Mollie Campbell to propose it. She is a child still about what you call dressing up!"

"Perhaps we all are. I can answer for one, at least. What do you say, Mrs. Noyes?"

"Certainly, if we are still here—I am not sure—"

"Oh, you must stay for it." We cannot let you off. And about costumes: the dear mater and I talked it over in the carriage coming home. She is going to wear a great-grandmother dress that she has stowed away with a lot of others in those chests on the gallery, and I am to try on a particular one that she thinks will suit me. It is like the dress Lady Sibell wears in the picture, where she has on the heirloom pearls and that queer harp-shaped brooch. Oh, Ian,"—with a sudden thought, and striking together the pink palms of her pretty hands. "It would be just splendid if you'd lend me the pearls for that one night! Say, will you? I'd take the greatest care of them. That is, if you keep them here, and not lodged at the bank. Are they here at Dunowe?"

"Yes," he said, "I have them here." He did not refuse the request, but he met it gravely, and might have been divined unwilling by one less eager.

"Then you'll let me have them, won't you?"—the piquant little face eloquent with appeal, and the clasped hands held out. "I'd like—oh, I would like to be Lady Sibell, just for the one night. I'd say I was Lady Sibell come alive out of the picture, if they can't guess who I am. I might even pretend to be the ghost!"

"A good idea," he admitted, but still there was that air of a reluctance he would not put into words. "But I wouldn't call myself Lady Sibell, if I were you. She mightn't like it. Couldn't you for the same period find a different name?"

"Why, is Lady Sibell the—! But I must not ask you that! It's charming of you, Ian. I must tell Noel. I feel as if I could hardly wait for Wednesday. If they are here in the house, could you show them me tonight?"

"I have them here—yes. In fact, they are in the built-in safe in my den, for they are not allowed to leave Dunowe. They don't often see the light. But you may be disappointed in them. They are not pure white, and some of them are irregular. No doubt they are Scotch river pearls, not oriental."

The description, though depreciatory, seemed to excite interest in both his hearers. Mrs. Noyes was also listening.

"Tinted pearls, are they? I wonder what colour?"

"Pinkish—to the best of my recollection."

"Pink pearls!" Caryl clasped her hands again. "They must be lovely. And I may wear them, may I not? Just for the one night!"

He smiled now in giving consent; she looked so pretty and childish in her eagerness.

"Yes, you shall have them for the dance. They may only be worn by a MacIvor. An odd provision, is it not; but it is in the deed, which also says they must not be taken out of the castle. But now you are married, you are a MacIvor, Caryl. So that will be all right."

It is said that lookers on see most of the game. Mrs. Noyes, looking and listening, was aware that Noel, who also listened, was rendered uneasy by his wife's request. He was on the edge of a protest, Mrs. Noyes thought, but Sir Ian made a slight repressive sign. Caryl the bride was to have her way. Other MacIvor brides had worn the pearls, but they were wedded to the head of the house, and not to a younger son. Noel was aware that Ian thought himself too poor to marry: was it in the elder brother's mind that Caryl in the future would have the right to the pearls as the reigning lady of Dunowe.

"Could you let me see them tonight?" Caryl persisted.

"And may I see them too?" put in Mrs. Noyes. "I admire pearls, and I may not be here when Mrs. McIvor wears them at the dance. Our plans are uncertain. I daresay Reginald told you?"

No, Noyes had said nothing: in fact, he had had no opportunity since the conversation in the bedroom. Sir Ian hoped, conventionally, that nothing would hurry them away so soon. In the husband's case, it would be with him a genuine matter of regret, but he would be able to spare Mrs. Flossie with perfect equanimity. He had no great liking for the lady: the surface of her was smooth enough, but he had an instinctive feeling that something unpleasant might be encountered underneath. He would be happy, he said, to show the pearls to both ladies, if they would honour him by paying a visit to his "den."

While dinner was in progress the wind was rising, buffeting round the many angles and turrets of the house; and now and then there was a roar in the wide chimney of the hall. It was evident that Lady MacIvor was listening, and listening with apprehension, though was it not the saying that when the ghost wind blew in the castle, the outer and mundane weather was wont to be a dead, calm? The old dame was never high-coloured—(old she was, to be the mother of those two stalwart sons). Hers was the ivory pallor of age, but a change of tint might have been noted on her cheek and lips, as she sat at the head of the table trying spasmodically to converse. On observing this, Sir Ian remarked, in a voice so far raised as to be sure to catch her ear:

"We are going to have a wild night of it. I could have forecasted as much when we were out today. The equinoctial gales have given us the go-by this year, but now it seems as if one of them was setting in in earnest."

Only an equinoctial gale, a natural feature, and Ian cheerful in the forecast. Surely that should have set her mind at rest, and she contrived to smile back at him down the length of the table. But there was still a quiver about the proud old head, and as she smoothed her lace mittens it was palpable that the thin hands they covered, trembled. And when she heard of the display about to be made in the "den," it seemed as if her uneasiness increased. She said, however, no word to oppose. Lady Sibell's pearls must be shown and worn, as Ian had given his word. She was a fatalist in her way: what must be, must be: but Heaven grant showing and wearing might bring no evil on the house, which in the past had been stricken enough and to spare.

It was in truth a stormy evening, a gale sweeping over from the western ocean, and buffeting the old castle as it had been smitten many times before during its centuries of existence. But the wind was external, not within the walls, except for such natural draughts as found their way through undefended chinks and crannies. There was a huge fire in the castle drawing-room of logs and peat, but despite of it, Lady MacIvor shivered, and drew a voluminous white cloud of Shetland knitting close about her shoulders as she sat alone.

The two younger women had betaken themselves to Sir Ian's den, and there he had the safe set open, and was displaying the contents of an antique casket made of some dark foreign wood, cornered and clamped with steel. Within, on a velvet bed, lay the pearls of Dunowe.

Both ladies admired the string, which was just long enough to encircle a slender throat, and had a ruby clasp. Caryl declared that the faint rosy flush upon the pearls was even more exquisite than the purity of white. She took them out of the case for closer view, and then passed the necklace over for Mrs. Noyes also to examine. But when they came into unrelated handling, a queer thing happened.

The room was lighted by four candles in tall holders, two on the table, and two set high on the mantelshelf. These lights were not extinguished nor did they flicker, but the illuminating power of them died down till each showed only a faint point of bluish flame. The room was almost in darkness, and the three persons grouped at the table could scarcely distinguish each the face of the other in the sadden gloom.

"What is the matter with the candles?" Mrs. Noyes exclaimed: *esprit fort* as she considered herself, she was for the moment appalled.

201

Sir Ian took the pearls from her hand and replaced them in their case, and, as he did so, the lights gradually brightened until they burned as before. He did not answer the question or give any explanation: he appeared not to have noticed the darkness and the return of illumination.

"You shall have then on Wednesday evening," he said to Caryl as he turned the key. "I am glad they come up to your expectation."

"I think they are exquisite," she said, "but I am almost frightened of them now. Ian, I know you won't tell me, but is it that Lady Sibell does not want them worn? Was it her doing to put out the candles, and make them burn again when you took back the necklace? No, you needn't answer, for I have found out! You may keep it as secret as you like, but I am certain now she is the ghost!"

Mrs. Noyes was awake that night when her husband came up to their rooms; she had also something to say.

"You need not be in too great haste over arranging our departure. The fourteenth will do for me. I have made up my mind to stay over the dance."

"You will stay for the dance, and leave the day after: is that it? Rather a mistake if anything should happen to be missing, and there is a hue and cry. Better make it the end of the week, the day set for us, and let me have another good shoot."

"You think of nothing but your shooting, Reginald. I never knew any one so selfish."

"This time, my dear, I am thinking of something quite other than myself. I am thinking of you, and the risk you are running, or are about to run. For of course this change of plan is because you have seen the pearls."

"Don't speak so loud. Heaven knows who may be outside the door."

"I am speaking with all discretion, and I want to know. You were there when MacIvor took them out of the safe. What are they like?"

"I had no time to look them over—of course, and there may be flaws. I had them in my own hands less than a minute. But I should say there were twenty at least the size of a large pea, and a dozen that would double that, all faintly tinted pink. The back of the string seemed made up of small ones, an odd and end lot, quite negligible. Whether those at the back were pink I could not see: there was a very bad light. But the middle ones would sell for a fortune in New York, if we can get them there. The latest craze of the Five Hundred is for pearls, and pink pearls head the market."

"You'll never get them out of this house without detection and exposure, let alone across the Atlantic. Give it up, Flossie: your scheme is a bad egg. I'm off on Monday, and I shall take you with me. That's my last word."

It might be Reginald Noyes's last word, but it was not Flossie's. Many words followed on the lady's part: indeed, discussions and re-criminations raged till the small hours, of which the result only need be noted. The couple would remain over the dance and until the following Saturday, and Mrs. Noyes held herself at liberty to pursue the course she had planned, and possess herself (if she could) of the pearls. And the following instructions were issued to the obedient Reginald, a little later on.

"Look here. I want you to engage Mrs. Noel for the fourth dance: it is a *valse*. No, I know you don't *valse* well, but that does not matter. The big saloon is cleared for dancing on account of the oak floor, but the flirtation nooks and refreshments will be in the hall. Get her to sit out with you, and take her to the nook right in the corner, left of fireplace, the one from which you see the stairs. It is shut in at the back with palms and evergreens, and there is a high-backed seat. Take her there while the dancing is still going on, and the hall is empty: tell her you want to confide in her: keep her engrossed."

"I can take her there—good: but as to confiding! What the devil am I to confide? She's the last sort of girl to stand lovemaking, and we haven't an idea in common. As you said once before."

"Talk to her about the ghost. Tell her you've seen it, with the tallest story you can make up—sulphur and brimstone, horns and hoofs, and all the diabolical horrors. She'll believe you, for on that subject she would swallow anything. If you do that, you'll have her fixed—for as long as will suit my purpose. You understand?"

The morning of Wednesday, Mrs. Noyes developed a headache. It was most tiresome of it to come when it did, and she accepted sympathy freely, and swallowed the offered remedies, which was heroic. To lose the dance would disappoint her, more acutely than words could say. No, not the actual dance; she must give up that in any case, for it would be impossible with such a giddy head. But if she could get better—ever such a little better—she would still hope to watch the spectacle from some quiet corner, where she would not be in the way. She was sure dear Lady MacIvor would excuse her arraying herself in the elaborate costume which had been arranged, and in which she was to be a *poudré*. But she happened to have with her a dark *domino* and half-mask, which would do well enough, and this she could throw on at the last moment if she felt able to come down. She would be inconspicuous so attired, and could slip away when fatigued.

So, when the evening came, she assumed a close-fitting sheath-like dress of black satin, in which her spare figure would occupy the least possible space, even when covered by the *domino*. She would not venture down till the dancing was well begun, but the right moment would find her ready and the headache cured.

Noyes hated the whole business, but had so far fallen under his wife's domination that he was prepared to play his part in the drama. He took the opportunity to acquaint himself with the special flirta-tion nook she had indicated, to which he was expected to lead his partner. It could not have been better arranged for Flossie's purpose. A large Chesterfield settee was placed across the corner, backed by an apparent grove of tall palms and evergreens, which masked the door into a side-passage. This door was not to be used in the service of the night, as the passage did not lead to the kitchens, and indeed commu-nicated only with the gun-room and a side staircase. Flossie would do her part, there was no doubt of that: it only remained for him to act up to the role for which he was cast, and whisper to a lady psychically interested some thrilling particulars about an imagined ghost.

He foresaw difficulty. The American bride was curious, but she was also an indefatigable dancer, and determined to enjoy herself to the full. Would she be tempted into that retirement, even by a hinted confidence as to ghosts seen at Dunowe?

Caryl was in wild spirits when the hour arrived, enchanted with the effect of her old-world costume, now completed with the heir-loom pearls, and a quaint harp-shaped brooch which also figured in the picture. Her hair was dressed after the fashion of Lady Sibell's por-trait, and Caryl made the painted lady a mock courtesy as she passed her in the gallery.

"No, you mustn't say you know me," she said laughing to her intimates. "I'm not Caryl MacIvor tonight, or Noel's wife. I'm his lady-ancestress instead." And then, in a following whisper: "I doubt if the dear old mater really approves of the travesty, though she would not interfere to spoil my fun. You know she's very superstitious, and in dressing up as Lady Sibell I strongly suspect I'm also impersonating the ghost."

The Dunowe dance being an impromptu, there were no printed

programmes; but those who had pockets—only the men had pockets—carried cards in them, and little stubs of pencils. In this way Noyes had Caryl's name down for Number Four, but when he came to claim it, that young person seemed to be deeply engaged with another partner.

"Do you really want to dance with me?" she queried." Because I'm enjoying myself very much with Freddy." (Freddy was one of the "guns.")

"I do really want this dance, and you know you promised. If you wish, I'll let you off the other; but do try me first."

She yielded, and they swung off together on the well waxed floor.

"I know I *valse* badly," he said presently, "and I am unpractised in the new steps. What I really want is to get you to sit out with me. I have something to tell you: it's—it's about a ghost. I have just had a horrible experience, and you'll be the first to hear of it: I have told nobody else. We shall get the hall to ourselves—for five minutes—if you don't mind coming this way."

"About the ghost?" There was quickened interest in her repetition of his words: his fish was rising to the fly. And perhaps she was not wholly unwilling to cut short her gyrations with an unskilled partner.

"You'll be comfortable sitting here, and that other fellow won't think of looking for you behind this screen. I really want to consult you—ask your advice. For I've had the fright of my life this afternoon."

She sank down on the soft cushions, leaning well back, which was what Flossie wished. As he took his seat beside her, he heard a slight rustle in the bower of foliage at the back of the couch, and it did not help to steady his nerves.

"I suppose it would not do to say anything to Sir Ian. My first idea, of course, was that it was a real man. A fellow with bad intentions, and no business where he was. In short, a burglar."

"A burglar—in broad daylight!"

"Ghosts are not supposed to like daylight, are they, any more than burglars? Though I know next to nothing of the habits of ghosts. But the daylight wasn't—wasn't broad."

Noyes felt he was floundering, and wondered what Flossie would think of his efforts at narration, in her hiding-place at the back.

"I mean it was getting dark—dusk, you know. If it hadn't been, I could not have seen the flame so distinctly. Yes, there seemed to be a flame about him, or at least a light. It came out of his eyes, I think, but

205

really, I don't know. You see, I've had no experience."

"You thought it was a man first, and then you saw it was a ghost? No, I wouldn't tell Ian: he does not care for these things, and I think they make him uncomfortable. But I would like to hear more about it. Ah-h-h, what's that?"

"Did you see anything?"

"No, but I thought something touched me—at the back of my neck—like a finger!"

Noyes noticed that her hand went up at once to feel for the safety of the pearls. Flossie's first attempt had been a failure, and he was nearly at the end of ghost-invention. Flames out of the eyes: he had better say next that his apparition breathed them out of its mouth.

"What touched you was a camellia leaf: see, I have broken it off. What were you asking me?"

"Was it the flame made you think the appearance supernatural? Or was there anything else?"

"Well—you see a real man couldn't be on fire, and yet be still and give no sign of pain. But a ghost might look like that, if—if it came from the wrong place. But what made me sure in the end, was that it vanished. It just went right out—while I stood there."

Noyes was facing sideways as he sat, and, with attention apparently riveted on his companion, he saw with half an eye the two hands again come forward out of the bower of greenery to attack the clasp of the necklace—this time with a lighter and defter touch, which did not alarm the victim. The string of pearls dropped one dangling end, and then was cautiously withdrawn. He made a desperate effort after self-control, continuing to look his partner steadily in the face, as if absorbed in their conversation. The scheme had worked well, Flossie had secured her prize, and now the best thing he could do was to lead Caryl back without delay into the thick of the throng. It would not do for her to recognise too precisely when and where the heirloom disappeared.

"If you'll come a little further out into the room, I can show you whereabouts in the gallery the ghost stood. You never heard of anything like it haunting Dunowe? But you see, they will not speak of the Dunowe ghosts, so whether familiar or not we cannot tell. There is the music ending, and I suppose I must take you back to the dancing-room. Thank you for giving me a hearing. Think it over, and tell me what conclusion you come to. At supper, perhaps; or tomorrow."

He offered his arm, and at the same moment a slight click of the concealed door informed him Flossie had escaped from her hiding-place. Caryl rose, and presently he was pointing out to her an imaginary spot on the gallery above the hall.

"I was just turning out of the corridor on my way down, when there he was straight before me. I give you my word it was horrible. And then to go like that, snuffed out in a moment!"

He had not told his story well; he was conscious of its lack of *vraisemblance.* And it left on the listener's mind an impression of insincerity, eager as she was to believe. Yet there was about Noyes a kind of subdued agitation which was curious: he would hardly have been so moved, she thought, by what was exaggerated or untrue. Yes, they would take an opportunity to speak of it again, and he might tell her husband if he liked, but no word must be said before Ian—As they crossed the hall, a car drove up with late arriving guests, and now the double doors of the entrance were being set wide. Servants came hurrying forward, and Lady MacIvor at the entrance of the ballroom was ready to receive her guests. Noyes and Caryl passed her going in, and but for the expectation and look beyond, probably she would at once have noticed the disappearance of the pearls. But the moment following a strange thing happened; one likely to be memorable ever after in the annals of Dunowe.

Did the gust of air rush in from those opened doors, or whence did it originate? A whirlwind blast tore through the house, extinguishing lights, swaying the pictures on the walls, tearing down wreaths of evergreens with which the saloon had been decked for the festal night. A wind which blew upstairs as well as down, shrieking through corridor and gallery, bursting open doors and whirling into closed rooms, so that no portion of the house escaped. There were cries of terror from the women guests, but the blast ceased as suddenly as it began, and Sir Ian's voice was heard above the din, begging everybody to be calm. The room would be quickly re-lighted, and the dancing would go on.

But the lights when they were brought, revealed pale faces which looked questioningly one to another. This was a strange thing which had happened, and beyond nature. The ghostly wind of Dunowe had hitherto been a joke in the neighbourhood: after the experience of that night, it would take rank as an article of faith.

The renewed illumination, however, brought with it a diversion, Caryl's loss was noted. Mollie Campbell exclaimed: "My dear, where are your pearls?" and the bride put both hands to her neck in uttermost dismay.

Had they been torn off and whirled from her by the ghost-wind—the act of an affronted ghost? But common sense suggested they had dropped to the floor, and had been swept away into some corner by a trailing skirt: this was advanced as the most likely explanation, though in these days all dancing gowns are sufficiently abbreviated. The necklace must be close at hand—Caryl was positive she had it in safety not ten minutes before—her dancing-partners could testify they had noticed it about her throat. The idea of theft occurred to nobody: theft was impossible in that secure house, and in the midst of friends.

"Oh, Ian, I am sorry: I am miserable to have lost it," she said, almost in tears. "I had no notion that the snap was weak: had I thought of it, I would have tied it on. I ought to have taken more care."

"You must not let that trouble you," he said to her kindly. "It will not be lost—it will come back to us": the last words *sotto voce* to Noel, who was as distressed as his wife. But what he meant by them he did not explain.

Noyes was among the searchers, round the floor and beyond, though well aware it could not be there. The ghostly wind, the darkness, had not helped to steady his shaken nerves, but in a way, he welcomed the diversion. Everyone was talking and thinking of the strange event, and if Caryl had been robbed, that darkness would be held thieves' opportunity. No suspicion could rest on Flossie, sick in her room.

But some half-hour later Sir Ian came to him.

"Noyes, I am sorry to tell you your wife is ill. We have a doctor here among our guests, and, if you are willing, I think it might be as well for him to see her. The matter? Oh, only a fainting-fit, but it seems to be obstinate. Some of the women found her lying in the corridor after the rush of wind, and I fear she may have been frightened. She was carried to bed, and the housekeeper and my mother's maid are both with her. If you will go up, I'll send Rawlins. He will know what to do."

Noyes went upstairs at once, his heart heavy with apprehension. Not so much on account of possible danger, though he was honestly fond of his wife, despite her outbreaks of temper, and the domination of the grey mare. What he dreaded was, discovery of what she had done. She must have fainted on her way back to their room, with the pearls upon her. And these women who found her in the corridor, who carried her to bed, would be certain to unfasten her dress in trying to recover her, and there would be the fatal necklace—doubtless well-known to both of them, housekeeper and maid. Neither would suppose it a guest's possession, even if unaware of Caryl's loss, and the search going on below. As he hurried upstairs, he felt like a man under sentence, who has just been informed that his hour has come.

He found Flossie laid upon the bed, moaning faintly.

"Madam is coming round nicely now, sir," said the housekeeper. "It was the faint going on so long that frightened us. I don't think she will be the worse."

The woman spoke cordially, not as if she knows them for discovered criminals; but there could be no further interchange, as the doctor was at the door.

While Dr. Rawlins examined the patient, Noyes looked round the room. Flossie's dress had been undone as a matter of course, and her few ornaments were unpinned and laid on the dressing-table, but the pearls were not among them. When he drew near the bed on the opposite side to the doctor, Mrs. Noyes turned her head on the pillow and looked at him. That she recognised her husband there could be no doubt, but there was a dreadful apprehension in her eyes. No word, however, could then be interchanged.

"Your wife has had a shock of some kind, and collapse has followed. Most likely the wind frightened her. I understand the people here consider it supernatural, and I am ready to confess it was odd, though I don't give in to spooks. You had better let the maid settle Mrs. Noyes comfortably for the night, and I daresay Mrs. Holbrook, the housekeeper, will sit up."

"No, no," Noyes objected." Nobody need sit up. I can look after her: the women need not stay. You think there is no danger?"

"No danger that I foresee: she is reviving quite satisfactorily. But I will come up again before I leave. I shall find you here?"

Noyes assented, and expressed his thanks. Then, when he had shut the door upon the doctor, he went back to the bed. His wife's eyes met his, filled with the same agony of fear.

"Are—the women—gone?" she panted.

"Yes, for the moment, but they are coming back. Where are the pearls?"

"I don't know—I don't know!"

"You had them. Where did you put them when you left the hall?"

"Inside the bosom of my dress—within everything—next to the skin. When I came to myself, all my clothing had been opened. They must have found—! Unless, indeed, the pearls were taken—when—!"

Speech failed, a violent shudder convulsed her, the apprehension in her face deepened into horror. The hand he had taken in his clutched him hard.

"Why— what?"

"The wind came: it was more than wind—it was anger, fury. It seems, when I look back, there was a face with it; or I dreamed the face after. A face that was terrible. I was so near safety when it came: a few more steps: and I was full of triumph. The wind struck me down. I knew no more till I found myself in here, and the women with me. Do you think the pearls—were taken—when I fell?"

After the fateful interruption of the wind, and a general dismay over Caryl's loss, the dance was not kept up late. The first gay frolic of it was only half-heartedly renewed, and the guests did not find much appetite for the excellent supper. It was but little after one o'clock when Sir Ian closed the great doors upon the last departure, and retreated to his den. Caryl had put in his hands the quaint antique brooch worn to fasten her dress as Lady Sibell, and again she made tearful expression of her sorrow over the loss of the pearls.

"I think they will be given back," he said: this and no more.

His errand to the den was to replace the brooch. He unlocked the safe with his own key, a key that had no duplicate, and never left his possession. He opened the steel-clamped casket to lay the brooch within, and there, safe and unharmed, was the gleaming roseate string, the heirloom pearls of Dunowe.

A few minutes later he knocked at his brother's door.

"Noel! it is I, Ian, I want to speak to you."

Noel opened at once: he was in pyjamas, and had been on the point of getting into bed.

"What is it, old fellow?"

"Only to tell you that the pearls are found. Let Caryl know. She will sleep all the better."

"By George, I should think she will, and I, too! Where did they turn up?"

"In their place, in my locked safe. I unlocked it to put the brooch away, and they were there."

"In your locked safe! Did you leave it undone?"

"No. And I had the key."

"Then how—who?"

"No mortal hand, I think. You know, there is a saying—! I tell you, but I shall slur it over to the others. Better so. Goodnight."

Iras: A Mystery

1

I have become subject to a failure of memory, the partial consequence of recent severe illness. Already, as I look back, a confused mist
obliterates certain portions of the past; and names and dates have a
trick of deserting me at the moment of requirement. I am told this
naturally results from the weakness I now suffer; but in my hours of
depression, I fear that mist with a deadly terror, foreboding how it
may gather more thickly and blankly about me, until, from my lonely
standpoint on a ridge of the dark mountains, all the land of Beulah I
have left will be blotted out.

Therefore, that a certain experience may be forever preserved to
me, being in my sane mind and telling truth as on oath, I, Ralph
Lavenham, write.

I think it well to preface the narrative with a few brief particulars,
which—should this manuscript after my death fall into the hands. of
a stranger—may assist in a better understanding of what follows. I am
singularly devoid of near ties. I have no certain knowledge whether
the name I bear is mine by right or mine by adoption: I never knew
father or mother. I was placed at school by a guardian who showed
no disposition to cultivate a nearer acquaintance; and from school I
passed to college, where I made few friends and took only a moderate
degree. At twenty-three I attained the control of my modest fortune,
a few hundreds yearly; not enough for wealth, but enough to set me
free from the necessity of adopting a profession.

The next ten years I spent aimlessly enough partly in foreign travel,
and in writing one or two descriptive books which met with some
degree of ephemeral popularity. And then I found at last the absorbing
interest of my life in Egyptian exploration, and threw in my lot with
a certain well-known body of workers. From 1877 to 1882 I laboured
in the Nile Valley, working with hands as well as with brain, uncover-
ing temple sites, opening tombs, deciphering hieroglyphics, driving

fellaheen, and building up theories like the rest. But in the early spring of 1882 a misfortune befell me, and I was laid aside with sunstroke and fever.

I had only myself to thank for it so my friends were kind enough to tell me. I had presumed on long immunity and a naturally hardy constitution, and exposed myself over-recklessly to the increasing heat. We were then at work on the temple of Kom Ombo, examining the remains of that earlier foundation which dates from the Pharaohs of the Third Period, as well as the later structure which bears the symbols of the hawk and the crocodile. I had been absorbed in the discovery of some unknown and deeply interesting particulars, relating to the temple service and with allusion to its mysteries, and was proportionately annoyed at having to relinquish my share in the work; but there was nothing for it but to return home. It is natural to call England home, even when, as in my case, home is an empty name.

I took steamer from Alexandria, and arrived in London so much restored by the sea-breezes that I resolved at once to set about the book I had planned, and for which I had already amassed voluminous notes. I found my former publishers open to negotiations, and, having given an undertaking it should be forthcoming by the winter, I hired rooms within easy reach of the British Museum. I still suffered at times with my head, but not in a degree to debar me from work; and I spent the greater part of the summer and late autumn days sitting at my desk. The book grew, and by the end of August I had several completed chapters, and my friend Knollys was at work on the illustrations to be developed from my own rough sketches, reproducing inscriptions and depicting certain curios, a collection of which I had brought with me from the East.

My rooms in G—— Street were moderately convenient, and my landlady would serve me there with a sufficiently palatable dinner when I was not disposed to go out to the club. I had a bedroom and sitting-room on the ground floor, the sitting-room behind to insure greater quiet, though the outside traffic was not great. They had formerly been in the occupation of an artist, and their chief attraction to me had been the permitted use of a temporary outer room in the garden-court at the back, built there as a studio with top lights, and entered either by a glass door at the end of the hall or from one side of the projecting window of my study. In this I found convenient stowage for my collection, and Knollys would come to work there as a rule-passing in and out without disturbing me unless communication became necessary. In that early October of which I write-the October of 1882-he began to look in rather often, with an expression of concern on his kind, quizzical face.

"I tell you what, Lavenham," he would say; "you are overdoing it, that is where it is. You will have your fever back again, and the devil to pay besides. You are working like a packhorse, and I believe you hardly knock off even to have your meals. I should like to get a doctor to give you a talking to."

I looked up at my kind monitor on about the eleventh delivery of this diatribe, which had become an almost daily formula; and I was conscious, first, that my head was paining me worse than usual; and, secondly, that the passage I had been striving for the last hour to elaborate would be better shut away till I could go back to it with less wearied brain.

"You look like a ghost, Lavenham. You had better take my advice, and you know it. You cannot make any real advance till that precious consignment of Turkey sponges comes to hand, and that will not be for another ten days at earliest. Lock up the pens and paper, and give yourself a holiday. Is there no one you could take a run out of town to see, for the week-end if no more?"

No, there was no one. I had forgotten my former associates, and had been forgotten by them; and there was not a single intimacy I felt disposed to revive. I had been away too many years, and since my return had inclined only to bury myself more and more remotely, like a hermit-crab in its shell. I shook my head over the suggestion.

"I would offer to go with you, but you know how I am tied at the present time. But I have for once a free evening, and I am going to throw it away in what will seem a sufficiently fantastic fashion to a grave and reverend *signor* like yourself. I'm going to Mrs. Bevis Payne's, and I want you to dine with me at the club and come too."

"My dear fellow, I don't know her, and I am sure she will not want to know me."

"You are quite mistaken. She likes lions, and I will introduce you as one of the first blood: my friend Lavenham, author, explorer, Egyptologist; engaged on a work which will be the book of the season! I've got a card for self and friend; and, to tell you the truth, there's a little girl there I want especially to meet."

I should have had no hesitation usually in negativing such a suggestion; but this time Knollys looked so kindly eager over his proposal, as he began to hunt his pockets for the letter, that excuses faltered on my tongue. When the card at last was found and laid before me, my unreadiness had sealed my fate: it was tacitly understood I would go to this leonine reception with my friend. The card was somewhat peculiar. Below the announcement of "Mrs. Bevis Payne at home" was written, in a rather dashing feminine hand, "Psychological Evening. To meet Madame St. Heliers."

"Oh, it's just one of Mrs. Payne's fads!" said Knollys in reply to my inquiry. "Sometimes it is theosophy—sometimes it is a mission to the heathen-sometimes it is art. Just now it is palmistry and clairvoyance and all that—so Madge tells me. I believe this Frenchwoman is rather an extraordinary person, ready to turn you inside out, analyse your character, and predict your future as soon as look at you. Madge is afraid of her, and so I am going to mount guard. She receives in the back drawing-room, and you need not go near her unless you like."

This was all the preparation I had for what was before me. When Knollys was gone, I so far obeyed his injunctions as to fold together my papers and put them away, together with the flimsy pink telegram which advised me of the despatch of the case of Turkey sponges to which he had alluded. The sender was Jack Skipton, a friend in Alexandria, and the curious consignment really enveloped and concealed a widely different one, which I had requested him to procure for the purpose of some experiments necessary to my work. The true enclosure was a mummy of the superior class, still sealed in its original casings and unviolated by the wholesale system of robbery which has prevailed in Egypt for centuries; a system by which the dead have been despoiled—not only of such valuables as it was the practice to bury with them, but of the very spices with which their bodies were embalmed—stolen in former times to figure again in the market, and take a fresh turn of service with the modern dead.

I was in this case to be the despoiler, as I wished to submit these spices, or what traces remained of them, to the analysis of an expert. I had for long suspected that in the higher walks of the embalmer's art—as mentioned by Herodotus and others—existed certain secrets both of ingredient and method; and to trace these, as far as might now be possible, was part of the design of my book. It is in these days no easy matter to procure such a mummy as would serve my purpose, as there are certain restrictions which are difficult to evade. But I knew, if the thing could be accomplished at all, Jack Skipton was the man to put it through for me; and the coming of that flimsy pink paper with the brief message, "Expect sponges," had that morning assured me of success.

I had certainly awaited the intimation with. some anxiety, and was gratified by its reception; but the singular excitement which agitated me from that time forward was quite unexpected and wholly annoying. It must be due, as Knollys said, to overwork together with the pain in my head, and the sudden inability to string together a dozen connected sentences of what before had been ready to flow from my pen. I could not count on many vacant days if the manuscript were really to be completed within the terms of my engagement; but it might, after all, be the wisest economy of time to try what rest would do for me over the weekend, at any rate—leaving a shut desk behind in G—— Street, and spending a solitary Sunday by the sea.

It was a somewhat haggard countenance which faced me in the glass as I made my evening toilet—a ceremony I did not often perform; but Knollys, when I joined him at the club, professed already to see improvement. I could not honestly say I felt better—the pain in my head still continued, together with the over-rapid, unequal pulse; but I told him of my projected visit to Brighton, and he was on the whole well satisfied.

We were early arrivals at Mrs. Payne's probably Knollys was pledged to be punctual; and I imagine he had in some way contrived to sound the leonine trumpet before me, as I was received with effusion. Mrs. Payne professed herself honoured, and volubly regretted having so small an assembly to meet me—so few people had yet returned to town, etc., etc. The drawing-rooms were certainly empty on our arrival, but in another half-hour, they began to fill up as if the psychological entertainment promised attraction; and I noticed that Knollys managed to keep a remarkably pretty girl at his elbow in a recess, the hostess's attention being mainly directed to me. This no doubt was Madge, who, I discovered, was a companionable poor relation and guest, not a daughter of the house.

I did not expect to meet acquaintances, and stood about in solitary fashion when Mrs. Payne was not plying me with dexterous flatteries, or questions about the East and my forthcoming work. She introduced me here and there; but conversation all ran in the same groove, about the mysterious Madame St. Heliers: had I consulted her before? did I know if she had arrived? Was it not possible. she might fail Mrs. Payne at the last, she was said to be so very uncertain? Or was she all the time behind the heavy velvet *portières* which shut out the inner room? I need hardly say these queries were feminine; indeed, the feminine element largely prevailed at the gathering, only four or five black coats keeping Knollys and me in countenance.

The sibyl did not fail us; the expectation had hardly become strained when I saw our hostess turn to the door to greet a new arrival. This was a small person dressed in brown—a soft gown which trailed after her on the floor—and who did not attempt, as so many short women do, to ape a higher stature by an exaggeration of *coiffure*. She was elderly enough to be grey-haired, and only redeemed from plainness by a good pair of eyes. The eyes had, I thought, a peculiarly intense and magnetic look about them; and, while Mrs. Payne was whispering instructions, she deliberately surveyed the room, and looked curiously at me as I stood against the wall behind the arm-chairs of the dowagers. What she thought of her audience I cannot say they were not a particularly attractive gathering; but she shrugged her shoulders and spread out her hands with a foreign little gesture of pro-test in replying to Mrs. Payne, who forthwith conducted her behind the closed *portières*, and both disappeared from view.

With this the stiff order of the room was broken up, and small groups began to press nearer to the curtains in the hope of an early interview. Mrs. Payne when she reappeared was at once besieged. As I looked on from my post of observation with, it must be confessed, only a languid interest, wondering how soon I could slip away with Knollys, my attention was arrested by a totally unexpected figure. This was a man in the sacerdotal costume of ancient Egypt, such as I have seen portrayed in temples and tombs, and associated with the blue complexion which is the conventional sign of the priestly caste.

His garment of white linen partly covered the head, which I saw was shaven: he was tall in stature, lithe-and upright, and his distinctly Egyptian features would have been strikingly handsome but that they were disfigured by so intense an expression of malevolent anger. He came into view from behind a knot of people near the doorway, some twenty feet away, across the width of the room, and stood for a few seconds in the vacant space, his eyes blazing into mine and his hand clinched, while I remained transfixed with astonishment.

It may have been half a minute before he moved, slipping behind another group nearer the recess his face turned on me to the last with the same look of scathing hatred. With his withdrawal came an instant impulse to follow; but it is impossible to rush across a room full of people, elbowing them right and left, and treading recklessly on the trailing skirts of women. I had to thread my way with caution and courtesy, and, tall as was the figure and peculiar the attire, I completely lost sight of it in the crowd. When I gained the recesss no one was there but Knollys and his *inamorata* and two elderly ladies, each engaged in conversing into the ear-trumpet of the other.

"Which way has he gone-the Egyptian?" I said, *sotto voce*, to Knollys. He gave me a bewildered look, totally at a loss to guess my meaning. "You must have seen him from here you can see down all the length of the room. A tall fellow in white linen, like a priest."

"My dear Lavenham, there is no such person here; we don't go in for fancy dress. Unless, indeed," with an appeal to the girl beside him—"it is some satellite of Madame St. Heliers'?"

Madge shook her pretty head and looked puzzled. *Madame* had a black page, she thought; but no—she had never brought him here with her; and she too had seen nobody. I did not think that very surprising in either case, as probably she and Knollys were both engrossed with affairs of their own. I could not cross-examine the deaf ladies, so I strolled back into the larger room to keep watch on the doorway; but the singular figure did not appear again. Could it have been somebody masquerading? But who would take the trouble for such an instantaneous appearance, and in a costume of which perhaps I alone of all those present would comprehend the meaning?

And it was not as if I had been a specially invited and expected guest. I had been brought there as an impromptu afterthought by Knollys; unless, indeed, Knollys was in the plot, an idea quite untenable. I tried to anchor myself on the conviction that the man was a confederate of Madame St. Heliers' it was easy to suspect a fortune-teller of any amount of charlatanry; but the dress and the stare of anger, and the fact that he seemed to attract no attention from the persons surrounding him, unusual as had been his appearance, still remained unaccountable by any explanation I could guess at.

In the meantime, several people had penetrated one by one behind the drawn curtains, returning-some graver than they went, others giggling (these were mainly the younger ones)—when Mrs. Payne appeared to be summoned to a conference. On her return she waved away the eager aspirants. "I must beg of you all to wait a little," she said. "*Madame* has seen ten ladies, and she now asks for someone of the opposite sex. She says it prevents an undue drain on her power to have an alternation. This time I am to send a gentleman, and she asks for the gentleman with a beard who was opposite the door when she entered. That must be you, Mr. Lavenham. You'll go in, of course?"

It had been far from my intention to consult the oracle; but it occurred to me on the instant that here was my opportunity to solve the mystery of the Egyptian—doubtless I should discover him in the back drawing-room in conjunction with the rest of the *diablerie*. I thanked Mrs. Payne, and came forward at her bidding, disappearing in my turn behind the curtains.

2

The back drawing-room had been effectively arranged in semi-darkness; a single lamp with a deep-red shade burned in the farther corner, and under the circle of its illumination sat Madame St. Heliers. She wore a black lace scarf thrown over her grey curls, possibly because the room felt chilly with only the embers of a dying fire left in the grate; and she sat propping her chin on her hand, and looking fixedly and in silence at the entering victim. I made my bow also in silence; I would wait, I thought, for the sibyl to address me, and abstain from leading questions. The Egyptian was not visible; but my eyes were still dazzled with the glare of the outer apartment, and might not penetrate his hiding-place.

Madame maintained her silence and her serious aspect sufficiently long to make me feel somewhat foolish; then a bright smile lashed from eyes to mouth, irradiating her small, pale face, and she drew aside the velvet folds of her dress, pointing to a low seat at her side.

"You did not want to come to me-I know that; and you have no opinion of this sort of thing—I know that also. But I was attracted to you directly I saw you, and determined I would have a talk with you. You are a man with a history—it is either made or yet to make. I shall soon find out which it is, little as you credit my methods. Give me your hands."

I held them out, palm upwards, scarred and roughened as they were with the manual labour of the past. She took them with her soft ones, and held them closer to the circle of red light, poring intently over them for a few moments. Then she released me, and leaned back in her chair, looking rather grave.

"I have seen hands by the hundred, and read spheres by the hundred also; that is, the personality, as perhaps you would term it, which is often more indicative than the lines. But I never knew a parallel case to yours. I am glad I made you come. You are unique."

It was now my turn to smile. jargon, I thought, which was comers? Was this the ready for all comers?

"There is plenty of history. You had an unhappy childhood. Your life has been solitary—you have travelled far across seas—you are a writer. Someone might have told me all this, might they not? though I do not know even your name. Am I right so far?"

I assented briefly, but I had the thought she indicated. Much of this might have been known of me through Knollys to Mrs. Payne.

"But the history I see is to come. Your solitude is nearly over. You are an affectionate man, though you do not know it. You are capable of passionate devotion, and you will throw your all at the feet of a stranger, who will become suddenly, in a moment, the ruling influence of your life. Whether this will be for good or for evil I cannot determine; it seems to me that you are under the shadow of a great calamity, but I am unable to say if it comes to you with your love. You have the gift of clairvoyance, but I imagine it has hitherto been dormant; you may in this way receive warning. And I would warn you also that you have an enemy, and a powerful one, who will strike you through your heart's dearest, and strike home. That will be the blow which shatters: see here! it is marked already, through your heart and fate. Beware of the snows of winter and Orion low in the east. Now Mrs. Payne will expect you back. Have you anything to ask before you leave me?"

I had risen, accepting my dismissal, and she rose also as I stood before her. My eyes by this time were focused to the dim light, and I could be sure we were alone in the room, which was a small one. "Tell me this," I said—"Who is the Egyptian?"

"The Egyptian?"

"Yes; the man in white linen, shaven like a priest. What do you know of him? Did he come with you?"

"Then do you see him as well?" was her counter-question. "That is a danger the less. Beware of him; it is he that is your enemy."

She came close to me, speaking these words in an emphatic whisper, and then pushed me away from her with both hands as Mrs. Payne opened the curtains."

I forgot all about Knollys. I made my acknowledgments and excuses to our hostess—how, I can hardly say; for all is confusion to my remembrance till I found myself alone in the street under the night sky, facing the chill autumn wind as I walked eastward. I think it was that cold breath about me which cleared my brain and brought me to myself, for I felt as a man might who is drunk with the inhalation of a narcotic. What spell had bewitched me in that ordinary middle-class house, with its good-natured hostess and crowd of commonplace guests, credulous enough to be entertained by a fortune-teller?

I would fain have styled the fortune-teller commonplace as well, but the term did not fit Madame St. Heliers. I could not help suspecting that her magnetism had wrought about me this singular disturbance of the senses, and I was conscious the words of her ominous warning were burning themselves into my brain. The irritability induced by overwork had rendered me sensitive to impression–doubtless that was all; but I could not feel Knollys's prescription of a social evening, however well meant, had met my case.

I went to bed and to sleep without opening a book, and woke late, though unrefreshed, as I had been harassed by dreams. After breakfast I went as usual to my desk, resolving to limit myself in the way of hours, but was aghast to find I was incapable of the effort of composition. I sat with the pen in my hand staring blankly at the unwritten page, and at last flung it from me in despair. Knollys was right—whatever the sensitive intellectual machinery may be on which we depend for origination, it was clear mine had been overstrained; and, for a time at least, I must try change of scene and rest.

I dashed off a line to leave for Knollys, and in another hour had taken train for Brighton. I should perhaps have done wisely to seek a quieter place with more of country surroundings, rather than go in this way from a town to a town; but, with all my usual occupations cut away, it seemed to me that I should feel less *ennui* in a crowd, even though it would be a crowd of the unknown.

I arrived there on a Friday afternoon, and spent that evening and most of the following day dawdling up and down the esplanade, or propped against the railing puffing tobacco-smoke. As I looked out over the heaving plain of green water, I heartily wished myself back again, spade in hand, among my comrades in the East—battling with our enemy the sand, at once the great obliterator and the great preserver of those relics of a dead past. Welcome the hot wind like the breath of a furnace, the torrid sun, the plague of flies beyond the power of even a Moses to remit, could I have exchanged for them England and inaction such as weighed upon me now.

There was beauty in sky and sea, and music in the wash of the waves on the shingle, wet higher and higher every moment by the advancing border of foam; but my eyes were dull to the one as my ears to the other. I could not get up the faintest interest in the endless procession of Bath-chairs, the overdressed women, the riotous children, the abounding dog-population, the smart equipages and equestrians in the ride. Possibly I was all the more disposed to dwell on the events of my last evening in London, and the expected consignment from Alexandria, than if my mind had been otherwise occupied.

I had seen too many mummies to be sanguine as to Jack Skipton's capture being a real treasure-trove of historical interest; but I hoped it would prove to be an unopened one of the higher caste, such as I stipulated for, and suitable for the desired experiments. I had strolled down to the shingle on the Saturday afternoon to while away the last hour before *table d'hôte*, scrutinising the boats hauled up above the tide-line, and picking my way among waifs of seaweed and debris, but with the pink telegram shut up in G—— Street always the rallying-point of meditation. The very sky seemed to have taken the hue of it, flushed as it was now with the decline of day; but when I at last turned hotelwards my thoughts were scattered by the shock of a sudden surprise.

A man was standing some yards behind me, higher up the steep shore, and nearer to the steps leading to the promenade; the same white-robed figure I had seen in the London drawing-room, and with the same expression of vindictive anger the features and the fashion of the linen garment, for twilight had hardly yet begun to follow sunset. He stood for about the same space of time as before, and then, turning on his heel, began rapidly to mount the steps.

I plunged upward through the heavy shingle, bent on following and accosting him. He had reached the top of the steps ere I had more than gained the bottom, but, as if he had no desire to escape me, he turned and waited, facing me once more. If his motive were attack, he would thus have had me at a disadvantage, as I was armed only with a light cane; but I was too intent on solving the riddle to hesitate. I was near enough to see the gleam of his eye, and to recognise the figure of a crocodile displayed upon his breast, when my foot caught on an uneven stone and I stumbled forward. It was only a moment before I recovered myself and was at the top; but the man was gone, and had disappeared as completely as he had done before at Mrs. Payne's.

The esplanade was thronged with people enjoying the fine evening, but not so crowded as to afford concealment for such a figure, and in the moment of time which had passed since. This time the hand was raised with a threatening gesture, and in it shone something which might have been a weapon. There was plenty of light to show I fell at its feet. I looked from side to side, at a loss which way to follow;

221

and no doubt appeared singular enough in my hurried rush up the steps and pause of bewilderment, for I noticed several of the passers-by turned to look, and a man leaning against the rail with a cigar was in particular regarding me curiously.

I put the same question to him as before to Knollys. A man in a white dress had come up the steps in front of me would the stranger tell me in what direction he had gone?

The man stared incredulously. He had been looking at the steps—had seen me rush up them from the beach and stumble forward, but there was no man in white. It must have been an optical illusion—of light on the notice-board, which I could see was at the top, and which probably misled me. So far with courtesy, but as I moved away, I saw he turned to his companion and tapped his forehead significantly.

That little action impressed me fully as much as the appearance, and I walked back to the hotel inexpressibly discomforted. Was that the true explanation, after all? Was my brain no longer to be relied on—not alone for the faculty of work which had deserted me, but to show me in their true shapes the common surroundings of this common world? If so, the end might come—must come; life would be impossible, I thought, under conditions such as these. And then there floated across me again the recollection of the fortune-telling woman in London, and her mysterious words, "You see him too?" That implied community with another; another who might help me, and explain—where reason told me no explanation could stand which was not more fantastic than the fact.

That was a dismal evening. I did not care to go out after dinner; my experience of the afternoon and the doubts which followed it seemed to have filled all the outside world with an atmosphere of pain into which I hesitated to plunge. I broke through my usual reserve, and tried to talk to the men in the smoking-room. I even attempted a game of billiards, at which I was once somewhat expert. But my companions did not interest me—the green cloth had lost its charm; I could not fix my attention on the spheres of ivory; and I went early to bed, hoping to find forgetfulness in sleep.

I did sleep for the first hours of the night, and then woke and lay listening to the distant rhythm of waves on the shingle, fully audible in the stillness. My room was to the front of the house, an old-fashioned one in an avenue running westward at the northern end of the parade, not far from the sea. After a while the darkness grew oppressive; and as a glimmer between the drawn curtains suggested moonlight, I got up, pulled them apart, raised the blind, and looked out.

The pavement opposite was alternately silver-white and black with shadow; the sky was clear, the night fair and still. I seemed to be the only creature awake and astir in all that somnolent world; the fleecy cloud just showing above the smokeless chimneys hung motionless, as if the winds also slept. A town at night looks more dead in its repose than the country ever can; more suggestive of something wanting—the full life which throbs through it in the day.

I raised the window-sash—softly, for fear of disturbing sleepers in the vicinity, huddled on a coat, for my tropical experiences have left me chilly, and proceeded to light a pipe: tobacco and cold air taken conjointly might perhaps prove soporific. A few congenial whiffs had soothed me into a placid train of thought, when, as I bent forward to knock out the ashes before refilling, I was attracted by a movement amongst those still lines of shadow to the right.

A figure had turned into the short street or court at the top, and was passing on the opposite side of the way, soundless-footed as a cat. A dim shape only in the shadow, but when it moved on into the moonlight—good Heaven! was it a somnambulist taking an airy stroll in his nightshirt, or the same enigma which had been visible half-a-dozen hours before on the sea-shore? Was it only my own imagination which figured the clean shaved Eastern face with the delicately chiselled features and terrible eyes upon that which looked up into mine at the moment of passing out of dimness into light, and forward again into shadow? It may have been so, but in that breathless instant it seemed to me that I again saw the Egyptian.

I was a late breakfaster the next morning, though not a solitary one; but the coffee and bacon had scant relish as a preliminary to the long empty day stretching before me, full of self-doubt and self-communing which I could not evade. I am not an habitual church-goer, and I believe it was some impulse of early superstition which suggested to me that I should thus take sanctuary, as it were, from my enemy; the same feeling which prompts an old crone to put a Bible under her pillow as a safeguard against hobgoblins. I consulted the waiter, and found I could hardly reach any of the fashionable churches in decent time; but there was one not more than a street's-length away where service would barely have begun. I care nothing for candles and ritual; the consecrated place and the occupation were all I desired; so, I followed the direction of the waiter and found the church he indicated.

It was certainly not a fashionable one, but the old-style high box-pews were well filled. As I was ushered into one of them by an official on the watch for sixpences, the dismal appearance of the place struck me with an ominous chill. Pulpit and reading-desk were draped with black cloth, and the same funereal emblem of woe was festooned along the front of the heavy gallery: more than two-thirds of the visible bonnets were black, and pocket-handkerchiefs were liberally displayed. A severe-looking individual, who noticed my destitute condition, handed me a prayer-book, and I ventured on a whispered inquiry.

"For the late incumbent," was the reply-whisper. "A funeral sermon."

I had truly chanced upon an admirable remedy for depression of spirits! I forget the late incumbent's name—I am not sure if I ever knew it—but I remember the discourse in which he was eulogised, and the sniffs and sobs which presently arose in my vicinity. How the world went on before that admirable man embarked on the task of its correction, how it would continue now his guiding influence was withdrawn, were alike left to conjecture. The preacher was very impressive, very flowery, and—very long-winded. I listened in a species of warm drowsiness which had succeeded my wakeful night and was perhaps further induced by the notion of a security under that roof greater than I could feel under any other; and when the concluding "And now" brought the congregation to their feet, I was almost sorry the sermon had ended and it behoved me to turn out into the street.

I stood at the pew-door, letting the stream flow past me before I followed it, and looking towards the point of exit, when a face turned back to me in the crowd, magnetizing my gaze to it on the instant—passed on and disappeared in the porch. It was again the Egyptian, and again the same shock as in the night thrilled through nerves and blood. But another surprise was in store for me. Had I been disposed to follow, it would not have been possible to leave the pew at the moment, as there was a temporary block against the door. It was caused by a stout woman who had dropped a cargo of small books in the aisle, and they were being gathered up for her by a polite stranger, and a young girl who blushed very much, and was, I think, her daughter. Stepping from an opposite pew on the farther side beyond the block was the person to whom beyond all others I desired to speak—Madame St. Heliers.

She looked at me without apparent recognition, but it was she beyond the possibility of mistake the same small, pale face and intent eyes and grey curled hair, though now surmounted by a bonnet instead of her laces; and she wore brown velvet of the same hue, though this time it was a feathered mantle. She passed quickly to the door, following the Egyptian; and by the time I had at last struggled out of my durance and was in pursuit, she too had disappeared. But I was able to tell myself she at least was no delusion. *Madame* was in Brighton, and this might explain—must explain—the coincidence of the Egyptian. To find and question her was now my purpose: not for a few apportioned minutes, as at Mrs. Payne's, but for the explanation which I divined she could give of the unwelcome mystery that had come into my life.

I went back to the hotel a new man: the definite aim lifted for a time the cloud of despondency which hung darkly over me, and I did not at first appreciate the difficulty of the undertaking which lay before me. There is an old-world saying about searching for a needle in hay; and seeking for one woman in a wilderness of streets and houses is nearly its parallel. I did my best both that day and the Monday morning, calling at one hotel and boarding-house after another, and asking for Madame St. Heliers, only to meet with an invariable negative.

Of course, it was quite possible she might be staying with private friends, and possible also that the name under which I knew her might only be adopted professionally, while her real cognomen was commonplace Smith or Robinson. I had all along intended returning to London on the Monday: I would still do so, see Knollys and ascertain her address, which he could discover for me through Mrs. Payne, and then again take train for Brighton and the interview I desired.

3

I sent a wire from the station to Knollys, "Come round to my diggings this evening," and took the afternoon express up to town. Months instead of days seemed to have elapsed since last I travelled through that autumnal country: the sear woods with their brilliant leafage hardly yet despoiled, the golden stubbles broken here and there by the fresh lines of the plough, the flat pastures and the grazing flocks. I can feel the beauty of rural England, though it does not appeal to me through associations of a happy past, which no doubt makes its chiefest charm to the many. Those long days at Brighton had brought with them strange experiences, painful doubts, acute depression; and I felt an older man for all I had gone through. I was still revolving the same hideous perplexity, still arraigning my own sanity at that inward bar of judgment, as the panorama of open country shifted to suburb, and the question was yet unsolved when the train glided in under the echoing roof of the great terminus.

There is a certain element of comfort in most things which habit makes familiar like an old shoe trodden easy to the foot, or an old coat stretched to the curve of one's shoulders; and in this way there was some amount of comparative home-likeness in my return to G—— Street. Mrs. Mappinbeck received me with smiles, and had a cheerful fire alight in the sitting room; and I felt hope stir within me as I looked at the shut-up desk in the corner. If I could work again, I thought— the work round which all my interests centred—I might well afford to put away into oblivion that harassing enigma.

I had finished my solitary dinner and after-glass of claret, and had read through the evening paper from beginning to end before Knollys made his appearance. It was cheering to see a friend's face; and he came in full of kindly interest, a bit of wholesome fresh reality to be the touchstone for sick fancies. I had resolved to make a clean breast to him of my trouble; he was not the man to betray my confidence, even to a woman; and with him I should be safe.

If we had been a pair of Frenchmen, I suppose we should have embraced; but being only unemotional Britons, "Halloa, Lavenham!" and, "Here I am again, you see!" was the extent of our greeting. I pushed across the claret to the clean wine-glass side, and he threw off his overcoat and drew in to the fire, giving me a glance as if not wholly satisfied with my appearance.

"I doubt if you have given Brighton a long enough trial," he said. "I would have been round earlier, but I got behindhand with an off-day last week, and am trying to make up for it with longer hours. I could not even afford to keep Sabbath yesterday, and go and see Madge, as I wished. I am glad to see you back, old fellow; but you haven't taken enough of my prescription, and I had rather you had stopped away. There's a paradox for you!"

"Very likely I shall go back to Brighton tomorrow; that is, if I can get an address I want there. But I'm afraid change of air won't meet my case. It is harassing me a good deal, Knollys; and I would like to have your opinion, if you have patience to go into symptoms."

"Patience enough for a dozen doctors, but the usual amount of lay ignorance. I am capable of much sympathy, but of very little advice. But tell me what is up. Have you been worse than I thought?"

With that I began my story—the story which is written here. Never in my life before had I experienced a spectral illusion, not even when delirious with fever, if indeed that were the true explanation of what I had seen. At my first sight of him in Mrs. Payne's drawing-room, I had no suspicion whatever that the Egyptian was any less a creature of flesh and blood than I was myself. I had confidently taken him for a satellite of the fortune-teller, and part of her *mise en scène*; and the first idea that he was in some way associated with her had been strengthened by the singular reply she made to my question—or counterquestion, to be more accurate.

"I don't think anything of that," Knollys broke in at this point. "Those people are nothing if not mysterious. No doubt she seized the opportunity of impressing you, without the least real knowledge of what you referred to—or the fellow was her confederate all through."

"Wait and hear the rest." And I went on to tell of the apparition on the beach, as solid in appearance as the other; of the deliberate pause made on the steps, the disappearance at the instant of my stumble, and the man who, looking on, had seen nothing save me alone. Knollys did not interrupt again or express incredulity. I told of the midnight passer-by, of the face in church, and of the presence of Madame St. Heliers; and when my narrative came to an end, he made no immediate reply. It was not easy to find anything reassuring to say to a man who has been the victim of such an experience; but after an interval of staring at the fire and tugging at his moustache, he spoke with confidence.

"Look here, Lavenham, I'll tell you how it strikes me. I think there has been a mixture of fact and delusion over this, which accounts for some of the difficulty. Of course, you know you ran a risk of knocking up when you settled to this literary work directly after such an illness as you had abroad. What you have experienced is just the result of an overtaxed brain—all on the lines of what has occupied your mind, if you consider: you are writing about ancient Egypt, and your phantom is naturally an ancient Egyptian.

"The affair at Mrs. Payne's may very well have been a bit of masquerading *hocus-pocus* on the part of the French woman; I did not see anything myself, it is true, but then I was not looking out for it. That made an impression on you, your nerves being all wrong at the time—that, and *Madame's* patter which followed it—an impression of which your brain or your visual nerve, one or other, was retentive, and externalized to you the first opportunity. No doubt that first opportunity was your solitude on the beach; and on the other occasions the same thing happened, but less perfectly. I dare say there was a real night-prowler going down the street, and you reflected on him the face which was in your mind, and the highly inappropriate costume into the bargain. The same upon some unsuspecting individual in church; and Madame St. Heliers' presence was a mere coincidence—"

I shook my head at this, but he went on:

"You have asked my opinion as a lay doctor; my advice is, go and consult a real one. Tell Messrs. Travis & Co. they must extend the time for your book—there will be no difficulty to speak of; and take a couple of months' complete idleness. It is what you ought to have done when first you came home."

"I may consult a doctor after a while," I said, "but I am going to someone else first."

Knollys's eyes made the inquiry, if not his lips, as I paused over filling my pipe.

"I am going to consult Madame St. Heliers. You may be quite right, Knollys—I dare say you are; but before I do anything else I must get to the bottom of that woman's connection with the mystery. I failed to find her at Brighton, and now I want you to help me. Find out from Mrs. Payne where she is staying and let me know."

"I believe you are on a wild-goose chase; and you'll find she won't do anything for you—because she can't. But if it is understood you will see a doctor after, I don't mind helping you to this first, but you will have to make haste. I know from Madge that Madame St. Heliers is going abroad for the winter, and is on the point of leaving England; for that was a sort of farewell appearance the other night at Mother Payne's. I've no doubt I can get her address, as she and Mrs. Payne are very intimate—birds of a feather, as the saying is; but it is not a feather I have a fancy for. I'll drop a line to Madge if you'll give me pen and paper, and post it as I leave here. I shall get an answer by the afternoon, and I will bring it round to you if it tells what you want. Will that do?"

He wrote the letter before he left me—a longer one than the shaping of the mere inquiry; but that, I suppose, is the way of lovers. His explanation was plausible, though I could not feel it altogether met the case; but to have eased my mind by the avowal and to have shared my burden with another was much; and his cheerful conviction that all lay within the realm of the physical and the reach of a doctor's prescription comforted me in spite of myself. I slept soundly that night, and the next morning rose to find Jack Skipton's letter on the breakfast-table.

I have it by me, and shall transcribe such portions of it as bear upon my narrative.

"Dear Old Chum,—Your precious consignment is safe through the custom-house and *en route*; and I am enjoying—in company with a bottle of India pale—the first moment of real ease which has visited me since I received a certain commission. Never was there such a job in the doing as this which I undertook at the call of friendship; and I doubt if even friendship such as ours would stir me up to the undertaking of a *ditto*. As for myself, I ought to take rank as Orestes and Pylades rolled into one; and I only hope, friend Lavenham, that you appreciate yours truly at his proper value.

"That the valuable shipment really is what it professes to be (not in the bills of lading, by-the-way !)—an unopened mummy-case of the Twentieth Dynasty or thereabouts-rests on the assurance and testimony of that old Arab thief, Abd-el-Moluk of Thebes. And that he believes it goes without words'; for does not the promised remuneration—which, by-the-way, touches the outside limit of what you empowered me to offer-depend on the consignment satisfying you on every point? Till I get your assurance that all is on the square, that money remains on deposit, suspended, like Mahomet's coffin, between heaven and earth. So, wire me back when you get the thing open, that I may put the old fox out of his misery. Not that he will own to any doubt about it; on the contrary, he seems particularly confident.

"I knew if anyone could put the thing through for us, he could, being up to all the tricks of the trade, the real and the false together; and, what is more, I have his neck in a noose through a certain past-and-gone transaction not suitable for daylight. However he may swindle others, I did not think he would draw the feather over me. So, I sent for him, and he came up to my rooms, looking as pious and venerable as you please—the old fox, and swearing by the beard of his Prophet that he only breathed to serve me—and all that rot. I told him what we wanted, and made him understand, in language more forcible than polite, that none of his cooked-up shams would go down in your case—it must be the real Simon Pure. Well, he took to muttering a string of things out of the *Koran*, as they do when they are afraid of the evil-eye, and then he went to the door and looked out; and finally, he came close up to me—a good deal closer than I liked, for your Arab is odoriferous. He could put his hand on the very thing for us, provided I would keep counsel; but there were difficulties in the way—of course; and it would cost much money-also of course; and might lose

229

him his soul into the bargain.

"This was an item I did not expect, but as he is certain to be damned any way, it ought to have been light in the balance. I asked for particulars, and he came out with a truly extraordinary story, which you can believe or not as you like. For my own part, I am inclined to believe a good deal of it, the man went such an awful colour over telling it, and the sweat stood out on him in drops. It seems, about eighteen months ago or rather more, he was engaged as head over a gang of workers for the Government among the cliffs out there by Luxor—a lynx-eyed official to look after him, it is needless to state, or else the Government would have bagged little.

"Among the tombs of the priests, they opened one of a fellow named Savak, after the lesser deity of the Sun. It turned out a rich yield—a *papyrus* or two, a very fine funerary statue, and other things, which went to the Boulak Museum; Abd-el-Moluk says so, at any rate. It was not so highly decorated as some of the others—probably the proprietor was cut short in the days of his youth; and he seems to have died a bachelor. While this place was ransacked, Abd-el-Moluk noticed signs of carefully concealed working in the limestone at the back, indicative of a tomb within a tomb, which is, as you know, not unusual. Instead of pointing this out to his 'boss,' he kept his suspicions to himself—for good reasons, doubtless; and when the search had passed on to other quarters, and the place was deserted again, he and four of his myrmidons returned there secretly and fell to work at the back of the Savak excavation—with the result he anticipated. here was an inner chamber hermetically sealed, with a *sarcophagus* of alabaster, and within it the identical mummy-case which is now on the high seas, hidden away among your sponges.

"Of course the object was spoliation, and the mummy would naturally have been examined then and there for valuables and *papyri* ; but there was some sign or inscription in the inner chamber (if an inscription, it was of course in the Hieratic; but Abd-el-Moluk reads that after a fashion) invoking a curse so terrible on any who should violate its sanctity, or disturb the sleeper within, that he was glad to get off with his prize; and he and his men beat a hasty retreat, carrying off the mummy-case. Here Abd-el-Moluk's story failed in clearness. Something happened which frightened the whole five of them out of their wits, I could not make out what, but evidently, they supposed it to be supernatural; and, concluding the mummy was bewitched, they resolved upon abandoning it, first giving it a hasty reburial. A hole was dug in the sand at a point Abd-el-Moluk could mark down, the thing was shovelled over, and the conspirators fled. There Abd-el-Moluk believed it still remained; and this bundle of malefic influence was what he now proposed to offer you—for a consideration.

"I thought the affair seemed promising. It was evident, the superstition of these body snatchers having been so strongly aroused, that the mummy was really inviolate; so, I signified to Abd-el-Moluk that I was willing to treat on the conditions I mentioned in the beginning. He also advanced conditions. I was to hire a *dahabeeyah* and crew of my own, and go up myself to Luxor; and the crew were to have the privilege of disinterring the mummy and putting it on board. Abd-el-Moluk would accompany me to the spot and point out its whereabouts, but he was not to be required to touch the thing so much as with the tip of his finger, nor would he return to the *dahabeeyah* when it was shipped.

"Once I was in possession, he and I would part company; and except for the after-question of payment—or which he has already begun to hang about—see each other's face no more. The whole artful contrivance was to shift the ill-luck of that mummy disturbance onto my convenient shoulders, and to get off scot-free himself—plus the cash, if you were satisfied.

"The whole thing was an infernal nuisance. I did not want to go up to Luxor. I did not want to be caught red-handed in the possession of an unlawful mummy. Any man in his senses would have said no, and left the old Arab fox to bring it down at his own risk, bad luck and all. But there was, after all, something attractive in the spice of adventure; and this, and the strong considerations of friendship aforesaid, sufficed to prevail. So, I consented, and stood committed to *dahabeeyah*, expedition, and everything else, at Abd-el-Moluk's dictation.

"I need not dwell on the preparations; you are an old Nile voyager, and can fill in my sketch with details from recollections of your own. Suffice it to say that *dahabeeyah* was sunk as a preliminary, and all the vermin took to their boats, and came on board again expectant the instant of its reappearance. It was one of the four-cabin ones, with a single saloon; the *reis* was a friend of Abdel-Moluk's, and we had a picked crew. I invented an errand at Luxor which would serve as a reason for going up there should anybody be inquisitive; and accordingly put in a couple of days at the place, and interviewed some of the officials. Abdel-Moluk had chosen his night, clear starlight with a late moon; and the evening before we dropped down a mile or two below the village, and came to anchor. We left the *reis* with two men on board, and took the rest of the crew with us, Abd-el-Moluk and I, setting out soon after sundown, for the distance was considerable.

"That was a queer expedition, I can tell you; and I believe it had begun to get on my nerves as well as Abd-el-Moluk's; he had been praying all day like a fasting *dervish*. As we went, I tried to shake off the eerie feeling by indulging in a little jocular conversation, but he would have none of it, and hinted the greater prudence of silence. It had not been possible to secure anything to ride without betraying our errand, and I was dog-tired with tramping through the sand when we got to the foot of the cliffs. The moon was just then coming up behind the mountains to the east; and, by Jove! there was something in her cold white light that night which gave me a chill down the back; she wasn't the jolly old moon that used to light us home from frolics, but quite a different sort of luminary.

"Abd-el-Moluk found the place—there seemed to be nothing to mark it from the other sand-hillocks—and the men set to work digging in the loose stuff. The temporary grave was a shallow one, and it was not long before the spades struck substance, and they began to uncover the mummy-case—a finely decorated one of sycamore-wood, which you will appreciate. It was easy to see by this time that Abd-el-Moluk was horribly agitated; he turned quite livid, and kept glancing up at the rock openings above us, either fearing surprise, or else his superstitious terrors were getting too much for him. And it would not have been difficult to fancy anything in that scene and by that light, with weird moving shadows all about us.

"The men had brought some striped cloth and padding to disguise the shape, in which they rolled the thing like a bale of goods, turning it over and over and fastening it with cords; and when ready it was hoisted on their shoulders, and we prepared to follow back to the shore. I don't fancy they half relished what they were about; but they had been offered the bribe of double wages for the job, and for holding their tongues. We were back at the riverside much faster than the outward journey, and my prize was hauled on board and installed in an empty cabin; while the *reis*, according to promise, despatched a boat upstream to convey Abd-el-Moluk back to Luxor.

"So far all was well, but the very quintessence of bad fortune seemed to have come on board to us with that mummy. I know not if any of it followed Abd-el-Moluk, or if the whole farrago stuck to me. We fell under no suspicion, it is true, but I never had such a dropping down the river in all my experience. There was not a single sandbank which that *dahabeeyah* did not run her nose upon, and everything it was possible to foul she fouled. Once we were in imminent peril of sinking, mummy and all, and were saved as it were by a miracle. The *reis* was in despair, and the sailors began to mutter among themselves with evil looks both at me and my cargo; I believe they thought they had a Jonah on board. One man went the length of deserting, and the *reis* had a panic all the rest would follow. I was afraid they might make away with the mummy, which would not have suited my book after the trouble of the capture and indebtedness to Abd-el-Moluk.

"I put some screws of my own in the shutters of the cabin, and at night, hot as it was, made up the door of entrance and the door into the saloon, and lay with mine open and a revolver handy. I am a light sleeper, and kept a sort of dog-watch; the least noise and I was up. The last night but one I had an adventure—which for the life of me I can't explain, unless it was a particularly vivid nightmare. There had been no noise—I can be sure of that; but I woke all of a sudden flat on my back in my bunk, and there was a man's face close to mine. It was a strange face, mind; none of our crew, and many degrees lighter-coloured than any of them; and there was a murderous look about it which made me feel I had but the moment to strike for my life. Pah! I can see the glitter of those eyes whenever I shut my own. I had my revolver close by me, and it was ready loaded; and in less time than it takes to write about it, I pointed it full at the face and fired.

"I am a pretty dead shot, as you will remember, and that bullet ought by rights to have blown the top of his head off—he wasn't more than two feet away. The little place was full of the smoke of the discharge, but I was up in a moment looking for my victim, and, now that it was over, half ashamed of my panic. But the fellow was clean gone, and not a trace was to be seen of any one having got in. My bullet had blown a hole in the upper-deck-that was all, except the disturbance on board as if bedlam had broken loose with the alarm. The doors were fast, just as I had left them, and the *reis* could not explain matters; he did nothing but mutter spells out of the *Koran*, after the fashion of old Abd-el-Moluk. There is a sensation for the finale all that came after, and the risks encountered over transport and shipment, would be only an anticlimax, so I will end here. One word more. I am not a dab at hieroglyphics, but, so far as I have been able to make out, the mummy on its way to you is that of a woman—the virgin daughter of the priest Khames. Send me that wire without fail, to relieve my

233

mind as well as Abd-el-Moluk's, and believe me, dear Lavenham, your devoted—J. Skipton."

I got back to work that morning, and was greatly relieved to find the capacity for it had returned to me. Not that I was able to take up the broken thread of the previous Thursday—there an invisible barrier still withstood me; but, contrary to my usual plodding custom, I passed on to another branch of the subject, and found my pen again fluent. Except to be amused by it, I did not think much of Jack's letter, nor did it occur to me till later to connect his experience with my own. I had done a fair day's work by the time Knollys looked in, and was feeling better satisfied with myself and my world.

He seemed to have taken on my mantle, for he looked harassed and ill at ease, and faced me on the hearth-rug instead of subsiding into his usual seat by the fire. I thought, too, that he scrutinized me with greater solicitude than he had shown the day before.

"I am all right, old fellow," I said, in answer to his look more than his words. "I have set to work again; and I believe, after all, that was what I wanted, for I feel a new man. Have you got the address?"

"I have heard from Madge," he said, taking a letter from his breast-pocket and opening it with a reluctance palpable even to my slow apprehension. "I am afraid you will not be able to consult Madame St. Heliers, for she has gone abroad. And, Lavenham, it must have been someone like her in the Brighton church. She spent the whole of Sunday at Mrs. Payne's, and was there to lunch; and they saw her off yesterday by the boat-train to cross from Folkestone."

4

My hallucination, then, was double—of the fortune-teller as well as her confederate; unless, indeed, it had been, as Knollys tried to persuade me, a mere case of mistaken identity with the former. He argued that a spectral illusion would have shown her to me as I saw her that first evening—the Egyptian had maintained the same appearance throughout—and would not have added the bonnet and mantle *I* had described to him. He took a slip of paper out of the letter, on which was written in a pretty girlish hand; "11 Avenue du Nord, Hyères."

"Madge sends the address to which letters are to be forwarded, but *Madame* will not be there for three weeks—so Mrs. Payne says. She will be moving from place to place and visiting friends, and her plans are uncertain. But you can write there if you like."

I took the paper and thanked him mechanically. My mind was

running on this new development, and I was striving to put behind me the ominous impression, the awful doubt of my own sanity, which confronted me afresh. I could see Knollys was anxious, and had feared the effect on me of the communication he was bound to make. "Do you think of writing to her?" he said.

"I may do so; I am not sure. I want to force the truth from her, and it is easier to evade a written question than one put eye to eye."

"You still think she had a hand in it, though the coincidence of her presence on Sunday has broken down?"

"I know she spoke as if from knowledge of the man and his connection with me, and, sooner or later, I will find out what she meant by it."

"Well, as things have turned out, it will be later, unless you write. I have done my part of the bargain, Lavenham, and now I want you to do yours. You will go to a doctor?"

I put that inward argument aside to smile at him—he was such a good fellow, and he looked so much in earnest. "A specialist for mental cases?" I asked.

"Good heavens! no; not that, in the sense you mean. A clever all-round man, who will find out just how your nerves are out of order and the best way of putting them to rights. Don't mistake my urgency, or imagine that I have such a thought of you."

"Very well; if I find the trouble continues, and comes between me and my work, I pledge myself to see any doctor you like to name. But I must choose my own time. I can't submit to a possible ordering away till Skipton's crate comes to hand and I have ascertained it is what I bargained for. Then I will put myself in leading-strings, shut up shop, and keep holiday if the faculty advise."

I made a double condition in the foregoing—not only of the interval till I received the mummy-case, but also of the continuance of my malady with the former disabling result. And in the days which followed I saw nothing of the Egyptian. I slept ill, it is true, and was harassed by disturbing dreams, and I had little appetite for the fare Mrs. Mappinbeck provided; but I was haunted by no hallucination, and I found myself able to write. I could not work as before, confining myself to a planned system, and what was written at that time is fragmentary; but I thought then, and I think still, it has a higher literary merit than anything I have yet attempted.

It was as if a feverish exaltation was upon me, temporarily increasing the powers of the mind as such a condition does sometimes the

powers of the body. My desk had a fascination for me, and I tore myself away from it with difficulty; but, mindful of my former collapse, I
kept the hours of labour within bounds and took daily exercise—long
evening walks into the suburbs, prolonged perhaps unduly, but my
object was to tire myself out physically, and thus compel sleep.

Knollys was not wholly satisfied with these proceedings; he would
look in now and then, and ask when I was going to the doctor, and if
my sponges had come to hand; but he never inquired whether I had
written to Madame St. Heliers. And, indeed, I was at first undecided
whether to write or no, and for three or four days I kept the address by
me and did nothing. But in the end, I did write—a carefully worded
letter, and despatched it to the address in the Avenue du Nord, to await
her arrival there. It was many long weeks before the answer reached
me, and by then my view of the situation had radically changed, as
will be seen later.

By the time I posted that letter I was in daily expectation of Skipton's consignment. I had made arrangements for its reception in the
studio; setting certain low trestles in a convenient light for the better
display of the mummy-case, which—if as fine as represented—I wanted Knollys to sketch as one of the illustrations for my book. It seems
strange now to remember those preliminaries, and the unmoved and
business-like view I took of the great packing-case when first I beheld
it—through my bedroom window to the front—being lifted off a
dray by three men, who seemed to have as much as they could do to
get it up the two steps and within the hall door. I had a carpenter at
work in the studio, putting up a shelf or two of which I was in need,
and I pressed him into the service. But the noise and scuffling were
considerable, and the men, being awkward with the crate, brought it
in damaging collision with the wall of the passage—peeling off a long
strip of decorative paper which was dear to Mrs. Mappinbeck's soul;
and that, too, just as the worthy lady arrived on the scene of action.

Generally speaking, I was high in her favour; but I found it was
possible she could be tart— and on this occasion she was very tart
indeed. Her wrathful eye marked the torn paper, and mentally entered
it to my account; but she made no open complaint of it, nor did she
notice me as I stood by. Her objurgations were all addressed to the
men. She would trouble them to make less noise, and bring that great
awkward thing in more carefully: she had an invalid lady on her first
floor, a lady of title (the widow of a city knight), who would be seriously annoyed by all this disturbance, and she was bound to consider

236

her lodgers. And so on, in shrill *falsetto*, while the case was propelled through the glass door into the studio, and I followed to make the necessary arrangements with the porters. It was certainly large; and when they vanished, perspiring, I was left contemplating it in company with my carpenter, and planning a united attack.

The lifted lid disclosed a close layer of sponges, which, besides giving a title for the customs, had made excellent packing to preserve the more valuable contents from any damage in shipment. When swept out by handfuls, a bale of striped cloth became visible, tied with cords; evidently the mummy-case just as it had been wound up for transport at Luxor, as described in Skipton's letter. I did feel a growing excitement as the carpenter and I lifted it out on to the floor, undid the careful wrappings, and finally exposed it to view.

It was a very handsome one, as Skipton had said—fashioned in resemblance to the human figure within, though so much greater in bulk; the lid pointed at one end to indicate the upturned feet, and at the other carved into the similitude of a face, and of crossed hands above the breast. The wood was beautifully finished and in excellent preservation, and covered with hieroglyphics and figure-subjects, in which a great part of the colouring still remained, and the face and hands were finished with a kind of yellow varnish. It was doubtless a somewhat gruesome object to the uninitiated. My British workman looked at it in silence, and scratched his head; and an aggressive small rap at the studio door was followed by an exclamation of alarm.

"I just called in, sir, to ask—O Lord! whatever's that?"

What my landlady had called to ask I never discovered; the sight before her seemed effectually to scatter her ideas. With an instinct that propitiation might be politic, I indicated the litter on the floor, and asked if she had any *penchant* for sponges. "These are the best Smyrna ones, I am told; and pray help yourself to as many as you like. Why, Mrs. Mappinbeck, this is what is called a mummy-case, and it has been sent me direct from Egypt by a friend. It is a fine specimen; and Mr. Knollys is coming to make a drawing of it one of these first days. It is probably about three thousand years old—perhaps more." I was going on to descant on the rock tombs and their contents, when the indignant horror deepened on the face of my auditor.

"Are you meaning to tell me, sir, as how there is *a body* inside of it?"

"What was a body three thousand years ago. Probably not much in human likeness at time present."

Thereupon ensued confusion, out of which I managed to understand the following. She was a lone woman and a widow, and had taken me in as a gentleman; and now I was taking her in by turning her respectable lodgings into a charnel and a dead-house for disreputable heathen corpses. Lady Wilkinson—just now her trump-card—didn't in general go where there were gentlemen lodgers, but had consented to put up with me, seeing that I was such a quiet gentleman, with never any goings-on. Lady Wilkinson would be with her for the winter certain, if all was what she expected; but if she found there were corpses about, she would walk out of the house that very moment. She had left her last rooms after two years just because, there happened to be a death in the family-a death as couldn't be helped, being just the will of Providence. And now here was a body brought in under her very nose; and who was going to make the loss good to her, Mrs. Mappinbeck? And so, on *da capo*.

"But, my good woman," I said, as soon as I could put in a word, "how is she to know there is a corpse here unless you tell her yourself? Lady Wilkinson is not likely to come into the studio."

"Oh, it was all very well to talk; but where there was corpses there was death-smells; and if Lady Wilkinson would not go into the studio, there was no answering for Lady Wilkinson's maid, who was an inquisitive sort of person—here, there, and everywhere she wasn't wanted, and not above tale-bearing either!"

"She won't get through a locked door, Mrs. Mappinbeck. And so long as it is needful for my purpose to keep the mummy at hand, I will undertake it shall be locked and the keys in my pocket. And if the room needs cleaning it must wait for it." I might have added that it often did want cleaning, and was quite accustomed to waiting. It was some time before I got rid of the landlady; but when she did depart, it was on the understanding that the mummy should remain under lock and key while on the premises, and that I should use all reasonable despatch in getting it removed elsewhere. She had no objection, she said, to the case, but it was—with one last long shudder in departing—*the corpse!*

My British workman had stood by grinning during this altercation, and when the last bellicose whisk of the landlady's petticoats vanished through the doorway he asked if I wanted him to assist in opening—the box, or whatever it was! That had in reality been my intention before Mrs. Mappinbeck appeared on the scene; but the passing annoyance had cooled my ardour, and I experienced a sudden disinclination to have the man meddle with my treasure. I possessed the requisite tools, and could do the work myself at my own leisure; and possibly it might be better to let Knollys make his drawing before it was disturbed. So, the carpenter got his *congé* after helping me to lift the weird-looking thing on to its trestles, and making a summary clearance of the packing-wood and sponges. Then I took the keys of the two doors, according to promise, and left it in sole occupation of the studio.

There was nothing in all this to upset the nerves—a fracas with a vulgar woman, the arrival of an expected purchase; but, as I sat down to my desk, I became again possessed by the peculiar agitation and excitement which had befallen me on the arrival of Skipton's telegram—the day of the reception at Mrs. Payne's—and it had the same result as before. I found myself utterly incapable of adding a single line to my manuscript. I began a letter to Skipton, to be finished after examining the mummy-but with that also it became impossible to proceed. Of what new seizure was this the precursor? I felt minded to rush off at once to the indefinite doctor so often preached to me; but I had promised to leave the choice to Knollys, and must await the result of his inquiry. At length I dashed off a line, informing him of the coming of the mummy-case, and asking if he could come. round the next day to make his drawing.

With that I left the locked-up studio and went for a walk—out in the Highgate Rise direction, past the old church and churchyard on the hill. I walked till the mid-October afternoon darkened down upon me and the stars came out; and then, finding myself near a station, and pretty well tired out, took the train back into London.

I had an answer from Knollys next morning. "Glad you have got your sponges, old fellow," he wrote, "but I can't come round and draw them till Sunday. I have a new piece of work on hand needing urgent despatch, and it may lead to something good and permanent; so, you'll forgive me putting you off. Sorry your landlady makes a fuss, but you must soften her heart into giving the deceased one house room for another week." I had been careful to say nothing of the return of that symptom of excitement, and the letter contained no allusion to my health. I felt I had done well to be reticent, for something had befallen me in the night so inexplicable—except on the dream hypothesis—that I hesitated to communicate it even to Knollys.

It was, I knew, just possible that I might be exaggerating a vivid dream into a reality. The precautions taken to satisfy Mrs. Mappinbeck and secure the studio from observation might very well have recurred to me in sleep distorted by grotesque anxiety; and then the impression on the nerves, which Knollys talked about, might again have projected the Egyptian figure in conjunction with this disturbance. But, as it seemed at the time, I waked from snatches of uneasy sleep sometime in the small hours—starting broad awake in a moment under the spur of an intense anxiety, as if some threatened danger were close upon me or upon the house.

I raised myself on my elbow to look and listen the room was not perfectly dark, as the street-lamp shone into it between the venetians; but nothing was there to cause alarm—I was alone in the comparative stillness of a London night, and the sole sound other than usual was the thick, hurried beating of my own heart. Then the anxiety, which had at first been vague, took shape in the direction of the studio, suggesting something wrong there with Skipton's mummy. It was not a likely object for a burglar to make away with, but I believe that was the ruling idea; the men who delivered it—the carpenter—even Lady Wilkinson's maid, might be in communication with a gang of burglars, and have surmised possible treasure in that still inviolate *sarcophagus*.

It seems to me that I did not surrender at once to these misgivings. I lay still, the one-half of my mind in argument with the other, administering dose after dose of self-ridicule, all utterly without effect, for the uneasiness grew. At last, the mental picture of the great case, in its semi-human form and grotesque colouring, lying defenceless under the stare of those unshaded upper windows, so wrought upon my fancy that I felt there was nothing for it but to proceed to the scene itself and make sure of its safety.

I got up, huddled on some clothing, took a lighted candle with me, and the key which opened the door leading from the sitting-room. The place had that eerie look which even familiar rooms will acquire when we revisit them dark and deserted in the night. The gas flamed up at the touch of a match; and so, leaving illumination behind me, still with the lighted candle I went on.

That one candle shed only a feeble light into the large bare room full of shadows. There was the night sky looking in through those shadeless windows, as I had pictured to myself; the grim, half-human shape of the *sarcophagus* lay on its trestles as I had left it, but what upon that? What was the white form stretched upon it stark as a corpse as I entered, but which moved as the light flickered, gathered itself together to rise, and turned on me—the face of the Egyptian?

I am ashamed to say the shock utterly unnerved me. For once

I knew what it was to be afraid, with that extreme of terror which holds the very springs of life arrested for one awful moment. What I did with the candle I know not. I did not drop it, but it was suddenly extinguished, and there I was alone in darkness with that inexplicable presence—that face of fiendish hatred which had just looked into mine.

Thank God! the moment of panic passed—moment or age, which was it?—and in the reaction I was myself again. I found the shut door behind me, from which I had not advanced many steps, flung it wide, and retreated into the gas-lit sitting-room. To relight the candle was the work of a moment, and armed with a stick—the revolver in my bedroom was too far to seek—I re-entered the studio.

There was, be it remembered, another exit, but this was locked and the key in my possession. Except by this, and those high windows in the roof, the man could not have got out save by passing through the lighted room in which I was, and yet he had absolutely disappeared. I set every gas-burner in the place aflame and made the strictest search, but could find nothing. When I had seen anew to the security of all the fastenings, I went back to bed, and after a time to sleep, waking in the morning to ask myself whether what I had experienced in the night was fact or vision—vision in the sense of dream.

I write of the feelings and doubts which beset me at the time. I know now of a certainty who and what it was I saw.

Through the following day I strove to employ myself actively, and banish from my mind as much as possible what had gone before. I went round to the experimental chemist whom I designed to employ for the various analyses of the embalming process, and spent the best part of the morning arranging the direction of these with the expert. He also undertook to relieve my G—— Street lodgings of the custody of the mummy as soon as Knollys and I had done with it.

On my return I made a careful copy of the inscription on the case and of the emblematic figures; this will be found among my Egyptian papers, so I need not transcribe it here at length. It set forth that the case enclosed "the sole orphan and virgin daughter of Khames, high-priest of Amen-Ra and one with Osiris; beloved of the priest Savak." There was, however, a peculiarity in the phrasing of the inscription. All Egyptians believed death would be a temporary sleep, after which the mummy would be reanimated by its *ka*—the vital principal—and again fitted for the habitation of the soul. But in this case the insistence on the term sleep was somewhat out of the common; perhaps

241

paralleled by that departure from usual custom which sometimes appears in newspaper announcements, describing our own dead as having "fallen asleep" on a certain date, instead of the more ordinary term.

The task of copying and translating was not a long one. I completed it in the course of the evening, and then felt utterly disinclined for bed and hours of forced inaction, during which the feverish excitement that still possessed me would keep me wakeful, and flash its searchlight unrestrained into all the dark places of my soul. I wanted the shield of occupation between me and those fears—for myself and of myself—which I desired to keep at bay; and I resolved to spend the night in making examination of the mummy. I lit the fire which was ready laid in the stove that warmed the studio, saw to the lights, and desired the servant to place for me in the sitting-room the tray with materials for making coffee and preparing a light meal, which I was accustomed to have at hand when working unusually late.

The studio warmed and lighted presented a very different aspect from its appearance the night before; and the spectral form seemed to be effectually exorcised by the cheerful accessories of fire and gas.

Working as silently as might be—for had I not to consider Lady Wilkinson's aristocratic slumbers?—and with extreme care to avoid damage, I unfixed the great lid, sealed in its place in ages so remote that the bewildering procession of centuries and generations makes one dizzy in retrospect. Underneath was the protecting *cartonnage* smeared with bituminous resin, hard and thickly coated, so that the task of cutting through it was both slow and laborious. I worked gradually round it till I could remove the whole upper part corresponding with the lid of the *sarcophagus*. It did not appear to be moulded as closely as usual to the form, and a glimpse within showed something different from ordinary mummy cerements. When lifted away it disclosed a wrapping of some costly fabric resembling gold tissue, and fastened upon this was a thin tablet coated with wax, on which an inscription had been engraved or scratched with a stylus.

It was enough to make the eyes of an Egyptologist glisten. I no longer thought Abd-el-Moluk's bargain a hard one—probably the tablet was worth it all. What precious historical testimony might not be enshrined therein? or domestic detail of a bygone age, setting in familiar light before us the dead-and-gone actors which trod that stage of the world? I broke the fastenings and carried it to the light, not heeding that the rotten stuff which shredded away with it was left partly open.

Unfortunately, I have no exact copy of the writing, and the tablet is not now in my possession. I left it behind in the studio during my absence, carelessly omitting to secure it among my papers; and neither Knollys nor I could find it when we returned. I am obliged to trust to the memory of that night. To the best of my remembrance, it ran as follows:

"I, the priest Savak, servant of Sebek, have sealed the virgin, the daughter of Khames, in trance according to the Voice of the Oracle. Not of this land or generation is her lover, but he yet unborn that awakes her from sleep before the seven ages have passed over, his she will be. And if the seven ages pass without awakening, she is dust and she remains mine. To this she submits with knowledge, having denied herself to me in marriage; and, being obedient to the Voice of the Oracle, goes down alive into the tomb, willing to sleep. And I, Savak, do seal her in the inner chamber to be mine; for were it seventy ages instead of seven, and were the land perished under our feet that abides continually, I would pursue her until she turn to me. And I, Savak, do seal the inner chamber with my curse, and with the curse of my God, which shall dwell with terror upon him that meddleth and upon him that openeth. And to him, the lover—in the ages to come, and the generations to come—should he find her over my body and the guard of the tomb and the guard of the curse, I do set against him wager of battle that his days be not long in the land; neither hers to whom life returns and youth returns for seven spaces, according to the ordinance of the eternal Gods."

5

This was indeed an extraordinary piece of archaic romance on which I had stumbled; and in the elation of discovery, I went over it a second time to ensure correctness before the full horror of what was signified smote me with comprehension, and I became aware of a certain consequence that touched myself. Not that I could be the foredoomed lover; but that the *sarcophagus* held no mummy after all, but the body, or what had been the body, of a girl who had met with the horrible fate of burial while yet alive—doubtless through the jealous vengeance of this rejected lover, this priest of the crocodile god. But that, if the tablet spoke truth, there had been no embalming and could be no analysis was clear.

As I sat at the table with the inscription before me my back was turned to the coffin. I pushed the chair sideways and glanced round at it, when all power of movement was arrested by surprise. Thrown carelessly out of the disturbed wrappings, and hanging over the edge, was a woman's arm—slender, exquisitely rounded, warm with life. Was it believable that a human creature could have existed under such conditions and in such suspension for three thousand years? the trance of a toad shut in a rock paralleled by enchantment! The first shock of conviction past, I started to my feet—I would look nearer at this wonder. The rotten shreds of tissue had been torn apart by the movement of the arm, and there within lay the sleeper in the perfect bloom of her young womanhood, white-robed from throat to foot, the darkly fringed eyes still closed, the soft breathing just stirring the linen folds which veiled her breast.

The face I looked upon was beautiful, but it was a marvel the more that I did not regard it in the least as one looks upon the beauty of a stranger. I knew my heart's one love when I saw her face to face. All the aching loss of my solitary life—all I had lacked hardly knowing—was present to me in that moment, as I recognized a need filled, an incompleteness suddenly made whole. Will that be the fashion of those meetings in a world beyond to which some strong in faith look forward? Speechless with the wonder of it, new born into joy, and into a rarer atmosphere where it was difficult at first to breathe, I stood and looked upon the sleep which I alone from the beginning of the ages had been ordained to break. Was it moments or hours before I took the warm small hand in my own, before the red lips parted with a sigh, the dark-fringed eyelids lifted, and the eyes and the soul behind them looked into mine?

At first with a question in them. Then came knowledge, recognition, joy in the sweetness of a dawning smile, though the lips were still serious. "Oh," she said, "I am not dreaming! I am awake at last; and it is you—my lord."

Now here was a fresh wonder. This girl, who had lived her waking life when the savage dwellers in our islands of the sea were grubbing in fellowship with the cave-bear and gabbling some dialect of Norse, had spoken to me in perfect English, and understood when I replied to her in the same tongue. It seemed then to come by nature that we should be one in language; but the surprise of it struck me after. I believe my ear was so attuned to the soul of her speech that I heard this rather than the form of words; between us two the confusion which fell upon the builders of Babel had been done away. I noticed later that she hesitated to address anyone but myself, and did so in the imperfect speech of a foreigner; while at first, she seemed unable to comprehend what was said to her, unless a touch completed the link with my understanding of it. But I am anticipating.

Can I tell what I replied to her—can I remember what expression of words rose to the surface of that driven sea of feeling which had been stirred to the very depths? Her lord! nay, but her slave and servant; hers absolutely by the right which love has over love. A thought expressed itself between us as conceived, and mine involuntarily had been—would she turn from me? Her radiant youth, though so incredibly the elder of my own, assorted ill with that weather beaten scarecrow of a countenance which I saw daily in the glass, and the grey streaks in my hair. Her delicate, fine hand, which lay in my work-hardened palm, accentuated the contrast.

She had raised herself by this time, and was sitting up in the coffin, while I knelt beside her; and she laid the other hand with a momentary touch on that same grizzled hair.

"You are wanting to change yourself for my sake, but where is the need? It was your face as I see it now that I saw in the divining-cup, and in the smoke above the altar. It was your face as I see it now, that gave me strength to go down alive into the grave, and has been with me as I slept and dreamed. O my master, is it true I am awake at last? or is this but one dream the more, sweeter than all?"

It was reality, I told her: she had waked to truth and life. Not a moment longer should she linger in her prison, which was broken forever. And I lifted her, she permitting, and set her beside me on her feet. I held her guarded for the first uncertain moment in which she wavered and clung to me, but when it passed, she stood up firmly, a lithe, slender figure, tall above the common stature of woman. As she drew herself erect, the coils of hair which had been banded round and round in the coffin dropped loose, and fell a dark veil about her, hanging almost to the knee. Did this transgress some ancient rule of etiquette?—for she flushed all over her lovely face, and, stepping back from me, began to coil it up again into a great Greek knot.

Ah me! if I had the artist's gift of portraiture, I could paint her now as she stood there, gowned in pure white with gold thread-work in the bordering and about the girdle, twisting her long hair, with that flush under the rich tint of a cheek hardly darker than an English brunette's. "Tell me a name to call you by," I pleaded.

She paused, with her hands still twisted in her hair, as if she were listening for some faraway echo, and then a smile lit her up like sunshine. "I am born again into life," she said. "I do not want to go back to my old name—it did not bring me happiness. You shall give me a name."

"I will give you my own, if you will take it," I answered. She looked at me with a sweet half-comprehension, like a child at once perplexed and confiding. I liked to meet her eyes, they gave me so strange a thrill; but this was a glance and no more. Some aroused consciousness dropped the screen of dark lashes over them, and she turned away to look round the big bare studio with its shelves and packing-cases and general litter—Knollys's and mine.

"Is this your home?"

"It is only my work-room—in temporary quarters. I will have a better home than this to share with you, dear heart. There are lovely spots in our island of the north; or I could take you back to your own land— Egypt—after a while."

"Not to Egypt—not there. I am afraid."

"Afraid—with me! Afraid of what?"

Her reply was hardly above a whisper, as if she had suddenly grown fearful of her own voice. "Afraid that *he* may separate us, after all."

"Tell me who you mean."

She was standing close to the table at which I had sat to decipher the inscription; the tablet lay upon it, and the low-breathed confession had hardly left her lips when she started and bent forward to examine it. "That is the name," she said, laying her finger on the words in the hieratic writing—*Savak the priest*. "I dare not say it: it is he who is my enemy, and will be yours for my sake. O my master, put it away—cover it; the words seem to evoke him from the air."

I tossed the tablet away, face downwards, and took her hands, for she was trembling. The events of that night had swept away from me for the moment all recollection of my former trouble and of the Egyptian; besides, doublet and hose was bound to show itself coura- geous to petticoat. "You have been wonderfully preserved to me, dear heart; but the man who was your enemy has been dead and dust for centuries. It is beyond his power to harm you or come between us, either in Egypt or here."

Her gaze followed the tablet as if fascinated—she did not appear to heed me. I looked also, constrained by her example; and there before us, right above where it had fallen, there floated a light film of cloud, and out of this looked for a moment—looked and vanished—the face which had haunted me by the sea-shore and in London. She gave a

246

shuddering cry like a creature in extremity, and hid her eyes against my breast: I knew she saw as I did. Her enemy might be dust, as I had boasted, but I could no longer deny there was survival of that personality for harm.

I did my best to soothe her; and as she seemed to shiver with fear and cold, I drew the settee nearer to the fire, and found a warm travelling plaid to fold about her. But after a while the natural bright spirit of her seemed to reassert itself, and she in her turn became the comforter. "He cannot do us serious harm so long as I keep this perfect," she said, putting her hand to her neck. "I was afraid for the moment it was gone—that he had taken it, and the end had come."

I looked as she indicated, and saw she wore round her white throat a necklace of that delicate antique workmanship of which I had before seen specimens recovered from the tombs. There were three chains of gold and silver links, connecting small lozenge-shaped stones, which I think are emeralds; and from the lowest chain hung seven tiny lotus-buds, either carven in carnelian or moulded-in some imitating composition.

"This was given by command of the Oracle, as a pledge of my restoration. These seven drops are seven spaces of time—whether long or short I know not; the time I have granted me to spend with you. So long as I can keep them, I live in the life of this world, were it a hundred years; but when they go, I die and am a spirit. While they are safe, I am yours."

"A hundred years!" I said, jealously. "Then it will be my fate to die and leave you—perhaps to another!"

"Not so;" and again, as her eyes sought mine, soul met soul for a moment as at first. "If you go before me, it will be mine to throw the toy away and to follow. It is not my life that will divide us."

Ah me! if there is a cloud on my memory, it does not rest over the sayings of that night. They are clear to me as when first spoken, as her lovely face is distinct in my remembrance. And yet they would have me believe it was all a fever-vision; that there were no sweet words and looks and vows—no wife, nothing but delusion and a corpse.

I could have sat forever listening to what she had to tell; but in an interval of silence the hall clock struck three, reminding me of the advance of the new day. I thought of the coffee tray in the next room, and that my dear one, being of this world again, must need food to sustain the new-found life. There was sweetness in that practical touch, and in the thought that I could serve her; that I, even I, had someone of my own to serve.

I left the magic of her presence for long enough to prepare the meal—surely with something sacramental about it, that first meal we were to share; and as I boiled the "*ætna*" and made it ready, the necessity for other considerations pressed on me. To shield Iras—I will call her at once by the name I gave her later—from the faintest breath of the world's censure was surely my first duty towards her who trusted me with such childlike confidence, such complete innocence. I cared little for the world; but in it she was soon, as soon as I could make it possible, to have her assured place as my wife.

Never to anyone, unless it were to Knollys, could the extraordinary chain of circumstances which brought us together be made known; and even if there were any good woman to whose keeping I could confide her till our marriage could be arranged, I should have feared to surrender her on account of that mysterious spiritual persecution which she so greatly feared, and from which she seemed to feel safe only with me. To allow her to remain in the G—— Street lodgings was out of the question; I seemed at once to see Mrs. Mappinbeck's face of outraged virtue, and divine the coarse conclusions she would draw from the presence of such a guest. I had heard of Scotch marriages, though I confess I knew little about them; and in my perplexity this seemed the best solution of the difficulty in which I found myself. Iras and I would travel at once to the Northern capital, and there, in the speediest manner possible to an easier law, she should be made Mrs. Lavenham.

I took the tray into the studio with the coffee I had made, and had the delight of seeing her drink it. She ate the biscuits too, though the sandwiches seemed unpalatable to her; and as she sat by the stove with my plaid about her shoulders, warming her pretty feet in their quaint sandals, the *sarcophagus*—which it seemed already incredible she could ever have occupied—pushed away in the background, a fresh perplexity occurred to me. Her white robe with the loose sleeves, modestly as it was fashioned, was utterly unusual and conspicuous, as well as unsuitable in texture for such a journey as I purposed to take with her—turning our faces northwards at this autumn season. I noticed how she shivered and drew about her the warm folds of the plaid; and, in the midst of trying to explain the vast changes which had converted the Egypt she remembered into the Egypt of today, I was revolving the problem of how this manifest need could be supplied.

I knew nothing of women's fashions; and a less observant person than I of the garments displayed in the streets on the shoulders of passers-by, or set out in the shops for the temptation of purchasers, could hardly be found in the length and breadth of London. But as I thought over my puzzle there rose before me, like a mental dissolving view, the front of a certain shop at the corner of Oxford Street. I had been button-holed on that spot, an unwilling victim, by a persistent bore of my acquaintance some day or two previously, and while listening to his strictures on the policy of the Government I suppose I had stared vacantly through the plate-glass window in front of me.

The picture supplied by an involuntary recollection was of a lay-figure equipped in what I think is termed a *paletot*—a long garment of brown cloth cut for a tall, slender figure like that of my dear, and bordered at all its edges with thick glossy fur which matched the dark tint of the fabric. It was arranged on the frame partly open, so as to show a furred inner lining of grey and white, warm enough and dainty enough for a Russian princess. I remembered that a turban head-gear, also of fur, accompanied the coat, and that a large gilt placard, setting forth the number of guineas for which the garment might be purchased, was displayed against it. This would be what I wanted for Iras, and I resolved to send a check for the immediate purchase as soon in the morning as the great emporium would be open.

The hours were nearing dawn when I persuaded her to rest, urging the length of the journey which was before us. She laughed, and pleaded she had so lately reopened her eyes upon life that she did not want to waste any of her time in sleep; but finally, she laid her head upon the pillow I brought and slept, covered with the plaid, till the first greyness of the morning broadened and brightened into full daylight.

"*And the evening and the morning were the first day.*" That fragment of the Mosaic account of creation floated through my mind not inappropriately; for had I not come upon new heavens and a new earth, and was not all my life created afresh? I could well believe that Zion's message had come also unto me—that my warfare was accomplished, my iniquity pardoned, and, with the dark days of my solitude, sorrow and sighing had fled away. To have one belonging to me, depending on me, how sweet the possession!—how welcome the burden which, with all loyalty of a glad heart, I would carry! Such thoughts were mine as I sat there in the grey dawn, watching my love sleeping profoundly as a child, and smiling in her sleep as a child might. Her breath was drawn so lightly that more than once I bent over her, fearing I knew not what. But all was well; and so, as I wrote before, came up the day.

That was a morning full of occupation. I had my things to put hurriedly together for an indefinite absence—letters to write, arrangements to make in preparation. I wrote out a cheque in advance for Mrs. Mappinbeck, and directed my bankers to transfer a certain credit to me in Edinburgh. I wrote to the publishers for whom I was working, explaining that it might not be possible for me to keep to the set terms of the agreement, as failing health and "family affairs" combined made it imperative I should leave London for a time. The forfeiture must be at their option, but I still hoped to have my book ready early in the new year. But the letter of which I have clearest recollection was to Knollys. Would he undertake, I wrote to him, to settle certain affairs (which I enumerated) out of the enclosure; and also, to telegraph to Skipton at Alexandria that I was "satisfied with the purchase," and that the money might be paid over to Abd-el-Moluk?

"You will find the mummy-case in the studio," I wrote, "and I would like a sketch of it made for an illustration, as we planned. There is, however, no hurry over immediate completion. I am taking your advice, my dear fellow, about the needed holiday; but I have imported into it a new element for which you did not calculate. I am going to be married. Do not be too much surprised until we meet, when I will give you all the particulars I now withhold, and make my wife known to you. I can let you have no certain address for the present, but letters may be sent to the post-office at Edinburgh."

Iras spent the morning in the studio, guarded by the locked door and my presence in the outer room. I brought her there a makeshift breakfast from the meal prepared for me, and we made merry over the inconvenience; though without my enlightenment she would have taken it all as natural to our Northern manners. Whether our voices were audible I know not, but Mrs. Mappinbeck had a suspicious air about her when she came in answer to my summons; the cloudy sky of the day before had not altogether lifted. She received with equanimity the news of my probable absence and the advance cheque. Yes, she would see that nothing was disturbed while I was away, and Mr. Knollys should have access as usual to the studio. Might she inquire, however—very severely—whether she would be expected to keep *that corpse* on the premises.

"That corpse!" I nearly laughed in her face when I thought of Iras; but I contrived to reply soberly, "No, it was not expected of her; in fact, it had been already removed." Whereupon the latent suspicion became on the instant broadly apparent. I imagine a pretty close watch had been kept on the comings and goings of the house, and Mrs. Mappinbeck could have ventured to take her *affidavit* that nothing so grizzly had been removed from it. No doubt the studio and all the premises were subjected to a strict search as soon as my back was turned, even with scrutiny of the flooring! But I felt too light-hearted just then to care for suspicion other than what might turn to annoyance for Iras. I wanted an early luncheon, I told her, and a cab fetched to take me to Euston by two o'clock. "And prepare the table for two," I said. "I shall have a friend with me."

Iras would be seen to leave the house; and as I was momently expecting the return of my *commissionaire* messenger with the furred wrapper, I thought I might very well produce her openly at luncheon as a friend who had called in. Mrs. Mappinbeck withdrew, still looking unutterable things over the corpse; and the next ring at the bell announced my purchase—my first purchase for my wife's adornment. Iras was woman enough to care for beauty in garments, though the fashion of them might be strange to her; and the warmth and softness of the furs attracted her at once. I know not which of us was the more pleased as I put on the warm coat over her thin Eastern dress and fastened it from throat to foot. It fitted her to a marvel, and converted her at once from the sculptor's dream she had been previously into the likeness of a woman of fashion. I crowned her with the fur toque, and brought a glass in which she could see herself. The parcel held also furred boots to slip on over the bare sandalled feet, warm gloves, and a wrap for the journey.

It was a fair reflection that she saw in the glass, and I believe it pleased her, however unfamiliar the array. But she was more intent on looking her gratitude for what I had given than over any thought of vanity. "There is one thing I want," she said, timidly, "if people are likely to see me—something to cover my face. I do not want any eye to rest on it but yours."

I was proud, and I told her so, for all the world to see it; but she shook her head doubtfully; and I bethought me I had among my possessions a thin gauze veil, which I had formerly used as a precaution against dust and sun-glare in the East. I brought it and she accepted it, still with those grateful eyes, and twisted it deftly round the hat, so as to shade her face without wholly concealing it.

Lunch was ready by the time these preparations were complete, and with it Mrs. Mappinbeck, hovering about in a state of uneasy curiosity. I think this was at once gratified and increased when I led Iras in, looking like a princess as she did, and seated her at the table. The servant betrayed an unusual inclination to linger and wait on us; but I dismissed her, and myself did the honours, admiring the quick way in which my dear caught up the unfamiliar fashions, and the gentle dignity of her bearing. She did not care for meat, and refused the wine I offered her; but she drank water from the clear crystal of the tumbler, which greatly attracted her, and enjoyed some stewed fruit which Mrs. Mappinbeck had fortunately added to the repast.

Then came the announcement that the cab was at the door. My portmanteau was placed on it, and Mrs. Mappinbeck was in the hall when I went out with Iras. "You will find the keys of the studio in the two doors," I said to her as she curtsied with her eyes on my companion; and with this valediction I helped my dear girl into the hansom. Directly after we were turning out of G—— Street—prosaic G—— Street! which had become all unconsciously the scene of so strange a romance—in the direction of the northern train.

<h2 style="text-align:center">6</h2>

I was glad for my wife's sake that no chance acquaintance happened to be on the platform to witness our departure, and possibly set fire to gossip. Iras was very silent in the noise and roar of the great terminus, but I felt her cling closer to my arm as we entered under its high glass roof and when the first fire-breathing monster of an engine passed out before our train was ready to move. She said, as I rejoined her after buying our tickets, "I thought we were going by a river!"—an idea, no doubt, born of her recollection of the Nile, the great highway of Egypt then in those far-away years even as now. And that silent sliding of river-travel under warmer skies would have been more appropriate for all we had to say, drawing into closer knowledge each of each, than the throbbing rush of the train and the close-smelling cloth-cushioned carriage in which we were presently shut.

The rapid movement seemed at first to affect Iras, and she hid her dizzy eyes against my shoulder; but when I moved her to face the window, and opened it to admit more air, she gradually lost the sensation of giddiness, and became amused by the green landscape flying past us—the moving panorama of fields and woods and streams, churches and hamlets—so widely different from any view she had ever looked upon in the past. "It is a beautiful world," she whispered more than once. "I am glad to be alive to see it, and to see it with you."

That day's sun went down in glory; the west put on its fairest tints of rose and gold and pearl to receive him, and flushed the floating clouds up towards the zenith with a tint of faint scarlet. Iras and I together watched the deepening and fading of that transfiguration, and she evidently derived from it an observation of our direction, for she presently said, in a tone of relief, "Yes, we are going north!"

"Not very far north, and not for long. You do not fear the cold?"

"In this warm dress you have given me? Ah no; and the farther north the better, were it to the frozen seas. The farther away from *him*, and from his power."

It was curious her association of Savak with everything southern; and I found later on it had become a fixed idea.

The afternoon was darkening by the time we halted at Crewe. I wanted her to go with me for some refreshment, but she seemed afraid of the bustling platform; so, I brought her out a cup of coffee to the carriage. We were not disturbed there by intruders—I think the guard had marked us down as probably a bridal couple, despite my grey hair and my shabby coat. But at the next stoppage, which was Preston, an elderly man came running down the platform, bag in hand, after the bell had rung for departure, wrenched open our carriage door, and was pushed in puffing and breathless, the train being actually in movement. He stumbled past Iras to the farther side of the carriage, and plumped down to recover, presently beginning to swell with triumph over his achievement. "A near thing that, sir," he said, unbuttoning and throwing back his overcoat, and diving into some underpocket for a travelling-cap.

I found it difficult to repress a reply the reverse of civil. Iras shrank back into her corner, and pulled down the veil she had partially lifted; and a whispered monosyllable now and then was all I could extract from her during the rest of the journey. I had plenty of conversation, however, to make up for the lack of hers. Our stout fellow-traveller proved maddeningly communicative, secure in the conviction that his affairs and his experiences must needs be interesting, even to a stranger. It transpired that we had a mutual acquaintance—a man who formerly held a Syrian consulate, and had the misfortune to be related to our stout friend; and on the strength of this, midway between Carlisle and Edinburgh, he handed me his card of address. I reluctantly took it and put it away in an inner division of my pocket-case, and now mention it only because of an after-use which Knollys made it serve.

He did not address Iras, as she sat with her face turned away, looking out through her veil as long as there was light to see the barren hill and dale on the outskirts of the Lake District. But that he did notice her presence I was sure, for after a while he took from his bag an illustrated paper and passed it to me, suggesting that "perhaps it might amuse the lady." I went through the form of offering it to her—what she thought it was I know not, but she shook her head in rejection; so I glanced through it myself, just as a matter of courtesy, before handing it back to the owner. To see me thus occupied did not stop the conversational torrent, and I had been too engrossed with other matters at our start to care to provide myself with book or paper of my own. The man talked on through the long miles and weary hours of that journey, while I began to grow uneasy about Iras, fearing she must be very tired, and picturing to myself how, if only our fellow-traveller would have bestowed himself elsewhere, I could have contrived for her a more restful position, and pillowed her head against my shoulder.

The clocks were on the stroke of eleven when at last we glided into the Edinburgh station. I had telegraphed from Rugby to a hotel I knew by report, to secure rooms and supper; and a porter with the name-badge was on the lookout for us, and seemed surprised to have only my one portmanteau confided to him. It would be necessary to provide Iras with luggage, that I could see—for the sake of appearances, as well as for the hundred and one things she must need.

The rooms had been reserved and were warmed and lighted, a suite on the second floor—private sitting-room, where supper was presently served to us, and a chamber for Iras adjoining my own. She promised to call to me if anything happened to alarm her, but in the fact of our having come northwards she seemed to find security; and, content to see her light burning through the partly opened door, I fell asleep myself in the darkness—suddenly aware that I was weary, and that the strain of all those wakeful hours of excitement and action had been great.

I wrote our names in the visitors' book next morning—Mr. and Mrs. Lavenham. If not a truth, it was very shortly to become one; and, leaving Iras at the hotel, I set out to find that necessary factor in what we had to do—a respectable lawyer. I had run my eye down the hotel directory, and picked out an address by chance; and it was as I turned out of Princes Street into one of the numerous inter-sections at right angles, inquiring my way to it, that it suddenly struck me I must be prepared to give my wife a name.

I wished then it had occurred to me earlier, so that I might have

254

consulted with her what name she would bear; but I would not now make delay by a return, and that my decision would have ruled hers I knew. It was necessary for me to invent a maiden surname as well as the familiar prefix; and probably some boyish recollection of Shakespeare grafted itself on to the idea of her nationality, by suggesting the names of the great queen's handmaidens in "Antony and Cleopatra." She should be Iras Charmian as a preliminary to her conversion into Iras Lavenham.

Mr. James Macpherson, Writer to the Signet, was an elderly man with a conical bald head, very Scotch, and somewhat laconic. He was engaged with a client on my arrival, and for half an hour or more I had to devour my impatience as best I might, gazing out at the interval of broad street and the cold-looking grey-stone houses over the way. At last, the clerk called my name. I was shown in to tell my errand, and I thought a faint surprise evidenced itself on the attentive countenance addressed to me from the other side of the table. I suppose I did not look the part.

"If I understand you rightly, Mr.—Lavenham"—he glanced again at my card to refresh his memory—"you wish me to advise you on the contracting of an irregular marriage."

"By no means," I interrupted. "My anxiety is that all should be on a completely regular and legal basis."

"Certainly, certainly;" he waved aside my lay ignorance with some impatience. "The legal term for a marriage of the kind you mean is an irregular marriage, but it is perfectly valid in law. The lady will be as safe your wife as if you were married in all the kirks and by all the ministers in the land. I suppose the lady is of age?"

"Yes," I said. That particular at least I could affirm absolutely.

"You will just have to make a declaration before me—which I will draw out for your signatures, yours and the lady's both, and the signatures of two witnesses here in my presence. Then you go along to the sheriff-substitute, you and the lady together, and he signs the declaration. Then you go to the registrar and get a stamped copy; but the lady need not go with you there unless she likes."

"And can this be done today?"

The man of law raised his eyebrows and deliberately consulted a pale-faced elderly watch. "Hardly today," he said. "Lord Stair's factor is coming at the half-hour; and by the time I have the declaration ready, and you have brought the lady—I conclude she is not here now?— you will not be likely to find the sheriff-substitute at his chambers. I will make an appointment for tomorrow morning; and you can come here first at 10.30, if that will be convenient—you and the lady."

I had hoped to carry the thing through immediately, but the few hours' delay was no great matter; so, I signified acquiescence.

Mr. Macpherson adjusted his spectacles, spread a sheet of paper before him, dipped a pen in the ink and held it suspended. "You will now," he said, "give me the particulars."

"Certainly. I suppose you mean our respective names. Ralph Lavenham, bachelor; and Iras Charmian, spinster; both of age."

"Not so fast, my dear sir; not so fast. Ralph Lavenham, bachelor. Aged what, and of what address?"

"Thirty-nine. Of G—— Street, London, number 46."

"Parents' names?"

"Son of the late Thomas Lavenham and Mary Priscilla his wife."

This opened my eyes to what was about to follow in the case of Iras. I gave her age as twenty-two, which I thought would most nearly accord with her appearance. The question of address was puzzling, and in despair I said Luxor, Egypt, as having been the locality of the tomb.

"Parents' names?" again inquired the man of law, with another glance at his watch—I was evidently trespassing on the next appointment.

"Daughter of Khames Charmian. I do not know the mother's personal name, but both are dead. Is it essential to give it?"

"Preferable—preferable, not essential; but it can be inserted tomorrow. That will be sufficient. I wish you good-day."

He struck a hand-bell on the table, and the factor's entrance and my exit were simultaneous.

★★★★★★★★★★★★★★★★★

I had to tell Iras that the ceremony was postponed till next day; and as the weather was fine and clear, I hired a carriage and took her for a drive through the Old Town and the familiar round of Arthur's Seat. It was delightful to me to watch her bright ready interest in all she saw, and to explain to willing ears much it was necessary she should know about the present era. In returning I made the driver set us down at the head of Princes Street, and we walked the length of it together, past the rows of shining shops which attracted her curiosity. I wanted her to accompany me into some of them, that we might purchase together what was necessary for her outfit; but she shrank with such timidity from the proposal that I did not press it.

"I know nothing about the things that the women of this land have and wear," she said to me in explanation; "and I cannot speak your language to strangers, though I can speak to you. Tell one of these merchants to send what is needful to make me appear as you wish, but not in extravagance. This must have been costly, I am sure, it is so beautiful;" and she touched the fur on her breast.

So, on this expedition also I set forth alone. I had hardly appreciated the full difficulties and embarrassments of my task till I found myself, the only male creature in a warehouse given over to women's needs, struggling to explain to the astonished face of the lady presiding over the establishment that I wanted a ready-made outfit for my wife. I described her as an invalid and a foreigner, unable to enter upon the business for herself. Proposals were made, as a matter of course, that specimens should be submitted for the invalid lady's selection; but this I was obliged to negative, knowing it would distress and bewilder Iras. Therefore, it remained for me to wade as best I could through the printed lists and estimates laid before me, bristling as they were with unknown items, among which I felt myself utterly incompetent to decide. The presiding lady compassionately advised me on some points; I think my ignorance and my anxiety must secretly have caused her great amusement. The question of quality was easier—cambric and embroidery and lace would be more suited to my darling's dainty beauty than plain calico; so, I ended, as a matter of course, by putting my name to an alarming cheque.

I was asked for measurements, but could give none; and as a compromise indicated one of the shop-servers—a tall girl all bones and angles, as unlike Iras as possible—as being about my wife's height and size. The dresses were a further difficulty, though an amber tea-gown of shimmering Indian silk and a white dressing-robe with an inner lining of pale rose were comparatively easy of selection. I made some purchases in serge and homespun; the dinner and ball costumes pressed on me I negatived altogether for the present. I stipulated that shoes should be included, and that the whole should be packed in a couple of serviceable travelling-trunks and sent to Mrs. Lavenham at the address I gave. And then with a gasp of relief I found myself free of the bewildering place and under the October sky.

I had two more errands to discharge before returning. One was the purchase of a certain gold ring for use on the morrow, the other the selection of a travelling-bag with the usual toilet fittings. A boy-messenger carried the bag beside me to the hotel; and it is another memory of that day how I displayed its contrivances to Iras and watched her pleasure in them—the silver-backed brushes and mirrors, the scent-bottles and powder-pots, and—wonder greater than all— the tiny repeating-clock which fitted a case in the centre. The trunks were not long in following. Iras dined in her tea-gown that night, and arrayed herself in grey homespun the morning of her wedding-day.

The things once there, it seemed to come to her by nature how to wear them; there was nothing, save her uncommon beauty and grace, to distinguish her from an ordinary English girl. But I knew that on her throat, under silk and serge alike, the mysterious necklace kept its place and was never for an instant unclasped.

If this narrative should ever fall into other hands than mine, it may be wondered why I should dwell on so trivial a matter as the purchase of the outfit when so dark a cloud hung in the future. But I write to preserve the memory of our pleasure in it, and the joy it was to me to see it used and worn, as used and worn it was, despite after-evidence.

I have another remembrance of that evening, the eve of our wedding, which is also sweet to me; the remembrance of how I taught Iras to write her name in preparation for the morrow. I can see her now, with the laughter in her eyes and on her lips, and the flush on her soft cheek, setting herself to copy the bold letters I had written out—first with them placed before her, and afterwards from memory.

There were mistakes at first, of course, over which we laughed anew; but ere long she had her lesson perfect, for she was in all things very apt to learn.

I kissed her hand as I took the pen from it—I would not touch her lips till she was mine—and, still holding it, I said, "There was one piece of information the lawyer asked me for which I could not give. It was your mother's name. I knew your father's."

Her face changed to an older and graver face on the instant—it was always so when there was any allusion to the pastàand the fair brow took on a furrow, as if with the effort of memory. "The name was Suten-Mertetefs," she said. "I have heard my father say so, but I do not remember her. She was a king's daughter, and she died when I was born."

I took a card from my pocket and pencilled it down on the reverse side, ready for Mr. Macpherson. So, she was royally descended, my princess who had fallen on such a poor alliance in these latter days! I could well believe it, for that proud little head was noble enough to have carried the crown of all the Pharaohs.

The morning when it came was all sunshine, as a good omen for the bride, though the air was keen and ground crisped with a touch of early frost; there were rumours of snow already on the northern hills. It was a bright face I saw opposite me at the breakfast neither of us greatly cared to eat; and presently my wife came back, arrayed in her furs, to rejoin me in the sitting-room. "You are content to take me, Iras," I said to her before we started, "poor as I am, and not young to match your youth?"

"Content and glad—my lord, my love," she answered, whispering the addition so low that I barely caught it, and dropping before mine the eyes which told too much.

I had no words to thank her, but there was no happier man that day in all Scotland than I as I passed out into the street with her hand upon my arm.

I believe a certain amount of curiosity prevailed in Mr. Macpherson's office over the bride, for in the comings and goings during our few minutes of detention, what must have been his whole staff of clerks went in and out of the anteroom.

Iras had veiled herself closely, but the perfect figure and the big knot of hair were sufficiently conspicuous attractions, and the curiosity was evidently replaced by admiration.

Mr. Macpherson had set a special chair for her, and came forward with his best smile; and she responded to the introduction gracefully though in silence. There was the insertion of the missing name to be added to the document lying on the table, the old lawyer copying from my pencilling with some query as to spelling; and then he glanced at me over the top of his spectacles.

"Ye have not provided yourselves with the witnesses I spoke of?"

"No. I thought they might be supplied from among your staff."

"Quite so—as you wish it. But it is more usual—and perhaps agreeable—to have friends of the contracting parties. However, I shall be willing to serve for one of them, and"—striking the bell— "Elliott, send Mr. Miles to us—Mr. Miles will be the other."

Mr. Miles had been one of the investigators in the outer office, and—perhaps with a sense of his misdeeds on his head—he looked from me to Iras and from Iras to me, and blushed all over his pale forehead as his principal beckoned him forward.

"I will now, with your permission, madam, read over the declaration before the signatures are affixed."

Iras glanced at me, and I laid my hand on her shoulder as I stood beside her, so that my understanding of it could supplement hers. My signature came first, and then I handed the pen to Iras. She raised her veil a little, only a little—I do not think either of the men present succeeded in seeing her face—and traced in a rather trembling but legible hand the signature I had taught her the night before.

Mr. Macpherson and Mr. Miles signed after us, and then—an open carriage having been called and kept in waiting-the former accompanied us to the sheriff-substitute. He made one or two gallant remarks *en route* to the bride, and as I held her hand, she understood them sufficiently to attempt some faint word of reply; in her position a certain shyness was excusable. The official we visited must also have thought her rather silent; but he looked a very open admiration when, at the close of the proceedings, he offered his congratulations to Mrs. Lavenham and shook hands with us both. Mr. Macpherson preferred to walk back to his office instead of driving with us to the registrar's; and there Iras sat in the carriage while I went in alone, presently issuing, the possessor of an elaborately printed and stamped blue paper filled in with clerkly writing—the marriage-lines which proved Iras my wife.

I told the driver to take us out through the suburbs—any direction would be pleasant that bright breezy morning; and with his face safely turned in the direction of his steed, my wife and I could feel ourselves alone. Presently, when we were out in the more open roads, I saw her furtively uncover her hand to look again at the broad band of gold on the marriage-finger. And then with gentle insistence she pressed something into mine.

It was a ring I had noticed on her hand from the first—a tiny figure of the royal asp in gold, together with a gem which I believe is called an asteria, really a flawed sapphire, with a minute glistening star of white filaments. in the centre of the stone. "It is the star of hope," she said, "and it must never set for you and me." She tried to pass it on the finger corresponding to that on which I had placed her ring, but mine was too large and rough, and the little finger alone would receive it.

"You have given me so much, Ralph, my husband, that you will in your turn take this from me."

Ah, my darling! I wear it there to this day, with your marriage-ring above it; but our star has set as regards this world, and gone down in utter night. But I am beginning to know there is another firmament where still it shines serene, and when I pass beyond these voices it may be indeed from dark to dawn.

7

It is said that the nation is happy which has no history; and for the first seven days following our marriage my history is only that we were happy. There was not a cloud in the sky, even of the size of a man's hand, to forecast the coming tempest of clouds and wind; no prophet sat for us on the top of Carmel. On the day after that of which I have written we travelled to Melrose, in the valley of the Tweed and under the Eildon Hills; and there the last sands of October dropped away out of the glass of Time, and November came in with so soft a grace and so warm a smile that we could well believe ourselves in earlier autumn.

We found sufficiently good accommodation at the inn, and a carriage we could hire for our own use without being encumbered by a driver. Sometimes we trod the beaten track of sight-seers, but oftener wandered at will where the fancy of the moment led us, or the greater solitude proved a temptation. Those three cleft summits rise again on the horizon of my dreams, and that brawling river runs once more at my feet: I linger now over the blessed remembrance of the happy hours they witnessed—shrinking from what I have to tell of the beginning of anguish, the first chill touch of that advancing shadow of eclipse.

I did not wholly forget my work while we were making holiday; and to find Iras profoundly interested in all which concerned it was a delight the more. She was never weary of hearing how we laboured in the excavations, and of the treasures of antiquity restored to light, and the theories deduced from them. Touching these she—an eyewitness of that remote past—had much to say, both in correction and confirmation; and I began to note down various matters to be incorporated in the book. I was busied in this way the evening of the seventh day after our marriage, Iras sitting by. She had been singing to me some verses of the flower-invocation song of which I had spoken (the rescued *papyrus* is now in the British Museum, but in her day, it was familiar as our street music). After the song I had a history of the yearly festival at the great Theban temple, when the sacred boats made their pilgrimage; telling of a ludicrous incident that occurred in the last year of her remembrance, which was held to be ominous by the common people.

I was jotting down the lines of argument designed for my new chapter when her head sank on my shoulder with a sigh. Thinking she was tired with a long day in the fresh air—we had spent the afternoon at Dryburgh—I put my left arm round her to hold her supported, going on meanwhile with my notes, and presently bent my cheek against her soft hair, which always had about it some kind of flower-fragrance. I know not how it was that a sudden disquietude thrilled through me with that touch, but I lifted her face and looked at it. It was quite wan, the eyelids closed and sunk, the whole appearance more of death than sleep; she seemed hardly to breathe.

Much alarmed, I laid her down on the sofa, chafed her hands, and called for brandy; reproaching myself for letting her overtax that newly returned strength and vitality which it was difficult to measure. But before the brandy could be brought, she had revived enough to look at me with a puzzled, dreamy expression, and she gently put it away when I held it to her lips. It was not for some minutes that full intelligence seemed to return; and then terror came with it, for she clung to me with all her strength.

"Ralph — Ralph, hold me; do not let me go! They were taking me away."

I soothed her as well as I could, and assured her that she was safe. No one could touch her in my arms—what did she mean?

For a while she was too much agitated to explain, but at last she whispered with her face hidden. "I was there again—in the temple of the Oracle, and *he* stood by with his claim. I was crying to the high God to release me, and to save me pure for the lord of my heart; and the answer was, to achieve that I must die. Not go down alive into the grave as aforetime, but away through the great gate of death and the judgment of the balance. That I must leave you on earth, my beloved, if I would be forever yours."

"It was a dream, Iras. We had been talking of the old scenes and the old ways, and your mind went back to them—that was all. You are here with me; I hold you in my arms; there is no death, no danger. It was nothing but a dream."

"Would that I could think so!" she sobbed. "I am afraid—I am afraid. And oh! I cannot leave you, my love, my lord!"

Her nerves seemed thoroughly shaken, whatever had been the cause. I persuaded her to go to rest, for indeed it was already late; and I sat by her and held her hand till she slept. When her even breathing assured me of this, I stole back to the sitting-room to put together the papers that strewed the table, at which I had been at work earlier in the evening. I lingered, glancing over them to modify a phrase here, and there, jot down a forgotten detail; but the current of idea was broken, and I felt too much vague anxiety about my wife to settle back to sustained effort. The shabby inn parlour, which had been transfigured by her presence, looked empty and garish, now this charm was withdrawn. I folded away my manuscripts in the despatch-box, turned out the gas which flared above the table, and then, attracted by some suggestion of moonlight at the window, drew aside the curtain and looked out.

Another pen than mine has perfected forever a wonderful night picture of the grand old abbey; and from that window I looked upon the shadow side, silhouetted against a starry sky. The spell of Scott's recollected verse filled my mind, and no other thought; but this was disturbed by a widely different and unwelcome suggestion. Something, human or animal, was stirring in the dense shade under the walls; no form was visible, nothing but vague movement between the buttresses and among the grassy hillocks of the graves. I dropped the curtain and drew back, involuntarily recalling a certain night experience at the window of a Brighton hotel, and then smiled at my own faulty nerve and folly in entertaining the idea.

Later in the night I woke suddenly in the abrupt change of an uneasy dream. Iras was sleeping peacefully, and all was still. No light burned in the chamber; but the window was thinly shaded, and a flood of moonlight poured in across the bed, illuminating the opposite wall. I lay looking at this, and revolving sundry conjectures and recollections, when I saw a shadow projected on this space of light. It was the shadow of a man standing at the bedside and stooping forward, and at the same instant I heard my wife moan. I sprang up—the shadow disappeared, and there was no visible substance to account for it having been there. The small room was in silence and solitude, the door fastened as I had left it, the window undisturbed. Iras was still asleep.

I lay down again softly, so as not to disturb her; and until the moon set and the light faded, I watched the brightness on the wall. But no shadow crossed it a second time, and at last I slept also, dream-haunted by a conviction that the form in silhouette on the wall was identical with the phantom persecution before my marriage, the Egyptian priest who wore the crocodile on his breast on the beach at Brighton, Savak, servant of Sebek, the ancient suitor of Iras.

★★★★★★★★★★★★★★★★

The fears of the night took on insignificant proportions in the prosaic light of a November morning. A chill white fog had stolen up from the river, and was blurring the prospect outside the window of the dressing-room; pails and pattens were clinking on the yard pavement underneath; a horse was led clattering out of the stable. I was contemplating the unpromising outside world when another sound broke on my ear—a cry from my wife's room. She was standing before the glass, her white robe open at the throat, round which I could see the glitter of her necklace. Her gaze was riveted in pale horror on her own reflection.

"I have lost it!" she said, in a tone of acute distress. "Oh, Ralph, it is gone!"

Not the necklace, as it still clasped her throat; but she pointed to the lower chain, and then I saw that only six lotus pendants hung from it instead of the full number of seven.

I shared her concern at the loss, knowing the superstitious value she placed on this ornament; but I made the natural suggestion it might be found in the bed or about the room, and proceeded to search for it. She looked on, and even assisted me, in the faint hope I might be right; but when our effort failed it did not surprise her. "It has been taken from me in the night—I am sure of it. It was safe when I took off my dress. I looked for it at once, remembering the vision, and counted the buds. Ah, Ralph, if he has power to tear it from me now that I am with you, when and where can I be safe? Is this his revenge? They will be taken from me one by one, and then I must die."

It seemed a wild idea, and I strove to combat it and reassure her; but at the same time, I remembered with a shudder what I had seen in the moonlight—the shadow of the man at the bedside, stooping over the pillow where she lay. The little ornament seemed to have been wrenched away from the metal wire which suspended it, as a fragment of the composition still remained, as if broken short. All the other pendants were firm and perfect. It went to my heart to see her sweet face so pale and sad; and when at breakfast she urged that we should leave the place, I caught at the proposal, hoping that change of scene would divert her mind and remove any morbid impression caused by the loss.

"It is not that I want to go—we have been so happy here, and all is so beautiful; but I shall never feel safe again where *he* has become strong. Do you mind very much, Ralph, if we go away?"

No, I said, I thought it was the best thing we could do. I had planned a whole month's holiday, returning to London at the beginning of December, and it had never been my intention to spend it in one place. I wanted to show her the West Coast, which is mild even in winter: we would return at once to Edinburgh, and arrange next day for a journey beyond.

I spoke as cheerfully and confidently as I could, and said nothing of the Shadow; but I too felt relieved I had not to look for it on that moonlit wall through the wakeful watches of another night. We would leave by the mid-day train; and I rang to order the bill and a carriage to the station, and helped her to put together the pretty novelties of possession strewn about over her toilet-table, of which she was so proud.

Her smile came back, and a faint colour to her cheek, as the train moved out of the station and the last houses of the little town fell away in the distance. I think throughout the journey we both had the feeling that we were fugitives, and were glad when stately stone-built Edinburgh closed about us once more. We chose a different hotel for our one night's sojourn—this at Iras's suggestion; and while she rested, I bethought me I would go to the post-office and see if any letters had been sent from London.

One I had to prove identity by a receipted bill and a card, and then a couple of envelopes were hunted up out of a dusty pigeon-hole and handed to me across the counter. was a mere cover for some unimportant enclosures, the other the letter I thought would come from Knollys. He wrote:

"You have indeed taken me by surprise. I had no idea there was a lady in the case, or that you were keeping back from me so great a secret. I wish you joy, my dear Lavenham, and trust you are as happy as I hope someday to be with Madge. Let me know when you are returning to London, and if there is anything I can do for you in the meantime. I shall be glad to see you back, even as Benedick the married man, and though I fear my old bachelor crony will be transformed beyond recognition. But I hope you will not cut short the change and rest you were greatly needing through any mistaken idea of the obligation of returning to work. I have been to No. 46 G—— Street, and made two drawings of the mummy-case; you can have your choice of them on return.

"I was not quite satisfied with my first effort. Seeing it had been unfastened, I took the liberty of looking within, and own to some curiosity to know how you disposed of the mummy. I telegraphed as you directed to Skipton, so of course you had made the examination you talked of. Adamson the expert came round about it, and said you had arranged with him to do the analysis, and also to take charge of the thing itself, as your landlady objected to keep it at the lodgings;

but I was obliged to tell him it was gone, and I had no instructions. Mrs. Mappinbeck is queerer than ever. I asked her about it, naturally, and I believe she thinks it is concealed on the premises. She hinted she was disappointed in you, that you had not behaved as she expected.

"You gave her your word as a gentleman it should be taken away, and she can declare it never went out of the house after it came in—not unless you took it with you among your luggage. Not very likely, is it, that you would travel about with such an encumbrance on a bridal tour! Write to me at the old shop and clear up all these points—that is, if you like, otherwise they can stand over till we meet. Mrs. Mappinbeck tells me a very grand lady in splendid furs lunched with you the day you left, and that you went away together; I conclude this would be the present Mrs. Lavenham? The season keeps wonderfully mild, but do you not find it cold so far away north? Whatever made you elect to go to Scotland so late in the season? Yours, etc."

I folded up the letter and put it in safe keeping. I fully intended to answer it in the course of a day or two; but first procrastination and then increasing anxiety caused delay, and the reply remained unwritten to the end.

We left Edinburgh next day for Greenock, and there took one of the Clyde steamers down the firth to Largs. It was a foggy early morning as we crossed the country from east to west; but on entering the environs of Glasgow a yellow glow broke out through the hanging smoke above the busy city, and by the time the train arrived at Greenock pier the mists had lifted and the waters of the firth were sparkling in the sun.

The scene seemed to interest and delight Iras more than anything she had yet witnessed—the heaving water, the shipping, the open docks, the line of blue hills to the west, and the churning paddle wheels as we set out. She was so intent on looking about her that she forgot to draw her veil closely as usual, and a couple of men, who passed and repassed us up and down the deck with their cigars, looked at her with evident admiration, which it amused me to witness. She was unconscious of annoyance from it, or of anything but the wonderful new world and the ways of the great deep—resting with a child's confidence on my power to explain and make clear every perplexity.

The sea-trip to Largs is not a long one, and, November as it was, the air on the water was not chill; fortunately, the day was one of still weather. I wanted Iras to have an extra wrap, but she was warm—quite warm, she assured me—in her fur coat, and only sorry when we drew alongside the wooden landing-stage to go on shore. The little place in a nook of hills, with its clustered houses along the beach, looked almost as remote from worldly disturbance as in the days when it was said that you went "out of Scotland into Largs." I had no recommendation to quarters, so we left our baggage at the pier-head and went on a prospecting expedition along the line of town.

Now here occurs the first serious confusion of memory. When I revisited the place with Knollys, I could not identify the house where we stayed. The name of the people also has escaped me; and it is of the greater moment because, as it happened, Iras made friends with the woman, and she could have borne effectual testimony to her reality. I only know that for some reason or other we disliked the appearance of the hotel; and, farther on beyond, we came upon a house close down upon the beach, with an attractive bow-window, in which was displayed the placard of apartments. It looked clean and bright, and the idea of being so near the wonder and variety of the sea delighted Iras, the waves breaking within a stone's-throw of us. So, we rang at the bell, and were answered by a pleasant, matronly-looking person, whose face I remember to this day, though her name is a blank to me.

We took the rooms—a parlour on the ground-floor and bed and dressing room above—and were the only lodgers; but the house was not a very still one, as the patter of children's feet went about it out of school-hours, with a sound of merry voices which the mother-mistress was always trying to keep in check. I think the woman's husband was something in the seafaring line; but whether this was conjecture, on account of his absence, or an ascertained fact, I cannot now be sure. It was to this woman Iras made some timid advances in the speech that halted to others, though to me it flowed without a check: the children, of whom we caught occasional glimpses, were the attraction, and any manifestation of interest in them pleased the mother.

Some of the events of our stay I have clearly enough in memory, though the cloud rests over others. I remember well a showery afternoon when I had been abroad alone on some trifling errand, and on returning found Iras gone from the sitting-room. I drew a chair to the fireside, waiting for her faintly uneasy, as I was apt to be when my one treasure was out of sight—when I heard a ripple of musical laughter and a child's crowing shout in the passage, and Iras entered, flushed with delighted triumph, her eyes shining, her lips apart, and a big baby eighteen months old carried in her arms.

"See what I have here, Ralph; and he likes me—he will come to

267

me—he is not afraid!"

It was not wonderful that he should like her—at least, I thought not. I never saw her look lovelier than when she sat down opposite with the baby on her knee—a pretty child, it is true, with big dark eyes a little like her own. It was not a bit shy of her, but crowed and clutched its fingers in her hair; and she laughed tenderly over it with genuine woman's delight—especially when the little fellow shrank away from my bearded face as I bent near the pair, and hid against her breast. Ah me! if one day—one day—a child of mine could have come to fill her arms! but it was not to be.

The landlady presently made her appearance, laughing also and apologetic. She was afraid Teddy would tire the lady. But it was "just wonderful" the fancy he had taken—he was accustomed to be shy with strangers; and it was evident Teddy's favour was considered as a special boon. Mrs. Lavenham was "real kind," she said to me more than once in the days that followed—whether few or many I can hardly now tell; days during which I often saw Iras playing with the big baby when we were kept perforce indoors. But if more uncertain than at Melrose, the weather favoured us on the whole. I can recall strolls along the beach road either way, and drives to the higher level at the back; views of the mountains about Loch Striven to the north-west, and Cumbrae and Arran to the south—in sunshine and mist and driving showers, and sometimes with a gleam of snow whiteness on the Alpine outline of the Arran hills.

That whiteness of snow-peak would have been to most people a danger-signal to flee away southwards; but I knew Iras felt herself safer in this northern region, and it would be time enough to think about London at the expiration of my holiday. Since that night at Melrose, she had never voluntarily led the conversation to her past life in Egypt, though she was always ready with a reply when I appealed to her. One afternoon, when we were returning from a walk, I noticed she was unusually silent, and had drawn close to me, slipping her hand under my arm. I asked if she were tired, but she said no; and then, as I still looked inquiry, presently there came confession.

"I have been thinking today of *him*; you know who I mean. I have felt afraid again, as I did at Melrose; as if his power were closing about me, and his hand stretching out to touch me once more. When first we came here, I felt so free—in the midst of clear air and safety; but now it seems to be thickening and darkening again, as if the end were close upon me. What shall I do?"

I gave such counsel as I could—to turn her mind to other matters, and not dwell on a fancied danger; I would not own that I shared her fear. We would grow old together, I told her, and the end was far away yet, even from me.

"I wish I could think it," she said; and, the road being solitary, she clasped her other hand upon my arm and touched my shoulder with her cheek.

"It will be death indeed, and more than death, to leave you, O my dearest; but it is borne in on me more and more clearly that our happiness is not for long. But I have much to be thankful for. I have been preserved to see you face to face; and, as it says in the flower-song, '*An hour passed with thee is worth a space of eternity!*' I have no right to complain."

Words such as these would bring a sudden stricture to my heart. I know not how I replied, protesting there should be no parting—I would not, could not, let her go. A change of scene had before removed the impression; we would leave Largs as we left Melrose, and would be up and away on the morrow.

This was tacitly agreed between us; but soon after our return to the lodgings, Iras came to me as I stood at the window watching the light already fading in the west. "Do not say anything about going away to Mrs. —— tonight. Little Teddy is ill, and she is in trouble about him, and very anxious."

The baby was ill indeed, with one of those short sharp seizures of croup which are so hazardous to frail young lives. Through the night my wife could not be persuaded to rest, but sat up with the mother, anxious almost as she; while I waited about, with masculine incapacity for help, except as a messenger for the doctor should he be needed. When the crisis was abating the child grew restless, and struggled from his mother's arms to Iras, seeming easier as she carried him to and fro in his warm wrappings, raised against her shoulder.

I feared she would exhaust herself, but she was too happy in having won ease to the little patient to think of her own fatigue; and she paced to and fro in the lowered light, while the mother made ready a warm bed and emptied the bath which had been used in the height of the attack. This went on long after the first exhausted doze had deepened into real sleep; but at last, we persuaded her to lay him down. As she gently lowered him into his nest of blankets, and the small chubby hands left her neck, there was a slight crack as of something broken.

I saw my wife put up her hands as soon as they were free, in sudden anxiety for the necklace. She was wearing a dressing-gown which had fallen undone at the throat, and as she carried the child cradled against her, he must have grasped one of the lotus pendants; for, as she turned significantly to show me, another was missing. "Not lost," I said; and with as light a touch as I could contrive, I opened the curled-up baby fingers and took out the tiny ornament. The little fellow still slept, so I drew her away from the mother's thanks into our own room, where she, too, could rest.

"It is nothing but an accident this time—no omen at all. We will find a jeweller to repair the broken wire, and I can put it back in its place for you myself. My dear Iras, do not look so concerned!"

"It will be taken—I am sure of it. The virtue has gone out of it."

"It cannot be taken if I put it in safe custody, as I will show you." I unlocked the despatch-box, and taking out a tiny case of buffalo-horn, which I had been accustomed to use for steel pens, and which had been with me in all my wanderings, I shook out the contents, folded the lotus ornament in a sheet of fresh paper, and laid it within, turning the key upon it. "I have faith in a Chubb lock," I said to her. "Your trinket is safe this time, my darling; you need not trouble about it anymore."

I thought she looked weary and anxious next morning, more than the hours of watching would warrant. Little Teddy was better, and we arranged with the mother to leave the day after, crossing to Rothesay by the steamer. When setting out for our walk, I suggested we should call at the jewellers about the repair of the pendant, and confidently produced my despatch box and the key. There was the little case of buffalo-horn, it is true, and its lining of folded paper; but no pendant lay within. The paper held a little heap of fine dust, into which the thing had doubtless perished by some agency beyond my power to define.

8

The next stage of our pilgrimage was Rothesay; and there, as in every fresh place, there was at first the feeling of freedom, of escape and a temporary safety, and then there gradually darkened down upon my wife, and to my perception also in a degree, the same foreboding of a threatened danger. But we could at times forget and be happy. There rises again before me in sweet remembrance one clear starlight evening when I walked with Iras on the quay, the lamps and windows of the town a semicircle on one side of us, while on the other the lights of the anchored shipping were duplicated in the dark water. The fresh breeze had a salt taste on our lips, and below us against the shore the wash of unseen waves made a cadenced undertone in the stillness.

It was, I think, the fourth day of our sojourn. I had inquired about one or two expeditions into the interior of the island, and, as we paced up and down on the sea-wall, I told her what we were going to see, and why these places were thought of interest—some fragment of the long roll of the world's history which had written itself in achievement and suffering while she lay asleep in her rock-tomb in the cliffs beyond Luxor.

We were to set out after breakfast if the day proved fine; and I went down in the morning to see what might be the hotel capabilities of providing a carriage. I was absent only half an hour; but when I returned, I found my wife full of distress and excitement, and with my big portmanteau and her trunk before her, rapidly laying in the things which had been removed.

"Can we get ready in time for the steamer?" she said to me. "Don't ask me why, Ralph, but I dare not stay here any longer. You will not be angry, I know; you will help me to get away."

Whatever had happened in my short absence had greatly alarmed and distressed her—that was evident. She shook her head when I asked about the necklace, and I would not press any question when I saw how much she trembled, and that tears were difficult to restrain. The Fate before which we fled had overtaken us for the third time— so much was clear; and we had no choice but again to flee before it. There was time and to spare to get ready for the steamer, which called at noon; and, as it happened, we were on the quay nearly an hour before its arrival, as it was considerably after time.

There was the scene of our walk the evening before, looking far more prosaic in cold daylight than under that enchantment of night and stars. The lovely mountain view opposite was now hiding itself in gradually advancing mist, which presently drizzled down on us in chilly rain. Conditions had changed for the worse. I stood with Iras on the edge of the pier, holding her arm and feeling her shiver with distress far more than cold, as we strained our eyes for the first glimpse of the steamer round the point; and I confess my heart sank within me, failing for the first time before the horror of this intangible persecution—this enemy who struck in the dark, against whom I was powerless either to avenge myself or to protect her.

She said she would rather not come under shelter—"if I did not mind"—she would rather wait in the open and the air. A few people lounged about on the pier—one or two hand-barrows with luggage stood ready for the boat beside our own; but the autumn tourist stream had long ago been diverted to the south, and the traffic to and from the Bute seaport was not great. "I am safer here than within walls," she said, presently; "at least, I fancy so. But there will not be any safety till we are away."

"Can you tell me now, Iras, what it was that alarmed you at the hotel?"

"I ought to have told you then—when you asked me first; but the terror was so great and unexpected, and I was afraid of worse harm following—to you and to us both. Yes, I will tell you. I shall have courage to tell you now, for surely that is the ship."

The line of smoke against the sky, the gleam of red funnels far off in the rain, marked indeed the advent of the deliverer; and as we stood together watching its advance, my wife told her story.

"I went to the bedroom for the book you are teaching me to read—the one with the pictures, and the double alphabet you wrote out in the beginning; and I had just taken it from the dressing-table when I felt all at once faint and giddy and terrified—like a bird feels when the snake is looking at it before it darts: you have seen that in these days as I used to see it in the time long ago. The room changed about me, although I had the book firm in my hand to remind me who I am now, and where; and I was wearing this Englishwoman's dress that you have given me, which belongs to the present, not the past. Instead of the bedroom, it was like a hall with pillars—and gods and kings on the walls, and written words that were terrible. And there before me among the pillars, unchanged, implacable, commanding, *he* was looking at me as the snake looks at the bird—"

"Don't go on now, my darling. Wait and tell me later, if it distresses you so much."

"I thought I was lost—I thought I had seen you for the last time. I put both my hands to my throat to cover the necklace, and turned to rush away from him. But what seemed an opening in the court between the Osirides was no opening really. I struck myself against the wall—the real wall of the room—and fell on the floor. I was half stunned, I believe, for the blow was a heavy one."

"You are hurt, then, and I did not know it!"

"There is a bruise, I think, but it does not matter. I was glad of it then, for it seemed a deliverance. The temple was gone—the eyes that compelled me were gone—and there I was in the bedroom with your coat lying over the chair. I took it and hid my face in it till I was calmer; it seemed to bring me nearer to you—to you and safety. But I knew the time had come for us to go; for *he* had gathered power against me, and would use it without mercy."

The steamer came gliding in against the pier, the gangways were pushed over, the bell rang for us to go on board. I said what I could to comfort her as we sat together on the sheltered side of the deck, and I held my umbrella to screen her from the rain, which now poured faster. But she knew, alas! and I was learning to know also, that there was little comfort to give or to be taken except in the knowledge we were still together—that, strong as our foe might be against us, the final stroke of parting had not come.

A third pendant was gone; but whether the loss was discovered when next Iras opened her dress, or later, I cannot now be sure. My recollection is also vague of a night and a day passed at Ardrishaig, and of posting on from there by two stages to Sonachan on Loch Awe.

I remember Sonachan, and the glassy beauty of the great lake with the peaked mountain at its head—the dark mirror of the water reflecting the burning reds and browns of the autumn foliage not yet fallen. The sunshine favoured us again here, and lit up the withered fern and heather on the lower hillsides and the barren rocks above with a golden glow. There was a charm in the still remoteness, the profound peace, unbroken as it seemed by either tides or storms in those dark depths of liquid blackness over which the boat glided so smoothly.

For we hired a boat, and I took Iras on the lake the afternoon we arrived, and again the day following. The air was mild, and neither of us felt any cold; but it is possible that a chill on the water brought about a renewal of my old fever, or the attack may have been some first symptom of the more serious illness which came later. I woke the next morning—the morning we had arranged to leave—with aching limbs and throbbing pulse, and a pain in my head which made vision dazzled and difficult. A cold sponge-bath and hot tea gave me temporary relief, and I would not acknowledge to such illness as would prevent our moving forward—the movement by which alone we seemed able to baffle the enemy.

Our journey on that day was neither long nor difficult. We posted to Taynuilt as a stage for Oban; but long before we reached our destination my malady had increased beyond concealment—at least from such quick eyes as my wife's, as her anxiety for me was easily aroused.

She arranged our wraps in the wagonette which took us on from Dalmally so that I could recline in the carriage; and I told her the probable course of the attack, and of the quinine treatment I had before found efficacious, directing her how to measure the powder I carried with me for these emergencies. At Taynuilt she must have given the necessary orders to the people at the inn, though I am told they do not remember her, for our arrival is a blank to me.

I was carried to the bed on which I lay for more than a week utterly prostrate—often, I am afraid, delirious, but most tenderly cared for through all those days of illness by my wife. She seemed never weary, never impatient; and her cool hand on my head would call me back over and over again when I was wandering away into mists of delusion. Delusion did beset me; but her presence at my side was a blessed reality, in the after-time most sorely missed and longed for.

I must not dwell on that now—what she was to me, and how I have lost her—or my brain will go wild again and writing become impossible. I spoke of the delusions of that illness. I will write of one which partook somewhat of the character of a dream that found fulfilment; or was it a dim perception, exaggerated into grotesque form, of something that actually took place?

The bed on which I lay was close to the window, and from my pillow I could look up the corrie seamed in the side of the great mountain to the shoulder of Ben Cruachan, white with snow against the sky. I used to lie there, too weak and weary for speech, my wife's hand clasped in mine, and watch the white summit and the cloud-changes about it; but my sick fancy was annoyed and baffled by the crossbars of the window between me and it—especially at one point where the transverse woodwork cut across the snow. That black network seemed to press upon and hurt my vision; and when I wandered it was to beg impatiently that it should be taken away, and the white remoteness left clear before me.

One night, when I was at the worst, it seemed to me that I awoke and lay looking at the white mountain with some soft light about it such as stars or moon, when, between me and it, uplifted into space, I saw a cross. Not the window-bars, for they were gone, but such a form of wood as that with which painters have made us familiar in ghastly representations of the Crucifixion. To this instrument of torture my wife was bound, in the white dress she wore in the coffin, her arms and neck uncovered, and the green gleam of the necklace about her throat; while I saw plainly the four remaining lotus buds where they hung below. As she floated between me and the snow her eyes did not meet mine, but looked away into space with an awful expectation in them—a dumb dread and endurance which it turns me cold to think of even now. The light brightened as I looked, but only on the figure and on the beloved face; the depths of air and the mountain shape behind remained dim as at first.

It seems to my remembrance that hours went by, during which I gazed on the cross with anguish unutterable, nailed to the bed on which I lay—dumb with the oppression of nightmare, powerless to succour. A mysterious attraction drew my eyes to the necklace, and, as I watched, a single lotus blazed out into a star of flame, burned hotly for a few moments, and then died into a lingering spark; and there on the white neck a blackened and blistered spot showed the space where it had hung. Then came an interval which I cannot measure, and another pendant bud broke into flame, blazed, and vanished, leaving a second burnt spot; and two only hung upon the chain. The face on the cross moved for the first time, turned, and looked at me; and, as if those eyes broke the spell, the cry I had been powerless to utter broke from my lips and I awoke.

With that night the crisis of the fever passed; the next day found me better, clearheaded, nothing ailing me but weakness. Iras played the tyrant, and forbade me to speak or excite myself; I must lie still and obey orders, and take what she held to my lips. I was, I think, tolerably quiescent, but after another night anxiety began to stir. I had lost count of our sojourn, but we had been fully a week at the inn. Surely it was time, and more, that we were moving onwards; the enemy must be already on our track. I insisted on a carriage being ordered for the next morning to take us on another stage towards Oban, and Iras did not oppose, though she fenced and put aside my questions. On this our last evening at Taynuilt I was sitting up in a chair with pillows, watching my wife as she moved softly about, when something in her face and air—I know not what—struck me with a recollected fear. "Iras," I said, and she came instantly beside me. "Undo the collar of your dress, my darling; I want to see the necklace."

She tried to put me by on some soft pretext, but I would not take denial. Kneeling beside me, she unfastened the hooks which held her dress together and turned it back—dumbly, without a word, but with a mist of unshed tears in the dark eyes, and a quiver of sorrow on her lip. It was as I dreaded—two only of the lotus pendants remained, and under two of the spaces left vacant there were slight bruise-marks on her neck like the print of a finger—the very spots which I had seen burnt and blackened in my dream.

I would have set out from Taynuilt that hour had it been possible; but as it was, the night passed without disturbance, and we left early on the morrow. I have no clear recollection of the stages to Oban; it mattered little now where we went, so long as continued movement was possible. I no longer thought of any return to London or to work—nothing signified to me anymore save the desperate effort to keep Iras mine, and to prolong to the uttermost the time we could spend together.

I was better by the time we reached Oban, but the mantle of my weakness seemed to be falling upon Iras. I noticed henceforward that she did not care to walk any distance, and when we were not travelling, she would lie on a couch drawn to the window of our room, looking out on the hills or the sea. But in ministering to my comfort, she knew no fatigue, and her care for me never faltered till the end came—anymore than her love.

To my eyes her beauty was greater than ever, though a change was passing upon it; it was growing more ethereal under the advancing Shadow, though so gradually that it was only by comparison with that first revelation of her in the glow of renewed life that I fully realized how she was altering. She had something the air of a woman in a decline, and yet it was hardly ill-health, but increased spirituality, which was suggested by the change.

I mark our brief sojourn at Oban by the discovery, little as it impressed me at the time, that my wife was not perceptible to all vision as to my own. I believe it was not so at the first, and I note it now doubtfully and with a query in the light of what came after—asking myself if the gradual abstraction of the pendants took from her the power of impressing others with her living semblance as in the beginning.

When we entered the hotel where I had elected to stay, together from the chaise which had brought us, a smart manageress in silk gown and a display of gold ornaments came forward to answer my inquiry for rooms. Yes, she said, I could have what I asked for; they were not full now, as it was after the season; and would I put my name where she pointed. I wrote, as I always did, Mr. and Mrs. Lavenham; and she glanced inquiringly at the pile of luggage over which the hall-porter was hovering, and again at the names in the book. "You expect Mrs. Lavenham to join you here?" she said.

"Mrs. Lavenham is here with me," I replied; and indeed, Iras was standing at my elbow all the time. The woman looked puzzled, but said no more; and I drew my wife's arm in mine to lead her upstairs, following a chambermaid armed with the keys. I made a joke of it to her at the time, and indeed it struck me in no other light. "It all comes of my grey hairs," I said. "You see, they cannot believe you are anything but my daughter;" and all import of the blunder passed away in the sweetness of the eyes and the smile she lifted to meet mine.

I will finish the hotel incident while I am about it, though I have another instance to record during our stay. When we were departing, and the bill was presented for payment, I was about to settle it with this same manageress, when the total happened to strike me as unexpectedly small. I am somewhat careless about money matters, and seldom examine the items of such an account; but this time I did glance over it, and saw that dinner, breakfast, attendance, and so forth, were charged throughout for one, as if I had been alone.

I pointed this out, and requested correction; and again, came the same puzzled hesitation—almost an unwillingness to make any change. "You have not charged for Mrs. Lavenham," I said. "Please make the alteration at once, for time presses;" and thus urged, it was done, though the woman muttered "she had made out the bill as instructed," and accepted the additional sovereign with a bad grace.

The other incident occurred that same morning. Iras and I walked round by the harbour to look beyond the point at the unquiet sea—still roughened, even within the natural breakwater of Kerrara, after the heavy storm which had raged round the coast two days before. I got into conversation with an elderly Highlander who was superintending the landing of a smack, and heard from him some further details of an accident which had been the leading topic at the hotel on our arrival. A fishing-boat, driven on the rocks in the outer channel, had gone down with all hands—a man and boy—and the bodies were being watched for with every tide. The boy seemed to have been of small account—an orphan lad, no stay to anyone as yet; but the fisherman had left a house full of little children, and since that night of disaster one more had come to the widow in her agony. Iras stood by while the old man was giving me these details, and I could see she understood them enough to be moved to pity. I was not surprised that her hand came creeping under my arm when we had turned away.

"Oh, Ralph, that poor mother! Could we not send her something—for the little baby?"

The old Highlander had looked honest, and had, moreover, told his story with no hint of expected charity. I offered her the loose coins in my pocket, and she chose out of them a little gold piece. "Will you go back and take it to him?" she said.

"Come yourself, my darling. He will like it better from you."

"No—no." She shook her head emphatically. "I could not make him understand. Please go without me, Ralph, and I will wait here."

I went back, as she wished, and explained to the man the destination of the bit of gold.

"The lady had sent it," I said. This assertion seemed to perplex him, and he eyed the coin doubtfully. "Mrs. Macdonald would be ferry much obliged," he said; "but there would be friends raised up, and he had not meant to ask from strangers. And who might be the leddy?"

"The lady who was with me," I said, in explanation; "who stood by when he was telling me about the wreck."

The man looked completely mystified, and stared as though he thought either he or I had taken leave of our senses. "I never saw no leddy," he broke out at last; and then—perhaps fearing some lapse of manners—went on to repeat, in conclusion, that he was "ferry much obliged all the same, and Mrs. Macdonald she would be ferry much obliged as well."

9

The two last pendants were safe when we left Oban—that I remember; but I cannot say certainly in what direction we journeyed beyond. That treacherous cloud of memory has blotted out a portion of our wanderings, and the dates which intervened between the 25th and 29th of November. I can only now tell that in some out-of-the-way place, name forgotten, we were detained a day beyond our reckoning by the accidental failure of the conveyance which was to take us on. The afternoon of my remembrance was stormy and cold, and Iras had seemed so much tired by her last journey that I was not sorry for the rest for her, nor greatly concerned over the detention, as she had expressed no uneasiness. The inn was a small one, and had no private sitting-room to place at our disposal; so, we were forced to content ourselves with the common room at the service of all comers; but, as it happened, at this lonely season we had it to ourselves.

The name of the place is gone irrecoverably, but I remember the room: the peat-fire burning in the grate, the glass cases against the walls—with their contents of phenomenal fish and one royal eagle—the slippery horse-hair sofa on which Iras lay. I had been running over

the week-old newspaper at the window, and when that exciting occupation failed me, I stepped softly across to the chair by the fireside,
from which I could watch her as she slept. She looked very frail and
delicate as she lay there, and the soft oval of her cheek was growing
wasted. I realised this with a pang of fear; not of the supernatural this
time, but of failing nature. I had been wrong, I thought, to keep her in
the North, much as she loved it, and mild as had been the season hitherto. We were now on the edge of winter; henceforward our enforced
travels should be in search of a warmer climate. We would push on by
the cross-country route on which we were embarked till we reached
again the great centres of rail, and from thence our advance could be
by easy strides to the South.

The afternoon was growing early dusk, and the fire, all in a cave of
red heat, threw scant illumination into the room. It may be objected
in this case, also, that I dozed in my chair, and what I have to tell was
only dream. All I can say is, it came to me with the semblance of reality, and was followed by the same effect of loss.

Those who know what it is to be on the edge of parting—be it
the severance of distance or the severance of death—will understand
how I studied my wife's face, and with what contraction of heart—
striving to print indelibly on remembrance every beloved trait, every
fleeting expression, as a possession for the blank which would come
after. I surely foreknew that it must come, strenuously as I strove to
deny it both to myself and her. It is a possession; for through all the
failure of memory which besets me I can recall her face perfectly in
every change from grave to gay; can recall it as she lay lost in dreams
on that hard pillow in the winter dusk—the dark sweep of eyelash on
her pale cheek, the fine pencilling of the straight brows, the lips with
their sorrowful curve, as if *her* foreknowledge were a shadow upon her
even in her sleep. Her right hand was under her cheek as she lay; her
left, with the wedding-ring on it, hung down in the glow of the fire.
I saw both hands plainly, but what was this other?

A third hand came into sight over her shoulder—a slender hand,
longer and larger than her own, and darker in tint—the lean fingers
moving round the collar of her dress as if to pluck it undone. A hand
only in view, but with no appearance of detachment, it seemed to
reach over from behind her, as if the figure to which it belonged were
concealed by the back of the sofa and the arm passed through it. There
was something hideous in the contrast between those stealthy fingers
and her placid sleep—something devilish, horrible, murderous; and for

the first aghast moment I could only look in paralyzed astonishment.

The hand was quick in movement, and as I started to my feet it had already dived within the collar. I tried to clutch it, but was too late; the eel-like thing eluded my grasp, withdrew, and vanished. Indeed, that I ever touched it I cannot be sure; and there was Iras awake and looking at me in surprise.

Nothing earthly was lurking in the shadow; we were alone in the room. I drew her head on to my shoulder, and clasped her to me in an agony of dread under the semblance of a caress. I did not dare ask for the emerald chain to be uncovered as I had done before; I knew too well how it would be. The discovery came at night that the last pendant hung alone. Iras took it very quietly; the terror and distress she had shown in the beginning were all gone. I could divine she was trying to be resigned, and would not mar the time that remained to us by any open demonstration of grief. She said little, but the clasp of her arms about my neck was silently eloquent, and we kissed as we might have done if the parting hour had already come.

I knew what she expected—that the severance of the last pendant would bring about her death; and, witnessing the advance of the change in her as one after the other fell away, I feared it might be only too true a forecast. The resolve I renewed in the watches of that night was to keep moving onward, and to sojourn nowhere for a longer period than twenty-four hours; during that time, so far as experience had borne out, we might consider ourselves secure. It would be a weary life of perpetual journeying, and might tax her diminished strength; still, if it lengthened the span of her continuance with me, that was motive for all.

It was a piece of singular unwisdom, I reflected after, which had prompted me to embark on that cross-country journey, where the means of conveyance forward might often become difficult; but we were now so far advanced that to go on was preferable to retracing our steps. I calculated we could reach Inverardoch possibly in another day, and Callander by the following evening; and from there the railway would be available for Edinburgh and the South.

Was it only one day's journey from that nameless inn to Inverardoch? Here again I am obliged to confess a doubt. I remember our departure, and how, standing at the door, I had occasion sharply to rebuke the man-of-all-work who brought out my portmanteau and brushed roughly against Iras with it, pushing her aside. I called to him to stand out of the way of the lady; and his face is plain before me with its gape of wonder as I helped her into the vehicle and arranged our plaid over her knees.

I have no positive remembrance whether it was the evening of that day or the day following which found us slowly crawling along the hilly road that wound up through one of the less frequented passes towards the head of the great lake. If the same, we had somewhere changed vehicles *en route*, and were in an open wagonette—machine, as they call it in the North—and not a covered chaise. Anything wilder or more grand in its desolation it would be difficult to picture: I, with my travelled experience of other lands and heights of greater altitude, had been impressed equally with Iras.

We seemed to have penetrated into the very heart of the mountains, and the effect was enhanced by the covering of snow which rested on all the higher summits. That phenomenon of the snow was of unfailing interest to my wife; the wonder and mystery of its white purity, its soft descent, delighted her ever anew. The rain had charmed her when first it fell, and the clouds and mists about the mountains, with their soft veilings of distance and their sudden changes and revelations, and especially the pageant of the rainbow; but her delight in the snow was greater than all. If I live into the snow-time of another year, I shall never see it fall without the thought of her pleasure in it; but indeed, the thought of her is with me in all surroundings and in every act of life.

We had that day, what is rare in the Highlands, a communicative driver, who took upon himself something of the office of cicerone: probably the man had a strain of Irish blood in his veins later than the Scots extraction. It was he who pointed out the different heights by name, and drew our attention—my attention, for I do not remember that he ever addressed Iras—to the first opening in the landscape below us of the loch to which we were bound. It must be lovely indeed under the sun of summer. It was grand as we saw it, but lonely and awesome—black in the shadow of those girdling hills, and under the growing darkness of a sky pierced here and there already by the fire-point of a star. Iras stood up in the carriage to look, with my hand to support her, gazing silently and intently over the wide prospect. "It is beautiful," she said; "yes, it is beautiful—but oh, how dark! It is like going down into the night."

The driver was busy under the carriage scotching his wheel for the long descent which now began into the valley. About half-way down he pulled up his horses at a turn of the winding road; something had gone wrong with a strap, and the putting of it right paved the way for more conversation. "Ye see that hill on the left, sir, right below us? That's the Cruach-fruin; and some say it's rightly named because of the burying-ground there is there, right up against the kirk, for all this district round about. Ye'll be bound to see the roofs on the south side in the shelter—that's Cruach-fruin kirk and Cruach-fruin manse, and this is the Allt-fruin burn, which runs down from it, that the road crosses at the bridge below."

I looked where I was bidden, and saw the humble slated roofs against the hillside, with a glimmer of white gravestones about the farther one, but did not feel an interest keen enough to prompt me to ask for an explanation of the name. It was, however, supplied to us.

"It just means the Hill of Sorrow—Cruach-fruin does; the name has been that from all time; but it's a hill of sorrow it has proved to many a one going up there with their dead. No, sir, there's no village hereabout. The people come to the kirk from far and wide over the hills, and the only near house is Inverardoch, where ye are bound."

He climbed back to his perch and set the machine in motion. I looked at the lonely manse on the Hill of Sorrow, and wondered what manner of people spent their lives there in these solitudes. With books and a congenial companion, it would be possible, I thought, to be happy even in a place which called itself Cruach-fruin; nay, would I not be more than willing to change lots with that Free Kirk minister, if only I could find there a safe shelter for Iras, a refuge from persecution, which she could share with me! She had glanced at the place and away again without remark; and then, drawing off her glove, held out her bare hand to be touched. by the snowflakes, which now began to wander down one by one—flakes which proved to be the vanguard of a host. As she lifted her face to the darkening sky, I saw she was very pale. Yes, she was tired, she said, in answer to my question, and she felt stiff from the long sitting in the carriage; but the cold was nothing—she would be well when we got in and I could have tea.

As I have said, the stars were brightening on the eastern horizon, which was still clear from the snow-cloud that gathered behind us in the northwest. I looked up, as she did, and there, right opposite across the lake, was the great sign of the hunter—the stars of Orion's belt above the shoulder of the hill. It was long since I had given Madame St. Heliers a thought, but the words of her warning came back upon me as if freshly spoken—"*Beware of the snows of winter, and Orion low in the east.*" There was the sign of Orion fronting me with ominous clearness—the sign of the hunter, when we indeed were fugitives; and as I saw it the snows of winter were falling already around me.

The hotel of Inverardoch was a big, rambling place, full to overflowing, doubtless, in the early autumn, but at this season shuttered up and dismal. Our arrival seemed to be a surprise here, as at other inns along our route; I suppose a November tourist was something phenomenal. There was of course ample accommodation at our service, but it would be some little time in preparation. Meanwhile there was a fire in the bar-parlour, where tea could be served to us.

I went back to the carriage, but when I offered Iras my hand to alight, she said, in a whisper, "I am afraid you must lift me, Ralph, I feel so weak and stiff." I took her up like a child, and light indeed she seemed in my arms, carrying her in to the warmth and glow of the fire. I write of this because it was mentioned afterwards to Knollys. The rooms were made ready for us in about an hour; and at supper the waiting-maid announced with much unction that it was snowing heavily, as if the contrast of wild weather outside might be an enhancement of comfort within. When I crossed the hall later in the evening the host and proprietor was standing before the barometer.

"Lucky the storm did not come on till you got in, sir," he said to me. "Your man was bound for Innisfail, and has had a tough job to get there, I reckon, though it is but a matter of four miles. All the signs point to prolonged disturbance. Listen to the wind!"

We had driven through still air, but now the wind had indeed risen, and was shrieking round the house with a note of true wintry tempest. An outer door opened, and through it a gust of snow whirled into the light. A man entered, white over the head and shoulders, and stamping his feet to clear them. "A rough night, Mr. Fergus," he said to my companion. "The drifts are blowing up already, and will be deep and to spare before the morn."

Whenever I woke in the night it was to hear the same hurtle of tempest, and when the late grey light struggled into the room— the light of that last day—the gale had hardly abated. I called Iras to the window to look at the universal whiteness, which found contrast alone in the black waters of the loch and the murky sky above. No sharp outlines remained lower than the mountain summits; everything seemed rounded into billowy curves, and it needed only a gleam of sunshine to make the prospect dazzling.

"A white world for you, my darling," I said, as she gazed in silence and with caught breath. "You wanted to see a deep snow! Does it look

283

as lovely as you fancied?"

"It is wonderful," she said, presently. "There is something about it beyond beauty. A world with no sin in it nor wrong thoughts might look like that! Do you think the heavenly country you believe in will be built of snow?"

At first sight I had felt nothing but pleasure she should be pleased; soon, however, there awoke a new and keen anxiety. How would the roads be found for the journey of that day?—the enforced journey which we must not omit. I took an early opportunity of consulting the innkeeper, and he pronounced at once and unhesitatingly on the impossibility of getting forward. There had not been such a snow in the district for twenty years or more, and, as I could see, it was deepening every hour; and indeed, another squall tore down from the hills as we were speaking, driving before it a cloud of whirling white. The drifts would be shoulder-deep—ay, and more than that in places; there was a drift pretty nigh to a man's waist between the hotel and Cruach-fruin two hours back, for all it was to the lee of the hill. A messenger had waded through from the manse, as they feared being short of supplies. I must make up my mind to stay where I was, for a day or two, at any rate, till communication could be opened up.

I believe the man thought I was mad in my insistence, as again and again I returned to the charge. No bribe, and I offered a heavy one, would induce him to send out a carriage or launch a boat on the loch; the latter would, he said, be certain death in the teeth of such a storm. It might be possible next day, if the wind abated, but not now. He did not put the direct question what ailed me with Inverardoch that I could not remain where I was; but it was plainly in his eye, if not translated into speech, when I urged that the effort might be made at least to get us to the manse at Cruach-fruin. He was master of the situation and paramount, and my open purse did not tempt him. He became at length both short and surly in denial; doubtless he thought, who was I, a stranger, that life and limb should be risked in my service, even granted I had money for payment! Iras saw in my face when I returned to her that some disaster had arisen, but when I endeavoured to explain, it was she who was the comforter; it was she who was brave to face the threatened danger, and not I.

Shall I ever forget the passage of that long day? She asked me to wheel her couch to the window, and there lay looking out at the white landscape, the falling snow which had built round us so complete a prison. She had taken up the book from which I was teaching her—the study begun with eagerness on her side and pride on mine, both of us looking forward to a long life spent together in which such knowledge would be of service. Today we had little heart for the task, either I to teach or she to learn; and presently it was laid aside, and her head drawn to a resting-place on my shoulder. I strove to be dumb in my anguish, but I could have groaned aloud in this impotence to avert the fate which was stealing upon her with the passing hours. She put up her hand now and then to stroke my face—such a thin hand it was now, and the wedding-ring so loose upon it.

"Ralph," she said, "you must not be troubled. I have had the feeling there could be no long postponement—I think it will not have made much difference, after all. And to be with you to the last, for you to love me to the last, even had the time granted us been years instead of days, what more could I have asked than this? Since I have grown weaker, it is as if something had widened in my mind—as if a power were given me to look forward, and to see dimly that what seems the end may be only a stage of our beginning—not for me alone, in the great change, but for me and you together. When this little space of life drops away, and my body goes back to the dust it should have been by now, this Iras, as you call her, who loves you and feels and knows, will be close to your heart as the pulse of it; will be alive in your life, a double soul in one frame, till the time comes, the blessed time, when we can begin together. O my love! I am glad you are grey-haired—I am glad you are not a young man—so that the time may not be long."

I remember the utterance as if it had been prophecy; I have graven it, as it were, on the palms of my hands; and I think, my heart's dearest, you will prove right in this—the time will not be long.

The inn service went forward, meals were brought to us, and we made some pretence to eat them; noon passed over, and the day declined. There was no evidence of a spiritual presence in the quiet room, or of the stealing upon us of the enemy; but every nerve of me knew *he* was at hand. In the deepening twilight Iras fell asleep, pillowed as she was against me—peacefully at first as a child. might, but presently a wave of trouble seemed to pass over her dream. She struggled faintly, though without waking. "O Ralph," I heard her murmur—"O Ralph, my husband, save me!"

The appeal was unconscious, but it thrilled through me like fire. I could endure inaction no longer. The one scheme I had revolved again and again, and given up as impracticable, became suddenly transfigured into the possible. I would wade through the snow as the man had waded in the morning, and carry Iras to the manse. What matter if it had deepened? He had dared the passage, a hireling sent on an errand; and could not I dare it, when the stake was life and love? I was strong enough to carry her, light as she was, in my arms; and at the manse they could not refuse us shelter—the church would afford that for the night, even if the house were full. We would not delay another moment here in peril.

"Wake up, my darling. I have thought of a way. We are going to the manse. You will not be afraid to trust yourself with me? Stay here a moment, and I will fetch your things."

I brought her fur coat from the bedroom, with her hat and veil, and put it upon her as I did that first day of all our days, the morning at G—— Street. She looked at me bewildered, hardly awake, but passively obedient; and I carried her down the staircase and through the entrance, and out into the wintry twilight.

The air was growing keen with frost, and the snow proved deep to plunge into, even on the level. A line of loose-built wall helped me to keep the road, which here and there had been swept bare by the fierce gusts whirling drifted heaps against every obstacle in their track. This gave me an opportunity to set Iras on her feet for a brief rest before we went on. At the moment it was fine overhead and not yet dark, though there was no light of stars or moon. The depth of snow lay in the hollow and under the hill, but it was still soft; and I could just distinguish the outline, far above us, of the buildings at Cruach-fruin. It was something to have our goal in view, and by it I thought I could sufficiently steer our direction to keep the track. I bade my wife hold firmly to my shoulder, and, carrying her as high as I could, I plunged into the drift.

It was hardly so deep as I expected, but to battle through it taxed all my powers; fortunately, the great exertion of that first effort warmed my blood, and warded off for a time the paralyzing chill which overcame me later. How long the struggle lasted I cannot say; but we won our way through at last, and I set my precious burden on the parapet of the bridge and leaned there to recover myself, breathless and suddenly weak.

She made some protest that I should carry her no farther—she would walk as I did; but I would not hear. I took her in my arms again and began the ascent of the hill. The snow here was not so deep, except where I missed the track and stumbled into hollows, but in another way, conditions became less favourable. Another whirling storm of snow swept down upon us, confusing vision and making breath difficult to draw; and there was the increasing labour of the rising ground. But to turn back was not to be thought of—death lay behind us, and hope before; and if desperate resolve were ever sufficient in itself to keep life whole in a man and brain steady, that hope should be ours.

I cannot measure the time, nor say how long it was that I toiled upwards with heart throbbing as if it would break the prison of my chest, and pulses beating like hammers in ears and brain. The white storm smote me in the face, but I began to see dimly through it a faint light, like the light of a candle set in a window. Sometimes I lost it stumbling into a hollow, and then, emerging, saw again the feeble glimmer which told of a possible haven. But a horror of darkness was coming upon me, a confusion of strange shapes, a voice within which spoke taunting words, reminding me that this was the Hill of Sorrow, and I too was climbing it with my dead. The ache of all my limbs passed into an icy numbness; I could no longer feel where I set my foot. Iras lay very still, and the clasp of her arms failed from my neck. I feared she had fainted—nay, my fear was deeper rooted. I tried to see her face, but as I bent over her something seemed to snap within my brain, the blackness of utter extinction rose up and engulfed me like a wave, and I remember no more.

10

That wave of blackness engulfed brain and being, and sucked me out into the ebb and flow of an unquiet sea, wherein I was overwhelmed for many days and nights. Sometimes I would seem to rise to the surface for a few conscious struggles, and then be again drawn under to the depths. I had no knowledge of my surroundings beyond a dim occasional perception of faces which would bend over me and vanish—away into the blackness, or else I myself was withdrawn into it. So much for the outward; but with all I had the haunting consciousness of a purpose unfulfilled, a train of idea broken which I could not connect, a spur of necessity to arise and be doing, but I knew not the deed.

The knowledge of Iras and her danger seemed to be blotted out; and this country in which I was toiling up precipices, and through sandy wastes, and between the pylons of ruined temples, and into the chambers of the dead, was a country that knew no snow nor winter— a country of torrid heats and burning sands, of sudden darkness at sundown and the shining of strange stars. Such bewilderment and lapse of memory confused the inner citadel of the mind; and yet this outer husk of me remembered her, for I have been told that all the cry of my delirium was on the one beloved name.

There came a day when, on the edge of twilight, the divided consciousness was made whole, the two halves of my brain reunited, and I opened seeing eyes once again upon this weary and desolate world—an unfamiliar world which did not connect itself with any former experience. A narrow strip of a room with two lattice-paned dormer-windows and a sloping roof, a small iron bedstead on which I lay—or rather to which I seemed nailed in the prostration of utter weakness. I saw the flicker of firelight, the outline of a chintz-covered chair by the hearth, but I appeared to be alone. I suppose I made some noise in trying to move, for a large collie gathered itself up from the floor, approached the bed, surveyed me with intelligent scrutiny and a snuff or two from the long, fine muzzle, waved its bush of a tail, and disappeared through the half-open door.

A muffled bark outside seemed to be translated into a summons, for it was quickly followed by the entrance of an elderly woman wearing a muslin cap tied under her chin. The collie accompanied her, and had doubtless acted on previous instructions. "Good dog, Nell," she was saying, "to call me when he began to stir." She glanced at the fire and then at me, but not as if expecting any coherent address.

"Where am I?" I asked.

"Why, Lord save us, he's come to himself!" was her first ejaculation. "You are at the manse, sir, and have been this long while—ever since Nell here found you out in the snow."

In the snow! These words pieced together the broken chain of memory; it seemed but the hour before that I was struggling towards this very goal with Iras in my arms. I wrenched myself round in the bed in an agony of anxiety. "My wife?" I said. "Where is my wife?"

"Dear, dear! he's off again for sure! Now you must just keep yourself quiet, and take your medicine as the doctor said."

I put out a weak hand to grasp her dress, and I suppose something in my face convinced her I was a sane man expecting an answer, and not repeating the cry of my delirium. "Indeed, sir, I can't tell you," she said. "We know nought about you but that you were found as I say, and only your name off a letter—if it happens to be Lavenham?"

"But I was not alone when I was found? My wife was with me. Are you concealing from me that she is dead?"

"No, sir; I am concealing nothing, for, it's Heaven's truth, I don't know. You were brought in here alone, and for aught else ye'll have to ask the minister. And now lie still, for I must change the cloths on your head."

"Can I see the minister—now?" I persisted.

She shook her head. "He's out on his round, and will be this hour yet. And the mistress is lying down, for she's bad again with her lameness since the cold came; so ye'll have to be content with me for the present—I'm just Hannah, if you want to cry on me—and Nell here, who has taken an interest in you like a Christian all the time you've been ill. She thinks ye are her property, I take it, seeing how she found you; and it's been right down impossible to keep her from the room."

All this time Hannah was steeping the bandages in fresh water and laying them back with dexterous fingers, and I felt the relief of the welcome coolness about my aching, dizzy head. I put up my hand and discovered I was close cropped indeed under that wet turban. "Ay," she said, "we cut your hair as close as we could lay the scissors. The doctor said it was best so; but it will grow again, never fear, and you'll be even with the best of them."

She administered this piece of consolation so quaintly it was impossible to help smiling; but my powers of conversation were giving out, and, after swallowing the restorative she presently held to my lips, I was fain to lie still in the twilight—pressing no more useless questions, but consuming anxiety and impatience as best I might in face of the inevitable suspense. What had become of Iras? That my darling was lost to me—that the last pendant was gone, and the separation we feared had come about—I never doubted; but she was in my arms when I swooned, and must have been found with me, dead or alive, unless, indeed, the Power which attacked her life could remove her body also. The woman who called herself Hannah had mended the fire, and the glancing flames threw upward strange flickers of brightness and shadow on the bare walls of the chamber. The light within, though only of the uncertain blaze, was growing stronger than the light without, when an outer door opened abruptly, admitting footsteps and voices, and closed again as if the in-comers were glad to shut out night and cold behind them. The voices passed into the room below.

Not for long, however; for presently there was a noise of chairs pushed back, and the footsteps, two pairs of them, came treading up the staircase. A short man, moustached and bearded, was the first to enter. "There can be no objection to you coming up," he was saying. "There has been no sign of consciousness hitherto, and I shall be glad to know that you recognise him. Hannah, a candle."

The woman came forward with some whispered communication, and meanwhile the second taller figure approached the bed and bent over me. There was no mistaking that kind, ugly face, and at the moment only one other could have been more welcome. I gave a choked cry at the sight of it, and my hands went out wavering to grasp his. If I could find no voice to speak with in that first moment, my weakness must be remembered as a plea of excuse.

★★★★★★★★★★★★★★★★★

"Knollys, old man, are you here still?" This sometime later, when the room had been for a long time very silent.

"Close here, my dear fellow. I am sitting up with you tonight. But you must remember injunctions and keep quiet."

"Tell me this. How did you know where I was, and how did you manage to get away? I am afraid it will be a loss to you—in time and money both."

"As for the first, it came about very simply. They didn't know who you were or where your friends lived, so Mr. Colquhoun here examined your pockets for papers. And it seems you were carrying about with you the letter I wrote to Edinburgh; so he dropped me a line to say you were ill and all that, and asked me to come to you."

"And you came like the good fellow you are, and gave up your work and your prospects—for me!"

"Well—I had run down rather and wanted a change, and thought I would like to see the winter aspect of things up North. It will give me some hints for black-and-white effects, don't you know. And I have not left my work, I have brought it with me. Luckily, I am just now about a job that was movable."

"I shall be able to talk better to you tomorrow. I have so much to say."

"No doubt you will. And all the more chance of it if you lie still now and try to sleep."

"Knollys, you will promise me this. My wife—Iras!—I am in trouble. I have lost her. Help me to make them speak—to get to the bottom of the mystery—to find her if she is above ground—"

"I'll help you in anything and everything if you will be quiet now and get to sleep. And I'll hear all about it from beginning to end tomorrow, or as soon as ever you have strength to tell me. But I can't let you talk now, or I shall have that severe-looking female to reckon with, and be deposed forever from my post of nurse. I am going to wet these rags, and then you must lie still."

★★★★★★★★★★★★★★★★★★

It was neither the next day nor the next after that I was able to tell my story in its entirety. A few words now and again were all I had strength for, and these, I am sure, Knollys took at first for delirium, confused as they were by my very eagerness. It became familiar and usual to see him bending over his blocks at a table set in the small window; though at first such an astonishing and unreal importation of a bit of my London life into this new and strange existence—full of weariness and pain and loss. Hannah came to and fro on ministering errands, and I made the acquaintance both of my host and hostess, and of the small ferret-faced doctor whose skill had, I suppose, dragged me back out of the jaws of imminent death. A consultation with Knollys used to follow his visits; and I felt my friend came back from these less disposed to give credit to the story I was striving to tell, though there was no outspoken incredulity.

Mr. and Mrs. Colquhoun were kindly people; and to me they had indeed acted the part of the good Samaritan, taking in and tending the helpless stranger stricken down at their gates. They were neither of them young; and the children who had grown up under the shelter of the manse were men and women out in the world, leaving the father and mother solitary to go down the hill of life together hand in hand. Mr. Colquhoun had travelled in his youth, and was an exceptionally good talker, with plenty of racy humour despite the narrowing influence of his cloth: the Northern burr which characterized his speech is always pleasant to my ear. We got on well enough, and I liked him; but anything that touched on what he considered my delusion would always send him to the right about.

The wife was a small bright-eyed woman, a sufferer from sciatica, and frequently obliged to keep to her room or the sofa during the colder part of the year. She would come limping in to ask after me, and had a kind, motherly way with her, putting her soft hand to my forehead and on my pulse, as if I had been a son of her own. But here, too, was another sceptic, incredulous of my story. It was not to them that I could turn for help, though I might have looked for sympathy from a woman: it was in Knollys that my hope lay.

"You believe, do you not, that what I am telling you is the truth?"

We were alone together on the fourth morning, and Knollys had brought the despatch-box from Inverardoch at my urgent entreaty. He was to make out a cheque for such shaky signature as I could contrive; and I had another and further object in sending for my papers.

"My dear Lavenham, I feel sure of this—that you entirely believe what you have told me. But the view the doctor takes seems to be that your illness has been a long time threatening—possibly ever since the sunstroke in Egypt; and when this is so it is not at all unusual to find the patient subject to what he calls persistent hallucination. He knows your story only in outline—do not imagine I have betrayed your closer confidence; but under his theory you were hallucinated when you left London believing you had a travelling companion, and the same impression has continued since in your wanderings, till the attack culminated and spent its force in brain-fever. You must have patience with me, old fellow, but I want you to see the other side, and what will occur to people as the natural explanation of all this."

"I put out my hand, the left hand. "Am I hallucinated when I think there is a ring on that finger? How does it appear to you—as a ring or a shadow?"

"A ring certainly, and a curious one. But what has that to do with it?"

"It was my wife's gift to me on our wedding-day. It has never left my finger since she placed it there. And I maintain the giver is as real as the gift."

"I can see it is an antique, such as might be taken from a tomb. Lavenham, I may be unwise in speaking out to you so soon, but I think it is better you should know what it was which was found with you in the snow. It will be a shock, I doubt not, but I believe it will set your anxiety at rest."

I looked at him, and my heart began to throb in its weakness as it had throbbed under the oppression of that deadly chill. The suspense was too great for speech.

"It was a mummy—the mummy of a woman; a thing swathed and bandaged in cerements and dry as a stick, which had been dead for hundreds—nay, thousands—of years. *The* mummy, doubtless, that Skipton sent you to G—— Street, and that you took from there un-der—the impression you told me of."

I had no words in that first moment. Not that my belief was shak-en, but the wonder and horror of the revelation struck me dumb. So, this was how we had been parted, and the doom had come!

"The mummy had been wrapped from head to foot in a fur coat, and had a modern gauze veil tied over its own bands of long hair. And—-Lavenham, I asked the Inverardoch people about your stay there, and whether you had a lady with you, and they say expressly no. You arrived alone, but you carried a bundle wrapped in fur, of which you were very careful; and when you left the hotel to go out into the snow—some of the people about saw you leave—you had the same bundle in your arms."

I dragged myself up higher on the pillows, and signed imperatively to him to give me the despatch-box, and the keys from where they lay beside my watch. I could hardly see key or lock, but I got the lid open and put my hand on what I sought. It was the blue folded paper which had been given me in the registrar's office—the certificate of marriage in due form. "Show that to the doctor," I said. "Ask the witnesses and the officials in Edinburgh whether the wife I married was a living woman or no!"

Knollys unfolded the paper and spread it out. The spaces left blank in the printing were filled up in clerkly handwriting with the particulars I had given, and the document attested my marriage by declaration and warrant of the sheriff-substitute, on the twenty-seventh of October in the current year, to Iras Charmian, formerly of Luxor.

"This is very strange," he said. "There was certainly a marriage."

"I will prove it if I live—both her existence. and my sanity; for the two stand or fall together, I can see. The mummy you spoke of—where is it?"

He hesitated. "It was not brought into the house. Mr. Colquhoun had it put in a sort of loft or granary over the stables, and there I was taken to see it when first I came. I did not think the place a very secure one—"

A granary over stables! A horrible vision of rats and their depredations rose into mental view, and I could not repress a shudder.

"—So, I took it upon myself to order a coffin—the plainest possible—just to enclose and protect the body till we knew your wishes. There was some hesitation at first over supplying a Christian coffin for heathen service; but as the remains were once human, I brought Mr. Colquhoun round to agree with me, and the scruples of the Presbyterian carpenter were overcome. The box is to be here today, and it will remain in the loft, covered over, till you give directions for disposal."

"I must see it, Knollys. If it is all that is left of my darling, I must see it. Can it be brought to me here?"

"I'm afraid not. In fact, I know these good people would have a prejudice against bringing it into the house—some superstition, I suppose. I think they will be glad when it is removed even from the stables. Not Mr. Colquhoun, perhaps, but the women. But it shall remain where it is till you have seen it, and I will look to safe custody."

I lay staring before me, striving to realise the awful, ghastly change which had passed upon so much beauty. I was just in that mood of depression which can only see the earthly side of death, and I was yet but a stumbler at the alphabet of things spiritual. Could I bear to look upon it? and yet the dire necessity pressed me close that I must make myself certain the form was hers, and not a substitution. She spoke to me at the foot of the hill, her arms clung about me as we began the ascent; was the change in that remembered moment when they failed from my neck? or did she stiffen into this dread likeness after I was stricken and powerless to protect her? Knollys was still regarding the certificate as if striving to fit it in with a preconceived idea; it was a bit of evidence neither he nor the doctor would easily get over, and that I knew when I produced it.

I had struck that blow for the truth's sake; but just then the wound of my sorrow bled too newly and ached too sharply for me to follow it up by volunteered discussion. He turned the paper over and examined it closely, as if suspicious of fraud, but found nothing to cavil at. "There must certainly have been a marriage," he said again. "Can a real woman have taken advantage of your delusion and personated it for a time, afterwards leaving you with the body? Forgive the suggestion, Lavenham, but, as you said yourself, this is a thing which must be proved—one way or other. We must find out who it was you married, for your sake and the truth's."

I shook my head at this question, but he went on, more to himself than to me, revolving the idea. "It would have to be someone clever enough to act the part, and able to conceal the real mummy for the time being. There would be difficulties, I allow, and some strong motive must be conjectured. Was there no stage of the affair in which you noticed a change—that your companion seemed to alter?"

"I can only tell you, Knollys, that the Iras whom I found in the mummy-case was the Iras I married, and the Iras who was with me at Inverardoch. There was no change from first to last, except the change which might be seen in the same person under the influence of a wasting decline. You have had evidence of her living presence in London. What did Mrs. Mappinbeck tell you of the lady at my rooms? And I opened the case myself. I cut through the inner envelope of bitumen and resin, and the living woman was within."

"There must have been imposition from the first. Could Skipton have been in the plot, I wonder—or more likely that horrible Arab? What I should like to find out is when she ceased to appear to those about you as a living person; that would be the point of discovery—the weak place in the conspiracy, granted there has been one. Dr. Graham shall see the certificate, Lavenham, if you will trust me with it till he comes. It may stump him about his theory as much as it does me."

We were interrupted by the collie Nell, who all this time was lying at my feet on the bed, as she had taken to do latterly, proving very handy on occasions; for if Hannah was wanted—and the room possessed no bell—the dog would fetch her at a word, and take no denial. Nell had been sleeping, to all appearance, but now roused herself and looked eagerly at the door, as if at an entering figure—eagerly and in doubt, her silky ruff erecting and the hair on her back bristling up. She followed with her eyes invisible movement across the room, dropped from the bed, and seemed to approach what excited her curiosity, and then, with a satisfied wave of her tail, leaped back again, and curled herself once more beside me. That was the first time Knollys and I witnessed the little pantomime of what we called in jest Nell's ghost, but it was of frequent after-recurrence.

The next real entrance following that fancied one was the minister, Mr. Colquhoun. He drew a chair beside the bed, and, noticing Nell upon it in close attendance on me as usual, he said: "I think when ye are well enough to leave, Mr. Lavenham, ye will have to take the dog with you. She has fairly owned you, as the saying is; and she never has settled in thoroughly with us. She was left behind by a fine lad, Jamie Macfarlane of the glen, who got a travelling place with a gentleman going abroad all in haste like—one of those Americans who come crowding over in the season. He did not know what to do with the dog, so we just took her in at the manse till such time as a home could be found for her. You can have her if you will."

The suggestion pleased me: lonely as I was, there was some cheer in the thought of even a dog's company. I put out my hand and she licked it as a seal of our alliance, and so the bargain was concluded.

"Ye'll have Graham here before long," he went on. "I met him driving over the hill to Neil Anderson's, and he said he would look in here on his way home. The road is passable all along, now the drifts have been cut through; and indeed, the snow is disappearing fast with this warmer change. We have it on the ground for weeks together at this season as a rule; but I believe it is going to prove a mild winter, for all the rigorous beginning."

"And what do you do about service with the country in such a state?" said Knollys. "I suppose you shut up the church?"

"I have been here thirty years and over, and I only mind one occasion when the doors were closed all day through on the Sabbath; and that was when I was ill myself and unable to rise from my bed, and the weather was such we could not get a supply. Otherwise there has never failed to be a reading of the Bible and a prayer and a short expounding, if no more. But in the depth of winter, as now, it has often been to no more numerous congregation than our own household—just the women-folk, and the children, if they were home for the holidays, and Madeline to lead the singing. That is my wife, you must know, and she has a sweet voice yet. It's a small place, and doubtless would seem a poor place to you, who are accustmed to the grand cathedrals and fine churches of the South; but to us who are used to it, God's ear seems nearer to us under that low roof—readier to hear and we to speak—than where there are so many fine gauds to take off the attention.

"Ay, and there is something impressive about the stateliness, I grant you—fit to stir an enthusiasm; but that is a poor staff to help ye to salvation. I have been there myself, with the music rolling like a sea, and sweeping up the heart with it, as it were, to the throne, and everyone singing out their prayers on the right note. But to me, who am a plain man, 'tis like that God Almighty would prefer them spoken best, as a man speaks to his friend when he means what he says and wants what he asks for, not sing-songed out in intoning. Music was meant for praise, I take it, but it's out o' place in prayer. And how are you getting on, Mr. Lavenham? Better since Mr. Knollys came, I am glad to think."

"When you wrote to him on my behalf, you added one more kindness to the long list I can never adequately repay. I am ashamed to think of all you have done for me, you and Mrs. Colquhoun both, and the trouble I have brought upon you."

"Tut, tut! Madeline and I are well pleased to help our fellows when we have a chance, or assuredly our Christian profession would not be worth much. And it is a boon to us to see a fresh face. We find the winter with just our two selves in the house, long now that the boys and girls are all away. An empty nest—that is what it is here, with all the young brood flown; and we feel it lonely at times. But it is the way the world goes on, and God's ordinance no doubt."

I suppose when a man has been granted the mingled delight and care of children, their affection and companionship are a solace sorely missed when they go. Perhaps I too might have felt as this Colquhoun. did, in years to come, had Iras been spared to me and to wear her crown of motherhood. But at the moment it seemed to my sorrowful envy that the man whose wife remained was rich beyond expression, and could have nothing to regret in any other loss.

Mr. Colquhoun got up and went to the window, the one opposite the bed foot, which, I found later, commanded the path of approach. "Graham has been quicker than I expected; I suppose there proved not to be much amiss at Neil's. I thought I heard wheels, and there he is coming up the brae. I'll go down and meet him at the door, for I want him to take a look at Madeline when he's had his crack wi' you."

11

The doctor's step was presently heard ascending the stair, and Nell promptly got off the bed—she has a fine instinct about those to whom she is unwelcome—and disposed of herself and her tail in a remote corner, unlikely to be trodden into. He amused me, this Dr. Graham, with his abruptly positive ways and his sharp questions; but a doctor who is self-reliant inspires confidence, and with the patient's belief enlisted on the side of his remedies the battle is half won. I smiled to myself the dreary smile which perceives humour without mirth, as I thought of the theory he had evolved respecting me—the theory with which he had inoculated Knollys—and recognised the drift and direction of some of his inquiries. He thought me better, he told Knollys after; I did not wander in conversation into any track of delusion; and now the fever had left me, he believed I should rapidly gather strength. The consultation below seemed to be a long one; I heard the two voices rising and falling in argument, doubtless over the certificate. I was curious to know what had passed, and ready with a question when my friend returned to me.

"Well, what is the result? I heard you wrangling down below. Have you convinced him there may by chance be a thing or two in the universe not included in his knowledge-box?"

"I have shown him the certificate." Knollys was not good at beating about the bush, and presently it all came out. "He thinks, with me, that certainly there was a marriage, but he is stout in holding to his point of the delusion. But now he is inclined to make it retrospective. The intention of this marriage was concealed from your friends—

297

from me, at any rate, and I think I know you more intimately than anyone else in England. It was probably a hasty and ill-advised step, and upon it may have come some accident of discovery and disunion, which would be a shock to you and send your brain astray for the time. And upon such a condition he thinks the hallucination took root and grew. You know, my dear fellow, it is impossible to expect him to believe that the dried-up corpse in the granary, centuries old as it is, could have been alive a month ago and your wife. Considered from that point, I cannot believe it either; though I do think there is some strange mystery at the bottom of all this that none of our conjectures have touched as yet."

This was my furthest point of advance with the doctor. He believed—on the evidence of the certificate—that I had married Iras Charmian, with the conviction I had gone mad after the ceremony instead of before.

He was right about my improvement. I did gain strength rapidly in the days which followed. I was anxious to be up and doing, and forced myself to eat when food was dust and ashes to my palate, and abide by every rule which could further my purpose. Presently I was able to crawl from my bed to a chair, then to pace the room, Knollys giving me an arm; and after a further day to get down to the unknown regions below—to Mrs. Colquhoun's sitting-room, where she lay on the sofa, a warm coverlet spread over her inactive feet, but with the glancing knitting-pins ever busy, and a bright word and smile ready for all comers. Finally, to get out.

I was wrapped up in coat and comforter as carefully by Knollys as if he had been a woman, and his arm steadied me as I drew in my first free breath of the keen air from the hills. The wintry landscape, which I had last seen dark with storm, now smiled under a glimpse of sunshine. The lower ground was crisped over with frost; the mountains still were white with those remembered snows, but the wide loch rippled steel-blue beneath a brighter sky. I took one turn up and down under the shelter of the house, and then checked my companion.

"You know, Knollys, where I wish to go."

"I was afraid you would wish it. Leave it today, however. You are not strong enough yet."

"I can wait no longer. I am stronger for action than suspense. Take me where she is."

We crossed the yard and went up an outer stone stair which led to the granary. Knollys undid the door and held it open, and I entered. A bare garret in the rafters, partly dark, for a piece of sacking hung over the unglazed window nailed to the upper beam. He drew this aside, and light flooded into the place, showing the coffin lying on the floor covered with a coarse sheet. At the other end over the stable hay was heaped up, and winter roots; there was, too, some lumber and litter of boxes, out of which he drew one forward as a seat for me. I was glad to sink down on it, and for a brief moment I covered my face. Was it indeed Iras that the cloth and the coffin-lid hid from me? A rude death-chamber this for my princess, daughter of Pharaohs as she was, and a sorry resting-place the pauper's coffin from which Knollys drew the sheet. This was spread on the floor to receive the body, and then together we raised the lid.

There was not much to shock in that first view. The fur coat covered the straight lines of the form, the gauze veil which had once been mine concealed the face. With Knollys's help I lifted her out of the coffin for the examination on which I was bent—remembering in vivid contrast how once before I had raised her from such a resting-place. And even as then, the coil of long hair slipped undone from beneath the knot of the veil and fell over our hands—the same lengths of silky dark hair I had so often seen her twist up, and almost undimmed in its beauty. I cut off a tress to keep, and it lies before me now.

"Of course, recognition is impossible," Knollys said, and he was right as to the face. That had changed and perished, as if from contact with the air; and so, had the slender feet, which protruded beyond the wrappings, still bound into their sandals. The exposure of face and feet appeared to be the only disturbance of the original wrappings, which wound round and round the body in a regular pattern, securing the arms to the sides.

"I recognise the hair. And I must look further: I want to examine the left arm. There was a lump on the bone above the wrist; it had been broken when she was a child, and set crooked. That is a mark which must remain."

"But, Lavenham, cannot you see the thing has never been opened any more than this? It is just as it was left centuries since. What is the use of looking for an arm you can never have seen before? Don't put yourself to further pain, but come away."

For all answer I began to unwind the stiffened bandages, which became softer and finer in quality after the outer layer. The usual small amulets were disposed amongst them, and they were to all appearance entirely undisturbed. As I unwound the second strip from about the neck, the gleam of an ornament came into view; and there round the shrivelled throat hung the chain of emeralds I knew so well, showing the broken wires of the seven pendants—the first with a tiny fragment of composition adhering, as I had noticed at Melrose. I pointed this out in dumb show to Knollys, who had heard its history, and thenceforward he made no further protest. I am aware the evidence is inconclusive, and that it may be said by those who are skilled in objection that I had unwound and prepared and then rewound the body, copying the fashions of the ancient embalmers, which I had studied; and all this for some occult purpose of self or other deception. But, conclusive or not, it was sufficient deeply to impress my friend.

These upper bandages fastened the arms to the sides, and when released each was rolled in its own separate swathes, concealing the hands. When undone, these were of more natural appearance than the face, or the feet, which were almost those of a skeleton; and they retained to a great extent the flesh and form. It was the left wrist I wanted to examine, but Knollys's exclamation drew my attention to the hand. There on the attenuated finger, still a finger and not a bone, was a new broad wedding-ring of shining gold.

As I looked at it with that dead stick of a hand in mine, the slender small hand I knew so well, it slid from the nerveless finger by its own weight and dropped into my palm. I passed it to Knollys, that he might see for himself the modern hall-mark, that it was really a Victorian ring on the hand of a mummy three thousand years old; and, more than that, it bore our two names engraved within, as had been done for me in Edinburgh. The special token of identity for which I looked, the distorted bone, was plainly visible through the shrunken yellow skin which covered it; and made Knollys examine it as well. "Yes," I said, "there is no doubt of it. This is my wife."

Had I kept alive till now, unknown to myself, some hope not utterly extinct that the body would prove a substitution, that Iras in the flesh might somewhere and somehow be living still!—for it seemed as if I had suddenly and for the first time plumbed the full black depth of my despair. I laid her back presently on the floor, for at the moment the light weight seemed more than I could hold; and then I remember Knollys dragging me to the air of the window and holding a flask to my lips.

"It has been too much for you. I was afraid of this. I blame myself, for I ought not to have let you come."

I shook my head. "It has done me no harm. I wanted to see for myself; it was better than suspense."

"Let me lay her back in the coffin"—he said *it* no longer—"and then come with me to the house. Do not try yourself any more—to-day."

I have regretted since that I did not investigate further, and set at rest the question whether the body had been prepared in the usual way by incision and with spices, or wound whole in its wrappings in a living trance, as had been declared. But I could not depute any such examination to another, and to proceed with it myself was out of my power. After an interval, and with Knollys to help me, I rewound the bandages about her as smoothly as I could, but with vastly different effect from the art we had disturbed; wrapped her again in the shroud of her furs, with the veil about the perished face, and laid her back in the rough coffin. He had unclasped the necklace, and I put it in my breast with the ring and the tress of hair, and then we stood up to go. "I may fasten the coffin now, may I not?" he said, and I signed an assent.

I think he went back to do it, but I am not sure when the closing actually took place; all that night the hammering of coffin-nails seemed to pursue me in my dreams. The question next to be decided was the question of a grave. Mr. Colquhoun consented that one should be dug at the edge of the burying-ground of Cruach-fruin, where it verged upon the open moor, and promised that the spot should be undisturbed. No Scottish burying-places are consecrated, so there was no objection on that score to a heathen interment. The grave was prepared overnight, and early on the morning of the second day, before it was fully sunrise, Knollys and the man who acted as sexton carried the rough coffin between them down the granary stairs and across the yard on to the hill, and I followed with Nell at my heels. I neither expected nor desired other companionship, but Mr. Colquhoun came across from the house when all was ready and joined the procession. Perhaps his presence was as well, as it overawed the sexton into silence, and spared me remarks which might have given pain. I was known in the district, it seemed, as "the mad gentleman who thinks he has lost his wife"; and the man's looks were inquisitive, if his tongue was mute. But there could have been little in my dull apathy of sorrow to gratify the curious.

The sun came up with a flush of crimson behind the mountains on the east of the loch, but on our western side the cloud hung heavy about the hill-tops, and began to descend in snow. The feathery flakes she loved fell softly on the uncovered coffin as it was carried before me, and into the open grave dug deep in the sandy soil—a hard task, doubtless, in the frost. There was no delay; the coffin was lowered immediately, and the sexton began to fling the earth in over it in heavy spadefuls which rattled on the wood. I stood and watched him, the dog pressing close against me, and looking up in my face now and then with a low whine. Finally, the mound was heaped up and shaped, and the man took himself and his spade away; and then, as I did not move, Knollys and the minister, who had waited at a distance, came up and stood beside me.

"His mercy is over all His works," said the minister as he stood at the foot of the grave. "It was by His ordinance that the soul which once inhabited this body was called into existence in those early ages which knew not the light of the Gospel; and we may surely hope that such ignorance will not be laid to its charge. Let us look to it that we with our knowledge fall not into the greater condemnation."

Such was the funeral oration over my wife.

★★★★★★★★★★★★★★★★★★

I bade farewell to the manse that morning, expressing my gratitude as well as I could to the Colquhouns for their timely succour and generous hospitality. I would fain have repaid the charges they must have been put to by my illness, but this Mr. Colquhoun would not hear of, and insisted on considering me as a guest. I could only resolve in secret that a certain Eastern carpet of mine should travel northwards, where its rich tones would brighten the homely parlour, and the thick warmth of it be welcome underfoot. My expressions to Hannah were less difficult; and, the farewells accomplished, I turned my back on Cruach-fruin, and, leaning on Knollys, walked slowly down to Inverardoch, Nell following my fortunes.

We were to stay that night at the hotel, and cross the loch next morning to a point where a carriage was ordered to be in waiting to take us on by easy stages to Callander. The rooms prepared for us were those I had occupied before; and still in the window of the sitting-room was the couch on which Iras had lain through the hours of our last day. I sat down on it and gazed round me with that dreary realization of change and loss under which the heart sinks low. There on a side-table was the very book she had laid aside, and in which, as I showed Knollys presently, I had written her name—"Iras Lavenham, from her husband."

A meal was presently served to us in the sitting room, and again I had to run the gantlet of curious glances; doubtless I had been a subject of gossip here, as at the manse. As we sat at table, we were reflected in a pier-glass at the side—a bit of decoration which, as I remembered, had amused Iras formerly; and I was able to judge of the alteration in my person that had come about since last I saw myself thus doubled. A haggard object I was truly, with my cropped head and sunken cheeks, and shoulders bowed by weakness into the similitude of age. But my appearance mattered little: she could not now be pained by any change in me. I was glad to go back to the sofa and lie there while Knollys went out to make some needed arrangements for our journey on the morrow; it was not long before he returned.

"The people here say they have had some boxes of yours in charge, Lavenham, and that you will find them in the bedroom. I thought we had had all your things up at the manse?"

I had totally forgotten Iras's belongings. Surely here would be another fragment of evidence for her reality! Before I could explain a knock came at the door, and it partly opened. "Could I speak to Mr. Lavenham himself?" a voice said.

It was the innkeeper, Fergus Macgregor. I had not seen him since the interview in which I offered almost all my worldly wealth for means of transport, and he refused me. I know not whether that recollection dwelt in his memory as it did in mine. He looked somewhat scared or shocked at my appearance, and though he glanced at me now and again in furtive fashion from under his shaggy eyebrows, the cloth cap he had removed on entering, and was now twisting in his fingers, seemed to have the main share of his regard.

"It was just the trunks I had to speak about, Mr. Lavenham, the two trunks and the big bag which ye left behind with us. Being in charge by the accident, as it were, of your absence, I thought it right to look to them; and seeing none of them were fastened, I put some strips across and sealed them at the two ends, so as to prevent meddling. I shall be glad to know, sir, that you have found them all right before you take them on with you. That is what I wished to say."

I thanked him, of course, for the attention, and Knollys offered him a glass of his own wine, which was on the table; but my presence, or some other cause unknown, seemed to strike him with discomfort, and after another furtive glance or two in my direction he made us an abrupt *adieu* and took his departure, closing the door behind him with great care and gentleness. When he was safely out of earshot Knollys burst out laughing. "Would you not say, to look at him, that he had stolen half your valuables instead of locking them up for security? That face and that manner would be enough to hang him if he were in the dock on a criminal charge. And yet I know from the Colquhouns that he bears the character of being an upright, honest-dealing, God-fearing sort of person, and is respected all over the district. Mr. Colquhoun had only one thing against him, and that, as I said, might be forgiven to a Highlander. He has an odd leaven of superstition about him, and is supposed at times to have the gift of second-sight, seeing corpse-candles, and shrouds breast-high about people, and a few other pleasant trifles of that sort. You will have to look into those boxes before we go."

I nodded assent, but chiefly present to my mind was a query whether the innkeeper's gift and the innkeeper's discomfort were consequent the one on the other, and whether he had seen any shroud breast-high upon me.

Knollys had some work to finish ready for despatch when we were again in the neighbourhood of railroads; and through the early after-noon he was diligently occupied, while I lay idle with a book before me—the book from which I had taught my wife, and which was made sacred by her use and her name. Something of the faint exqui-site perfume that pervaded all her belongings still seemed to breathe from it; it was only a hornbook, but I looked at it with dim eyes. The light had already begun to fade when my friend got up from his task and stretched out his long arms in a refreshing yawn.

"That is done with, thank goodness. I can put the package under cover by lamplight, so what do you say, Lavenham, to opening the boxes now? I suppose a glance into each of them will be enough. Are the contents of value?"

For answer I told him what they contained—the outfit I had bought in Edinburgh for my wife. They stood in the bedroom which had been prepared for me; and, as Macgregor said, they were strapped only—the locks were loose. I wondered at this, remembering Iras's ex-act particularity about her keys and pride in them; and then it struck me how the keys must have gone with the dress she wore when I car-ried her out into the snow. We broke Macgregor's seals and raised the lids; and there a surprise awaited me—a shock even, which perhaps might be thought disproportionate to its cause.

The trunks were full. Layer on layer within them we found the dresses and the linen I had bought in the Edinburgh shop—new, un-worn, undisturbed—the keys which should have fastened them en-closed in an inner envelope. The very grey homespun she had worn continually, and in which she was dressed at last, lay untouched in the box, folded in wrapping paper, as it had been sent. To all appearance no eye had looked at the things, no hand had unfolded them, since they were put up and packed to my order. And yet day by day my wife had worn and used what I had given her—how, I cannot explain, and can only testify to the fact with most solemn asseveration of its truth. Have inanimate things souls—spiritual doubles? and could it have been these she used and I saw?

One solitary token of the dearly remembered past alone repaid my search: a tiny spray of white heather with a silver pin to fasten it, which I had bought for her in Rothesay, was still brooched among the ruffles of the yellow gown. I had pinned it there, with a kiss for payment, the evening of our arrival; and the bit of dried flower, frail as it was, had outlived our brief happiness. But that was all. Everything else, the yellow gown itself, was unused, creaseless, fresh as prepared for sale. Even for me a deeper shade of perplexity had gathered round the mystery, and the chances of vindicating the truth to others seemed yet more remote.

12

Certain points of time stand out more clearly than others in retrospect, like the hill-tops of a submerged country. I can recall vividly our passage across the loch next morning; the heavy ferry-boat, wide in the beam, conveying us and our baggage, while I sat with the dog at my knee looking back at the receding shore-looking my last at the Hill of Sorrow, and thinking of the grave I left there, and how the sods had fallen heavy on that coffin only four-and-twenty hours before. My eyes will never again look upon Cruach-fruin in the flesh; but a day will come when this worn-out body of mine will return there, and be carried feet foremost, step by step, up the way along which I struggled in vain. "You will bring me back when the end comes, and lay me beside her?" I said to Knollys. He tried to say I was like to be the survivor, so his word would count for little; but I think something in my face checked him, and he gave the pledge—gave it gravely and fully as I desired.

We reached Callander that afternoon, and Edinburgh the day following, driving from the station to the same Princes Street hotel at which Iras and I had stayed at the time of our marriage. I turned back the pages of the visitors' book as far as the end of October, and showed Knollys our names written; and the account-register of the hotel afterwards proved that two persons had been charged for in accommodation, and meals served to a private sitting-room. Individual recollection of us could not be expected in that large place, full of an ever-changing multitude of comers and goers. A packet of letters was given out of the office pigeon-hole to Knollys; and then I was glad at once to go upstairs to my room, for the two days' travelling had been a heavy tax on what strength I had regained.

Knollys came to my bedside later and read me those letters. They were replies to inquiries he had written—on my behalf, but in his own name—from Cruach-fruin to such places on our tour as my shattered memory could recall. He made some business pretext for the need of information, and asked —first, whether it was correct that a person of my name had stayed there between certain dates; secondly, if accompanied by a lady; and, in the third place, for a personal description of my companion. He also wrote to our fellow-traveller in the train going up to Scotland—the man who had pressed his card on me, which was still preserved in my pocket-book. The testimony of his reply was complete my voluble friend remembered me, remembered a pleasant conversation which—confound him!—had whiled away the tedium of the journey, remembered also that I was travelling with a lady. Here the letter evinced some curiosity and a disposition to be facetious; but described Iras as tall, of an elegant figure, dark-haired, and closely veiled.

Another affirmative reply was from the inn at Melrose: Mr. and Mrs. Lavenham had certainly stayed there between the dates named. Mrs. Lavenham was a lady of dark complexion, tall and good-looking, and apparently much younger than her husband. The charges at the inn were certainly for two persons, and were paid by Mr. Lavenham on departure. From Rothesay the hotel-keeper replied that the names asked for were signed in his book, and the account would doubtless be rendered correctly; but he was unable to trace items, and had no personal recollection. I have explained before that it was impossible for me to write to Largs, and from Ardrishaig no reply reached us. At Port Sonachan there was again the record of the written names, but no description could be given—only the testimony that the lady and gentleman had hired a boat and gone out rowing on the lake.

The letter from Taynuilt was curious. Here was the point of my first breakdown with illness, and no entry of name could be traced; but it was remembered that a gentleman, who seemed a great invalid, arrived posting from Dalmally as described, and was laid up at the hotel several days. He came with a quantity of luggage, but was not accompanied by any lady. It was, however, declared by the servant who attended to his rooms that a lady was with him on several occasions, who more than once shared such meals as were served to him, and was of course charged for. It was not known who this person was, but they concluded she had come in from some house in the neighbour-hood; and then followed a description based on the maid's recollec-tion, which agreed substantially with that given by others.

This was the last link. From Oban came a letter of some length written in a woman's hand, detailing how a gentleman had inscribed the names Mr. and Mrs. Lavenham in the book, though he had arrived alone; and how, on departing, he insisted on his bill being altered to charge for two persons instead of one. The writer concluded at the time that he was insane; and if his friends wished to claim for the sur-plus charge, it should of course be refunded.

Here was food for thought in the wakeful watches of that night. Did the evidence point to a gradual dissolving and withdrawal—save in its manifestation to me—of that personality which at first was pal-pable to all, becoming less and less apparent as the pendants were abstracted one by one? But even from this view there were discrep-ancies which it was difficult to reconcile. Neither from Taynuilt nor Oban came any mention of the mysterious long bundle wrapped in fur which was observed at Inverardoch, which I was said to have car-ried in so carefully from the carriage, and to have borne in my arms when I departed. Next day Knollys and I were to have gone together to the lawyer, but I found it all I could do to dress and crawl into the sitting-room. The expedition for me was out of the question; but time pressed, and so I consented that my friend should undertake it alone. As he was departing, he turned back from the door. "Give me an au-thority for the post-office, Lavenham. There are letters lying there for you, I know, for I forwarded a second and third packet from town, not knowing any further address."

I did as desired, and was left shivering by the fireside with a plaid about me; for Edinburgh can be chill in early January—colder by far, I thought it, than at Cruach-fruin. Nell sat beside me with her chin on my knee and her wistful eyes on my face; the unusual surround-ings must have been strange to the country-bred dog, and that may have drawn the bond of our alliance closer: she would not leave me for Knollys. Sometimes I wonder whether in the clear instinct of her canine mind she has a foreboding knowledge that our companionship will be brief—that the master she has chosen to follow is nigh to setting out on a journey she cannot accompany, by a path into the unknown dark which he must tread alone, without even a dog's fellowship!

That strange trick of hers—that pantomime of watching an unseen entrance—had been displayed here as well as at Cruach-fruin, so it had no dependence on locality. I had been thinking of it, doubtless, as I sat over the fire and dozed in my weakness, so it was not wonderful the idea should still have possessed me as the doze deepened into a dream. In the dream Nell looked round at the door with the same rising of the hair and interrogative bearing I had noticed at the manse, left my knee, and went forward the usual half-dozen steps; and then I became aware that a lady had entered and was standing just within. A stranger, for I knew no one who could be wearing the deep-mourning garb of an English widow, with a crape veil hanging over her face. As the dog approached her, she lifted both hands and put it back—and lo! the face revealed was the face of Iras.

A cry broke from my lips in the overmastering surprise—love and anguish and yearning blent in one—and with the cry I woke. The entering figure was Knollys, and he was stooping down to pat the dog.

"Well, I have seen Macpherson, and he is as positive a witness as even you could desire."

"He remembered the circumstances?"

"Perfectly. When I got to the office there was some demur about showing me up—I had no appointment, and Mr. Macpherson was going out; but I wrote on my card, 'About Mr. Lavenham's marriage—urgent,' and I think curiosity prevailed. He is a queer old file; but he seems to have had an impressionable spot in his heart, and your wife found it out."

Not wonderful that, I thought; but I did not interrupt his story with remark.

"Did I come from you? he asked when I was planted opposite. I said yes, and that you would have accompanied me but for indisposition. I had your authority for the questions I was about to put to him. Then I unfolded the certificate. 'You are one of the witnesses named here, Mr. Macpherson,' I said, 'and I conclude you can bear testimony that all was in due form.' He assented, and I went on to say what we agreed upon. That you had married a person unknown to your friends, and had since experienced a severe illness with partial loss of memory; and as your wife was not now with you, it had been suggested that the marriage was a delusion, and there had been no real woman in the case at all. He would be doing you a service, I said, if he could give conclusive testimony one way or the other, either for the fact of the marriage or against it. That was how you permitted me to put the case, was it not, if needful to give reasons?"

"Yes; as much of the truth as was necessary. To explain the whole would be impossible."

"He did not waste many words on me in replying. 'I should have thought the certificate here was vara conclusive evidence in itself,' he said in his slow Scotch speech. 'But you can tell Mr. Lavenham I will come forward at any time to give testimony. I drew up the declaration as between the parties, and witnessed their signatures, together with a clerk of mine whom I can produce; and I went with them before the sheriff-substitute. It was all in due order, Mr. Knollys. There can be no doubt whatever that Mr. Lavenham was legally married on the day named.' Of course, I expected this reply; the gist of the matter was to come.

"Had he observed Mrs. Lavenham, and could he describe her for me? Did she appear to understand what was going forward, or did she behave in any way with peculiarity or like a foreigner? 'Do you want to upset the marriage on the ground of insanity? was his counter question; and I think those small eyes of his are the very keenest I ever encountered. I answered that I wanted to upset nothing; my motive was solely to sift out the truth from an accidental confusion; and your anxiety was altogether for incontestable proof that the marriage had taken place. 'I should have been sorry to hear the contrary,' he said,' or that there was anything adverse to that pretty young creature, who seemed so confiding and gentle, and all that a young bride should be. I did not get a good view of her face, Mr. Knollys, for she wore her veil down, as was doubtless natural; but she had dark eyes and pretty hair, and a clear complexion, though maybe a bit brown, with the blood showing up in it when the ring was put on her finger. Ay, she understood it all well enough, and I noticed no peculiarity except that she seemed to turn to her husband about everything, as a wife should. That she was a foreigner born you can see here in the particulars; and when she spoke it was in a hesitating way, like one choosing among unfamiliar words. Now and then when I spoke to her her husband touched her shoulder to make her attend; I noticed nothing more.' That is all about our interview, as nearly as I can remember to tell you. You can see the original document with the signatures if you like to make application."

The old lawyer's words, as repeated by Knollys, brought that notable morning vividly to mind. It was plain to see Macpherson's testimony had weight with him. I had surely succeeded in proving my wife's reality beyond doubt, though there was still the unaccountable confusion and conflicting evidence of those last weeks of gradual withdrawal, still the broken link which failed to connect the Iras I had married with the body coffined in the grave at Cruach-fruin.

But I was in no mood for argument; I could do nothing then but turn my face to the wall in keen realisation of my loss. I think Knollys saw how it was with me, for he talked on about indifferent matters—the newspaper in his hand, the latest intelligence on some point round which popular interest was just then astir, and last, but not least, his own impressions of Edinburgh, which he was visiting for the first time. I was sorry the royal city had not put on a brighter aspect. The outside world was grim and cold; a northeast wind swept the streets and shook the windows of the room in which we sat; the fine outline of the Castle and St. Giles's crown on the hill opposite were veiled and dim with mist. It was not till later in the evening that he put his hand to his breast-pocket with a start of sudden recollection.

"I had quite forgotten your letters, Lavenham. Here they are; the two covers I sent on; stale news by this time, no doubt."

With one exception the letters were unimportant—the usual accumulation of circulars and small notifications of indebtedness which come in the common course of post. The exception bore a foreign postmark, and was addressed in a woman's hand—written thick and large, as if with some affectation of importance. The signature at the foot of the last page was Amélie St. Heliers.

My life had changed so utterly in current and horizon since all the early trouble of threatening appearances that I had completely forgotten the letter I sent to Madame St. Heliers' address in France, and the elucidation I expected from her reply. I knew more now than she could tell me. I knew now that what I saw in London and on the seashore was Savak the priest, dead to bodily life, but alive for evil across all the gap of centuries—my wife's enemy and mine.

Though I had ceased to expect it or to look for enlightenment from this quarter, I turned back to the commencement and read the letter with some interest. I have it by me, and will transcribe it here.

"You ask a question it is difficult to answer," said the letter. "I can but tell you facts, and leave you to draw your own conclusions.

Any explanation I might give of them would be based on theories of which you are probably ignorant, and a system of belief with which you would wholly disagree. I am a clairvoyant, which means I have by nature that opening of the inner eye which is spoken of in the Scriptures. I do not exercise the gift at will, as we open our natural eyes when we desire to see; the faculty is fitful, and not always a source of pleasure to the possessor. For some occult reason the dwellers on the threshold are nearer to our perceptions than the ministers of grace. But, granted that drawbacks exist, I would not forego my advantage and be dim-eyed like my fellows.

"The gift is of great service to me in my practice as a palmist. I read the chart of the lines, it is true, but I also am able to look intuitively into the sphere of the personality and perceive something of the spiritual affinities which each draws to himself, or which are drawn to him by the operation of other laws. I knew nothing of you when I saw you at Mrs. Bevis Payne's, neither name nor history; but directly I entered the room my attention was drawn to you in a way I shall not easily forget. Close to you, within your sphere, stood the man you call the Egyptian, and I knew instantly that you were menaced by a great danger. Whether when you read this, it will have come and passed I know not, or whether it may still be in the future, but it seemed to me that it pressed very near. I determined to speak to you, to give you warning if possible; so, on some pretext I induced our hostess to send you in to me, for an interview: I knew you would not seek me of yourself.

"What I saw further confirmed the first impression; I spoke as plainly to you as I dared, and I would now repeat the warning in case it is not yet too late. But of information I can give you little. I am ignorant, as you profess to be, who the Egyptian is and why you are persecuted. I do not even know certainly whether he belongs to the next world or is some spiritual projection of an enemy yet alive. But a point of change is come or coming which will render you vulnerable to his attack, and he will smite and not spare. I would advise you to walk warily and set your expectations low, and neither love nor hate: the affections as well as the passions disarm our defences. I know and have seen nothing of you beyond the one evening, and now the history of your letter; and I certainly never was in any Brighton church. I can say no more"

★★★★★★★★★★★★★★★★★

I was able to accompany Knollys the day before we left Edinburgh, when he went to examine that original document of the declaration of marriage which he had made requisition to see. There was one notable peculiarity about it when produced. While my signature and those of the witnesses remained plain to read in all the ordinary blackness of ink, that of Iras was faded so as to be barely legible. I could just distinguish the faint brown characters I had taught her to trace, but the beloved name was without doubt gradually disappearing; a few more months and the paper will be blank. It matters little; there is one place where her name is written indelibly, and that is my heart.

I wished to revisit Largs before we went south, and Knollys was considerate enough to put aside his own urgency to suffer me to do this. I felt positive that once there I could find the house at which we stayed, and I was especially anxious the lodging-keeper's testimony to my wife's reality should be added to the rest. Her name had escaped my memory, though at the time I certainly knew it; the name of the house, if indeed it owned one, I may never have heard; for while there I neither wrote nor received letters, so was not concerned with the address.

The aspect of the little place, the rough stage on which we landed, were all familiar enough, and I set out confidently along the shore, Knollys accompanying me; but the house had so disappeared, or changed from the recollection I preserved of it, that identification became impossible. As a last resource we inquired at each door along the sea-front which advertised lodgings, asking if a married couple named Lavenham had stayed there in the previous November; but we were everywhere met by an invariable negative, and none of the house mistresses whom we disturbed from their vocations in the least resembled the landlady of whom I was in search. I went back to Glasgow profoundly discouraged, and from there we took the night-mail up to town.

I was glad we travelled back by night—that the darkness hid from me the changing panorama of landscape on which I looked last with Iras when she found the world so fair. It was only a broken sleep which visited my narrow couch amidst the swing and rattle of the train, speeding southward as if the great metropolis drew it like a magnet; and in the watches of that night, I had time to realise what the dismal home-coming must be, and what the effort which would lie before me. It behoved me, for the sake of my manhood, to piece together what shattered fragments remained of the hope and purpose of my past; to take up life anew out of the grip of despair. I had put the contemplation of it behind me; yet now that the hour was at hand, I knew I had dreaded it in secret for days and weeks.

London looks inexpressibly dreary at seven on a still, dark, early morning of mid-winter; wet pavements were shining under a pale glimmer of gas, and the air was thick with the drizzle of a falling fog. Knollys went with me to G—— Street, and there Mrs. Mappinbeck had fires and breakfast prepared for us—a breakfast I could not touch. He was loath to leave me when that was over, but he had business to attend to—business which had for too long been neglected for my sake. It was necessary I should face the long, lonely day, and the procession of its kind which must follow before the end comes—that end which still delays.

"I will look in this evening and see how you are getting on," he said, as at last he got up to go. "And tomorrow we must see about consulting some first-rate doctor, who will cure you up in a trice, and make you fitter than you have been for months. Try to get some rest in the interval, for I do not expect you slept much last night, any more than I."

It was a long day, but it wore to an end at last. Late in the afternoon I went into the studio, overcoming a first reluctance, determining to face alone the sight of the empty *sarcophagus*. The lid was upon it, and when raised there still remained within the resinous inner case I had cut through, and the rags and shreds of the wrapper in which Iras had lain. The husk which had enclosed her through that mysterious survival by which she was preserved to me had a certain lingering touch of her presence about it, which made me feel for the time less desolate—the sort of dreary comfort I might have had in sitting by her grave. I rang for the servant and ordered fire and gas, and settled myself there for the evening with Nell lying at my feet.

The room was eloquent to me of that former scene—of her revival and of our meeting; and as I mused upon it there came sharply to mind the evidence of the tablet. I wished to see again the lines traced by my enemy, and to have it at hand for exhibition to Knollys; and, as well as feeble strength would permit, I searched the place, but failed to find it. I remembered how I had cast it from me face downward, at Iras's entreaty, and how there had appeared above it for one fleeting instant the awful similitude of the face. Mrs. Mappinbeck and the servant professed to know nothing of it when I came to inquire, and possibly it may have been thrown away as rubbish when the room was swept after our departure. I drew paper and ink before me, and it was then I began to set down from memory the words I remembered to have read. I have written them once already in these pages, but I will repeat them here:

"I, the priest Savak, servant of Sebek, have sealed the virgin, the daughter of Khames, in trance according to the Voice of the Oracle. Not of this land or generation is her lover, but he yet unborn that awakes her from sleep before the seven ages have passed over, his she will be. And if the seven ages pass without awakening, she is dust and she remains mine. To this she submits with knowledge, having denied herself to me in marriage; and, being obedient to the Voice of the Oracle, goes down alive into the tomb, willing to sleep. And I, Savak, do seal her in the inner chamber to be mine; for were it seventy ages instead of seven, and were the land perished under our feet that abides continually, I would pursue her until she turn to me. And I, Savak, do seal the inner chamber with my curse and with the curse of my God, which shall dwell with terror upon him that meddleth and upon him that openeth. And to him, the lover—in the ages to come and the generations to come—should he find her over my body and the guard of the tomb and the guard of the curse, I do set against him wager of battle that his days be not long in the land; neither hers to whom life returns and youth returns for seven spaces, according to the ordinance of the eternal Gods."

Wager of battle!—if that had lain between us, who was the conqueror, he or I? The life was broken within me and I was left solitary; but the Iras who had turned from him had loved me, and I could be confident that wherever she might be, and however it might fare with her in the dimness beyond, she loved me still. There passed into my mind in that hour some apprehension of how the power of the enemy had spent its permitted force against our union on earth, and could touch us no more: the Hereafter—that Hereafter of which I, a doubter, had received such tremendous evidence—alone would decide with whom victory lay.

I remembered the words Iras had spoken when first the Shadow touched us which was to widen into black eclipse—how through death she was to be preserved mine, as at first through centuries of its semblance. The wound of the foe had smitten deep into my life, but, were the veil of earthly illusion withdrawn, it might show him defeated by his own act, and the triumph not with the strong. Was this stirring of the soul to perceive the aspects of eternity a whisper from a source beyond itself? or was it born only of the craving of a sick fancy? Was the victory hers and mine? and, after all, was there hope in mine end?

I questioned to the void: no voice answered; my head sank on my breast. But in the stillness the dog got up from my feet again as if recognising an entrance, followed across the room to the *sarcophagus*, and then returned to me. I had grown to attach little importance to this demonstration, for which there was never any visible cause; but now I rose, and by some instinct again pushed back the lid of the shell in which she had lain—the elaborate carven lid, with its strange semi-human form and grotesque decoration—and lo! in the empty hollow, green and fresh as if just divided from the tree, there lay a branch of palm.

★★★★★★★★★★★★★★★★

Since then, months have gone by; winter is no more; spring is upon us, and the earth rejoices; we shall soon be in touch with summer. I was told at first that the more genial weather would bring back my strength; but now the doctor looks graver—talks of persistent anaemia, and says my heart must have been injured by the struggle through the snow. I swallow his horrible compounds and his marrow-grease, and am generally biddable—because Knollys is anxious; and in these days I abstain from argument. I know the great man's theory about me, and how he disposes of my "delusion" on the score of previous entanglement and conspiracy—with Skipton in the plot doubtless, and probably Abd-el-Moluk to boot; and how he considers the Egyptian sunstroke affected my brain, and wove a chain of perfectly accountable circumstances into a supernatural romance.

Knollys hangs suspended between us like Mahomet's coffin—he can neither quite credit me nor wholly believe the doctor; the narrowing faculty which he calls common-sense is with him a stone of stumbling and rock of offence, as it is to so many. But no brother could have extended to brother greater kindness than he has shown to me, and we are not likely to quarrel because he is unconvinced. Mrs. Mappinbeck is much softened, and sees to my comfort with solicitude. I am now her only lodger, as Lady Wilkinson of aristocratic memory has departed to other climes. I do not think she would object in these days to the introduction of a dozen mummies if I desired to have them; and she even tolerates Nell, which at first was a difficulty.

Knollys has promised to take care of Nell when the end comes. The doctor has certified me sane enough to make a will, and indeed I have no kindred to dispute such disposition as I choose to make of my little property. I think it will please me afterwards as well as now to know that Knollys and Madge can be happy without the long waiting they have made up their minds to endure, and that the matter of employment will cease to be so anxious a necessity. This wasted body of mine is to be taken the long journey northward; the grave on the Hill of Sorrow will be opened once more. Knollys has promised to lay me beside her, and to set up a white cross over us, writing upon it, plain for all to read, the names of Ralph Lavenham and Iras Lavenham, his wife.

www.ingramcontent.com/pod-product-compliance
Lightning Source LLC
Chambersburg PA
CBHW030406030726
47497CB00002B/505